ATLANTIS AWAKENING

ATLANTIS RISING

continued . . .

THE WARRIORS OF POSEIDON SERIES
BY ALYSSA DAY

Atlantis Rising
High Prince Conlan's Story

"Wild Hearts in Atlantis" from *Wild Thing*
Bastien's Story

Atlantis Awakening
Lord Vengeance's Story

"Shifter's Lady" from *Shifter*
Ethan's Story

Atlantis Unleashed
Lord Justice's Story

Don't miss *Atlantis Unmasked*, Alexios's story,
and *Atlantis Redeemed*, Brennan's story,
coming soon from Berkley Sensation!

ATLANTIS UNLEASHED

The Warriors of Poseidon

ALYSSA DAY

BERKLEY SENSATION, NEW YORK

THE BERKLEY PUBLISHING GROUP
Published by the Penguin Group
Penguin Group (USA) Inc.
375 Hudson Street, New York, New York 10014, USA
Penguin Group (Canada), 90 Eglinton Avenue East, Suite 700, Toronto, Ontario M4P 2Y3, Canada
(a division of Pearson Penguin Canada Inc.)
Penguin Books Ltd., 80 Strand, London WC2R 0RL, England
Penguin Group Ireland, 25 St. Stephen's Green, Dublin 2, Ireland (a division of Penguin Books Ltd.)
Penguin Group (Australia), 250 Camberwell Road, Camberwell, Victoria 3124, Australia
(a division of Pearson Australia Group Pty. Ltd.)
Penguin Books India Pvt. Ltd., 11 Community Centre, Panchsheel Park, New Delhi—110 017, India
Penguin Group (NZ), 67 Apollo Drive, Rosedale, North Shore 0632, New Zealand
(a division of Pearson New Zealand Ltd.)
Penguin Books (South Africa) (Pty.) Ltd., 24 Sturdee Avenue, Rosebank, Johannesburg 2196,
South Africa

Penguin Books Ltd., Registered Offices: 80 Strand, London WC2R 0RL, England

ATLANTIS UNLEASHED

A Berkley Sensation Book / published by arrangement with the author

PRINTING HISTORY
Berkley Sensation mass-market edition / June 2009

Copyright © 2009 by Alesia Holliday.
Excerpt from *Atlantis Unmasked* by Alyssa Day copyright © 2009 by Alesia Holliday.
Cover art by Don Sipley.
Cover design by George Long.
Interior text design by Laura K. Corless.

ISBN: 978-0-425-22041-2

BERKLEY® SENSATION
Berkley Sensation Books are published by The Berkley Publishing Group,
a division of Penguin Group (USA) Inc.,
375 Hudson Street, New York, New York 10014.
BERKLEY® SENSATION and the "B" design are trademarks of Penguin Group (USA) Inc.

PRINTED IN THE UNITED STATES OF AMERICA

10 9 8 7 6 5 4 3 2 1

To Debbie Wooley,
who came up with the title Atlantis Unleashed.
Thank you!

To Cindy Hwang, who is wonderful beyond words.
May you have hotel breakfasts three times a day
forever and ever.

And, always, to Judd, Science Boy, and Princess:
I love you bigger than chocolate.

Acknowledgments

To the best editor and agent on the planet, Cindy Hwang and Steve Axelrod. What can I say? You're like dark chocolate and little fluffy bunnies all rolled up into one. Except not chocolate-covered fluffy bunnies, because that would be gross. And wrong.

To Prudence Scott, friend and archaeologist from Australia, who helped with scientific details about Keely's profession. Any errors are entirely mine and were made in spite of her careful and detailed assistance.

To Leis Pederson, Lori Antonson, and Elsie Turoci, who do the heavy lifting.

To the friends who keep me out of the rubber room during cross-country moves, leaking roofs, and mommy crises: Barbara Ferrer, Cindy Holby, Michelle Cunnah, and Eileen Rendahl: none of my books would ever get written without you.

And especially to Ann Thayer-Cohen and my wonderful reader group at alyssaday@yahoogroups.com and my friends at MySpace who keep me laughing, keep me inspired, and keep me supplied with wonderful titles for my upcoming books—you *rock*.

Dear Readers,

Welcome back to the world of the Warriors of Poseidon! Thank you for your patience while I worked on this book—Justice is a complex man, which made for a complicated book! Thanks also for continuing to read my books and for writing to let me know how much you're enjoying these stories of the Atlantean warriors and the women who've touched their hearts.

Although the important archaeological find of the Mayan mural at San Bartolo is real and was discovered by Dr. William Saturno as I described, I have taken liberties with the location of nearby villages (and, as far as I know, no rogue vampires have taken over the site in real life).

You can see amazing streaming video of the Mayan mural at www.pbs.org/wgbh/nova/sciencenow/3401/03.html, under the Nova ScienceNOW section, if you're a history and archaeology junkie like I am. Scientists speculate that the Mayan civilization in that area at one point exceeded the population of modern-day New York City. But then, over a few short decades, almost everyone simply vanished—and nobody knows exactly why. One theory is that they overbuilt their natural resources. (I'm pretty sure I'm the first to think that vampires had anything to do with it, but then again, I write fiction, so I can imagine anything I want.)

Creation myths, art, and ancient legends from vastly disparate cultures all around the world have so many unexplainable commonalities that it is plain to me that one overarching, advanced civilization, such as that of Atlantis, could have played a part in these astonishing similarities. They say truth is stranger than fiction, but for me, truth infuses fiction and makes the world of Atlantis so exciting. Thanks for coming along for the ride!

Please be sure to look for Alexios's story, *Atlantis Unmasked*, and Brennan's story, *Atlantis Redeemed*, in bookstores soon and visit me at www.alyssaday.com for excerpts, bonus short stories, and downloadable screensavers for members only, or friend me at www.myspace.com/authoralyssaday!

Hugs,
Alyssa

The Warrior's Creed

We will wait. And watch. And protect.
And serve as first warning on the eve of human-
ity's destruction.
Then, and only then, Atlantis will rise.
For we are the Warriors of Poseidon, and the
mark of the Trident we bear serves as witness
to our sacred duty to safeguard mankind.

Chapter 1

**Four months ago,
a cave deep underneath Mt. Rainier,
Cascade Range, Washington, United States**

Justice took inventory of his condition, his weapons, and his chances, as he'd done so many times before in his centuries as a warrior, and came up with:

1. bad
2. worse
3. odds-on favorite to be a dead man in the next five minutes

Condition, physical: Currently lying flat on his belly on the cold, damp dirt of the cavern floor. Face smashed down on the side of a wet and soon-to-be seriously enraged tiger. Peacock-egg-sized lump on the back of his head from rough handling by the vamp and the wolf shifters who'd carried him down the long dank tunnel from the surface. Possible cracked rib or two. The ketamine they'd darted him with was mostly worn off, due to the nature of his Atlantean immune system, but he wouldn't bet any gemstones on his ability to transform into mist.

Condition, mental: Fury bordering on homicidal rage. In other words, standard operating procedure. *Ha.* SOP. Poseidon picked his warriors carefully, or so he'd always heard.

The sea god must have been multitasking the day he'd decided to add Justice's name to the list.

Weapons: None. The sword he'd worn for hundreds of years—indeed, since the king of Atlantis had given it to him with not a single word of explanation but only a look steeped in contempt—gone. One of the two shape-shifters standing guard over Justice and his furry tiger friend Jack stood off toward the mouth of the cave, fondling Justice's sword like he couldn't believe his luck. A faint glow from the cavern beyond silhouetted the guards' shapes against the utter dark of the small cave in which they'd dumped Justice, and he watched in impotent fury as the shifter raised his sword in the air as if admiring his new toy.

Sure, it was all fun and games until an Atlantean warrior sliced your guts out.

Justice would have smiled if he wouldn't have ended up with a mouthful of wet tiger fur. They'd taken his daggers, too.

The better to kill them with.

He tried to reach out toward his brother down the shared Atlantean mental path, but nothing but a harsh static buzzed through his mind. The drugs were probably still interfering with his access to his powers over water and energy, too. He'd assume he was helpless. Better that way.

Never rely on the unreliable when you're otherwise weaponless against two wolves and a potentially drug-crazed tiger.

Chances: He'd bet on himself against most shape-shifters, even in close quarters like this, but five hundred pounds of tiger? Even Jack, who was sort of a friend when he walked on two legs.

He'd have to call it even odds. And that was before he ever got to the two wolves. So maybe he'd have to take out the wolves first.

Because Justice knew one critical fact: he'd rather spend eternity roasting in the lowest of the nine hells than spend one more minute with his face pressed into the rank animal stench of a wet tiger.

The shifters finished their muttering about sneaking out to see the action and moved off, as stealthy as a couple of drunken water buffalo. Before today, Justice would have bet a Roman-emperor-turned-vampire as powerful as Caligula would have hired a better class of help.

He'd have been wrong. No wonder the Roman Empire had fallen.

All the better, though.

Justice waited long enough to be sure they weren't faking the move, then leapt up and away from the still-unconscious but ominously twitchy tiger. Maybe the action knocked something loose in his drugged brain, because he suddenly knew his brother was finally arriving. Lord Vengeance to the rescue, just freaking great.

Of course, Vengeance didn't know that he was Justice's brother.

"I could tell you, but I'd have to kill you," Justice growled; then, more loudly so he could be heard, "Damn, Vengeance better appreciate this."

He whipped around to see Vengeance standing at the tunnel entrance, sword at the ready. Ven said something about cat hair and tiger pillows, but Justice barely heard it, because the booming sound of an unseen bell smashed through the air. He covered his ears, but the percussive waves of noise threatened to crush his skull beneath their power.

A flash of foreknowledge swept through him and he somehow knew—just *knew*—that the next hour would change everything.

Everything.

Then the goddess walked into the room clothed in the body of Ven's woman, and everything inside of Justice that was not the primitive, savage descendant of his Nereid ancestors shattered. Insanity and battle lust washed in a blue-green haze across his vision and, as he stared at the brother he wanted so desperately to acknowledge, his last rational thought was one of regret.

Had it been minutes or hours? Justice crouched on the stone ledge, hidden from sight and surveying the carnage. Dead and dying shifters and vampires littered the stone floor of the cavern. The stench of the acidic decay of the vamps combined with the coppery metallic tang of blood to rot the very air they were breathing. The flickering lights of the torches on the walls illuminated garish displays of broken and torn-open bodies.

He'd done his part, but had been careful to stay out of sight, drawing his opponents behind the cavern's many rocky outcroppings. Even the preternatural senses of the vampires had been overwhelmed by the wash of blood, and nobody had seemed to notice him.

Nobody still living, at least.

Justice was planning to be the trump card, and any good gambler knew the value of never revealing his hand. He glanced down at the blade of his sword, gleaming wetly in the flickering dark.

No trump card had ever dealt such a deadly hand. He was the joker, and the queen of death was next on the list.

He heard her voice then, and knew he'd failed. The vampire goddess Anubisa had captured Vengeance and his woman in spite of Ven's strength and Erin's powerful witchcraft.

Justice had failed them.

He'd failed his *family*.

As he listened, options, strategy, and desperate measures swirling through his still only semilucid brain, he heard her say it. The words he'd dreaded. Anubisa was going to take Ven with her. She was giving the rest of them to Caligula as a little gift.

A *snack*.

Justice shot up and began to show himself, then stopped, frozen, when he saw Anubisa holding Erin while Ven dug the point of his sword into his own heart.

"If you truly wish for my voluntary service, release her now and swear the oath for her safety. Or I will run this sword through my heart, and you will be cheated of your goal," Ven said, grim determination hardening his features.

Justice nearly staggered as the truth of what he must do slammed into him. To save his brother—to rescue Erin, who might possibly be able to heal his second brother's unborn royal heir—he must make the ultimate sacrifice.

Worse, he had to make them believe that he *wanted* to do it.

Acid washed through his veins as he prepared himself to face an eternity of torture. He almost laughed at the thought. It was no less than he deserved.

No more than he'd expected.

Below him, on the cavern floor, they were still talking. He couldn't hear it, though. Couldn't make out the words. Nothing but a vast ringing noise smashed through his skull, until he heard the bloodsucker goddess issue her demand, in a voice sheathed with blood and ice that sliced through the haze of his mind.

"Do you voluntarily accept my service, Lord Vengeance, blood kin to Conlan?" Anubisa demanded.

Justice forced down the grief and bile threatening to make him puke and stepped farther out from behind the shielding rock and onto the ledge directly above and across from her. This needed to be a performance to outshine all performances.

Good thing he had the best poker face in Atlantis.

He sucked in a lungful of air and called out to her. "Of course he doesn't, you evil bitch. You're holding his girlfriend as collateral. He has no choice."

The shock on her face pleased him. He'd surprised a goddess. Maybe he had a one-in-a-thousand chance to stay alive.

Maybe.

Anubisa shot across the cavern floor, and he leapt down to meet her, standing braced and silent until she jerked to a halt, only inches separating them. The burning red of her eyes deepened until they glowed, and then she freaking sniffed him, inhaling his scent like a beast, and his skin tried to crawl off his body.

"Blue hair," she said. "And yet you smell like—"

"I smell like the blood kin of Conlan and Vengeance," he said, flashing a smile that tasted like death. "I'm their brother, and I offer myself in Vengeance's stead."

Ven exploded in denial, but Justice barely heard him. The *geas* was kicking in, biting into his nerve endings. He'd been cursed to kill anyone he told the truth of his birth. Either kill them or his mind would shatter.

He picked option C. Shacking up with a vampire goddess. At least maybe he'd have a little fun before she killed him.

Everybody was staring at him. Right. Time to start acting.

He laughed. "You think I'm lying, don't you? Precious pampered royal princes, never imagining that dear Daddy may have done the nasty with someone who wasn't their mother. Someone who wasn't even their *species*."

Anubisa shook her long black hair away from her face, staring intently into his eyes as if to discover if he were telling the truth. Ancient vampire goddesses didn't show emotion. But there was something—just a flicker—in her eyes that allowed him to believe she was buying it.

"The mating I forced on Conlan's father bore fruit? Oh, that is entirely too delicious!" She threw her head back and laughed, and the shifters who were still alive began to howl.

"Yeah, well, this delicious fruit is going to start killing everyone in this room, thanks to the *geas* laid on my ass, if you don't get me out of here," Justice said, trying to think of a way to convince her. "You wanted voluntary? Well, trust me, after centuries of having to take orders from my brothers, with their overblown sense of entitlement that came with being the royal heirs, I'm more than ready to try out the other side."

Ven protested again but Justice cut him off, then sheathed his sword and smiled down at Anubisa. "Me for him. Willing service."

Then, though it took every ounce of courage he'd ever even dreamed he possessed, he put his hands on her shoulders, yanked her to him, and kissed her. It was more challenge than kiss, and she shuddered beneath his touch, first stiffening, then melting into his embrace.

So the vampire goddess was at least something like a mortal woman. He could use that, and he might yet survive. Soul intact or not.

When Justice finally raised his head, Anubisa's eyes had faded from glowing red to black. The world shifted into insanity as, for one single moment, she appeared to be almost mortal. A woman whose beauty was so dark and terrible that any man would willingly dive through her frozen depths to his own destruction.

"No man has kissed me of his own volition for more than

five thousand years," she whispered. "I accept your offer, Lord Justice, blood kin to Conlan and to Vengeance."

"No!" Ven shouted, but he was too late. Anubisa put her arms around Justice's waist and soared upward toward the far-distant ceiling of the cavern. As they rose, Justice remembered the healing ruby that she carried—the gemstone that might save his unborn niece or nephew. He caught her lips in another kiss and moved his elbow so that it knocked the cloth-wrapped bundle from her arms, figuring that was when she'd kill him.

Shock number three thousand or so of the day: she didn't even seem to notice.

So be it. Ven and Erin would be safe—Prince Conlan, his woman, and their unborn child would be safe.

Justice had—*almost*—gained a family, and his actions this day would keep them safe. His ruined soul for the innocence of new life. Death or insanity was the smallest of prices for such value.

But he wanted to say it. *Needed* to say it. Just once. He bent his head and gazed at Ven, and uttered the word he'd been forbidden to say for so many centuries. "Brother."

Then Anubisa whispered something in a long-dead language, and his reality fractured, kaleidoscoping into the Void.

Chapter 2

Dr. Keely McDermott unlocked the door to her office, glad
that the few students wandering the long, fluorescent-lit hall-
way didn't pay any attention to her. She didn't feel much like
answering questions after the long flight from Rome.

As she hauled the heavy bag containing her precious tools
into her office, she made a mental note to order a new Marshalltown trowel. Hers had seen better days and, like most
archaeologists, she counted her tools among her most prized
possessions. She'd keep the old one for sentimental purposes,
maybe. It had been her first, and it had brought *him* to her.

Her warrior.

She glanced down at the tiny wooden carving of a fish that
rested against the front of her T-shirt, hanging on its silver
chain. The old Marshalltown had discovered the delicate
carved fish for her. Since first touching the fish three years
ago, she'd spent more time than she probably should have lost
in visions of her very grown-up version of an imaginary
friend: the blue-haired warrior from hundreds of years in the
past. He'd carved the fish while he sat next to a campfire,
laughing and talking with friends. She'd caught her breath in
wonder at that first image of him. He was beautiful, so primi-

tively male that the sight of him had quite literally taken her breath away.

From the silken wonder of his multihued hair to his high cheekbones, strong neck, and the broad shoulders topping his muscular torso, he should have been posing for a sculpture, instead of forming one from wood. The lines and muscled curves of his body had been so clearly defined in the flickering firelight of her image as he sat there, wearing only pants, head bent to his carving.

Even now, probably hundreds of years after that campfire had been extinguished, the emotional resonance of his touch shone through, sparkling through her nerve endings with an almost tangible caress each time the fish came in contact with her skin. No matter that her warrior had been lying in his grave for a very long time. Trust her to be the kind of freak who lusted after a guy who'd died centuries ago. But when she touched the carving, it offered a kind of comfort. And still, even now, a shiver of heat raced through her, bringing sensual longings she'd thought were as dead as the civilizations she studied. For him. Never for a living, attainable man.

Always for him.

She caressed the odd little fish's wooden fin and, yet again, it was almost as if he were there with her. One of the few benefits of being a touch psychic. Her face twisted in a bitter smile. Lose all of your real friends, but find a hunk of a phantom warrior to keep you company.

She sighed and wished for the thousandth or so time that she even knew his name. Anyway, whoever he was, it wasn't his fault that she was a friendless freak. She'd definitely keep the trowel.

Finally snapping out of her private daydreams, she closed her office door behind her, glancing around at her space. Mementos of her travels and digs—casts from some of her finds and a few cherished gifts from the local citizenry. Colorful pottery and small carvings jockeyed for space on the shelves, while framed stratigraphic drawings lined the walls, each showing the layers of history within the dig it represented.

Her precious books overflowed the crowded and dangerously bowing shelves of her bookcases and lined the walls in precarious piles. From the looks of the inch or two of dust on every available surface, the department secretary had followed Keely's instructions to make sure her office was left entirely undisturbed while she was gone.

Keely breathed a shuddering sigh of relief at finally returning to the closest thing to a home she'd had in many years. The sterile apartment where she stored a few personal possessions had never been home; it was simply a place where she could go to shower and change clothes. She was always here in her office, in the classroom, or on a dig, living out of a suitcase.

But here, she'd carefully chosen every single object. Nothing that could disturb her—not a single object that could send her swirling into someone else's emotions—was permitted anywhere in the room.

Here, she could finally remove her gloves.

Peeling them off, she dropped them on a corner of her desk, and a puff of displaced dust shot into the air to tickle her nose. Okay, undisturbed was fine—excellent even—but now that she was back a little housekeeping was in order.

Later.

She dropped into her chair and closed her eyes, letting the waves of exhaustion wash over her. Even after all these years, all these trips, she'd never gotten the knack of sleeping on planes. She had to be vigilant against unwanted touches. Too much of a chance that her head would drift to the side as she napped, her cheek might brush against the airplane seat, unleashing the emotions of thousands of angry, impatient, terrified, or otherwise overwrought fellow flyers directly into her vulnerable brain.

She eyed the ancient red-and-green-plaid couch that stretched its lumpy shape against one wall, wondering if a nap wouldn't be a good idea before she tackled the piles of paper, hundreds of voice-mail messages, and everything else that usually piled up during months of absence.

Sighing again, she lifted the phone. She'd get a little done now, and then feel more virtuous about napping. She punched in her code, which only took her a few seconds to remember, found a pen and paper, and waited for the flood of messages to begin.

"You have no new voice-mail messages."

Keely blinked, then shrugged, figuring she'd messed up her code. Checking the bottom of her desk blotter, where she'd penciled it against just such an occasion, she started over.

"You have no new voice-mail messages."

Slowly lowering the phone, she felt the familiar acid begin to stir in her stomach. Bad airplane food and no sleep didn't help when one was wondering why none of her colleagues had bothered to call her in more than three months.

They'd known she was gone. Of course. That was it. Just because she'd always come home to a torrent of messages didn't mean anything. Or at least it only meant that people were finally wising up and calling her on her international cell phone instead of here, where she wasn't.

Where she hadn't been.

Except . . . she hadn't gotten many calls in the field, either. Of course, she'd ignored a few calls from George in the early days of the dig. The excitement of the discovery had taken every ounce of her attention. The famous Lupercale—the very sanctuary believed by ancient Romans to be the cave where the founders of Rome, twin boys Romulus and Remus, were suckled by a she-wolf.

When the team had lowered the probes, and they'd seen the outline of the imperial eagle, exactly as described in sixteenth-century texts, right there at the apex of the vaulted ceiling, everyone in the room had started screaming.

Chills danced down her spine even now, at the memory. One of the greatest archaeological discoveries of all time, and she'd been there. Naturally she hadn't had time to return calls from her boss. Very few of her colleagues bothered to call her when she was out; they understood.

Didn't they?

Except, everyone else in the department always seemed to call each other when they were on digs. Sharing the excitement and the wonder of discovery. She'd overheard conversations in the rare staff meetings she managed to attend. But somehow she wasn't included in that circle of collegiality.

Sure, she tended to keep people at a distance. It wasn't the gloves; in this age of *Deal or No Deal*, with Howie Mandel openly talking about his OCD issues, nobody thought a self-professed germaphobe was too far outside of normal. But still, when people became friends, they hugged. Touched. Wanted her to touch things. Hold their baby. Pet the dog. Admire the new object they'd acquired.

It was too hard to avoid it all. Too hard. Too conspicuous.

She couldn't tell them the truth. She could never tell them the truth. She'd learned that the hard way with a few close friends in high school, and then with the one man she'd ever thought she loved. He'd left her. Called her a freak.

She hadn't been able to deny it back then. Still couldn't, now.

But it didn't matter when she worked. Who needed personal connection when the ancient world unfolded before her very eyes? She'd counted on at least another six months at the Lupercale.

She should have known better than to count on anything, or anyone.

Now that the shape-shifters were out in the open, it had put a whole new spin on the Romulus and Remus mythology. Not to mention changed the face of jurisdiction. The Italian contingent of the European werewolves had taken over, throwing her team out.

"We'll call you if we need you, Dr. McDermott," one of them had all but sneered at her as he shoved her out of the dig headquarters. "Don't hold your breath."

The laughter that had followed her out had echoed disturbingly with an edge of moonlight-induced madness, and mindful of the twilight hour and the nearness of the full moon, she hadn't argued.

She hadn't gotten as far as she had by being suicidal, after all.

Shaking off the memory, she realized she still held the now-buzzing phone in her hand. She replaced it in its cradle, looking around her dusty office again. Undisturbed welcome or abandoned neglect?

Funny how such a simple thing as the lack of phone messages could change a person's entire perspective.

Phones worked two ways, she reminded herself, reaching for the phone again. There was one person who would always take her calls. With her free hand, she ran a finger over the dusty edge of the only framed picture on her desk. The woman nervously smiling at the camera looked so much like Keely. The red hair was a little less vibrant. The laugh lines more pronounced. The athletic build had softened over the years, but she was still a beautiful woman.

Once, Keely had thought her the most beautiful woman in the world. Before the doctors, the disbelief, and the doubt.

The phone rang four times before the familiar click came through. Something about the phone lines out in the woods of eastern Ohio always made the connection sound like she was talking inside of a jar.

Either the bad connection or the resonance of twenty-eight years of mutual disappointment.

"Hello?"

Keely swallowed, then managed to speak over the sudden obstruction in her throat. "Hi, Mom."

"Keely?"

Keely stifled the familiar impatience. Who else could it be? Her parents hadn't wanted to risk a second pregnancy, since Keely had been . . . defective.

"Yes, Mom, it's me. How are you? How's Dad?"

"Oh, are you finally home from that terrible place? We just saw on the news that the vampires are trying to take over the Russian throne. That woman said something about being the princess Anastasia, who was turned vampire when her family was murdered. Do you think that could be true? You stayed inside after dark, didn't you? We put in a whole second crop of garlic and are selling it like hotcakes, although who would want garlic hotcakes, right? Did you—"

"Mom," Keely interrupted, marveling that her mother hadn't seemed to take a single breath during the barrage of questions. "Mom, yes, I'm home and I'm fine."

She knew from experience not to answer individual questions, or the conversation would never veer back on course. "But how about you? How's your arthritis? How's Dad?"

"Well, we're fine, honey. But Daddy's worried about you, especially since we haven't heard from you in so long. Have you been suffering any from . . . your condition?"

Guilt mixed with pain bit into Keely. Somehow her parents could always cut her the deepest, even though they meant well.

Especially because they meant well.

"Mom, you know my *condition* is not a disease. I'm just a little bit psychic. When I touch objects, I get impressions—Mom, we've been over all of this for years and years."

There was a silence on the phone, and then the quiet sound of sniffling, as though her mother were trying not to cry. Again.

Keely wondered how many other daughters caused their mother such heartache simply by existing, but tried to shove the thought away when the acid in her stomach lurched its way up to cyclone force.

"Do you still have to wear those gloves to avoid touching anything? Have you seen Dr. Koontz? He says if you'd try the hypnosis again—"

"No, I'm never going to see Dr. Koontz again, Mom. He thinks I'm crazy. He refused to believe me, even when I gave him proof by reading that pencil holder his son made for him."

"That wasn't very nice, Keely. Making up stories about his poor little boy locking his sister in the closet," her mother said, voice chiding.

"It wasn't a story, and if you'd watched him closely when I told him my vision, you'd know that he'd suspected his son of bullying for some time. Anyway, I couldn't go back even if I wanted to. Dr. Koontz fired me as a patient."

She hadn't known shrinks could do that—fire people—but evidently they could. Like most people who'd seen her "talent" up close and personal, he'd never wanted anything to do with her again. Maybe some irony there. Even the shrinks thought she was a freak. Maybe she didn't need to go there, even in the privacy of her own insecurities.

She hoped he'd at least gotten his son under control.

"Can I talk to Dad?"

"Well, he's, um . . ." Her mother's voice faltered. "He's having a little nap."

Right. The lump in Keely's throat was suddenly back, and bigger.

"Dad's never taken a nap in his life, Mom. Couldn't you at least try to come up with something believable?"

"Keely, you know that he loves you. He just doesn't know how to deal with your . . . your problem."

"Right, Mom." She tried to keep the bitterness out of her voice but could tell she was failing badly. "My problem. Well, hey, I need to go. Hundreds of voice-mail messages to return, letters to answer. You know, from the people who *do* want to talk to me."

"Keely! That's not fair. You know I'm always so happy to hear from you."

Keely softened. "I know, Mom. I was thinking I might come by for a visit this week. We could drive up to—"

"Oh, honey, this isn't a good week. We, ah, we're just so busy. I'll call you this weekend and we'll have another chat, okay?"

"Right, Mom. Okay. This weekend. I—" Keely's voice faltered, but she took a deep breath and forced the words to come. Forced herself to say the words to the mother who didn't even want to see her. "I love you, Mom."

"I love you, too, baby. We'll talk soon."

After she hung up the phone, Keely put her head down on her arms, there on her dusty desk, in the middle of her silent office, and finally gave in to the tears.

Chapter 3

Present day, the Void created by Anubisa,
goddess of Chaos and Night

Justice floated in a dark dimension composed entirely of pain, his mind cannibalizing his memories for some sense of himself. Viscous as a thick, murky potion conjured by a dark sorceress, the pain surrounded him, taunted him, buffeted him, and cradled him until he no longer existed other than as a supplicant, a slave, an unwilling participant in a twisted and torturous game.

His consciousness had dwindled down to the barest pinprick of flickering light. He knew his name, knew he was Justice in a vastness of injustice, knew that his sacrifice had saved others whose names had long been torn from his mind. But nobility was as nothing against the pain; the pain ate nobility, consumed strength, devoured pride. Ate the Body until what was left of the Body burned in acid rebellion against the Mind. The Mind screamed and howled, silent shrieks of protest against an unyielding evil that licked his blood, feasted on his terror, and laughed a dark, breathless humor of longing.

But the memories flashed, taunting him with their evanescence. First, a glimpse of the beginning. There was the cavern, and then there was after. After had been when the pain began. Of that, at least, he was sure.

Rousing slowly to consciousness, Justice had woken to a nightmare that must surely exist in the lowest of the nine hells.

As designed by Vegas.

He stared up at the canopy of the biggest bed ever made, which was draped in—no kidding—black and red satin. No overkill there. The bedpost carvings of satyrs and mutant-looking nymphets, performing perverse sexual acts that must have broken at least a few laws of physics, didn't even surprise him after the satin.

"Who are you kidding with this? Did you hire some B-movie porn set designer? If the bowm-chicka-bowm-bowm music starts up, I'm out of here," he said.

The words were no sooner out of his mouth before he remembered. The cave. His sacrifice. He was supposed to have been willing.

Anubisa hadn't forgotten, though, and regardless of her taste in boudoir décor, she was no idiot. Evil, murderous, twisted, and obsessive, but not stupid.

Goddesses rarely were.

Even those who reigned over their own fiefdom in the nine hells.

She sat on the edge of the bed, which sank perceptibly, as though the sheer force of the fury and death that rode her soul added weight to her slender frame. Almost against his will, he touched a lock of her mass of hair that hung down to her hips. Or maybe it was against his will. Maybe she was manipulating him so expertly that he didn't even realize it.

But if he really believed that, he'd give in to his fate. Try to kill her and go out in a blaze of suicidal stupidity.

He wasn't a god, but he wasn't stupid, either. He'd bide his time.

"If you do not care for the furnishings, I will change them," she said carelessly, with the air of a benevolent parent bestowing a gift on a child. Then her voice turned almost coy. "Is there anything here that you like?"

Justice hadn't lived for centuries without learning a few things about women. It amused and somehow calmed him to find that this goddess, the scourge of Atlantis for millennia, had at least a superficial resemblance to mortal woman.

He wondered if she'd ever been one.

Wondered if he'd ever dare to ask.

"You know that there is," he growled as, rolling the dice that she wouldn't kill him for his temerity, he grasped her arm and yanked her down next to him. "Your beauty is flaw-less, and well you know it."

A scarlet light flashed deep in the centers of her pupils as she slowly smiled. "There is much about me that is flawless, warrior. Shall you discover more?"

Her smile widened, and her fangs descended as she lifted her head to strike.

~~~~~~

Knowledge shot Justice into consciousness even as pain ate the memory. So he'd cooperated? Had pretended to desire her? His skin tried to crawl off of his body at the thought.

At what point did evil permeate one's soul? Lie down with dogs . . . So what if you lay down with dog goddesses? Visions of mutant fleas the size of mountain lions eating his liver did nothing to reassure him of his sanity, but the brief flare of black humor reminded him of someone.

Of something.

Perhaps of himself?

But sanity dwindled, and his brief return to lucidity faded under the pain. He was Justice, and he had been buried in the pain for years or centuries or millennia—or merely minutes?—but the pain existed outside the reality of time until only the insanity of stretched and tortured perception remained.

But the flickering point of light that was all that remained of his Being waited and watched and plotted. Because he was Justice and—no matter the eons of time that passed before his time finally came—Justice would be served.

As if to reward the courage flying in the face of utter futility, hope crouching in the shadow of utter hopelessness, a window opened into the darkness and he saw through the shadows to a face. The face was Other, not his face, not his mind, not Justice. The face was Female, but not evil. Not female death or destruction or despair. As he watched the face, watched *her*, entranced by the vividly green eyes that shone so brightly they cast a shimmer of light into his eternal darkness, his vision expanded to include her upper body and her hands, which touched something at her throat.

A wooden carving?

She held it up and pressed it against her lips, even as tears shimmered in the emeralds of her eyes and slowly traced a path down her cheeks.

Suddenly the flash of recognition struck him, nearly enough to yank him back to sanity. The carving was a small wooden fish, an oddly shaped species somewhat like a clownfish, but one he'd only seen in the very depths of the ocean. They clustered near the base of the dome covering Atlantis and seemed to entertain the children who loved to watch them.

As he had, in long ago, far more innocent days.

No landwalker would have seen that fish. So none could have carved it. Whoever she was, she held *his* carving. As he watched her cry, alone and silent, a single, crystalline tear dropped onto the carving she still held to her lips. Somehow, even though it was impossible, he felt the pain of it dig into his chest.

Impossible or not, the carving connected them. He shouted out some wordless noise of longing or loss or loneliness, and through whatever magic or hallucination that swirled between them, she heard him.

Just for an instant, she gasped and blinked those beautiful eyes and seemed to stare straight at him.

Then as the vision or mirage of her vanished and he was plunged back into the darkness but not into the despair, he realized one undeniable truth.

She was *his*.

Or she was a figment of his imagination. Suspended alone in the unending dark, Justice began to laugh.

Chapter 4

Rowes Wharf, Boston

Alexios stared up at the enormous brick-and-granite-clad building that gleamed like new money and old arrogance in the moonlight. He whistled, a low, piercing sound of disbelief, and turned to Brennan. "Are you kidding me? This is the HQ? Whatever happened to the good old days when the Apostates of Algolagnia skulked around in abandoned warehouses and damp, leaky basements?"

Alexios almost laughed at himself, although nothing about the situation was funny. They were just having a normal conversation between a couple of guys.

If the guys happened to be centuries-old Atlantean warriors who'd called to their power over water to ride air currents rich with the sharp tang of seawater and diesel fuel that mixed over Boston Harbor.

Christophe shot up through the air to join them, his *Firefly* T-shirt and faded jeans contrasting vividly with the dark clothing Alexios, Brennan, and the rest of the Seven routinely wore on missions outside of Atlantis. High Prince Conlan's elite guard and fighting force wasn't really supposed to look like Goth college kids playing rebel, after all.

As if he'd heard the thought, Christophe turned the full

force of his gaze on Alexios, who suddenly realized that the clothes meant nothing. The weight of power, barely leashed, that glowed in Christophe's eyes made the question of his attire irrelevant—the warrior was a killer as icy as the ocean's most isolated depths.

It wasn't really the time to ponder Christophe's morality, conscience, or lack of either, though. They needed to find Justice, before all hope that he was still alive vanished under the harsh reality of passing time.

"Let's check it out," Alexios called out quietly. Shimmering to mist, the three rose farther into the air until they hovered thirty or so feet over the icy winter waters of Boston Harbor.

Poseidon's warriors, preparing to play Peeping Tom.

The thought sickened Alexios, especially given what they might see from the members of a cult that experienced pleasure through pain. No matter, though. He'd give his life to find Lord Justice. They all would. Tracking down a few sick perverts for information seemed a small price to pay.

"Even if the venue seems so unlikely," he added out loud.

"Catch up, already," Christophe said, sneering. "Anubisa's twisted cult owns the lives and rotted souls of members with big bucks and bigger connections. The humans call this complex of buildings the 'Gateway to Boston.' What better way for Anubisa's acolytes to stake their claim to the rest of the new world?"

"*Stake* their claim. I get it. Vamp-worshipping cult. Stake. Funny man," Alexios said, not in the least bit amused. "Where are they?"

Brennan cleared his throat, as if stretching rusted vocal cords. Lately the warrior had been prone to longer and longer periods of silence. Alexios wondered, not for the first time, if the centuries of having no emotion were finally wearing Brennan down. "When Quinn sent word to Atlantis, she indicated that the cult held its rites in a penthouse suite of the Boston Harbor Hotel, which is contained within this building." He pointed to a section of the multistoried arch that spanned a large area.

Alexios narrowed his eyes. "Freaking luxury hotel to play their sick games in. What's next? The White House? Maybe the Lincoln bedroom?"

"Abraham Lincoln would have been sickened by the weakling who holds his office today," Brennan said, his utterly calm voice giving no hint of whether or not he shared the sentiment. "There is no evidence that President Warren has joined the Apostates, however."

Christophe threw back his head and laughed. "Yeah, who needs to join a cult devoted to finding sexual pleasure through intense pain when you're already married to a ballbuster like this country's First Lady?"

"Perhaps we should leave the political speculation for the time being," Brennan said, a hint of command in his quiet voice. "We are the Warriors of Poseidon, and it is not our purview to speculate on the humans and their leadership choices, much as we may dislike those choices. It is our honor and duty only to protect them from those predators who formerly kept to the shadows of the night."

"Right. The pride of Atlantis protecting the damn sheep who invited the wolves in to dinner," Christophe sneered. "In the decade since the shifters and vamps declared themselves to humanity, they've taken over. Vampires in Congress and now in the British parliament. Shape-shifters controlling the media. Every one of them walking around as though they owned the place. Oh, wait—they do."

Christophe snarled a phrase in ancient Atlantean and sliced a hand downward. A funnel of churning water spiraled up through the air at his command, climbing high enough to spray water at their boots before Christophe released it.

Alexios gritted his teeth against the urge to reprimand the younger warrior. After all, Christophe was only acting out the maddening frustration they all felt. "No time for any of that now. This sect may have some knowledge that can help us find Justice. That's all we care about tonight. The mission is to get it out of them, any way we can."

As the three warriors shimmered into mist and silently soared up toward the rooftop, Alexios forced the toxic memories of his own time as Anubisa's captive from his thoughts. Memory was such a pale and impotent word, anyway; it was more like a full-on, lights-and-sound flashback to the torture that had seared through his body and mind. Almost as though he yet again endured the lash of her metal-tipped whips or the agony of her mind rape.

Two years of imprisonment to the vampire goddess, in payment for some wrong she believed Poseidon had done to her so long ago that any memory of it was lost in the waters of time. At least to anyone mortal.

Goddesses had very, very long memories.

Two years of being brought to the point of death and beyond, over and over and over again. That he'd survived was no testament to his own strength or courage, but rather to how low he'd been on her list of priorities. She hadn't been around to play her twisted games with him very often, or he would have been dead.

Or worse than dead. A pathetic toy to do her bidding. A man couldn't outplay a goddess, after all. Not even a man who was also an Atlantean warrior.

As the memories shuddered through his soul, he forced himself to focus. On the mission. On Justice—his colleague and friend. And tried not to wonder if, after four long months of Anubisa's very personal attentions, there would be anything left of Justice to find.

It took them only minutes to find the right window on the hotel's top floor. Shamelessness, or the exhibitionist tendencies of its inhabitants, meant that the curtains were thrown wide. He felt his lips curl back from his teeth as he stared through the phantom reflection of his own scarred face on the glass at a scene straight out of something Dante might have written.

The hotel furniture, probably high quality and all kinds of expensive, was shoved against the walls to make a roughly square open space in the center of the suite. Dozens of naked, sweat-slicked bodies twisted and contorted into impossible positions. The gyrating forms of several red-robed Apostates whirled from victim to victim. Each of the red robes carried whips and other, darker-purposed steel implements with which they slashed out in precise movements.

The worst part of it was that there was a deliberate rhythm to it: choreographed pain in a perverted dance.

The blood dripping from every player and soaking into the pale cream color of the carpet was shockingly vivid and almost too bright to be real. But even as Alexios watched, the robed figures sliced new gashes into flesh, causing the nude humans to cry out and writhe on the floor.

Alexios snarled an ancient curse in his native tongue and shimmered back into his corporeal form, still wrapped in shadows so the ones inside didn't see him as he unsheathed his daggers.

Brennan's thoughts swirled through the air toward Alexios, stopping him mid-motion. *Hold, Alexios. We wait for the leader. These humans do not react as you might think and will not welcome our interference, in any event, so we do no good by rushing in at this time.*

"What in the hells are you talking about? They're having their skin shredded by those whips. I'd say that it's a pretty good time to welcome some interference," Alexios returned, keeping his voice low.

Christophe shimmered into shape next to him, his eyes already glowing hot with power. "Look at the sick bastards, Alexios. They're enjoying it."

Alexios swung his head back to stare in at the humans writhing in pain on the floor. "They're not—"

But then he stopped, the words frozen in his mouth. He'd seen it often enough from the Apostates during his captivity. They'd made a cult out of sexual pleasure through pain—that of others and their own.

But the worst of them were bloodsuckers like the dark goddess they worshipped. Part of her blood pride.

These were humans.

Humans. And they were screwing each other as they bled, right there on the carpet.

Alexios felt the bile roiling in his gut. "Poseidon save us. That's the most disgusting thing I've seen in a long—"

Christophe cut him off. "To each his own, Alexios. Just because you didn't enjoy whatever Anubisa did to scar your pretty face doesn't mean that some of us don't like to play a little rough sometimes."

Whirling to face the other warrior, Alexios didn't even realize he'd drawn his fist back to strike until Brennan caught his wrist in one powerful hand. "Christophe's words, as is often the case, outpace his thoughts, old friend," Brennan said calmly. "But we are only three and cannot countenance dissension between us if we are to learn any news of Lord Justice."

Alexios nodded, still boring a hole in the side of Christophe's head with his gaze. "You're right, Brennan. But when this is over, there will come a reckoning time."

Christophe never even turned to face him, but remained staring into the window, his hands clenching and unclenching at his sides. Power rolled off of him in waves, until Alexios thought the inside of his skull would burst from it.

"Christophe, ratchet it down. Now."

Christophe didn't bother to respond, but the pressure in Alexios's head diminished as Christophe's entire body stiffened and he pointed at the glass. "I bet that's our slimeball. Look at the way all the red robes are bowing and scraping."

The man—no, the *vampire*; anybody with a face that color of fish-belly white could only be the undead—striding into the room had to be at least six and a half feet tall. His bald head gleamed as though oiled, as did the rest of his body. Or at least what they could see of it, which was way too much for Alexios's taste.

"What is he wearing?" Christophe said, disgust dripping from his words. "The newest thing in leather and chains?"

"My eyes are bleeding," Alexios groaned.

"Deplorable taste in clothing or not, we perhaps should act now," Brennan murmured.

Christophe raised his palms, and two glowing spheres of pure blue-green energy instantly formed, the power of Poseidon searing through him like channeled electricity. "Now works for me," he said.

"Don't hurt the humans," Alexios shouted, but it was too late. Christophe shot the spheres at the enormous wall of glass, shattering it inward in a thunderous explosion.

The cult members nearest the window screamed and threw themselves away from the deadly shards of glass arrowing toward them, scrambling away on newly bloodied hands and knees. Shrieks and cries filled the air as everyone in the room ran or crawled away from the window.

Great. *That* wouldn't alert hotel security. Alexios sent a

quick prayer to Poseidon that at least the security force wasn't composed of shifters, then shoved Christophe out of the way and flew through the jagged hole.

The cult members scrambled to put even more distance between themselves and the intruders as the Atlanteans soared into the room and landed on the glass-covered carpet.

Everyone but the leader. He stared straight into Alexios's eyes, and he smiled. "I expected you before this, weaklings. Do you wish to join the ways of Algolagnia? I, Xinon, would be delighted to demonstrate how pain can become pleasure."

"I think we'd rather demonstrate how pain can be nothing more than pain, bloodsucker," Alexios said, scanning the room for further threat. "Nice panties, by the way."

The vamp glanced down at the leather straps he wore in place of pants, and then he smiled again. "Yes, I'd heard that you enjoyed our games when you were our . . . guest."

The fragile control Alexios had on his temper after Christophe's idiotic stunt frayed near to snapping, and he raised his daggers. "You're closer than you know to the true death, vampire, so maybe you should keep your mouth shut."

Brennan started circling the room, throwing stars in hand. The sight of the warrior's icy features had a bizarrely quieting effect on the wailing humans who huddled in the corners. As he passed each cluster, they shrank back from him and muffled their sobs with their hands.

Brennan ignored them and called out a question. "This stinks of some form of mind control. Can you release them, Christophe?"

On the opposite side of the room from Brennan, Christophe stalked closer and closer to the leader, juggling more energy spheres—this time two to a hand. His eyes glowed so brightly with power that the humans shielded their eyes from the sight. "Maybe I'll just kill old Xinon here and see if that does the trick," he said.

The vamp just threw back his head and laughed. "Do you seek to intimidate me, Atlanteans? I have lived more than one thousand years and have survived war, famine, and village mobs with flaming torches." Xinon paused and shook his head, the silver rings that pierced his ears flashing in the light. "Such a cliché, that. But do you really believe that *you* pose any threat to me?"

"Tell us where that evil whore of a goddess is keeping Lord Justice, or I'll show you my version of a threat," Alexios growled. He sliced his dagger through the air in a prearranged signal, and he, Brennan, and Christophe all advanced on the vampire.

"From what I hear, your Lord Justice went willingly into the arms of Anubisa, most exalted goddess of Chaos and Night," the vamp taunted them, hissing a little as his fangs extended and he dropped into a crouch. "Perhaps he does not want to be found. Perhaps even now he lies in her arms enjoying her favors."

Before Alexios could move or even think, Brennan whipped his arms forward and down, and two of his silver throwing stars shot through the air so fast that even Alexios's Atlantean vision barely caught a glimpse of it.

One after the other, the stars drove into the vampire's neck with such force that the first sliced halfway through and the second completed the job. Alexios stared, caught between shock and fury, as the only hope they had for finding Justice dissolved into a sizzling pool of acidic vampire slime that burned through the carpet to the concrete floor.

He whirled to face Brennan. "What in the nine hells were you thinking? We needed to get him to talk, not to—"

The words shriveled in his mouth at the expression on Brennan's face. The calm serenity of centuries was nowhere to be seen. Brennan's eyes burned like molten silver and his face contorted as his entire body shook with what could only be rage.

Rage. In Brennan, who was cursed to feel no emotion at all.

Christophe's low whistle startled Alexios out of his trance. "What the hells? Brennan? Centuries of no emotion, and you pick now to go bat shit on us?"

Alexios couldn't even speak. It was as if up were suddenly down. As if fish flew and birds swam. Brennan, in a rage. The shock of it swallowed lucid thought.

Brennan evidently had enough words for them all. A torrent

of bitterness—harsh words made lyrical by the cadence of the ancient Atlantean tongue—poured from between the warrior's bared teeth. Brennan's eyes flashed that eerie metallic silver color as he spoke, but it wasn't until Alexios saw the blood dripping from Brennan's clenched fists that he realized the warrior still held the deadly sharp throwing stars in his hands.

Brennan seemed not even to notice the blood or the pain, because he kept ranting in low, hoarse tones, now turning in a slow circle to sweep the room and the cowering humans with his gaze. The haunting refrain spilled from his lips; still in ancient Atlantean, but of course Alexios understood every word. It was, after all, their native tongue.

"Kill them. Kill them all.

"Kill them *now*."

Chapter 5

October 1776,

the former British colonies in North America

Justice stood, silently watching, until the trail of dust kicked up by the horse's hooves had long since settled back onto the rocky ground. The last rays of the setting sun shimmered over the faint path like a benediction, Nature herself approving of the rider's news.

Independence.

Since early July, evidently, when these foolhardy and insanely courageous humans had declared themselves free from British rule. Free from the oppressions of a distant monarchy. Free to wrestle their existence from a land filled with both known and unknown dangers. Of course, then they'd go too far and try to conquer those who had resided in these lands long before the newcomers had landed from distant shores.

The pattern never changed. Battle and conquest. Triumph or surrender. Peace an illusory fantasy dreamed by a madman.

"We knew it was coming," Ven said, walking up beside him. "Damned if I don't like these colonists. All guts and grit. But the locals may have a word or two to say. Especially the Illini chief. He's a good man, a temperate man, but he won't be backed into a corner without a fight."

Justice sighed. "You're not wrong. I wish it could be different." Then he turned to confront the unlikely sight of a prince of Atlantis wearing a coonskin hat. "Guts and grits?"

Ven snorted. "Grit, not grits. Try to keep up." He liked to fit in with the local populace; now he was masquerading as a fur trapper. Justice grinned, remembering Ven's disappointment that nobody in Rome wore togas these days.

"Grit: another word for courage. Many of these men would make good warriors, should they decide to oppose the shifters and vampires."

"Grit or no, a gun and a bellyful of beans won't help them in a fight with that nest of vamps," Justice replied. "And no, I still won't wear a hat made out of a dead animal, so don't ask again."

"Fine, continue on with your tragically dull existence. You look more like a native than a French trapper, anyway."

It was true. The waist-length braid branded him as a native or—worse, to some bigoted minds—a half-breed. This had been kindly pointed out to him by the reactions of many of the more . . . *aromatic* denizens of the few villages they'd bothered to stop by on this mission.

One or two of the bolder ones had ventured a comment along those lines. Then they'd caught sight of the well-worn hilt of the sword sheathed diagonally across his back. Or maybe they'd simply seen the promise of an unmourned death in his eyes.

Either way, not one of them had ever dared a second comment.

Justice understood the inherent hypocrisy in his naming another a predator. But, then again, self-awareness was simply a more enlightened kind of freedom. If freedom could be claimed by one promised—sword, sweat, and soul—to the sea god.

"Imagine Poseidon's reaction if Atlanteans signed a Declaration of Independence," he said dryly.

Ven's mouth dropped open, and then he threw back his head and let loose with a belly laugh so loud and long that it made the horses restless.

"Why horses, again? When we can travel by mist with far

less struggle?" Justice deliberately stepped a few paces away. "Not to mention with far less stench."

"Vamps don't expect much resistance from a group of fur trappers," Ven said. "Be a lot different if a group of supes materialize in their midst."

"At least we'd have the element of surprise," Justice said, again. Knew he'd lose the argument. Again.

"Oh, they'll be surprised. Anybody would be surprised to find out a pretty boy like you actually knows how to use that sword." Parting shot delivered, Ven walked, still chuckling, back toward the campfire to join the others.

Justice couldn't help the smile twitching the corners of his lips. Ven was everything an older brother should be. Too bad they'd all be rotting in the lowest of the nine hells before anybody would learn he really *was* Justice's brother.

His smile died before it had had a chance to form. Much like any hope he might have harbored that he'd ever have a family.

❧——❧

Dinner caught, cooked, and mostly eaten, except for Bastien and his sixth or seventh helping, Justice settled in next to the fire to await full dark. Not knowing where the vamps nested, the best recourse was to wait for them to rise and go on the blood hunt. The small town that had served as the vamp feeding ground for far too long lay nearby.

This vampire's blood pride was strange enough to draw Atlantean attention, even more so than the usual type. Unlike most vamp groups that stayed small due to the natural disinclination of the bloodsuckers to form any kind of allegiance or bow to any authority, this nest was rumored to be enormous. Maybe hundreds of vampires, all in one spot.

The stories held that the vampire leader had a special weapon. A jewel that could destroy his own kind and worked as a great deterrent to any of them bold enough to want to leave him. Stories and gossip had a tendency to spread like wildfire out here on the frontier, but Conlan had wanted them to investigate. So here they were, camped out like real frontiersmen.

Or so Ven would have it, spurs, grit, and all. Justice shook his head, smiling, and looked around at the small, unobtrusive camp. They'd set it up as camouflage. Close enough to hear the prearranged church bell signal; far enough away to seem harmless to any vampire sentinel.

So now they waited. Seemed like more of a warrior's life was waiting than Justice had ever expected. It's why he'd started carving in the first place. A way to focus the mind before the clashing sound and fury of battle.

He turned the block of wood over and over in his hands, wondering what shape he'd discover in its smooth grain. The small wagon, the fat, round apple, and the horse he'd already finished lay on a square of Atlantean silk on top of his folded saddle blanket.

Bastien crouched down beside him, a plate of roasted meat and the ever-present beans in one giant paw and nodded his head at the block of wood, plastering an exaggerated leer on his face. "How about a nice, full-figured woman?"

Justice laughed and shook his head. None of the settlers who tended to run from the sight of Bastien would believe his penchant for joking around with his fellow warriors. The mere sight of the nearly seven-foot-tall warrior was often enough to stop any trouble before it began. At least any *human* trouble. It took more than the sight of a few Atlantean warriors to make any of the native shifter folk raise so much as an eyebrow.

And the vampires? They were already dead, and probably figured they didn't have much to lose.

Ven tossed another branch into the fire. "Are you saying the only way Justice can get a woman is if he carves his own?" he called out.

Justice ignored them, letting the ebb and flow of their banter wash over him as he tried to see inside the wood. Tried to feel and hear what it was telling him.

He wasn't carving a woman. It was something far more basic.

Simple.

Something that felt like home and resonated with the cool depths of the sea. A memory of belonging, held captive in the mind of a warrior bound by duty to patrol this dusty, rocky barrenness.

He closed his eyes and traced the outline of the chunk of wood with his fingers. Suddenly, he knew, like he always did.

A fish. It was a *fish*.

He could almost feel his ears turning red. Poseidon's balls, they'd mock him to death for this one. A godsdamned fish, of all the ordinary things.

But it was what it was; he'd learned long ago not to try to force a carving into a shape different from the one shown to him by the wood itself. This fish was different, in any event. One that traveled the deep vastness of the trench where Atlantis lay, hidden and waiting.

Waiting these long millennia for a day that might never come.

He'd focus on the fish, though. Not politics. Not now. This fish had never seen even the barest sea-filtered glimpse of sunlight. Schools of them swam near the dome, and children loved to watch them swirl into view. When the lights from the Seven Isles touched them, they glowed a rich, translucent green.

Emeralds infused with moonlight.

As if summoned by his thoughts, a face appeared in his mind. A woman. Laughing, but carrying a weight of sadness in her eyes.

Her emerald-colored eyes.

Bastien nudged his shoulder, jolting him from the vision. Justice didn't know whether to feel relief or regret. Settled on neither.

"Dreaming about that wooden woman, my friend?"

"Not a woman. Just a fish."

Tuning out their laughter, he bent his head to the wood. He could see it now. See the elegant curves and angles of her face.

No. Not her face. The fish. Just a fish.

And yet . . .

And yet somehow far more. Somehow, something—some*one*—who gleamed like emeralds in the corner of his mind.

He'd finish it in the next several days and then perhaps gift it to one of the native children. No point to keep it. No reason to carry it back to Atlantis.

After all, fancies of emeralds aside, it was just a fish.

Chapter 6

Present day, the Void

Sound grated through darkness to ears grown unused to listening. A distant bellow, a nearness of shambling sighs. Something large stirring in the dark.

The Void. Justice knew those words held meaning, meaning he could not decipher. He was Justice of . . . of Atlantis.

But what Atlantis might be crouched slyly under the mist inside his mind.

The *geas* was broken—he had broken it. Centuries of being bound by a curse never to reveal the circumstances of his birth unless he immediately killed anyone who had heard him do so. Cursed forever to be separated from his two half brothers. He'd shattered that curse in those final moments when . . . when . . .

But the memory was lost in shadowed histories of pain. Sanity had waved its final farewell so long ago. Now duty and revenge beckoned to his consciousness, called out to what was left of Self. Isolated Names that carried weight and resonated with ravaged emotion, both light . . .

Ven.

Conlan.

Erin.

Riley.

And dark . . .

Anubisa.

Justice flinched, wheeling backward in the blackness of limbo. Anguish battled rage in the murky confines of his mind. *Anubisa*. Better not to think of her.

The sounds again. Something large moaning wetly in the dark as it lurched closer and closer.

But the face. The light. *Her*. The name. He fought for it; screamed silently into the endless emptiness of Night. Failing, always failing to achieve it. Her name.

Her.

The beast—beast? Monster? The nameless evil that approached him grunted out a series of growls, growing louder in its eagerness.

Focus. A name, not hers. Ancient wisdom passed down. Archelaus. A voice in his head.

Use all of your senses. Never rely on your mind alone. To underestimate your enemy's potential to create illusion means death. Focus, or die.

Death. Was it his time? Would he even regret life's passing? Philosophical thoughts unsuited for the eternal dark of Void, perhaps. Why not let death approach and conquer? End the ceaseless pain.

An arrow of golden light shot through the dark, blinding him. Light after eons of darkness, burning through his retinas and stabbing into his brain, trapping him in its glory. Refusing to let him retreat.

The light centered around a face. *Her* face, surrounded by a flaming corona of red hair. Green eyes alight with a fierce intelligence, yet shadowed by remembered pain.

She was a conundrum. She was hope personified.

She was *his*.

Justice knew, and he was transformed. He roared out a challenge to the monstrous creature that approached him, even as the golden light seared through him again, nearly doubling him over with its heat and flame.

She was *his*. And her name was Keely.

Chapter 7

Archaeology Department,
The Ohio State University, Columbus, Ohio

Keely folded her arms, realizing that both of the men in her cramped office could read her body language like a red warning flag, but not giving much of a damn. "I don't care how prestigious it is, or what an honor, or which government is asking. I need a vacation."

The powerful-looking man in the black suit opened his mouth to speak, but she held up a hand to stop him. "Look, Mr. Liam—"

"Just Liam," he said, a trace of impatience in his voice.

She studied his chiseled cheekbones and the waves of silken black hair that were just a shade too long for him to be a standard-issue government flunky. The breadth of his shoulders and chest combined with his towering height didn't add up to cubicle jockey, either. Not with that kind of muscle. But since when did civil servants start looking like ancient warriors?

Ancient warriors? Where did that thought come from?

Keely blinked, and suddenly she knew. The carving resting against her chest seemed almost to burn her skin. This Liam looked like *him*. Like her warrior. The one who had carved her fish. Something about the angle of the cheekbones, or the arrogant command stamped in the planes and angles of his face.

They could have been brothers . . . no, cousins, maybe.

Then again, jet lag could be making guacamole with her brain waves.

Almost as if he could see through her skull to her thoughts, Liam's midnight-blue eyes narrowed and, for half a second or so, seemed to flash silver at her.

Right. The amazing changing-eye-color trick. Sheesh. She wasn't just tired; she was at a whole new level beyond tired. Zombified, maybe. She suddenly felt in need of protection and glanced at her discarded gloves, which lay on her desk. But she didn't need them; everything had been cleared. She was safe in her office. "Okay, Liam. Here's the thing."

She lifted her shoulders and rolled her neck to try to alleviate the tension that had knotted her up into hunchback status. "I spent eighteen months out of the past two years working the Lupercale, in three-month stints. Eighteen months, three cave-ins, one mugging, and two trips to the emergency room." She shook her head. "You'd think my Italian would have improved more by now."

George Grenning spoke up from where he hunched in a chair by the door, seemingly trying to fit his lanky frame into the smallest possible space. She'd worked with him for five years. George was a renowned researcher, frequent publisher, and Indiana Jones wannabe. Even though he was head of her department, therefore her boss, and had fifteen years of age and experience over her, he still didn't have any self-confidence. "The Lupercale. The actual cave where a she-wolf nursed Romulus and Remus, the twin founders of Rome. I'd give my left arm to have been invited on that dig."

Keely's eyes narrowed, but George's open, affable face showed only a touch of awe, no envy. Archaeology was a small world, and academic politics sometimes lent themselves more to backstabbing professional jealousy than any true camaraderie, as she'd learned, painfully, through her own experiences. Even though he outranked her in the office and in the field, her special . . . talent . . . meant that she was highly in demand.

Highly in demand, in spite of the fact that nobody she'd ever worked with had known that she was anything but normal. They all credited her with "amazing cognitive leaps" or, less generously, "women's intuition."

If she'd told them the artifacts literally talked to her, she'd be coordinating her future digs from the loony bin.

Liam turned the full effect of his "I am in command" stare on George, who shriveled even further. "Dr. Grenning, while I appreciate professional curiosity, I have very little time. Perhaps you could excuse us while Dr. McDermott and I discuss the parameters of our request?"

Keely almost laughed at the sheer nerve of the man. He'd just dismissed George from *her* office. "George stays," she said flatly, lifting her Diet Coke and downing a healthy gulp. Maybe a little caffeine would help. "And you're not the only one with very little time. I said no, so perhaps you should be on your way?"

Liam clenched his jaw, and the illusion of pleasant persuasion he'd worn like a mask faded, leaving stark arrogance and command stamped on his features. "I would be more than pleased to accept your denial, except that my high prince has tasked me with this mission," he gritted out. "We are aware of your Gift, Lady Keely. We know you are an object reader, and as such you possess a Gift believed long lost in the waters of time. For that reason, and because of your reputation as a brilliant archaeologist of impeccable integrity, it is my honor to invite you to Atlantis."

Keely's laughter got trapped in her throat as she looked into his eyes, which now smouldered with pure liquid silver, distracting her. "How do you do that thing with the eyes? And, seriously? Atlantis? The lost continent? You—"

The beginning of his statement suddenly registered, and she shot an alarmed look at George, who was staring avidly at the psycho who claimed to be from Atlantis. "My gift? I don't know what you're talking about, and clearly you're a nutcase. Atlantis, right. Sure, let me pencil that in."

She pretended to scan her desk calendar, but the phrase "object reader" whirled in her mind, scratching at something buried deep. Ignoring it, she smiled sweetly and utterly insincerely at Liam. "I can fit Atlantis in two weeks from now, right after I excavate Oz."

Liam never cracked a smile. "I know not this Oz, but your priorities just changed."

"Look, I'm going to call campus security," she began, standing up and scanning her desk for anything she could use as a weapon if he got violent. The marble bust of Philip of Macedonia had possibilities, but it was too far away.

"Of course you must call whomever you wish," Liam said. But in a movement too fast for her to actually see, he leaned across her desk and pressed something into her hand, then folded her fingers around it.

Instantly, the sheer age of the smooth stone in her hand registered in every one of Keely's nerve endings. "No! No, my gloves—you don't understand—"

Then the history enveloped her. Centuries of presence whirled her into the maelstrom, and her body arched into a painful spasm as she fell across her desk, crying out, her last sight the slight hint of regret shadowing Liam's face.

Unprepared—completely and utterly unprepared—she went under.

∼⌒∼⌒∽

"I need you, my darling." The words came from Keely's lips but the voice was not hers. She looked down at the blue silken gown she wore over a voluptuous body and realized the body was not her own, either. As often happened, she was trapped in the vision—an active participant in the life of someone who'd had vivid emotions involving the object she held.

The object. Liam.

Memories of her office wavered in the back of her/their mind, misty behind the curtain of the vision. She looked down at the object, to see that she held an enormous sapphire that glowed as if tiny universes sparked to life inside it.

The sight of her/their hands drew her gaze away from the jewel. Rings adorned every finger and silver bracelets chimed like bells on her wrists as she moved her slender hands. Pale white hands that weren't tanned or scarred with the remnants of countless scrapes from countless digs.

Hands definitely not her own.

Keely looked around the sunlit room, marveling at the exotic strangeness of it. Marble columns in corners were decorated with inlaid gems and a glittering copper-like metal. A bed large enough to fit ten people graced the center of the room, hung with sheer silk draperies in white, blue, and crystalline green. The room was open to a balcony that looked out on a city of crystal and marble towers and spires.

Then, beyond, a . . . dome. She/they knew the dome. It shielded the Seven Isles from the depths of the ocean. The Seven Isles.

Atlantis.

She dropped the gem from suddenly nerveless fingers, and a whisper of cold air sliced through the room to materialize before her as a man. Tall and outrageously handsome, his masculine beauty shivered a thrill of dark desire through her. He caught the sapphire before it touched the mosaic floor, then held it out to her. It caught the light and radiated sparkling shimmers of light from its heart. "It is unusual for you to be so clumsy, *mi amara*. Especially on such an important day. We crown our new king today."

As if his words opened the gate to her other senses, she became aware of the distant sounds of many, many people shouting and calling out. Not in anger, but with a celebratory tone. The scent of roasting meat wafted through the room, unexpectedly making her stomach rumble a bit.

The man grinned, his eyes lighting up with wicked humor. "We must do something about your hunger, love, although it is other hungers I had hoped to satisfy before we must leave."

Keely felt her cheeks warm, but she smiled at him, a bystander inside someone else's body. "There is not time. You crown the new king, my love. As high priest to Poseidon, it is your duty and honor."

He bent to press a kiss to her lips, and she caught her breath at the melting heat that swirled through her body. "It is my joy. As it will be your joy, I know, to gift this small complement to the Star of Artemis to his queen. Even as the Star itself is said to heal a warrior's fractured mind, this has the power to soothe a wounded heart."

"But what will heal the wounded heart of a kingdom that must remain buried beneath the sea?"

His brows drew together as his expression turned grim. "Not even Poseidon will venture an opinion on that. The seven gems of the Trident were scattered to every far corner of the earth before the Cataclysm. Until they are returned to their rightful setting, Atlantis cannot rise. The magic will turn against itself and the dome will be destroyed.

Keely gasped, the man/her husband's words drumming a dire threat through the room. For an instant, Keely was positive that his words held great significance for her own time, but the realization faded as her host's mind wrestled for control of its own consciousness and Keely's own scientific mind perked up at the idea of gemstones with powers.

He grasped her shoulders lightly. "You must never speak of this, for none but the king and I, and now you, know the truth of the Trident. If it were to be widely known, our populace would lose all hope."

She instantly thought of a dozen questions, and when better to ask them? Searching her host's mind for the knowledge she knew was there, she formed the name on her lips. His name. "Nereus."

As if the name held power, her host body's consciousness took command of Keely's speech. "Nereus, my love, my life. I wish them every happiness that we have enjoyed."

As the man took her into his arms, his black eyes began to glow with a blue-green flame in the exact centers of his pupils. "As do I, Zelia, my wife. As do I."

Keely lifted her face to receive his kiss, and when she closed her eyes, the world swirled down to black.

∾⌒⌒∾

"Dr. McDermott! Keely!" Someone was shouting at her, the sound muffled by the ocean waves rippling across the surface of the dome. The dome . . . Atlantis.

Keely opened her eyes to the sight of Liam's face framed

by the shabby ceiling tiles in her office. Shocked to full awareness of where—and *who*—she had been, she stared into the
dark eyes of the man who'd put her through it. "You look just
like him."

Liam's arms tightened around her, and she realized that he
held her in the air, cradled like a child. Her face burned with
embarrassment. "Put me down, Atlantean. Now."

With obvious reluctance he lowered her until her feet
touched the floor. "Are you well?"

"As if you cared, you bastard. Do you have any idea—" She
cut off in midsentence, a horrible thought crossing her mind.
George. If he saw . . . all of her years of careful hiding . . .

Keely frantically scanned the room and was enormously
relieved to see that George was gone. Unless he'd gone to find
the people from the funny farm.

That would be bad.

She returned her fury to the man who deserved it. "Do you
have any idea what it does to me to touch ancient objects with
no preparation?"

She took slow, deep breaths to try to prevent the reaction,
but it was hitting her hard. Her entire body shook so fiercely
that she could barely stand, but when Liam reached out to
steady her, she flinched away from him. "Take your damn sapphire, too."

She threw it at him, and he caught it with the same preternatural speed and reflexes that the man in her vision had
demonstrated. "Nereus. You look just like him," she repeated
bitterly. "Too bad you're not a gentleman like he was."

The Atlantean flinched back as though she'd struck him,
then leaned toward her. "Did you say Nereus? You actually
saw Nereus? There were rumors, but . . . that memory would
have been embedded in the gem more than eight thousand
years ago."

She shivered and tried to make it to her chair, but he
caught her and lifted her gently onto the battered old couch in
her office. Before she could protest, he'd whipped his jacket
off and placed it around her trembling shoulders.

"What can I do, my lady?" he asked her, crouching down
before her. "What helps in this situation? Be assured you will

have my utmost apologies, but they must hold until we have secured your well-being."

She blinked, bemused by his sudden concern. "I don't . . . well, tea. Actually, some hot tea with lots of sugar would help. George can—" She looked around, remembering that George was gone. "Where did he go?"

Liam's mouth flattened into a grim line. "He ran like a scared rabbit when you collapsed. I assumed he wanted to go in search of an authority figure or for medical assistance. I was compelled to prevent that."

She was instantly alert. "What did you do?"

"I did him no permanent harm, my lady. He is merely resting, and his memories are somewhat altered. It is a small talent that I possess." He gestured with one hand, and she whipped her head around to see George lying flat out on the floor behind her desk, passed out cold, his skin bearing an alarming resemblance to the stark white of his shirt.

"You're sure he's all right? We need to call—"

"I swear to you on my life and honor, and we will call for assistance for him in a few minutes."

She subsided, since he was clearly able to stop her from going for help and George's complexion did seem to be pinking up. A couple of minutes later, after the trembling subsided enough for her to be sure she was thinking coherently, she went after the facts. "You picked an interesting way to try to persuade me to accompany you."

He raised his head in an arrogant gesture that made her suspect he really did have a high priest in his bloodline. "You have been chosen as one of only five human scientists to be allowed into Atlantis while we prepare to make the announcement of our existence to the world. Do you really need persuasion, Dr. McDermott?"

She stared at him for a long moment, knowing there was no way she could turn him down. *Atlantis.* What archaeologist wouldn't drop everything to be among the first to explore its wonders? She'd give everything she owned for the opportunity, just as she'd always done. Sacrificed friendships and relationships for the thrill of the quest. The excitement of the discovery.

If she'd do that, maybe risking her job by ignoring her boss, for the Lupercale, what wouldn't she do for Atlantis?

There was no doubt that it existed. Not after that vision. Or at least it had existed, thousands of years ago. Keely's visions had never, ever been wrong.

Still, believing it was there to be found today was a leap in both faith and logic. The former was no strength of hers; the latter told her to stay put and escort Liam to the door.

But . . . *Atlantis*. The mere thought of it caused her jet-lag-induced exhaustion to vanish. Even the chance it was something more than a fantasy-fevered dream of every archaeologist, historian, and scholar in the world was worth pursuing. She knew she'd made her decision the moment she'd seen those crystal spires.

Still, it ticked her off to give in so easily, especially after he'd knocked her sideways with that trick with the sapphire. "I'll give you my decision in forty-eight hours," she said firmly.

A gleam of amusement lit his dark eyes. "Unfortunately, I need your decision in the next forty-eight seconds, or I'll have to wipe your memory clean of this encounter and go on to the next archaeologist on my list. A man by the name of Lloyd, I believe. He does not have your Gift, but . . ." He left the threat hanging, unspoken, in the air.

Outrage flooded Keely, burning out the last remnants of residual shock. Dr. Lloyd was always one of the first to make patronizing comments about her "female intuition," usually from the front row of the audience whenever she was presenting a paper at a society meeting.

Usually while he stared at her breasts.

No *way* was he getting his skanky hands on a single speck of Atlantean dirt. She put her hands on her hips and glared at Liam. "Lloyd? He couldn't excavate his way out of a paper bag! His theories on . . ." Her voice trailed off as his lips quirked in a smile he was unable to entirely suppress.

He'd been playing her all along.

"Right. *Nice*. Not very high priestly, but effective. Very well, Mr. Liam. I'm all yours. I just need to gather my gear and handle some personal things."

He shook his head. "As to your personal affairs, you will give me a list, and any tasks you need to accomplish will be handled by one of our stewards. All the gear you need is already prepared, and I'm assuming this bag on the floor contains your own tools?"

"How did you—"

He bent down and lifted her heavy bag as if it weighed nothing. Probably with muscles like that, it didn't. "Your graduate assistant was very helpful," he said.

Keely glared at him. "I just bet she was, once she got a load of you."

A wicked smile flashed across his face, and his resemblance to the high priest from her vision grew even stronger. "I believe the term was 'total hottie.' Perhaps you could explain it to me on our journey?"

"Figure it out yourself," she muttered, snatching up her gloves and pulling them on, then taking a last look around her office. "I'm on vacation, anyway, so nobody will miss me for a while. Lead on, McHottie."

He lifted one eyebrow. "I beg your pardon?"

"Yeah. You *should* beg my pardon," she said, but there wasn't much bite to it. As she followed Liam out the door, Keely wondered what exactly she'd gotten herself into, but she couldn't suppress a shiver of excitement. Atlantis. She'd seen it herself, and her visions had never, ever been wrong.

The adventure of a lifetime, and it was all hers. She nearly laughed out loud, imagining the expressions on the faces of the countless shrinks her parents had dragged her to see.

Overdeveloped imagination bordering on psychosis, my butt, Dr. Koontz. I'm going to Atlantis.

Chapter 8

Boston

Alexios stared at Brennan, who continued his litany of murder in low, hoarse tones. "Kill them. Kill them all."

Brennan lifted his hands, aiming his deadly throwing stars at a group of humans who huddled, naked and trembling, in the corner. The motion snapped Alexios out of his state of shock and into movement, and he flashed across the room to grab Brennan's shoulders, noticing with his peripheral vision that Christophe was changing position to protect the humans.

Protect the humans.

From *Brennan*.

It boggled the freaking mind.

"Brennan! Stop it now," Alexios shouted, shaking the warrior's shoulders. The pale green of Brennan's eyes had faded into silvery fire, and there was no sign of recognition on his face when he stared at Alexios.

For a moment, even as his mind recoiled from the idea, Alexios thought he'd have to fight the man who'd saved his life on countless occasions. Brennan's arms tensed under Alexios's hands as he strained to escape, but then the enraged warrior's eyes slowly subsided back to green as a gradual sense of awareness returned to his features.

"Alexios? What—" Brennan's voice trailed off as consciousness swam up from the secret depths behind his eyes. "The leader? Where is he? Did he get away?"

Alexios released his friend and stepped back, still wary, his hands dropping to the hilts of his daggers. "Not exactly."

Christophe strode up to them, his sword out and held at the ready, a snarl on his face. "Yeah, you dusted him. Which normally I'd be all over, but we needed this one to tell us what he knew about Justice. What were you thinking?"

One of the humans rose unsteadily to his feet and took a deep breath, trying to regain some semblance of control. He was built like a manatee, and Alexios randomly wondered why it was always the ugly humans who went to the cult's naked parties.

The pretty humans undoubtedly had better things to do. Damn shame, considering how many of these gatherings he'd busted in on over the past four months.

The manatee drew a layer of pomposity around himself like a cloak and dramatically cleared his throat. Probably some captain of industry when he had his clothes on. If only his board of directors could see him now.

"Look here, you three. I don't know what you think you're doing, but this was a private party, and I'm going to call—"

"Oh, shut up, Tiny Dick," Christophe snapped. "Just a tip, but maybe you'd be better off to keep your pants on in the future." Almost negligently, he waved a hand in the air in the direction of the man, whose eyes bulged out before his eyelids fluttered closed and he silently slipped to the ground, unconscious. Alexios shot a look at Christophe and was unsurprised to see that the warrior's eyes glowed a fierce dark green with the force of the power he channeled.

"Hells, while we're at it," Christophe muttered, "why not take care of all of this?" He took a deep breath and raised his hands in the air, then whispered an ancient incantation and opened his arms in a sweeping gesture that encompassed the room. Like a wave tumbling against the shore, the humans in the room fell to the floor in a graceful, rolling line of naked flesh.

Alexios narrowed his eyes. "They're unconscious, right? You didn't just kill a roomful of humans, did you?"

Christophe laughed. "Hey, not a bad idea. What, thirty fewer idiots we have to protect from themselves?"

Alexios nearly snarled. "Fool, if you—"

"Relax. I just put them to sleep for a while. But they'll all wake up with one miserable hangover. It was the least I could do."

Brennan shoved his throwing stars in some hidden pockets in his jacket and stared at the bleeding gashes on his hands. "What happened here? Why am I bleeding? Did I truly kill the one vampire who might have helped us to find Justice?"

Alexios blew out a deep breath. "Yeah. You did. You had some kind of meltdown and went crazy on us, saying the humans must die. And if I'm not mistaken, that was a giant helping of emotion crushing you down."

Brennan raised one eyebrow, but no other evidence of even the slightest surprise marred the serene calm that had returned to blanket his expression. "Impossible. I have experienced no emotion in more than two thousand years."

A shaky but determined feminine voice interrupted them, coming from the far corner of the room. "Well, that was a pretty good imitation of it, then."

As one, the three warriors whirled to face the threat, pointing raised weapons at the figure who peered out at them from behind a large red-leather sofa. A human female, wrapped in nothing but a torn length of fabric, stood up and stared at them defiantly. Her dark hair was tangled around her shoulders and one eye was swollen and bruised as though she'd been struck—hard—in the face. In spite of her disarray, she had a compelling beauty that drew Alexios, made him want to assist her in some way.

She lifted her chin and gazed at each of them in turn. "Unless I'm either hearing things, or I'm crazy, you're from Atlantis, and you hate these monsters as much as I do. So how about we make a deal? You help me get the story of a lifetime, and I'll help you find your friend."

Christophe laughed and lowered his sword. "Right. Naked

and beaten, in this room, and you expect us to believe you're some kind of reporter? You're as sick and twisted as the rest of them."

"That may be," Alexios said slowly. "But why is she the only human still conscious?"

Brennan made a strange growling sound and stepped forward, but Alexios shot out a hand to grasp his arm. Brennan stopped dead, but never took his gaze from the woman.

She shook her head, her slender fingers twisting in the fabric she held closed over her breasts. "No, you don't understand. I'm—"

"It's okay," Christophe said, leering. "Did I mention I like sick and twisted? We should definitely get to know each other sometime."

Brennan's growling throttled up into a full-fledged roar, and he broke away from Alexios's restraining hand and shoved Christophe halfway across the room.

"You don't understand," the woman repeated, with only a slight hint of nerves threading through the determination in her voice as her gaze darted back and forth between them. "I write for the *Boston Herald*. I know where your friend is. I heard them talking about him being in someplace they call the Void."

Alexios swore. "If Justice truly is in the Void, we cannot hope to find him. The way is—"

"Through magic," she said to Alexios, though she never took her eyes from Brennan, who had retreated into some sort of fugue state as he stood, hands clenched into fists, staring at her as if he would devour her.

"Dark magic. I know some people. Look, let me find my clothes, and we can at least talk. My name is Tiernan Butler, and I'm—" She suddenly stopped midsentence, her eyes rolling back in her head, and began to collapse to the floor. Either Christophe's magic had hit her with a delayed reaction, she was more injured than she'd let on, or the shock had finally caught up to her.

Before Alexios could move, Brennan flashed through the room, a miniature meteor shower of sparkling mist blasting through the air in his wake. He swept the woman up into his arms and turned to face Alexios and Christophe, baring his teeth. All that naked rage and fury was once again on his face, battling with an emotion shining and deadly, like an unsheathed sword.

An emotion Alexios had never once seen from Brennan.

But he'd definitely seen that look from someone else recently. When Prince Conlan looked at Riley, his bride-to-be. *Possession.*

"Damn," he muttered.

"Brennan, put down the nice human," Christophe said, grinning as if at some wondrous joke. "She's—"

"Mine," Brennan said flatly. "She's mine. Come near her and die."

Alexios lowered his sword arm and sheathed his weapon, then sighed and lifted his head to stare at the ceiling. "Great. Outstanding. So now I've got unconscious and bloody humans, Justice possibly in the Void, and Brennan losing his tiny little mind. Welcome to my nightmare."

An icy wind sheared through the room and materialized into the form of Poseidon's high priest. Alaric, clad in black that was only alleviated by the shimmering silvery green light of the power glowing in his eyes, took in the situation in a single glance. "You are in luck, warrior. I specialize in nightmares."

In the space between thoughts, Alaric lifted his hands and shot a pulsing blue-green energy sphere directly at Brennan, who flew into the air, still clutching the unconscious woman, to try to escape it. But Brennan, especially under the sway of whatever dark magic that had compelled his rage to the surface, was no match for Alaric. Sparkling light surrounded the warrior and his captive and inexorably lowered them until they hung, frozen, inches above the floor.

Alaric inclined his head, and Alexios rushed forward to lift the human from Brennan's arms. As soon as he pulled her away, the frozen state of her muscles relaxed into limpness. He carefully placed her on the couch and pulled the fabric over the rounded curves that had been revealed when he moved her. She was lovely, and she was trouble.

Why did the two always go together when it came to women?

"What happened here?" Alaric demanded.

Alexios brought him up-to-date. "So, this Tiernan claims to know a way to find Justice, but it requires black magic," Alexios concluded. "What do you think?"

Alaric closed his eyes for several seconds then slowly shook his head. "Poseidon offers me no guidance on this issue, although I do know that only death magic will open the Void. We must decide on a course of action, but Conlan and Vengeance will not rest until they have rescued their . . . brother."

"I still can't believe Justice is their brother," Christophe said. "Some seriously incredible secret he kept for all those years."

"It is the nature of the *geas* that was cast upon him," Alaric said. "He was cursed never to reveal the truth unless he then killed every living being who heard it from his lips."

Alexios shook his head. "But he didn't kill any of the ones who heard him during that final battle with Caligula. I never thought to ask you, in all this time we've been searching for him. What happens when you break a *geas*?"

Alaric's eyes darkened, all the green bleeding out of them until they were purest black. "You die, Alexios. You die, or you become utterly, irreparably insane."

"Then what are we searching for?" Christophe asked, all traces of mockery and humor gone. "What will we find if we ever do locate him?"

"That is the answer that even I am afraid to give," Alaric replied. "And Poseidon will not answer my queries on this matter."

A brittle silence filled the room for several moments, while time and terrifying answers hung suspended between them. Then Alaric shook his head and gestured to a space in front of the shattered window, and an iridescent oval shape began to form. "Now we return to Atlantis, where I can attempt to discover what dark force has overtaken Brennan."

"And the woman?" Alexios asked, staring down at her.

"She comes, too, and we will determine exactly what she knows."

With that, Alaric stepped through the portal, and Brennan, still frozen, floated through it after him as if pulled on a tether.

Christophe took a last look around the room and laughed. "Wonder how they'll explain all this to themselves when they wake up?"

Still laughing, he leapt through the portal, leaving Alexios to lift Tiernan into his arms and carry her through it with him. As he entered the magical doorway to Atlantis, he looked down at her pale and bruised face. "Lady, I hope you're telling the truth. Because if we don't find Justice soon, only Poseidon himself will be able to help him."

As the portal swirled shut behind him, Alexios's words—words he knew to be sacrilegious—echoed in the dark. "And gods? Just between us, they're not always all that reliable."

Chapter 9

The Void

Use all of your senses, the forgotten voice from an ancient past repeated in Justice's mind. He struggled to comply, marshaling formidable will to defeat surrender.

Took inventory:

Sight—useless in the blackness of the Void.

Scent—providing nothing valuable, no new information. The rankness of rotted carcass. The rusted coppery aroma of primordial blood.

Sound—the grunting and moaning grew louder, closer, more and more eager. Dark's denizen gaining on its goal.

The memory of a voice. Mocking. No, not mocking. Affection underlying camaraderie. "So, Justice, you gonna sit there and think about this monster, or are you gonna kick its ass?"

Facial muscles long atrophied moved in a parody of a smile. *Bastien.* Friend. Brother.

Home.

A harsh croaking noise rasped from his throat. Speech after unrelenting silence. Defiance after near surrender.

He was Justice, and he was going home.

"Kick. Your. Ass," he growled. As battle cries went, it was

lacking. As a directional beacon to the monster, it worked very well. "Come to me, then. Come to me and die."

The monster roared out in answering challenge, a harsh, gravelly noise paired with wet, sucking sounds. Heralds of grasping greed and insatiable hunger. Worse, somewhere in the nearly inarticulate noise, words existed. Garbled, twisted. Words spoken by one who had nearly forgotten the meaning of speech.

"For so long, my enemy. So long have I waited to feast on flesh and blood and fear. Defy me, I beg of you. Defy me, and your death will taste that much sweeter," the creature grated out in rusted syllables.

It took a moment to realize that the creature spoke in ancient Greek and to formulate a response in kind. Then for an instant—trapped between thought and action—Justice knew pity. "How long?" he demanded. "How long have you been trapped here, creature?"

It was a long, shuddering pause before the creature responded. "Longer than sentience, human. Longer than reality. There is nothing but the blood."

Before pity had opportunity to crystallize into empathy, the creature sprang, snarling in bestial rage. Justice reacted, body and mind moving into the dance honed by centuries of training and practice. His arm swept up, hand reaching behind his head to grasp the hilt of the sword that he hadn't even known until that moment was still sheathed on his back.

She'd left him a weapon, then. Even with his sword, he was too puny in her eyes to pose any threat. He'd prove her wrong.

"Then we dance, monster," Justice roared, finding full voice. "For Atlantis!"

In the next second, the monster hit him, hard, smashing him down onto rocky ground that he didn't remember having been under his feet. The weight of its body was unexpectedly light. What he could feel of his attacker felt disconcertingly like it was simply a man. But the sounds of it, by the gods. What man made sounds like that?

Justice rolled backward, shifting his body to accommodate the sword, and gained his feet in the space of a few heartbeats. Holding his sword in a two-handed grip, up and before him with tip pointing down, Justice charged forward. Brute force would have to suffice; the dark made elegance irrelevant. Judging his distance by the harsh, snuffling bellows of the creature's breath, Justice ran forward two short steps and drove the point of his sword at his target, rage accelerating the force of his thrust.

The monster shrieked and swung out with a stick the size of a tree trunk, deflecting the blade, smashing into Justice's side and possibly cracking ribs. But ribs would heal if death were defeated, so Justice pressed forward, putting his full weight behind the pressure he brought to bear on his sword, trying to pierce his opponent.

Bellowing sharp cries that burned like acid in Justice's ears, the creature switched tactics. Fetid breath his only warning, Justice leapt back and away a moment before the monster's teeth clashed shut.

A shiver of humor snaked through him, in spite of death and dark and Void. A shadow of the man he'd been before all three. "Brings a whole new meaning to 'don't bite my head off,' doesn't it?" he said, and then he laughed.

· In spite of madness and impending death, he laughed.

As if in response to the forbidden sound of joy, silver-blue sigils on his sword—symbols he'd never seen on it before—appeared and began to glow. First faintly, and then with increasing power, until a circle some dozen feet in diameter shone with the crystalline light of a moonlit night.

The creature screamed and dropped the stick. Shielding its face, it cringed from the light, and the sight of it twisted something deep inside Justice. The creature was humanoid, had perhaps even been human, once. Eons ago, before darkness and madness had taken it. Its ropy, muscled form twisted and bulged with pockets of barnacle-like encrustation, and the edge of the single eye that Justice could see was staring white and blind. The light from the sword seemed to be burning it, and it shrieked and shrieked for long minutes until its wild cries subsided into sobs.

Justice could not bring himself to execute it. He lowered his sword, which still glowed with the force of a new moon, though in a place where no moon had ever shone. "How long, then? How long since you have seen light?"

The hoarse sobs paused, then haltingly came to a complete stop. "I do not know. Anubisa found me on a battlefield, near to death, when my lord Alexander defeated Thebes."

Justice rocked back a step, the force of the admission more powerful than the pain in his ribs. "More than two thousand years? All here, trapped in the Void?"

A long, shuddering sigh greeted his words. But he waited, and finally the creature spoke. "I was near death from my wounds, and she promised eternal life. I did not know I would be damned for all eternity if I accepted. When I . . . refused her embrace, in fear for my soul, she cast me here, to become a worse monster than even she was."

Harsh, cawing sobs shook the creature again. "I have not seen light once in that time. Yet she will not let me die. Only a weapon wielded by a champion will release me, by the words of her curse. But no champion will ever find himself in the Void. So here I remain, for more than two millennia, as you tell me. Undying and never to find my eternal rest."

Pity and revulsion, both, combined in Justice, and he made a rash oath, not knowing how—or if—he could fulfill it. "I am a Warrior of Poseidon, creature, and by some measure all such stand as champions to earth's humans. We will escape this hell together." He lifted his sword again, to use as a beacon instead of as a weapon, and scanned the edges of the dark surrounding them, then turned his attention to his adversary. "If we are to fight together, I cannot call you *creature*. What is your name?"

The creature—no, the *man*—lowered his arm and squinted up at Justice, his face twisted painfully with what might have been hope. "My name? I have had no name for so long . . ." He wrapped his arms around bony knees and, keening softly, rocked back and forth on the ground until Justice feared the man had once again succumbed to madness.

"If you have no name—"

"Pharnatus," the man said, mouth falling open as one having a revelation. "My name was Pharnatus. I was foot soldier to Alexander of Macedon."

Justice inclined his head. "These thousands of years later, Alexander is still recognized as one of the greatest military leaders of all time. So you are no creature but a true warrior. I am Justice, of Atlantis, Pharnatus. Let us conquer the Void together, in the name of Alexander and Atlantis."

He held out his hand, and Pharnatus stared at it for a long moment. Then the Greek reached up with his own torturously gnarled hand and Justice gently grasped it and pulled him up to his feet.

Pharnatus inhaled a long, shuddering breath, then shook his head and stepped back, his white eyes flaring in the gleaming sword light. "The scent of your blood. It still pulls at me. I have only a phantom memory of being a man, but centuries of existing as a monster. What if—"

"You are a champion in your own right, Pharnatus. Remember Alexander and gain strength from his example," Justice commanded.

Command. Yes. It was coming back to him. He was Justice of Atlantis, and he had friends. Brother warriors. Home. Pain sliced through his soul as he remembered the *geas* he had broken. The truth he'd finally revealed.

Family. He had family. Brothers. Ven and Conlan were his brothers, and he must return to Atlantis. To his family. Yet another misted memory returned to him, breaking through the shrouds in his mind as the light from his sword broke through the darkness of the Void. He shouted out a laugh, and as Pharnatus flinched back from him, the sword's brightness gleamed even stronger.

"The baby! Pharnatus, I will be an uncle! We must find a way out of here. Now." He suddenly stopped, a face—*her* face—flashing into his mind. Keely. A tidal wave of renewed strength coursed through his body.

"I must find the woman I am destined to meet."

Chapter 10

Atlantis

The last shimmers of light from the portal flickered out as it closed behind what Alexios thought must be the oddest group ever to have entered Atlantis. He felt his lungs expand, as if the air itself were telling him he could relax now.

He was home.

The ornate marble platform they'd stepped onto was bordered by the thickest profusion of trees, plants, and flowers he'd seen outside of the Amazon jungle. Delicate orchids in colors never seen anywhere else grew to heights of four feet or more, impossible masses of blooms in so many shades of purple that only the palace gardeners could name them all. Trees topped with a symphony of blossoms, cascading through warm brown and shining silvery branches.

The gardens had been a touchstone for him during the worst of the torture. He'd leave his body and imagine walking through the paths of the palace gardens, and nothing they did to his body could reach him.

"You with us, Alexios?" Christophe's sarcastic voice snapped him out of memories he had no desire to revisit, and he realized that he still held the sheet-clad, bruised human woman in his arms.

Alaric stood, face grim, one hand held out toward Brennan, who floated unmoving beside him. Christophe smirked at the six portal guards, who crouched slightly, swords held at battle ready, awaiting command.

"You may stand down," Alaric said, voice quiet but resonating with authority. "Lord Brennan has been temporarily . . . incapacitated."

The more senior of the guards bowed to the priest. "As you say, then. Shall we notify the prince?"

Alaric gazed into the distance for a moment and then made a slight motion with his shoulders that may have been a shrug. "Prince Conlan is on his way with the Lord Vengeance." He turned his glowing green gaze to the captive warrior beside him. "Perhaps now, on the soil of Atlantis, Brennan will regain his faculties."

Alexios stepped back two quick paces, still holding Tiernan, as Alaric moved his hand in a small semicircle and spoke a word under his breath. Brennan's eyes snapped open, and he also dropped into a stance of battle readiness, scanning the area as if for danger.

"Atlantis? How am I here? Xinon—the humans—the woman—"

Alaric smoothly stepped between Brennan and Alexios. "Yes, Atlantis. Perhaps you would care to explain your actions in regard to the human female?"

Brennan slowly shook his head. "I know not to what you refer. There were many human females among the Apostates. Was there one in particular that required my assistance?"

Alexios stepped out from behind Alaric, but remained at a safe distance from Brennan. Tiernan was beginning to rouse from unconsciousness, shifting restlessly in his arms. "Yeah, you could say that, Brennan. This one in particular. The one you claimed for yourself and threatened to kill us over? Ringing any bells?"

Christophe casually rolled a green sphere of pure energy from palm to palm and shot a glare at Brennan. "Bells, hells. It should be ringing a big freaking gong in that tiny emotionless brain of yours, Brennan. Let's not forget the humans you tried to kill for no reason. Not that I'm not down with that; the only good human is a dead human and all that. Bunch of damn sheep. But, oh, yeah, sacred mission, duty as warriors, blah, blah, blah. Right?"

Before Alexios could snarl a reprimand at Christophe's insolence, Tiernan opened her eyes and stared up at him. "What— Oh. Right." She took a deep breath, which did interesting things to the curves concealed by the sheet, and then she spoke again, rather calmly, considering the situation. "Will you please put me down? I think I'm going to be sick."

Alexios hastily lowered her to her feet, and she took a shaky step and then crouched down, resting one hand on the grass and clutching the sheet to her breasts with the other. She drew in several deep, shuddering breaths, but apparently managed to calm her unsettled stomach. Finally, she looked up and stared around at the ring of warriors who watched her. Slowly, she rose, shaking her head at the hand Alexios held out to assist her. Her chin lifted as she stared up and up and up, and her mouth dropped open in an expression of utter awe.

Alexios followed her gaze and realized she was staring at the nearly transparent, faintly glowing dome that surrounded Atlantis. Or beyond it, at the deep, dark currents of the ocean under which the Seven Isles rested.

Finally, she spoke, her voice husky and richly compelling. "Holy Pulitzer, Batman. This is the story of a lifetime."

The priest's eyes narrowed. "It is a story you may not yet live to tell—" he began, before he was interrupted by a deep, almost animalistic growling sound.

"Harm her and die, Priest!" Brennan shouted, even as he sprang forward toward Alaric, unsheathed daggers in his hands. "She is mine."

In the space measured by Brennan's leap, three things occurred simultaneously. First, Tiernan fell back onto the ground, dark eyes gone enormous in her white face. Second, Alaric held up a hand and again captured Brennan, freezing him in place. Third, and most unexpected, a portal that was not *the* portal, but more like a window, shimmered into existence, no larger than a single pane of glass.

As they all watched, however, the window or portal expanded until it was the height and breadth of a man. It was transparent in a darkling manner and opened to a view that must be located in one of the nine hells. Reddish-orange light pulsed sullenly over a rocky, barren landscape that twisted as though formed from volcanic eruption or a game of boulder hurling played by bored gods. Nothing living existed within it—neither tree nor plant nor creature.

They stared at it and each warrior drew his weapons, prepared for the worst. Alexios tightened his hands on the hilts of his daggers. Always prepared for the worst, even in a life lived through centuries. Unfortunately, the measure of *worst* only stretched and enlarged as the years passed.

"It's like a window looking out onto insanity itself," Christophe muttered, shaking his head in apparent disbelief.

"Yet if it is insanity, at least two inhabit therein," Alaric replied, pointing to the upper-left corner of the transparency.

Alexios caught sight of two figures, tiny and moving slowly in the far distance as viewed through the distorted window. Light gleamed from an object held by the first of the two, who shuffled forward almost painfully.

"It's a sword," Alexios said. "And look. Look at the braid swinging behind him. It's Justice! It's got to be Justice!"

Alaric whipped around and pointed to the portal guards. "You two. Take Brennan to the palace. Carry him on your back if you have to. Install him in the healing rooms, and do not, under any circumstances, let him out." He snapped out a word and Brennan collapsed into an unconscious heap on the ground.

The guards rushed forward to gather him up, but Alaric didn't wait to see that they complied with his orders. "If that is truly Justice, then we are looking directly into the Void. Again, *if* what this human female tells us is correct. There is far too much supposition in the situation to make me comfortable."

"What if he's compromised?" Christophe asked, his hands on the hilts of his daggers. "What if he's leading some sort of army for Anubisa? How can he have opened a window directly into Atlantis? The wards protect the Seven Isles from any dark magic."

The female interrupted their speculation, rising to her feet from where she'd fallen on the grass. "He's in the Void," Tiernan said. "I saw someone die giving that information. A good man, who didn't deserve what they did to him." Tears rolled down her face, but she ignored them. "Your warrior is in the Void, and if that's him, you'd better prepare for some serious bad."

Christophe sneered at her. "Yeah, like we believe you, Apostate."

Alaric cut him off with a single raised hand. "As he says, female, we have no reason to trust you. When this situation is resolved, we will learn more of each other. Until then, unless you have further information that can help us seal this breach, remain silent."

"My name is Tiernan, not female," she said, defiance in her tone. But then, murmuring something that sounded like "Pulitzer, Pulitzer, Pulitzer," she inclined her head to Alaric. "Only one more thing, and you probably know this, since you seem to be the big boss around here. The only way in and out of the Void is with death magic, and I'm not talking animals," she said, adding a crucial fact to what Alaric had told them earlier. "A *person* has to die for someone to escape—a life for a life. So unless either you or he plan to sacrifice someone, neither of you is getting through that entryway."

Christophe raised one of his daggers and took a step toward Tiernan, a dangerous smile spreading across his face. "Well, how convenient that we have a sacrifice all dressed up and with no place to go."

Alexios unsheathed his own sword and stepped in front of Tiernan. "I know you're kidding, but she doesn't. Shut up and step away from the human, unless you want to seriously piss me off. Because, Christophe, I'm having what some might call a tragically bad day."

Laughing, Christophe whirled around to look through the entryway again. The figures had moved closer, and they could almost catch sight of the features on the man in the lead.

"It can't be Justice," Alexios said. "I can tell Justice from much farther away than this, simply by the way he walks. Nobody else strides along with that inborn arrogance, as though he owns the world. This man may sport his hair in a braid, but that shuffling walk cannot belong to Lord Justice."

Alaric, never looking away from the view, replied quietly. "And yet you yourself walked in just such a manner when you were healing from what Anubisa did to you. Near-fatal injuries can stamp out even the most determined arrogance."

Unable to form a coherent response to Alaric's truth, Alexios clenched his jaw and considered their options. As they watched, the figures trudged closer and closer to the shimmering distortion of the window. "Well, don't you always tell us that the simplest solution is usually correct?" he finally managed.

"Occam may have a prior claim on that teaching, but yes," Alaric answered. "Your point?"

"My point is that we haven't even tried to get through this yet. Maybe it's as simple as walking right through."

"Sure. Because there's no chance this could be a trap, right?" Christophe said, rolling his eyes. "No chance that this could be a 'fry the Atlanteans' game on Anubisa's part."

"The female—*Tiernan*—is correct. If this is a view onto the Void, it cannot be entered without death magic. I have no desire for my own death to become the platform for that entry, by way of touching one of Anubisa's constructs," Alaric said.

Alexios was tempted, in spite of the fact that he had never known the priest to be wrong. Justice was more than friend, more than brother.

They were the Warriors of Poseidon, and they *did not leave a man behind*.

Alexios had spent much of the past months, while ceaselessly searching for Justice, considering what the long centuries of silence must have cost the warrior. What breaking the *geas* must've done to erode his mind.

What Anubisa had done to further torment him. The shields Alexios had erected in his own mind to block those memories wavered, and he clenched his hands into fists as he built his shields back into impenetrable walls. "I will make the attempt, Alaric. I will test this barrier."

Before Alaric could stop him, Alexios placed a hand flat against the wavering surface of the window. An enormously powerful energy spike slammed into him, knocking him back nearly a dozen feet. As he lay on the ground, blinking, he noticed the smoke before he saw its origin. Stunned and speechless, with the air smashed out of his lungs, Alexios held up that same hand that had touched the barrier. The nerve endings screamed in pain as though he held his hand inside the hottest fires of the deepest of the nine hells. Yet the only residual damage was blackened fingertips and smoking fingernails. Still, though, the smell of smoke grew stronger.

"Fool," snarled Alaric. "Must I talk to you as though you were the rawest of untrained warriors?" The priest raised a hand, and then sliced it through the air toward Alexios, as though throwing an object. Instead, a stream of icy water arrowed through the air and slapped Alexios in the face, drenching his head.

He leapt up off the ground, spluttering and wiping water out of his face. "What was that for?"

Christophe started laughing. "Your hair was on fire, man. Alaric probably didn't want you to scar the other side of your pretty face, too."

Alexios almost involuntarily ducked his head, so his sodden hair swung forward to cover the hideously scarred left side of his face. "Someday you'll go too far, Christophe," he snarled. "Then I will be the one to teach *you* a lesson."

Tiernan, whom he'd almost forgotten, cleared her throat. "Um, not to break up your frat-boy testosterone party, but your friend is getting closer. If he *is* still your friend, after spending time in the Void. And, what exactly is that thing walking behind him?"

Alexios ran back to the dark shimmer of a window and saw what had become painfully clear over the space of the past few moments. "That is Justice!" he shouted.

A prickling feeling on Alexios's neck was his only warning before High Prince Conlan and his brother, Lord Vengeance, shouldered their way to the window. Tension practically vibrated from the pair of them as they caught their first sight of Justice. The warrior who had claimed to be their brother immediately before he'd sacrificed himself to the vampire goddess. Justice had saved Ven's life, and the life of the gem singer Erin Connors, who was Ven's chosen and a healer. By doing so, he'd also saved the life of Prince Conlan's unborn child.

Lord Justice was a hero.

But maybe he was a hero corrupted into a traitor. There was no way to be sure, until Alaric could test him.

As if he were thought-mining Alexios, Alaric began speaking quietly and quickly, filling Ven and Conlan in on the current situation. Conlan's obsidian gaze swept over Tiernan, and he nodded to her with all courtesy. "If you speak the truth, lady, you will be rewarded. Be welcome to Atlantis."

A strange expression, almost a grimace, crossed Tiernan's face at his words, but she merely nodded.

Ven snapped a hand signal to Christophe and Alexios, directing them to keep watch over Tiernan, but Ven himself barely glanced at her, his entire attention focused on the view through the dark magic of the window. "Truth, rewards, yeah, whatever. For now, what in the freaking nine hells are we going to do?"

Alaric finished his recounting, and Ven's hands dropped to the hilts of his daggers. "Death magic? Are you kidding me?" He barked out a laugh. "Great. We finally find out Justice is alive, and we've gotta kill somebody to get him out?"

Prince Conlan glared at his brother. "No one is dying today," he snapped. Then he returned his attention to Alaric. "Options?"

"If I had any options, I would have presented them," Alaric said, his voice so icy that Alexios was surprised Conlan didn't suffer frostbite. The priest was accustomed to solving every problem and having the last word in every crisis. Alexios figured it chapped Alaric's ass to be unable to solve this one.

"Perhaps," Christophe offered, "since Justice appears to have opened the first-ever window from the Void into Atlantis, *he* may have some ideas on the matter."

"What is that thing walking behind him?" Ven asked.

"Gee, I wish I'd asked that," Tiernan said dryly.

Alexios couldn't keep the grin from escaping. The woman had guts; he'd give her that.

As the two had drawn nearer, more and more of the figure

following Justice had been revealed. It looked almost human, although grossly deformed. As it shambled along in Justice's wake, it rarely looked up, but merely stared down at the path in front of it.

"Well, maybe we'll get lucky," Christophe added. "Maybe Justice brought his own sacrifice along with him."

A flicker of light in their peripheral vision was their only warning before the Atlantean portal, situated exactly on the opposite side of the marble entry platform from the dark window, began to shiver and elongate into its usual ovoid sphere.

Threatened on both sides with possible danger, Alexios ran to position himself in front of Tiernan, daggers unsheathed. Prince Conlan and his warriors drew weapons and Alaric called power, standing in a nimbus of silvery green energy, as Justice drew ever closer on one side of the group, and two people came through the Atlantean portal on the other.

Alexios recognized Liam, one of the most dangerously effective of Poseidon's warriors, leading yet another human female. This one had blazing red hair and the most intensely green eyes he'd ever seen on a human, and she was dressed casually, clutching a worn backpack to her chest with, oddly enough, gloved hands. Liam's head was turned to her as they crossed the portal. "Welcome to Atlantis, Dr. McDermott," he said.

The woman's stunning eyes widened and her jaw tightened but, to her credit, she gave no other sign of alarm at the sight of several armed warriors and one half-naked woman. She simply blinked once, held up a hand and waved, and then glanced up at Liam. "Well. I have to admit, McHottie, this is one of my more interesting welcome parties."

Chapter 11

Atlantis

Keely had learned, from long, painful years of experience, how to appear calm on the surface when everything was going clusterfark on the inside. Now seemed like the grand finale to all that practice; the PhD exam on maintaining order during chaos.

She'd never flunked an exam yet, and no way was she starting now. What would Gertrude Bell do? Not that one of the most famous female archaeologists of all time had ever had to contend with Atlantis. But Lawrence of Arabia had to have come pretty close.

She took a deep but unobtrusive breath, while she studied the group in front of her. Armed men and a woman with a bruised face wearing a—toga? sheet?—were standing, incongruously, on the greenest grass she'd ever seen. Jade melding into finest emerald, shading into nearly a dark teal beyond them.

Beyond that? Wondrous. Alice-down-the-rabbit-hole amazing. They stood on a worn, circular marble platform near the edge of the very same dome she'd seen in her vision.

Only deepest blue beyond the dome. A touch of claustrophobia strangled her for a moment, her scientific mind calculating the water pressure per square inch that must be pressing against that dome.

Thickly leaved trees clustered in small groves near the edge of the clearing and, in the distance, she could make out the tops of the same elegant domes and delicate spires she'd seen in her vision.

In spite of her deliberately measured breathing, her lungs hiccupped out her next breath. Atlantis.

It really was Atlantis.

Or at least someplace like none she'd ever been or imagined. Unbelievable. Even the scent of it was different. Exotic. Delicate floral hints overlay deep, lush greenery. Flora and fauna as imagined by ancient hedonism.

Except it was real.

Liam now held what looked like ancient daggers in his hands, although she had no idea where they'd come from. Hidden in his clothes, probably. It's not like the portal had been armed with a metal detector. Fascinated, she took another look at the daggers. The intricate scrollwork on the hilts dated from probably—

Focus, idiot. Now is not the time to try to place ancient weaponry, when a whole lot of the same is drawn and pointed at me by men who look like they know how to use it.

After Liam, she should have been prepared, but what could have prepared her for this? Five towering men, each one of them more gorgeous—more menacing—than the one next to him.

Plus the requisite damsel in distress standing behind them.

"It's like I've wandered onto a film set," she ventured out loud, hoping to defuse the tension so evident in the air. "Which one of you is riding to the rescue of the hapless maiden?"

She forced a slight smile and indicated the bruised woman with a nod of her head, as though it were an everyday occurrence for her to find heavily armed men surrounding a half-naked woman. A woman who'd clearly been beaten or else had been in a seriously bad car accident.

While wearing a sheet.

Yeah, lots of women head out for a drive wearing nothing but a sheet. A drive in, let's not forget, *Atlantis*.

Did they even have cars? Before she could scan the area for

any evidence of Atlantean transportation, the sheet-wearing woman snorted, her mouth quirking up into a half smile. "Tiernan Butler, not hapless, definitely not maiden," she said, with too much dry humor to be a victim. Something else, then.

Keely's tension lessened slightly, and she smiled in return. "Keely McDermott, lately of Ohio State. Go, Buckeyes, anyone?"

Years of anthropological studies, which complemented her archaeology, had shaped Keely into an astute student of body language. A certain nearly unnoticeable lessening of the tension in the men's stances signaled that maybe, just maybe, she wasn't about to get skewered on the point of one of those swords.

One of the men stepped forward. He was as tall as Liam, well over six feet, and had the same silken black hair. This man had the unmistakable bearing of command, however, and the aristocratic facial features to match. A general or leader of some sort. He was clearly as beautiful and as deadly as the weapons he carried and, although modestly dressed in a deep blue shirt and black pants, he may as well have been wearing king's robes or an admiral's uniform.

"I am Conlan, high prince of Atlantis," he said, and she felt the small warmth of expectations met flare inside her. "I bid you welcome, Dr. McDermott. As you may have surmised from our . . . appearance, we find ourselves unprepared for guests." His deep voice was courteous and surprisingly unruffled, as if he hung out with his friends, fully armed, all the time.

Which, for all she knew, he did.

Before she could speak, Prince Conlan turned his attention to Liam, dismissing her. "Please take Dr. McDermott and Ms. Butler to the palace."

A second man, who looked a heck of a lot like the prince, stepped forward, shaking his head. "Better if Liam stays. Depending on what's lurking in the Void to follow Justice, we may need another set of blades."

Liam bowed to them both. "Prince Conlan and Lord Vengeance, I am honored to serve as you wish, of course. However, you should know that Dr. McDermott saw Nereus in a vision when she touched the sapphire—"

"When you forced it into my hand, you mean, which is something we need to discuss," Keely said, smoothly cutting across Liam's report. "Warrior guy or not, you need to know that ambushing me like that did not exactly make me thrilled to accept your invitation."

The one Liam had called Lord Vengeance laughed, and his laughter changed him from forbidding warrior to pure, potent male. Every one of them radiated sexual magnetism so strongly that Keely felt she'd landed in some sort of fantasyland for women who'd been alone for way too long.

"Yeah, McHottie. Your bad, definitely," Ven said, cutting into her woozy mental meanderings. "Too bad we don't have time to hear all about it." He turned his gaze to her. "Call me Ven. Can I call you Keely?"

"Of course—"

"Great. Now is not a good time, Keely. As an archaeologist, I'm guessing you're pretty good at finding things. Head due north. In fact, just go straight toward that group of armed guards running toward us; see them?"

She nodded, assuming he was pointing to the slight haziness she could see in the distance down the tree-lined path to their right. Atlantean vision was superior to human, then, she noted and filed away the thought.

"Take Ms. Butler with you, if you would," the prince said, dismissing her as he turned back toward the strangely distorted mirrorlike shape with the rest of them.

Liam bowed to her, that Old World courtesy still in place in spite of the apparent threat. "Thank you for your cooperation, Dr. McDermott. We will soon—"

A shout from the group at the mirror shape interrupted him and a booming noise thundered through the ground like a minor earthquake. Keely had experienced cave-ins before and had an archaeologist's instinctive and healthy fear of anything that could bring tons of dirt collapsing down upon her.

This time, for a change, she was aboveground, but she scanned the area for any unstable structures that might topple over and crush them. Seeing none, Keely glanced at Tiernan and noticed that the woman's face had gone dead white, and the bruises on her face stood out in stark contrast to her pallor.

"Not a lot of earthquakes where you come from?" she asked, as she crossed rapidly to Tiernan's side. "Maybe we should take their advice and get moving."

Tiernan lifted one shaking arm and pointed. "I'm all for getting out of here," she said, "but the guy on the other side of that mirror seems to be headed straight for you."

Keely swung around to gaze back at the shimmering mirror, or window, or whatever it was, and gasped, taking a quick step back. Because the man she could see through it, covered with dirt and blood and worse, was snarling like some kind of feral predator. Her scientist's mind cataloged the details, even as she recoiled from the sight of him: His long braid of dirt-crusted hair swung behind him as he ran. The sword he held in attack position gleamed with cold, steely light from symbols on the blade. He was gaining ground, pounding across a landscape that couldn't exist in reality, and a ghoul-like creature shambled along behind him.

Although she couldn't hear him—the barrier must have trapped sound—he was clearly screaming. The eerie silence coming from the vision contradicted the evidence that was plain to see: his mouth was open, his teeth were bared, and the cords in his neck were strained taut as he screamed soundlessly. Or, at least, soundlessly to all of them on this side of the barrier.

Then she noticed one final detail, and her careful, dispassionate, scientific observation collapsed underneath the weight of a single fact. This predator, this terrifying attacker, was ignoring every one of the armed men surrounding the window and staring straight at her. And, somehow, he looked familiar.

∾⎯⎯⎯⎯⎯⎯⎯⎯⎯⎯⎯≫

The Void

First, there had been the faintest glimmer of light. Then, Justice and Pharnatus had seen what looked like a portal, in the distance. Stumbling at first, then moving more swiftly, they'd headed toward what would perhaps be freedom—or merely a mirage.

Justice could see Keely now. The sight of her inflamed and

overwhelmed the remnant of sanity that laughter and the light from his sword had briefly returned to him. Some core of reason knew it might be another mirage. A false oasis sent by Anubisa to torment him.

She had done it before, Poseidon knew. Sent him images of his fellow warriors in the Seven, visions that were similar to the sight of them standing by the entryway now. Conlan and Ven, the brothers he'd never been able to claim. Christophe, smirking with his usual bad attitude. Alexios, standing strong in spite of the scarring Anubisa had left on his face and in his soul during captivity. Even Alaric, with whom Justice had so often traded harsh words.

All of them standing there, standing in front of Keely. Standing in front of the woman he knew belonged to him. He shook his head, denial and rage clashing in the battleground of his mind. Keely was *his*. Not a figment of his fevered imagination snaked into his mind by Anubisa.

Keely was *his* woman. His salvation.

This vision was different, in any event. Bastien was not there, nor Denal, the youngling. Brennan was missing, too. His calm countenance had been in the foreground of the false visions Anubisa had sent him before. Brennan was a puzzle to her, one she'd laughingly told Justice that she planned to solve. Justice had played along, at first. Pretended to have defected to her side, claiming violent hatred of his brother's regime. All those years of playing subject to Conlan's prince. Forced to pretend that he, too, was not royal by way of blood flowing through veins that were only half Atlantean. Forced to deny his Nereid mother.

Closer.

He ran and ran and the entryway appeared to grow in size as he approached it. Closer and closer. *She* came closer, and the sight of her nearly knocked his feet out from under him. Pharnatus was forgotten behind him.

Anubisa was forgotten.

There was nothing but Keely, with her red hair and green eyes and soft, luscious lips. He screamed her name.

She looked at him—directly into his eyes—and she flinched. Even so far away as he was from her, he saw her reaction, and for an instant he hated her. He hated her and yet he did not; she was his. No matter what it took, he would claim her.

Reason called out to him, flickering in the darkness of his soul. Sanity tried to force its way through the scar tissue on his psyche. *She could save us,* it claimed. *She could save us from ourselves.* But the pact of peace that had long ago been settled between his Atlantean half and his Nereid half had shattered when he'd broken his *geas* in that dank cavern underneath the mountains.

The two sides of his nature—both alpha, both dominant—battled for control of his mind. He knew the scope of his powers as Atlantean, but was only just coming into the range of his powers as a Nereid. He would either become stronger than he had ever been, or sanity would self-destruct on the rocky ground of the battlefield fought entirely inside his mind.

"Keely," he screamed. "We are coming for you."

Still running, still screaming, he caught and held her emerald gaze with his own. She was afraid, he saw. She was terrified, and some small, foreign part of him almost reveled in her fear. Self-disgust choked him. Had the Void turned him so far from himself? From duty?

From honor?

But she wasn't backing away. She wasn't backing down. She didn't run, as if she realized flight would trigger his prey instinct.

Perhaps she thought that his fellow warriors would protect her. Perhaps one of them had already claimed her. The thought of it slammed into him like a spear in his stomach, and he stumbled and fell onto the rocks, hard, feeling the skin in his hands and face as it shredded. Ignored the pain. Ignored the blood. Both were irrelevant.

Scrambling to his feet again, he ignored Pharnatus's attempts to catch up to him, checking only that his grip on his sword was still firm.

The Nereid side of his soul howled wordlessly, and searing fury built in him until it reached explosive force. Not knowing or caring what could happen, Justice ripped loose the wards he'd held so tightly against the Nereid side of his nature for so very, very long.

Nereid magic, so long denied, blasted forth. Nereid power, claiming him for its own, nearly destroyed him. Hurricane-force winds whipped around him in the stark landscape, lifting boulders the size of blue whales like a youngling's toys and then dashing them to the ground with percussive force.

Behind Justice, Pharnatus screamed with fear but kept running, ever faster, to catch up to him. Justice realized this in the periphery of consciousness, in some part of himself that was not wind, not power, not rage. He ran, warm blood dripping down into his eyes from the cuts on his forehead. Must reach her. She was real. She was reality.

She was *his* reality, and if he could only claim her, he would be healed.

Chapter 12

Keely's heart thundered in rhythm with the pounding feet of the madman racing toward her through the twisted landscape that looked like it had come from a cheap graphic novel. He was gaining ground, and he was coming for her. It was in his eyes, swirling in the madness of colors that couldn't exist. Blue, green, and silver kaleidoscoped in his eyes until she felt dizzy—almost hypnotized—and had to tear her gaze away.

Still, in spite of the madness that twisted his features, there was something. Something so familiar . . .

Ice shivered down her spine. This had definitely *not* been in the program that she'd carefully constructed in her mind in the five or six whole minutes she'd had before she'd actually stepped foot in Atlantis. She'd envisioned ruined temples, maybe a few really, really old people wandering around as caretakers. A sort of archaeological dig in progress, in other words.

Instead, she'd walked into the middle of an ancient battleground come to life. Complete with magic, madness, and mayhem, not to go all alliterative or anything.

One of the warriors—Vengeance—turned and yelled something at her, and Keely rocked back a step on her heels, only to realize that he wasn't yelling at her at all. A short curvy blonde, dressed in jeans and a simple top, was running up behind her.

Vengeance leapt toward the woman, a truly terrifying scowl on his face. "Not a good time, Erin," he snarled. "I want you safely back at the palace. Now. You can take these two with you."

Instead of being the slightest bit intimidated, however, the woman laughed. "Alaric sent word that he might need me," she said. "And when has that he-man routine of yours ever worked with me, anyway?"

Vengeance turned the weight of his wrath toward the men surrounding the distorted portal. "Alaric, what in the nine hells are you doing involving Erin in this?"

The man who turned toward them and responded was one of the most frightening men Keely had ever seen in her life. He was definitely all man—like the others, he had that same alpha-male sexual magnetism. The force of his allure pretty much rocketed off the charts, in fact.

But this one was different.

Where Conlan had given the impression of royal command, and Ven was all rough-and-ready warrior, something in this one's eerie green glowing eyes and the harsh lines of his face spoke of dark deeds whispered in shadowed alleys. This one would draw blood before you even knew you'd been cut, and he'd enjoy doing it.

Keely shivered, suddenly more terrified than she'd ever been in her life.

"Do not challenge my judgment on this, Lord Vengeance," the man, presumably Alaric, said. "If we are to have any chance to save Justice from the Void, it lies with Erin and her mastery of the Wilding."

Ven stopped, mid-snarl, and tilted his head. "You really think that can work? Every time she tries to channel the Wilding in Atlantis, the results are, to say the least, unexpected. I'd hate for her to manage to pull nothing but his blue-haired corpse through."

The humor drained from Erin's face as though an unseen hand had scrubbed it away. "Don't mock me, Ven. If I can do anything—anything at all—to bring your brother home, after what he did for me . . . for us . . . I will do it."

As Ven and Erin continued to argue, Keely found herself inexplicably drawn back toward the portal. Toward the sight of the madman still pounding toward her. He was screaming something, screaming and screaming, but she couldn't hear what it was. The mirror was silent. But somehow, suddenly, she realized what it was.

She knew *who* he was.

What had Ven said? "*His blue-haired corpse.*" Blue. Hair.

It was him. It was the warrior from her visions. She closed her eyes as her hand involuntarily rose to grasp the wooden carving she wore like a talisman. It couldn't be. The fish was probably more than two centuries old. It was impossible.

And yet . . . and yet. Here she stood, in Atlantis.

She opened her eyes and immediately locked gazes with him again, inexplicably drawn to him with the sure pull of the moon tide. This time, she was sure.

It was him. Her warrior. And he was screaming her name.

Terror thrilled through her so intensely that she felt weakened by it, and a strange lethargy spread through her limbs. Always analytical, her mind studied her reaction as though at a distance. Was this how prey reacted to the sight of the predator bearing down upon it, claws unsheathed and fangs bared?

She snapped her head left and then right in an attempt to shake off the odd lassitude that gripped her. Then she realized Conlan was speaking.

"Decide now," he snapped. "We don't have time for this, Ven. If Erin cannot channel the Wilding magic to try to open this entryway, the only other way is through death magic. And if it comes to that, I pledge myself for our brother. He saved my wife and child—I can do no less."

A shocked silence fell. Even Keely, a stranger to the culture, instantly realized the significance of what the high prince had just said. He would sacrifice himself to rescue her warrior . . . no, not her warrior, *the* warrior . . . who was evidently trapped in this Void.

"No! You're meant to be king, you idiot!" Ven shouted.

"And did you forget the baby on the way? If anyone's dying here, it will be me. He's my brother, too, and he sacrificed himself to the vampire goddess for me."

The two of them—two of the deadliest-looking men she'd ever seen, although that seemed to be fairly common down here—squared off, looking ready to fight for the right to be the one who died. They were so alike they could nearly be twins.

The exact same dark fury clashing in two nearly identical pairs of eyes.

The exact same hardening of two identically chiseled jaws.

The exact same tensing of heavily muscled arms and shoulders, as they readied to spring at one another.

"Cut it out, you idiots," Erin shouted, sprinting up next to Keely. "What good does this do for any of us, especially Justice? We need to solve this. Nobody dies today."

Keely felt a wave of dizziness threatening to topple her from her feet. In the space of an hour, she'd gone from her nice, calm, bland office at Ohio State to a place where crazy people were fighting over who got to kill themselves to rescue more crazy people, who were running through a place that couldn't possibly exist, because of a vampire goddess who couldn't possibly exist.

"Of course, I *am* standing in Atlantis," she said out loud, staring up at the dome over her head. "Either that, or I'm having some sort of psychotic breakdown."

Erin patted Keely's arm. "It's okay. It affects all of us poor humans that way at first."

Then, her actions completely contradicting her words about being a poor human, Erin lifted her arms into the air, threw her head back, and began to sing. The song was wordless, with a melody so layered with darkness and power that it seemed as if it couldn't be coming from a human voice.

The notes almost physically plucked at Keely's emotions, calling forth long-hidden memories of pain and despair. Bleakness washed through her; the hopelessness of a life lived uselessly—potential unrealized, opportunity wasted. Regret and sharper pangs of guilt poured through her, lapping at her defenses through the waves of the song's currents. Every hurt she'd inflicted—every hurt she'd *sustained*—swirled around her in a miasma of remorse and misery.

She wanted to die. She *deserved* to die. Why were they all still taking breath? She found herself clutching fists full of grass that had shaded from vibrant green to dullest gray, like the colors of her pitiful, pathetic world.

A harsh voice sliced through the fog that gripped her soul in greedy claws. "Enough! Erin, that's enough. Your song is having no effect on the Wilding, but a harsher one than you realize upon everyone standing here in its vicinity."

Keely blinked as the song faded, coming back to some semblance of herself. She realized it had been Alaric who'd spoken, because he was gripping Erin's shoulders and gently shaking her. Silvery blue light surrounded the two of them, but as he stepped away, Keely realized that the light had come only from Erin.

Erin had somehow sung despair into reality. Hello, and welcome to Fairy Tale Central.

Keely stumbled to her feet from where she'd landed on her knees. She looked around and saw that the reinforcements had arrived. Another dozen or so warriors, but they'd all fallen to the ground as well. As she started to turn back toward the portal, she realized that one of the newly arrived warriors, a look of harsh determination on his face, was leaning on his spear.

The pointed end. And he was pushing it into his chest.

She screamed and started running, knowing she couldn't make it in time. "No! It was the music; it was just the music! Somebody stop him!"

Startled, the warrior looked up at her. In an instant, one of the others knocked the spear out of his hands. Keely was running too fast to stop, though. She skidded right into the two of them, knocking them both over. As she lay there, flat on her back with the wind knocked out of her, she started to laugh. Once she started, she couldn't stop.

Two faces came into her field of vision, looking down at her. The two warriors she'd bowled over with her not-so-graceful approach. They looked concerned, which made her laugh harder.

"This must be a nervous breakdown. I've been working too hard for too long, and so my brain is just taking a little vacation. This is a fantasy, which is why I'm surrounded with magic and vampires and gorgeous men, oh my," she managed to say, in between almost painful, gasping breaths.

One of the men grinned, but the other—the one who'd been on the point of shish kebabing himself—remained solemn. "I know not why the music affected me so, my lady," he said. "But I am forever in your debt that you would save me from my own actions."

He held out his hand for hers. As he pulled her to her feet, she tried desperately to regain control of herself. As the last of her laughter faded, she heard a different sound.

This time, it was definitely not music. It was a terrifying, soul-searing howl.

"It would appear that your magic has affected the entryway insofar as to remove the sound barrier," Alaric said to Erin, who had moved to stand near Ven. "I am not sure it is an improvement."

"I've never heard a sound like that come from Justice," Ven said. "Whatever Anubisa did to him—" He left the thought unfinished as he moved to shield Erin, drawing his daggers from their sheaths. "It's party time. Here's hoping he's at least a little sane, or that you can stop him before he gets hurt, Alaric."

Keely's gaze shot to the entryway, and any last vestige of laughter inside her disappeared as though it had never existed. Because her warrior—the one they called Justice—had reached the window, and his horrible screaming stopped, as if someone had flicked a switch. He caught her in his gaze, face hardening as if he dared her to look away.

Up close, he was even more terrifying. Under the blood, grime, and tangled hair, she saw that he resembled his brothers, except for the blue hair. Under all that filth, she knew it was blue. She knew it was beautiful. She'd seen his hair clean and shining, so many times over the years, as he bent to the task of carving her little fish.

Beauty was the right word, she realized, still trapped in his gaze. Justice had a dark beauty, as if a fallen angel had turned predator and stalked the earth. But more than that, beyond any physical characteristic, there was something in his presence—something in his eyes—that called to a primal part of her in a way that had never happened when she'd seen him in her visions.

The connection was so intense that she stumbled, forgetting how to breathe. Her entire body strained toward him, intent on anything he might say or do.

But he stood silently, simply staring at her, as the hideous-looking creature behind him shuffled ever closer. Then Justice raised his sword and pointed it directly at her, looking beyond his brothers, Alaric, and the rest of them as though they didn't exist. Justice simply stared at her, his face drawn in icy lines almost as though he knew her, almost as though he despised her. She shuddered in reaction, but was unable to speak.

He mimicked her silence, saying nothing for nearly a full minute longer.

Conlan glanced at Keely, then turned back to his brother. "Justice? Can you hear us?"

Justice's gaze flickered toward Conlan, but he gave no other sign that he had heard or understood the words before his gaze locked onto Keely again. After another breath of silence, in which nobody seemed to know what to do or say, he spoke, in a harsh, rasping voice. "You are her. You are Keely."

His words were a demand, not a question. She found herself nodding, as though compelled to respond. "Yes," she replied, voice barely above a whisper. "I am Keely."

He smiled a slow, dangerous smile, and the whiteness of his teeth was almost shocking in the darkness of his face. "We are Justice," he said. "And you are ours."

Chapter 13

Justice stared at the woman, wondering when and how she'd become the focal point of his universe. Wondering how she could be so beautiful that she glowed like a jewel in the setting of Atlantis. He was drawn to the courage he saw in her eyes and—for the barest instant—nobility and honor counseled him to turn away. To remain in the Void and never, ever attempt to find her again. She was light to his darkness, and he was twisted.

Everything about him was wrong.

For that single, frozen moment, the Atlantean side of him struggled against the compelling need, harsh demand, and bitter hunger that poured forth from his Nereid half. But his Nereid side had been too long denied.

It wanted. It *needed*. It needed Keely, and it would have her.

A wordless roar exploded up from his lungs and burst from his throat. He would take her. Now. He stepped forward to cross the entryway, but at the first touch of his hand to the glassy surface, a fierce electrical charge knocked him back half a dozen paces.

Behind him, Pharnatus, the poor creature he'd nearly forgotten, stumbled to a stop. "I understand not what is happening here, my lord. But any entryway from the Void is gated and shielded by death magic. As the vampire goddess created them, so must they be passed. Without a blood sacrifice, you cannot join yon fellows, nor they you."

Justice swung around, snarling, the sword still raised in his hand. Pharnatus cringed, shielding his face with one arm, his wild eyes rolling in their sockets. "What little sight I have left to me proclaims that you are near to taking my life," he said, with no little dignity. "At least let me say my final words to the gods of my fathers before you do so."

Before Justice could deny it, almost before he could check the impulse to strike out, the deformed creature who had once been a man bowed his head and knelt on one knee. He began murmuring a simple litany of prayer and Justice was shocked to hear that it was a prayer of gratitude.

Thankfulness.

He grasped Pharnatus by the shoulder and yanked him up. "What can you possibly have left in the way of gratitude? What can you be saying to those worthless gods of yours, who would leave you in this hell for thousands of years? They deserve neither your prayers nor your thanks, but only your hatred and vengeance."

Justice's Greek was almost unintelligible as he snarled it through clenched teeth, but the man before him seemed to understand.

"Perhaps you would have been right, once," Pharnatus murmured through cracked and twisted lips. "Perhaps I would have died with vengeance on my tongue and loathing in my heart, then. But you came, and you brought light through your holy sword. Light shone upon my face again, for one last time, after two millennia of darkness. How can I not be thankful? How can I not believe in my gods? For you are their messenger, and now, with your shining sword, you will deliver me to them."

Justice took a step back, all but screaming with frustration. "I am no god's messenger, you poor, deluded fool. I am naught but the cast-off bastard of a hypocritical king, and the unwanted bane of the sea god. Even my own mother abandoned me. So speak to me not of gods and messengers. I will not kill you. Though my name is Justice, I am no deliverer of it."

He turned back to the window. He would have no entry into Atlantis, then. He would never again set foot in his homeland. He had not known that the thought of it would wrench through him with such biting agony and rank despair, but he would give his own life before he would take that of this poor, miserable creature.

He could not bear to look at Keely again, so he was careful to gaze only at Conlan and Ven. "Brothers," he said, the word somehow shaping itself in Atlantean instead of the ancient Greek. "After all these years, I can finally call you my brothers, and then it is only so that I can tell you farewell."

The Nereid inside him howled silently with rage, but it was silenced by the Atlantean half of his soul when he saw the tears that fell from his brothers' eyes. Conlan and Ven, the brothers he'd never been able to claim, stood anguished before him, with the evidence of their regard for him tracking down their faces.

"Never farewell, my brother," said Conlan, his dark eyes flashing to silver. "Not when we have only just found you. I claim as king's right the sacrifice. Know that I do this in love for you, and be healed by it."

Before Justice could react, Conlan lifted a dagger to his own throat and pressed the blade into his flesh. Ven's reaction was much quicker, however, as he snarled out a warning and knocked Conlan's blade from his hand. "You will not, you damned fool! I told you, if anybody is sacrificing himself for our brother, it's going to be me."

With that, Ven twisted so that he was under Conlan's arm, and he forced Conlan's hand up until the dagger, still clenched in Conlan's fist, cut into Ven's throat. A line of vividly scarlet blood oozed from underneath the blade, mesmerizing Justice with its vibrant color.

Vibrancy. Life. The lives that both of his brothers were willing to sacrifice for *him*. The realization knocked him out of the strange trance caused by the sight of the dripping blood. "No. No! You cannot. I will not have it. I will not have your lives upon my conscience. I am not, and never have been, worthy of your sacrifice."

But either they didn't hear him, or they ignored him, because they were fighting over the dagger. Fighting each other over who would die so that he could return home.

Agony wrenched like cold steel through his chest at the thought of either of them dying on his behalf. "No," he shouted again. "I will not have it. I am returning to the Void, so any sacrifice you make would be in vain. Lower your blade, and do not continue with this course of stupidity."

He forced a mocking sarcasm that he did not feel into his voice. "You are such fools, the both of you. I am almost ashamed to call you my brothers. Leave off this madness now. I gladly return to the Void to escape your maudlin sacrificial tendencies."

And then, in an act of courage beyond any he'd known in all of his centuries, he raised his head to take one last look at Keely. He drank in the sight of her—the glorious red hair he would never touch, the lush body he would never feel next to his own. "Remember me, my lady. That is all I ask of you for this or any lifetime. Remember me, although you never knew me, for I feel that I have known you for all eternity and hungered for you for even longer, still."

With that, he turned to walk away, fighting every instinct that he possessed. His mind and heart and soul screamed at him that he could not leave her. And yet his honor knew that he could not allow his brothers to make the ultimate sacrifice for him.

As he turned, sword still held out in front of him, forgotten, Pharnatus blocked his way. "No 'cast-off bastard' would occasion such loyalty on the part of his brothers," he said, a simple dignity shining on his twisted features. "You are a messenger of the gods, although you do not know the truth of yourself. You are the emissary of my deliverance from darkness, from Anubisa, and from meaningless death."

At that moment, Pharnatus gasped and lifted his head to stare in wide-eyed terror at something over Justice's shoulder. Justice whirled around to see what new threat had arrived, but before he'd even begun to turn his body toward Anubisa's damnable portal, a sudden and ominous weight shoved itself onto him.

Reflexively, he bent his knees to catch Pharnatus as the man fell into his arms. But, looking down, Justice realized that his sword was buried to the hilt in Pharnatus's abdomen, and he threw his head back and howled his despair to the throbbing red sky.

"To any gods who are listening, know this," the Greek said, straining to shape each word, his face contorted in a shining combination of agony and exultation. "I do this of my own free will, and my sacrifice must release Lord Justice from his imprisonment."

Justice screamed and pulled the sword out of Pharnatus, as the man collapsed into his grasp. "No! Not for me! Never for me! I don't deserve your sacrifice," he cried out, his own tears pouring down his face. "You cannot do this."

"I have done it," Pharnatus said, voice fading. "And it is now for you to live your life with the knowledge of it. The knowledge that you are worthy, and the gods have chosen you for a reason."

With that, a joy suffused the Greek's face, and he held up his arms as though to an unseen herald. "Alexander, my lord, you have come for me," he cried.

With one last shuddering breath, Pharnatus closed his eyes and died.

A giant booming noise slammed through the Void like a shock wave, and Justice looked up to see that the distorted surface of the entryway had turned transparent.

High Priest Alaric leaned through the opening and held out one arm. "His sacrifice has opened the way, but only one living being may pass. I cannot come to you, Justice. You must walk through to us."

"I will not leave him," Justice rasped. "I did not deserve him, and I will not leave him."

"You may bring his body," Alaric said. "He is no longer alive, and thus is not subject to the strictures of the Void. But come now, before the gate closes."

Justice looked down at his sword and noted, with some corner of his mind, that it no longer glowed. In fact, the blade itself had turned black. "Black to match my soul, which was so unworthy of his sacrifice," he said bitterly. Through habit borne of centuries, though, he wiped it on his sleeve and sheathed it on his back instead of hurling it out into the wasteland of the Void.

"Now, you must hurry," Alaric urged. "We do not know how long the gate will remain open."

There was nothing else for it. If he remained in the Void, he would render Pharnatus's sacrifice irrelevant. He could not—would not—do that. He gathered the fallen man in his arms and stood. Then, in a single leap, he passed through the gates of the Void and into Atlantis.

As he crossed into the air of his native land, the fragile peace between his two natures shattered. The Nereid half of his soul screamed defiance, and his Atlantean side bowed its head in shame that the fallen man had sacrificed himself for such a worthless being as himself. His skull pounded with the raging fury of his divided psyche's battle for control.

But what matter was more pain after so long of nothing else?

He thrust his pitiful burden into Alaric's arms. "I would ask that you honor this man with the ancient burial rites. He was a Greek foot soldier in Alexander's army and survived two millennia in the Void."

Alaric inclined his head. "So it will be done, as honor and testament to his survival and for his sacrifice."

Justice threw his head back and shouted out a harsh bark of laughter that had no humor in it. "There was no reason behind his misguided act, although the selflessness is of itself worth honoring. But he should not have done it for me. Never for me."

Behind him, Ven and Conlan stepped closer. As one, they put their arms around him in a fierce embrace. In that instant, they were finally more than comrades or fellow warriors. They were brothers—*family*. For an instant, Justice allowed himself to experience what others had known. The warmth of belonging. But then he pushed them away.

"Do not think to include me in your royal lineage through a mere accident of birth," he sneered. "We are brothers in name only, and I would not have it any other way. I seek nothing now but to release myself from the burden of this man's unwanted sacrifice."

A soft noise caught his attention, the sound of denial made without words. It was her. It was Keely. The pain had nearly washed away his awareness of her presence. He looked up and directly into her eyes, greener than emeralds and deeper than the ocean currents that surrounded them. She was clutching one hand at her throat, and the silky warm skin of her neck entranced him. He wanted to hold her, to bury his face in the curve where her neck met her shoulder and never let her go.

When she spoke, the liquid cadence of her voice caught at something deep in his soul. In both of his souls.

"Don't do that," she said, in a husky voice that sang heat and fire down his spine. "Don't belittle his gift to you. In all of history, there's no honor greater than self-sacrifice, and this poor man gave his life for you."

He froze, both halves of his soul trapped by the sorrow in her voice. Every fiber of his being yearned toward her, desperate to know her. Desperate to hold her. Desperate to *have* her.

He would never, ever be worthy of her. But he was past caring.

"You wish me to honor him? Your wish is my command, lady," he snarled, losing all control—only able to focus on her. On taking her. "I honor his sacrifice with that of yours to me."

With those words, and nothing else beyond some vague knowledge of a Nereid power he'd never wielded, he sprang toward Keely, caught her up in his arms, and willed that they would be elsewhere. Just the two of them. Willed them to a sanctuary he had not visited in more than two centuries.

As a deep, blue-green mist swirled from nothingness to surround him, his last sight was of the shocked faces of Alaric and his brothers. Then, before she had a chance to protest, he tightened his hold on Keely and closed his eyes as the darkness claimed them.

Chapter 14

Atlantis,

a cavern underneath the Temple of the Nereids

Keely's consciousness shattered and re-formed, over and over, brilliantly colored particles of matter swirling around her like a sandstorm conceived by an insane artist. It lasted for mere seconds—somehow she knew that—even though her sense of time and space was thrown off-kilter. She existed and did not exist simultaneously in several different realities, but in every one of them, she was held by arms like steel bands against a rock-hard chest.

If steel and rock were to throw off heat like a furnace and smell like blood and dirt.

Suddenly, the vortex disappeared and she landed on her feet, hard, on a stone floor. Only Justice's strength and balance kept her from falling. She waited, eyes clenched shut, taking rapid, shallow breaths, until she could trust herself to talk or move without danger of losing the contents of her roiling stomach.

The arms around her tightened, pressing her closer into his embrace, and fear overruled nausea. Her eyes snapped open and she pushed against his chest with all the strength she could muster. She may as well have saved herself the effort for as much effect as she had on him. It was like pushing against boulders in a cave-in; the same sense of sheer immovable weight.

Fear turned into frustration and an overwhelming feeling of having had way, way more than enough pulsed through her head with the beginning of a whiz-banger of a headache.

"Let. Me. Go," she gritted out from between clenched teeth, staring determinedly at his chest. Although she was above-average height for a woman at five-eight, he was considerably taller, probably at least six-four. Somehow she knew she didn't want to look into his eyes. Not now. Not when he still held her trapped in his arms.

He finally spoke, still with that rusty hoarseness to his voice. "We are not sure that we wish to let you go, our Keely."

Her mind stuttered over his odd use of the plural, but before she could figure out a response, his arms loosened and, in spite of his words to the contrary, he released her. She immediately stumbled back and away from him, refusing to look down at her own shirt and pants, now also streaked with the blood from his body. Nausea was winning, and she didn't need to give it a boost. Instead, she scanned her surroundings to try to figure out where she was.

Figuring out how she'd gotten there could wait till later.

The dark space was enormous, with the roof so high overhead that she couldn't see it. The floor was an intricately patterned mosaic that reminded her of the floor she'd seen in her vision of Nereus. The faint, not unpleasant scent of minerals hung in the slightly humid air. It reminded her of the hot springs in California.

"Where are we?" She'd start with the simple questions, since she wasn't at all sure how sane the wild man who'd abducted her really was. Simply because he was the man from her vision—or his evil twin—didn't mean that she was safe with him.

She involuntarily touched the carving through her shirt. The man she'd seen, sitting next to the fire, carving her fish . . . he was like an oddly distorted photographic image of this warrior. It made her doubt her visions.

It made her doubt herself.

Maybe this man, Justice, was a descendant of the warrior from her vision? Maybe.

"A cavern deep beneath the Temple of the Nereids," he said. "Fitting, isn't it, since our Nereid half has finally assumed dominion over us?"

Okay. Time to tackle the obvious question. "Us? Who is us? Do you always talk about yourself in the plural?" Maybe not the best idea, to confront his psychosis head-on, but she was an archaeologist, not a shrink. After an entire childhood spent being dragged from one psychiatrist to another, she was uniquely qualified to know the difference.

Manic-depressive. Borderline sociopathy. Complete lack of any sense of reality.

The diagnoses, professional sounding or not, burned through her mind like acid. Had she spent all those years trying to convince her parents she really was normal—really was sane—only to lose her grip on reality now?

She pushed the doubts aside and drew in a deep, shaky breath. Gathering up what remained of her battered courage, she finally looked directly at him. Up close, he was even more terrifyingly feral and—though it made no sense at all—even more compelling. Although he stood straight and tall before her, he gave the impression of a predator crouched to spring.

Which brought her back to the uncomfortable sensation of being his prey.

All those years of studying the past, and now she was confronted with primitive savagery in all of its raging glory. The man was an ancient warrior come to life, not one buried in the sands of history, as she'd always assumed.

The rags he wore seemed to be the remains of a simple shirt and pants that either had seen battle or else had been run through a shredder. His thickly muscled chest was clearly visible under the tattered fabric, although both were streaked with blood and dirt. Her stomach flipped threateningly and she quickly looked away from the blood.

She was tough; she'd always had to be tough. But right now her equilibrium was not happy with anything about her situation. It didn't make her a coward not to want to stare at that poor man's blood.

A leather strap crossed his chest and attached to the top of the sheath on his back. He'd wielded the sword as though it were an extension of his arm, and it was evident that he'd used it many, many times before.

The strands of hair falling around his face and the ragged braid that hung to his waist were blue, as she'd known. But no simple blue, this. The hues of his hair ranged across the entire spectrum—from deepest midnight to the pale blue of a summer sky. At least from what she could tell, underneath the dirt and blood that covered almost every inch of him.

The taut lines of his face were classically perfect. She'd seen Roman statuary that would have suffered in comparison. And his eyes were either black or so darkly blue that light didn't touch them at all. His lips curved in the merest suggestion of a mocking smile, and she realized that she'd been staring at him like some starstruck coed for longer than she wanted to admit.

Or like someone in fear for her life.

"I can provide more light, if you would examine me further, my lady," he said, voice husky. "However, I find that my control is not what I might wish after the events of today, and your perusal is not helping me refrain from acting upon my baser impulses."

"You don't sound insane," she blurted out, then groaned. "I'm sorry. Really. I'm not trying to antagonize or upset you in any way," she said, trying for a calm and level tone, even as she stepped back a few more paces. "Although, you've gotta admit that you have some explaining to do. But let's start with how we got here and how we can get out, okay? Then we can move on to more complex questions, like how it is that you know me."

She considered showing him the carving and asking him about it, but decided against it. Not yet. Establishing some connection between them, no matter how tenuous, didn't seem wise considering his present state of mind.

Reason with the crazy man now; break down in hysterical panic later. Check. All those times she'd stayed up alone at night to guard against potential tomb robbers, she hadn't been scared then. Well, okay, she'd been scared spitless. But the experiences now allowed her to pretend a calm she was miles away from feeling.

He waved a hand, and a row of lanterns that circled the cavern lit up with softly glowing blue-green light. She gasped a little, not at the parlor trick with the lights, but at the vast expanse of space revealed, including a large pond-like body of water that must be the mineral spring she'd smelled earlier. Turning slowly in a circle, she studied the cavern and the sparkling gemstones built into the walls all the way around them, scientific curiosity almost overcoming her very sensible fear of what he might be planning to do with her. Or *to* her.

"Is it some kind of geode?" she murmured, mostly to herself, but he answered.

"Yes. Partially. The chamber directly above us is a geode and used in the healing rituals of the Temple. But this is a simple cavern, although the walls themselves are embedded with, as far as I remember, examples of every gemstone ever known to Atlantis," he said, slowly moving toward her. "You are more beautiful than I'd imagined."

The abrupt change of subject caught her off guard, and she snapped back into alert mode. "What? Why? Why did you imagine me? And why are we here, and who the *hell* are you? I heard the prince and his brother—the other prince?—say that you were their long-lost brother. So why aren't you at the big royal family reunion right now? Prodigal son and all that?"

His eyes narrowed. "You heard a lot. How long have you been in Atlantis? Long enough for one of them to claim you?" His words came out in a low, growling tone, and he visibly tensed, as if restraining himself from pouncing on her.

She backed up again, holding up her hands in an attempt to placate him and steer him away from whatever crazed ideas he was formulating. "Look, Mr. Justice, or Prince Justice if you prefer, I don't know what you're talking about. Nobody claims me. This is not the twelfth century. Your buddy Liam came to my office to offer me the chance to study Atlantis. I'm an archaeologist, and I—" She stopped, not really knowing how to explain.

He calmed somewhat, tense muscles relaxing for a moment, but then a wave of something that looked like either despair or loathing crossed his face, and he shuddered. "We seem to be unable to think clearly around you, Keely. Perhaps you might rest while we bathe, so that we can continue this discussion when we do not stink of the blood of Pharnatus's self-sacrifice."

"Rest? *Rest?*" She heard her voice rise into a near shout, but couldn't seem to help it. "Are you kidding me? You've just escaped from someplace that can't exist, a pitiful man killed himself in your arms with your sword, you kidnapped me, you're talking about yourself in the plural again, and about claiming and baser impulses, and you want me to *take a nap?*"

She clenched her hands into fists and looked wildly around for something she could use to defend herself, jarringly aware that it was the second time in one day she'd had to do so. "If I ever get out of this, I'm buying a switchblade," she snapped. "Or maybe a Taser. Or a gun. There is no napping. There is no resting. There is only *you*, getting *me* out of here."

He lifted the sheathed sword over his head, and she figured she was done for. Her mother had always warned her that her mouth would get her in trouble.

Moderately famous archaeologist killed by ancient warrior come to life: reenactment on YouTube.

But he simply placed the sword, sheath and all, on the ground, and then pulled off the remnant of his shirt. Blood and dirt streaked his skin, and she could see by the scar tissue in half a dozen places that he'd been badly wounded many times. Some of those looked like they should have been fatal.

"Are you hurt?" she found herself asking. "The—that blood—is any of it yours? Do you need medical assistance? I know some rudimentary first aid, if you can get us to some supplies."

He froze in place and stared at her, an expression she couldn't decipher on his face. "Did you just offer aid?"

Exasperated, she folded her arms over her chest. "Yes. Why? Am I breaking some kind of 'don't touch the royalty' rule? Because I have to tell you, I've got a good healthy dose of scared going on right now, but it's about to get overruled by what my grandmother always called 'pure cussed ornery.'"

He blinked. "You honor your grandmother, then, for you are both warrior women, are you not?"

It was her turn to blink, because that had almost sounded like admiration in his voice. "But—"

"No," he said, cutting her off. "There is no rule against touching royalty, although I claim no such heritage for myself. Half brother or no, I was merely the unwanted bastard forced on a captive king. It is rather that I could not believe you would offer to aid me when I have treated you so very poorly."

She tried to process the information, but she didn't have enough knowledge to form any theories. The soap opera drama of royal families throughout history seemed to be in full force with this one, too, and she needed more knowledge before she even wanted to speculate. "I did. I mean, I will. Help you if you need it," she managed to say, her breath catching in her throat as he started toward her. Then a thought occurred to her. "You said 'I' again. Not 'we.' Is that . . . Can you explain that?"

He walked slowly as if to show he meant no threat and finally came to a stop directly in front of her. "You honor me, Keely, and I will explain as much as I can. But first I must bathe and rest. You need rest, as well."

"Not that again! Look, I told you—" But as she looked up into his eyes, she forgot what she'd been thinking. Blue-green flames danced deep in the centers of his black pupils and, fascinated, she raised a hand to touch his face. Of course she needed rest. She was so tired, wasn't she?

So very tired.

When her fingers traced the sharp curve of his cheekbone, he shuddered underneath her hand, awakening a trace of potent sensual awareness in her body. But a tiny voice buried deep in her mind shouted at her that she wasn't tired at all. That she needed to escape.

As she stared into his eyes, the voice faded. Just as well. She was so very, very sleepy.

Her eyelids fluttered shut, and she felt her knees give way beneath her. He caught her as she fell. "You're holding me again," she murmured, sleep claiming her in waves of peace and restfulness.

"None other shall ever hold you, Keely," he said, and then she felt his lips lightly touch her forehead. "You are mine."

Something about his words—something *wrong*—tickled at the edge of her consciousness for a few seconds, but then she surrendered into sleep. She could figure it out later. When she wasn't so very, very tired.

Sinking down, down into gentle waves of slumber, she dreamed of swords, jewels, and a sapphire-haired man who wielded them both.

Chapter 15

Atlantis, the palace, the next morning

Conlan looked around his strategic planning room—he refused to think of it as a war chamber, when the subject at hand was his own brother—and wondered why a night of sleep hadn't seemed to refresh any of them. Darkness lay like bruises under the eyes of everyone entering the room, and he knew his own face reflected the same. Riley had suffered through a difficult night, again, and he found it impossible to sleep when she could not.

He glanced at her, to be sure she'd obeyed his command to remain on the comfortable couch, resting on mounds of pillows with her feet up. The pregnancy had not been easy, and as her due date grew nearer, she seemed to grow ever more pale and thin, except for the enormous mound of her belly.

She'd finally admitted to him only the day before that she was unhappy. Their wedding had been postponed again and again as the surface battle to protect the humans intensified. Then, of course, when Justice had vanished, all thoughts of planning a celebration had been put on indefinite hold. But, as she'd reminded him, the baby would not wait for the perfect time to arrive. He or she would enter the world at a time of nature's choosing, and if they did not make haste, the baby would be born without the blessing of legitimacy.

Or, as Riley had so elegantly put it, "Over my dead body." So, even if the official royal wedding, which by tradition and law had to follow or accompany the coronation, must needs be put off once more, there *would* be a wedding. Soon.

Whether they found Justice and Dr. McDermott or not.

As the last of the stragglers arrived, Conlan held up a hand for silence and then addressed the most senior of the servants circulating in the room, offering refreshments. "Thank you, Neela. If you will leave the trays, we can serve ourselves now."

It was an unspoken request that they be given privacy, and Neela instantly understood. She'd been with his family for decades and, unfortunately, knew well the requirements of wartime planning. With what seemed like nothing more than a nod of her head, she rounded up her staff and they were gone in the space of a few minutes, closing the enormous copper-and-orichalcum-inlaid wooden doors behind them. The sparkling Atlantean metal twined with the copper to form intricate designs on the door. Symbols of welcome or of warning, Conlan had never been sure exactly which.

Conlan took a long drink of the hot coffee and then put the mug down on a table. "Good morning, everyone. Thank you for gathering with me at such an early hour. We all know the situation, so I won't waste our time with the recap. We have three goals: First, we have to find Justice and Dr. McDermott. Second, Alaric must determine whether Justice has been compromised by his time in the Void. And, third, we're going to go on the offensive."

"It's about damn time," Ven called out from a spot across the room, standing next to Erin's chair. "Playing a reactive game against Anubisa's Apostates has gained us nothing but pain, pain, and more pain. If she hurt him . . ." Ven's words trailed off, but even from across the room, Conlan could read the agony in his brother's eyes. Justice had sacrificed himself to the vampire goddess for Ven, and the weight of that had been crushing Ven's soul ever since.

"I must agree," Alaric said. He stood alone, as always; separate and apart from the rest of them. Perhaps only Conlan knew the full extent of that aloneness—Conlan had been there with Alaric when the priest had first realized the full extent of his feelings for Quinn. But Poseidon's high priests all swore a vow of celibacy, and Quinn's role as coleader of the human rebels had forced her into her own state of solitude.

Never had a pairing been more impossible, but futility did not easily translate into the ability to forget.

"We need to work more closely with the human rebels and forge a comprehensive plan," Alaric continued. "The days and centuries of acting as a strike force are behind us. If Quinn— if Jack and Quinn are in a position to meet with us, we should make that meeting sooner rather than later. But our first priority must be Justice, of course."

Riley shifted on the couch and made some small noise of discomfort, and Conlan tensed, ready to leap across the room to her aid. She shook her head, though, and smiled at him. "I'm fine. Just stretching. Our son persists in wanting to sit on my bladder."

"Our daughter is never still, like her mother," he corrected.

"If you desire to know the truth of it, all you need do is ask," Alaric said dryly. "As much as we have all enjoyed this amusing interplay for the past several months."

Riley rolled her eyes at him, then wedged a small pillow behind her back and looked around the room. "There is nothing—*nothing*—more important than finding Justice and making sure that he's okay. Even before we knew he was your brother, we knew he was our family, just like everybody else in this room and each warrior in the Seven."

There were several nods of agreement. Conlan began to speak, but Riley shook her head again. "It's *my* turn to be selfish. I understood that everything needed to be put on hold for Justice when he was taken captive by Anubisa. I've done everything I could to support the search. But now, from what you tell me, he disappeared voluntarily. Not only that, but he abducted that poor archaeologist."

"Talk about your international incident," Erin said, wincing.

"Exactly," Riley replied. "Here's my point, although I know I'm making it badly. My baby will *not* be born until his parents are married. I understand that we can't hold the big brouhaha wedding, and I'm fine with that. I never cared about a big circus of a ceremony, anyway. But either we go to my church at home, we bring a minister to us in Atlantis, or we go to a damn Elvis chapel in damn Vegas. I don't care. It doesn't matter to me. I always loved Elvis, anyway. But one way or another, Conlan and I are getting married sometime in the next week."

The beauty of it, and one of Riley's most amazing qualities, was that she never raised her voice. She didn't have to. She was human, not Atlantean, and she'd once joked that the closest she'd been to royalty before she'd met Conlan was going to Burger King. But she wore the demeanor of a queen as though born to the role.

"Well, you've heard it. My future queen has spoken, and I can do no less than obey," Conlan said, smiling at her.

"She's correct that the child should be born to wedded parents," Alaric said. "He or she will face enough problems when the time comes for you to pass on the crown, as the first half human ever to take the throne in Atlantis. There is certainly no need to add the additional burden of illegitimacy."

"We can always count on you, can't we, Alaric?" Riley said, exasperation mixed with a grudging affection in her voice. "I meant that I want my baby to be born into the world knowing that his parents love each other enough to make the ultimate commitment. But thank goodness we have you to point out the legalities of the situation."

Alaric raised one eyebrow and looked puzzled. "Although I detect sarcasm in your words, I am unsure as to its cause. Although . . . oh. Of course." He bowed to her. "As you wish, my lady."

Riley narrowed her eyes. "If this is one of your 'Riley is hormonal' moments, Alaric, you'd better be glad I'm too huge to waddle over there and kick your butt."

"My butt, as you say, is infinitely relieved," Alaric replied. "But perhaps we might return to the subject at hand."

Ven crossed the room to the central long, wooden table, where stacks of maps and strategic plans had been piled on one side to make room for the refreshments. He helped himself to another cup of coffee. "Here's a quick status report. We got word this morning that there's a vampire uprising in St. Louis. Evidently, Anubisa is trying to crack the whip on how the vamps gather Apostates, but she's doing it through Vonos. Guy's got all the subtlety of Bruce Willis going after the bad guys in the fifth or sixth *Die Hard*."

Conlan nodded. "Alexios, Christophe, and Denal left before dawn to travel to St. Louis and meet Jack, Reisen, and the rebel faction there."

"Do we suddenly trust Reisen?" Alaric asked, his eyes suddenly glowing a fierce green as he drew power to him. "After he took it upon himself to steal Poseidon's Trident from the god's own Temple?"

"Whether we trust him or not is moot. Quinn trusts him, Jack trusts him, and they both reported that he's on some sort of quest for redemption," Conlan said. "He only takes on the most dangerous missions, going so far that they're afraid he may be suicidal."

"I don't care about his quest for redemption. I don't want him anywhere near Quinn," Alaric snarled. "I will leave for St. Louis as soon as we adjourn this meeting."

"We need you here, Alaric," Erin said. She'd been uncharacteristically quiet during the meeting. "I've been trying to reach for Justice—for some hint of his presence—ever since we got here. You know, I'm a gem singer? Protégé of the goddess of the Nereids? Since we discovered he was half Nereid, I was hoping that, somehow, I could use that connection to try to get at least a rough idea of where he might be."

She shook her head before they could ask. "No luck. Nothing. I may be a witch and a gem singer, but I apparently stink as a cell phone." She turned back toward Alaric. "That's why we need you. You're the only one with the power to locate Justice."

"I have no wish to offend you, Erin," Alaric said. "But you do realize, of course, that I've been attempting to contact or locate Justice constantly since he left us last night?"

Erin sighed and slumped a little in her chair. "I'm sorry, Alaric. I should've realized. I'm just exhausted. I don't think I've slept at all since Justice went off with Anubisa months ago. He saved my life. He saved Ven's life. He even saved my sister, in a way. But now we don't know where he is. We don't know where Deirdre is, or if my sister is even alive."

She stopped and scrubbed fiercely at her eyes with her fists. When she spoke again, her voice was husky with unshed tears. "I guess I'm just ready for something to go right."

Ven knelt beside Erin's chair and drew her into his arms, and the anguish on his face mirrored what sliced through Conlan's chest.

"I think we're all ready for something to go right," Conlan said. "We need a plan, then. Alaric will go to St. Louis, but continue to attempt to locate Justice. Riley and I will find either a minister or an Elvis willing to perform a marriage in Atlantis. Ven, you lead a team to try to figure out where Justice is with this archaeologist and then go bring them home."

A knock sounded at the door, and Liam put his head in and looked an inquiry at Conlan. Conlan nodded and beckoned him to enter.

"Perfect timing," Ven said. "We need to know about this Dr. McDermott. What is it about her that made Justice go nuts?"

Liam strode into the room, shaking his head. "That I don't know. But I can tell you this: Keely McDermott is a true object reader, though the Gift was thought lost in the waters of time. She read the sapphire, and she saw Nereus."

Alaric's head snapped up, and he leaned forward. "What did she say? What did she say about High Priest Nereus and the Star of Artemis?"

"Not much," Liam confessed. "I'd planned to question her more about it once she was safely in Atlantis. But she did say the strangest thing. She said I looked exactly like him."

Chapter 16

The cavern underneath the Temple of the Nereids

Justice woke instantly, climbing through waves of sleep to full alertness in the space of a couple of seconds. There had been no unguarded rest in the Void, and even less during his brief time with Anubisa. Her rage when he'd been unwilling—and, truth be told, *unable*—to consummate their relationship had been monumental. She was a goddess and possessed a dark beauty more exquisite than mortal eyes could even comprehend. But it was beauty rooted in evil and steeped in murder and damnation.

A wave of self-disgust washed through him. After all, it's not like he was all that particular. Over the centuries, he'd been with plenty of women, whenever he pleased. Unfortunately, nothing and no one had actually pleased him in several decades. There had always been something missing in his brief encounters. Something he hadn't wanted to recognize.

Until he saw *her* face. *Keely.* The thought of her jolted him into full memory of where they were and what he'd done. He leapt up from the pile of quilts and blankets that he'd fashioned into bedding the night before. The cavern had been a refuge for those of troubled mind before the rockfall and subsequent instability of the tunnels, and several trunks filled with blankets and random bits of clothing were stacked in a corner. He suddenly remembered making a similar bed for her, but where? Either the fog of his memory wasn't cooperating, or else she was gone. What if she'd escaped? What if he never found her again?

Panic raced through him at the thought. Panic and something deeper. Something darker. Something originating in the Nereid half of his soul. He was growing to recognize that side of himself, as it fought harder and harder to be released. Fought his Atlantean half for control.

He whirled around, searching the darkened cavern for a sign of her, and then sighed in relief, his muscles unclenching from the adrenaline-based fight-or-flight mechanism they'd shot into when he thought she'd gone. She was still there, asleep on the pile of bedding he'd created for her near one gemstone-encrusted wall.

He already knew her well enough to realize she'd be furious with him for daring to meddle with her mind. But she'd needed to sleep, and he'd been close to dropping from exhaustion, entirely unable to respond to her determination that had bordered on terror.

Right. He'd done it for her sake, he silently mocked himself. Of course. Villains always demonstrated exquisite talent at self-justification. Remorse washed through him again, but he dismissed it and tried to focus on his physical realities. A bath. He needed another bath.

Though he'd bathed in the hot spring–fed pool before he'd fallen asleep, simple joy in cleanliness after so long in the Void drew him to it again. He refused to consider that the filth touched him on a far deeper level than his skin.

He would bathe and then, properly attired in some of the clothing from the trunks, he would wake her. They had much to discuss. He wanted to know everything about her. Every single detail of her life. Also, he needed to convince her to give him time.

Time to prove that he wasn't a monster. Time to persuade her that she belonged with him.

Time to figure out for himself how he knew it to be true.

He didn't bother to dress, except for his sword. It was as much a part of him as his arm or his eye, in spite of the terrible death it had inflicted. It was what it was, and it was his. He quietly crossed the small space between them and, crouching down beside her, he was content merely to watch her sleep.

Keely's lustrous red hair was exactly the shade he'd seen in his original vision of her. It was flame melded with sunlight, and it was a perfect complement to the flawless golden glow of her lightly tanned skin. Her closed eyelids blocked his view of the almost-iridescent emerald green of her eyes, but his memory was happy to provide the exact shade.

She lay on her side, and one hand rested on top of the blankets. He'd removed her gloves after she'd fallen asleep, wondering why she wore them, and placed them near her. Her hand was slender, with long fingers that somehow looked sturdy and competent. Nicks and scrapes marred her skin, as though she'd done rough work quite recently. Perhaps that's why she wore the gloves.

Archaeology. She'd said she was an archaeologist. A student of the past. He almost laughed, but trapped the sound in his throat so as not to wake her. She was a student of the past, and he was a warrior who had lived through her past. Perhaps they had been destined to meet.

This time the bitter laugh escaped. He was the bastard son of destiny; now would he turn hypocrite and bless the very fates that he'd spent centuries cursing?

"What would I surrender for you, Keely?" he murmured. "My honor? My bitterness? Perhaps even part of my soul? What is it about you that has caught me like this?"

She sighed a little in her sleep, and the sound was like a torch to lantern oil, racing through him and igniting a burning trail of fierce, almost animalistic hunger. He wanted her so suddenly and so desperately that the wanting was a physical pain.

No, he *needed* her. *They* needed her, and they would not be denied.

Stop! He shouted the word in the silence of his own mind. *You cannot conquer me, although you are part of my very being.*

A voice, his but not his, whispered icy menace inside him. *You are wrong, Atlantean captor to my imprisoned self. I will conquer you, because you are weak. And when I gain control of our mind entirely, the woman will be mine.*

The Nereid—although it was part of Justice, it was Other, and he didn't know how else to think of that part of his soul—flashed images through Justice's mind. A boiling torrent of sensual images, each more explicit than the one before:

Keely, naked and kneeling before him in submission, those lovely tanned hands circling his cock.

Keely's pale limbs intertwined with his own as he pounded into her.

Keely, sprawled on silken pillows, her legs over his shoulders as he tasted her.

Keely, bent forward over his bed, as he held her lovely round breasts in his hands and drove into her from behind.

Keely, writhing in ecstasy, screaming his name as she shattered with pleasure in his arms, her slick, hot cream bathing his cock with its sweetness.

Keely. Keely. Keely.

The visions burned through him, over and over, faster and faster, until his cock hardened so painfully that he felt he must wake her and take her and make her understand how desperately he needed to be buried to the hilt in the warm, wet center of her. His hand reached out, almost against his own volition, to rip the covering from her.

Then he saw it.

The silvery tracks of the tearstains on her face. She'd been crying. Even in the hypnotically induced sleep, some part of her had known she was in danger, and she had been afraid.

She thought him a monster, and with good cause. He flung himself back and away from her, shuddering in self-loathing. He *was* a monster, but he would never touch her unless invited. He'd kill himself first.

You cannot win, he told the Nereid, or perhaps merely the greedy, lusting side of his own nature. *I will defeat you, or I will die trying. But I will never let you harm a single hair on her head.*

Mocking laughter rang faintly throughout the cavern, or

else it only existed inside Justice's brain. He was almost unable to distinguish any difference between the two.

A single hair on her head? You like her hair, too?

As Justice ran toward the pool to immerse himself in its steamy waters and wash the erotic images from his mind, the Nereid flashed a final image: Keely wrapping the long strands of her hair around the base of his cock as she pulled him into her mouth.

He dropped his sword on the ground and stumbled as he entered the water, wondering as he fell if perhaps a warrior of Atlantis who was half Nereid would dare, for the first time in his life, to ask the Nereid goddess—or even Poseidon himself—for assistance.

He was very much afraid that his sanity might depend on the answer.

∾————∾

An eerie sense of apprehension curled around Keely's dreams, tingeing them with shades of charcoal gray and burnt umber. She swam through darkened currents, battered and buffeted by oddities: a fat, wooden apple the size of a donkey, a poodle-sized wooden carving of a horse that turned and smiled at her as it swam by. A child's wooden wagon, buoyed by the waves, floated serenely beside her, keeping pace with the speed of her swimming in spite of the flotsam that jostled it. She felt a strong compulsion to reach for the toy, but was afraid that if she lost the tempo of her strokes, she would drown.

She knew she was dreaming—was almost sure of it—but had lost any sense of reality outside of the watery dreamscape. Her only purpose was to reach the opposite shore, where she knew salvation waited.

But she didn't know how, or why, or what it might be. Something smashed into her shoulder, and she turned her head to see a red metal tricycle, its handlebars caught in the tangles of her wet hair. Faltering, she wrenched her head to the side to release herself, and the tricycle fell behind. She turned back toward the shore she couldn't yet see but knew was there, and the toy wagon gently bumped against her nose, as if nudging her to take it.

"But I don't have a pocket that you'll fit in," she said help-lessly, and—instantly—she was awake and gasping for air, bolting upright and staring around her.

Out of a dream and into a nightmare.

Memory came flooding back in waves unpleasantly remi-niscent of the dream, buffeting her with the events of the previ-ous day. Atlantis. Warriors. The dead creature . . . who'd turned out to be a man from the time of Alexander.

Justice.

She scrambled to her knees, trying to stay low and incon-spicuous while searching the cavern for the wild man from yesterday's waking nightmare. Or maybe, something whis-pered wistfully inside her mind, the warrior from her vision?

Instead her gaze locked onto a vision from an entirely dif-ferent kind of dream. The kind of dream that ended up with her tangled in damp sheets, aching and unfulfilled, because the primal male warriors she'd sometimes seen in her visions, when she'd touched certain artifacts from ancient civilizations, simply didn't exist in modern times. They certainly didn't show up in the academic offices at Ohio State.

But she wasn't in Ohio anymore. The hard, muscled male proof of it was climbing out of the water, stark naked and drip-ping wet, not a dozen feet away from her. Keely had never thought of water as an aphrodisiac before, but the drops that clung lovingly to Justice's body might qualify. They caressed him in all the places she suddenly found herself wanting to touch.

With her tongue.

She closed her eyes for a moment at her own stupidity. Now she was attracted to her kidnapper? But he'd been so careful with her yesterday, and she'd seen his bitter grief over the man's sacrifice . . . Surely he couldn't be . . .

She opened her eyes, unable to resist another peek. He'd lifted his arms to push the heavy weight of his wet, unbraided hair away from his face, and the movement did things to the lines of his body that should be illegal. Justice was so long and elegantly lean and muscled that it made the bodybuilders she'd seen working out in the gym at OSU seem like squat trolls in comparison. His powerful arms, the right with an intricate yet simple tattoo high up on the bicep; his strong legs; the thickly muscled chest that tapered down to lean hips and . . . oh.

Oh.

She tried to swallow through a throat gone dry as the dust in an unopened pyramid. Either Atlanteans walked around in a perpetual state of intense arousal or Justice was seriously glad to see her.

A bolt of pure, sizzling heat flashed through her, turning her good sense to a silvery coil of liquid lust in exactly the place she'd like to . . . *Oh. Dear. God.*

He'd caught her watching him.

Frozen, she stared into his eyes, feeling the embarrassment burn in her cheeks. Common sense and self-preservation overruled zinging hormones, though, and she shot to her feet. "Stay away from me, okay? Just . . . put on some clothes, and let's talk like civilized human beings, er, Atlantean and human beings, now that we've gotten some rest and you're, um, clean."

He never moved or made any threatening motion, but suddenly she felt a thrill of trepidation shiver through her. Some nameless emotion burned in his eyes, changing them from darkest midnight to fiery sapphire blue. Slowly, ever so slowly, his gaze traveled from her face, down to her chest, where it lingered before continuing its perusal all the way down to her toes. The masculine arrogance and blatant possession in his gaze had her poised to run, even as her nipples swelled and throbbed in the lace cups of her bra.

No way would she respond to him. Nothing in her background or her fiercely independent personality would make her the type to be turned on by some naked, alpha-male throwback to the days when men were men and women were possessions.

Even as she told herself that, her body was turning traitor, evidently tired of lonely nights. As his gaze swept slowly back up her body, her skin tingled—oversensitized and desperate for his touch.

That tingling sensation, finally, was what snapped her out of the sensual trance he'd somehow put her in and back to logic, caution, and a little damn sense.

"Cut it out," she snapped. "Stop staring at me like I'm

the spoils of your own personal war, and get dressed. We need to talk about how we're getting out of here, okay? Where is the exit? Where is the passageway, or the tunnel, or the super-magical Atlantean elevator that will get us the heck *out* of here?"

He held his hands out to the sides, palms up, as if to show her that he meant no threat. Unfortunately, the movement only highlighted the strength in his muscled arms and made her realize that, her years of self-defense classes notwith-standing, and even though he was naked and unarmed, she would be no match for him.

Well, he was naked. *Not so sure about unarmed*, said the previously silent evil-seductress side of her nature. *That's a pretty big weapon he's got there.*

Great. She picked *now* to go all multiple personality.

The sane side of her went right back to its personal agenda of scared, terrified, and pretty darn frightened, if the goose bumps traveling up her arms were any indication.

"Keely, please be calm," he said quietly, as if soothing a wounded animal.

"I'll be calm when you get me out of here," she pointed out, proud of how reasonable her voice sounded, when her heart was thumping in her chest. "Not the way we got here, either. None of that 'beam me up, Scotty,' crap. A nice, normal tunnel. Or stairs. Stairs would be good."

"But—"

"And get dressed!" she shouted, out of patience. "I don't care if you look like some kind of Greek statue come to life. I want you to put your clothes back on!"

That slow, dangerous smile of his—it ought to be regis-tered as a lethal weapon, really—spread across his face. "You think I look like a statue?"

Keely scowled at him. "Clothes. Now."

Still smiling, he sauntered over to a pile of clothing and, not nearly quickly enough for her peace of mind, pulled on a shirt and pants. Her view of his tightly muscled behind, as he stepped into the pants, nearly made her groan out loud.

She was going to get years' worth of fantasies out of this experience, if she happened to live through it.

"Okay, fine. Now you're dressed. So you can lead me to the up arrow."

He shook his head as he crossed the mosaic tile toward her in a few long strides. "I would like to believe that I would release you if I were able, in spite of the dark desires of the Other inside me, Keely. But I'm not entirely sure how we got here, since the power of transport has never been one at my command until now."

"But—"

"I don't know how to use it again." He stopped, mere inches away from her, and stared down into her eyes, his own spiraling with vivid blue-green flames. "Unfortunately, the staircase that leads from the Temple to this cavern was blocked by rock and dirt in a cave-in some years ago. There is no way out."

Chapter 17

Keely had never suffered from claustrophobia, thankfully, even after some of the more outrageous treatments various shrinks had subjected her to in childhood, such as the sensory-deprivation tank that only lasted one session.

They hadn't known an eight-year-old could scream that loudly.

But the news that she was trapped with Justice in an underground cavern—underground in *Atlantis*, and no *way* did she want to even think about the possibility that the whole she-bang could spring a leak or something—took her to a whole new level of psychosis.

Her breathing sped up to hyperventilation, and she started trembling, fluctuating with each shuddering breath between fury and panic. "You . . . you . . . Are you insane? You brought me to a *cave—underground*—with no idea of how to get back out again?"

He raised one dark eyebrow. "Most caves are underground."

"I know that! I'm an archaeologist, you—"

Ignoring her sputtered words, Justice lifted a hand as if to touch her. Oh, no. Not going to happen, whether he was sex on a stick or not. She jumped back out of his reach, clutching her head in her hands and inhaling deeply. Tried to calm down, so she could think rationally about a plan. A plan, that's what she needed.

Not random, useless terror about what the archaeologists of the future would think when they found her crumbling bones lying beside a pair of gloves, another skeleton, and a damn sword.

She belatedly realized that her fingers were twined in her hair. Her *bare* fingers. "My gloves! What did you do with my gloves?" Her breathing sped up again until her lungs burned inside her chest.

He silently pointed to the floor near the pallet where she'd slept. She backed away from him and bent down to snatch them up, but he moved with that eerie, inhuman speed and caught her wrist before she could pull the first glove over her hand.

"Why, Keely? Why the gloves? Do you feel they offer you some protection?" A grimace twisted his face. "Am I so terrifying to you?"

He released her wrist and crouched down, then stood up with his sheathed sword in his hands. Before she could protest, deflect, or take any evasive action at all, he shoved it into her arms.

"Take this, then. Take the sword I've worn for so long it is a part of myself, and use it against me if you fear me so much," he said, his dark eyes and roughened voice coated with ice. "To kill a man, press the pointed end here." He placed his palm flat on his chest, over his heart, but it was too late, too late.

Too late.

The hilt of the sword fitted itself into her hand as though it were seeking her. Seeking her knowledge of it. She had a fanciful notion that it was laying claim to her mind, even as Justice had laid claim to the rest of her when he'd brought her here.

Soon there was no room for thought as the weight of ages crushed the whimsy, crushed her defenses. Ages of time and eons of violence. Violent, bloody death splashing through the unprotected corridors of her mind.

"No," she tried to protest, even as the resonance of the

sword's history beat her into submission. "No, no, no. Too much, too much. I can't . . . my gloves . . . I can't—"

"Keely!" He called out to her, but the sound was muted. Muffled. Yet again, he caught her.

Held her.

But it was too late. She fell, screaming soundlessly, into the blackness of her own personal void. As she fell, she looked into his eyes and managed one final sentence.

"I can't survive it."

∾⎯⎯⎯⎯⎯⎯⎯⎯∾

Keely smashed into the reality of the vision with actual physical pain. A great wrenching and tearing of the fabric of her existence manifested itself in the searing pain of broken and bleeding flesh, oddly focused on her face and throat.

She gasped and fell back, her attention captured by the floor—a very different floor than the one in the cavern. This floor was brilliantly white marble, inlaid with designs of gold and copper and another metal, similar to copper, but sparkling and almost gem-like. The wrenching pain began again, and she realized she might not survive the vision. Pain like nothing she'd ever felt wrapped around her throat as though it had been crushed. She gasped, wheezing in a breath, but a moaning cry came from farther into the room and she looked up to try to find the source.

It was a dark-haired woman, kneeling on the floor, clutching at her belly. Her enormous, rippling, pregnant belly. The woman was clearly in labor, and the agony of it made Keely rethink any random yearnings she'd ever had for children. She cried out again. It must be contractions. If they came this quickly, one on top of the other, didn't that mean something?

Oh, no. Oh, no, no, no. The woman was about to have a baby—right there on the floor. Keely started to call out, but the sharp, searing pain that sliced through her throat told her that the woman she'd become in her vision wasn't going to be talking anytime soon. What had happened to her? She gingerly felt her neck and flinched from the sting of torn flesh. Her fingertips traced the wound and discovered a long slice in her skin; it seemed to be shallow but was bleeding quite a bit.

From the way the side of her face hurt, someone had struck her quite recently, but her questing fingertips couldn't find any cuts on her cheek or near her eye, where the pain centered.

She wore a simple cotton dress and sandals. No jewelry or adornment. She was probably seeing the room through the eyes of a servant girl, then. But why a servant girl? Usually the visions took her to someone who had a close personal connection or deeply emotional connection to the object she touched. Would a servant girl ever . . . ?

Slowly, a horrifying thought crossed her mind. She lowered the hand clutching her throat and stared almost blindly at the bright red blood that stained her fingers and palm.

She tried to seek answers in the terrified mind of her host, but all she could see was an image of the sword, coming toward her—no, headed for the pregnant woman. The servant girl had only been unlucky to have gotten in the way of the backstroke, when the crazed man wrenched his sword up over his shoulder in preparation to strike. Whoever he was, he'd literally cut her throat, and now there was a pregnant woman going into labor right in front of her.

And there was absolutely nothing she could do about it. She was no more than an observer in her visions, unable to change actions that had happened long ago in the far-distant past. All she could do was suffer their pain, and pray that the vision released her soon.

The woman on the floor screamed again. She fell to her side and drew her knees up, curling into a ball, as if trying to escape. "Help me! Somebody help me," she cried out, pushing her tangled hair away from her face.

Her tangled *midnight blue* hair, Keely realized. What if this woman were related to Justice? She tried, in spite of everything she knew about the visions, to force her host body to go to the woman. To help her, in spite of the servant girl's obvious terror.

But it was like trying to move a pyramid with only her mind. She couldn't affect what was long over and done. No matter how much she wanted to do so.

When the contraction eased, the blue-haired woman managed to raise her head and scan the room. Keely did the same and gasped again. Marble columns lined the walls, and a golden throne graced one end. She must be in the palace throne room, then.

But she wasn't alone.

How could she have missed him? The man standing in front of the throne. His dark hair, aristocratic features, and regal presence had so much of Conlan and Ven in him, and she recognized the sword he held as the one that had hurled her into the abyss.

Except now it was wet with her blood. Drawn by some hideous fascination, Keely stared at the evidence that this man had sliced her throat. Her host's throat.

Their throat. Blackness began to whirl behind her eyes, and she didn't know whether to try to stay conscious or hope that fainting would yank her out of the vision. Would her host faint?

Would the man with the sword punish her if she did?

And since Keely couldn't affect the past, was she only experiencing the dizziness of her host, surely due to fear and loss of blood?

The pregnant woman cried out—a long cry filled with suffering and hopelessness. She stared up at the man, beseeching, from where she was curled up on the cold, hard floor, all alone. "Help me, please. I beg of you. This baby is coming, and now."

Distantly Keely recognized that she was somehow hearing and understanding ancient Atlantean. The cadence of the language was almost musical; it seemed wrong to use such a lovely language to describe such suffering. The harshness of English would be better.

Can't you see I'm in pain here? Or, *Help me, you bastard.*

Three contractions in a row swept over the woman, pressing her back to the floor with the weight of the pain. Her abdomen tightened, visibly hard as a rock, with each one. But whatever was supposed to happen didn't seem to be happening.

At least as far as Keely knew. She hesitantly glanced at the woman's legs, bare under some kind of silken skirt, praying that the baby's head hadn't breached yet.

Not yet. But Keely noticed something new. Something her shock had kept her from noticing before. The skin of the woman's legs and hands were the color of ivory tinged with the palest blue. She wasn't human. She wasn't even Atlantean. She was something . . . other.

The contraction seemed to ease again, and the woman was reduced to sobbing, lying on the floor. Keely tried again in vain to force her host to go toward the woman and help her. But the servant girl's fear was far too great to allow compassion to translate into motion.

Anger swept through Keely's consciousness in a blazing swath, and a single very determined thought popped into her mind: if she ever survived this vision, she was going to stab Justice with his own sword.

King SOB finally spoke. "I cannot believe you dare to come to me with your bastard child, Éibhleann. After what you and Anubisa did to me, you're lucky I don't strike you dead where you lay on the floor."

The pregnant woman bared her teeth and actually hissed at him, an alien sound that ricocheted off the walls. "It was not me. It was never me. I was as much a captive as you, Your Highness. If you, who are the all-powerful king of Atlantis, could not resist Anubisa's mind control, how could a simple Nereid maiden hope to do so?"

She threw her head back, clamping her teeth shut, but then giving in to the howl as another contraction hit. When she could breathe again, she continued. "You know that Nereids see the destined face of our true love as part of our vision quest. Believe me when I tell you that I never once saw yours. I, too, was sacrificed to Anubisa's jealous obsession, although I will not love our child less because of it."

The king's confusion almost overruled the fury that hardened his features. Just for a moment, but it was enough to give Keely a little hope that he would help the woman.

"If what you say is true . . ." he began, but then shook his head. "But, no. It matters not. I will not raise the bastard child borne of the vampire goddess's mind rape as my own."

As another wave of pain from the contractions smashed

into Éibhleann, something happened that had never before occurred in one of Keely's visions. She spoke out in her own voice, from her own knowledge, in a way that ran counter to her host body's every instinct.

"You are a pathetic excuse for a king," she shouted up at him, her voice hoarse. "Conlan and Ven would be ashamed of you if they knew about this. You need to help this woman before she has her baby right here on your floor."

The king snarled and lifted his bloody sword, taking a step toward Keely, but a new player entered the room. A shaky but determined feminine voice spoke up from behind Keely. "Yes, my husband. We must help her. Call for the First Maiden of the Temple of the Nereids immediately to assist with the child-birth."

Keely was almost afraid to try to discover who was speaking, although she had a pretty good idea that it was Conlan and Ven's mother.

"Thank you," she whispered, through her raw and injured throat.

The queen slowly moved into view, her face starkly white with either shock or pain. She barely glanced at Keely at first, but then jerked her head around, staring at Keely's host's wounded throat.

"You are welcome," the queen said, barely above a whisper. "Now we will find the healer for you and the First Maiden of the Nereids for this woman and her child."

Either relief, exhaustion, or both combined rippled through Keely, still locked inside her host's mind, and her tenuous grip on consciousness faded. As the edges of the room grew dark, she fell, twirling and spinning in the vortex of the vision that clearly was not yet done with her.

～～～

The door opened behind Keely, who stood in the darkened room staring down at a swaddled infant in a wooden cradle. A familiar voice murmured a hello. The queen.

A strand of silvery hair fell forward into Keely's face, and that and the absence of pain in her throat made her realize that she was not inhabiting the same woman as before. With the relief from the servant girl's injuries and terror, Keely was able to think more clearly.

Justice's mother. Éibhleann must have been Justice's mother, then. But where was she? And who was hosting Keely now? Tears welled in her eyes and clogged her throat as the knowledge filtered through her host's mind.

Éibhleann was dying. The birth had been too much for her. There was nothing further to be done but pray.

A wave of sorrow and pity washed through Keely as she stared down at the delicate curve of the infant's tiny hand, his fingers curled like a fragile sea anemone. This must be Justice, then. No wonder he was so damaged, with a start like that.

"First Maiden," the queen said, entering the room. She carried a candle, and the light from the flame illuminated the wildly spiking blue-tinged hair of the sleeping baby. "How fares the child?"

Keely realized the First Maiden was her/them, when her host responded to the query. "He does very well, Highness. But the mother . . . I fear that she is beyond my power to heal."

The queen turned to face Keely. Head held high, quiet determination in every line of her face, she spoke softly, but with definite purpose. "Although this Nereid female has known my husband, due to Anubisa's vile manipulations, I would not have any harm come to her. Do everything you can to heal her, please. For me and for this child, who is blameless."

"And if she does not live? She is very ill, and we have had no gem singer in the Temple for thousands of years. The legends say that a gem singer can draw upon the power of the goddess herself, more powerfully than even a First Maiden, in order to heal."

"Then I will raise him myself, as my own child," the queen said, her eyes carrying the weight of ravaging pain, but still dry. "He carries the blood of my husband and is kin to my son Conlan and to any future children I might bear. Could I do any less?"

"Could you love this child?" Keely asked, registering in the back of her/their mind the First Maiden's courage to dare to question a queen so. "He deserves to be loved and not made to feel unwanted."

"I will love him," the queen replied firmly, as though trying to convince herself. "I must love him."

The baby sleepily opened his eyes and looked up at Keely. She reached out to touch his cheek, and she fell, plunging back into the dark.

∾───∾

The visions came fast and faster; one after another. Brief snippets of memory the sword had gathered throughout its long existence. Blessedly, Keely was observing only as a bystander throughout, as she was thrown from moment to moment.

∾───∾

The throne room

"He cannot know," the king said to a man and woman who stared down, overjoyed, at the baby she held in her arms. "He can never know."

As they agreed, words tumbling over each other in their haste, the queen stood behind her husband with tears rolling down her face.

∾───∾

A rocky shore, in the midst of a thunderstorm

Waves crashed against the cliffs, and the king stood alone, silhouetted against a tempest-painted sky. A voice, somehow larger and louder than the waves, surrounded him. "You must tell him. His name shall be Justice, and he will serve as a reminder of the injustice that will result if Anubisa is allowed to extend her dominion over the human race."

The king bowed his head, his fists clenched at his side. "I cannot tell him. I cannot risk my sons, and the enemies of my sons, knowing of his existence."

The voice, again. The voice that somehow Keely knew—although it was impossible for her to know it, it was impossible that it was true—was that of the sea god.

Poseidon.

"Do not defy me in this. You will tell him, as I have ordered. I have set a *geas* upon him, and he is cursed never to reveal the circumstances of his birth, unless he should then kill everyone who has heard him."

"Then you have created a monster and a murderer," the king shouted, pointing his sword—*the* sword—at the waves.

"No," thundered the god. "I have created a weapon, unlike any that ever has been honed for battle. He will serve your sons, and he will serve my justice. When he is ten years old, you will give him your sword, and you will rename it Poseidon's Fury, to ensure that my fury at Anubisa's treatment of my chosen king is never forgotten."

Lightning crashed down on the waves, and a dark, undulating shape arrowed through the water toward the shore, but before Keely could catch a glimpse of it, she fell back down into the dark.

～～～⁓⁓

Outdoors, in front of a small cottage

The small, blue-haired boy looked up at the king, bewilderment on his face, then down at the sheathed sword that rested in his thin arms. "But, but I don't understand, Your Majesty. Why would you give me your sword?"

The king stared down at him with no tenderness in his expression. "There's something I need to tell you—"

And Keely fell.

～～～⁓⁓

Twisting, turning, and whirling through the centuries, Keely fell from vision to vision. The one constant was Justice, growing from child to man to seasoned warrior, always with the sword either strapped to his back or being used in battle. Battle after battle. Desperate fight after desperate fight. Vampires and shape-shifters, all of them with the goal of enslaving or eating humans.

All of them defeated by Justice, wielding Poseidon's Fury.

Keely fell, and fell, and fell, in a never-ending vision. Vision wrapped inside vision, bloody battle after bloody battle, until she couldn't remember anything but carnage, pain, and death.

But she grew to know him—oh, yes, she grew to know this wild man who'd stolen her away. The anguish that lived deep inside him. The loneliness. The bitterness that came from living for centuries as a tool in an angry god's quest for vengeance.

Her heart turned over, and Keely felt the helpless tears rolling down her face. "Enough!" she cried out. "Enough, already. Please, I can't take any more of this. Please, please. No more."

She fell, again, down into the dark. But this time, instead of falling away, she fell *toward*—she fell toward a blue-haired warrior with flames in his eyes.

Chapter 18

St. Louis

Vonos materialized in the roomy den of the mansion in St. Louis's nouveau riche suburb of Ladue, and it was clear that nobody had been expecting him. They'd been looking for the recently deceased Xinon, and they'd not expected *him* until later in the week. So they were totally unprepared for the vampire to show up in their midst.

Which was just how Vonos liked it.

Dressed in a meticulously creased custom-made Savile Row suit, complete with exquisite Zegna tie and Ferragamo shoes, he knew exactly the impression he made upon the polo-shirt-and-khaki-pants-clad humans in the room. He did nothing without deliberate purpose behind it, even down to the choice of what to wear to help these idiotic sheep underestimate him.

The *supermodel vampire*, the press had labeled him. The *Primator of haute couture*. They didn't know whether to admire him or ridicule him for his polished-to-perfection appearance. A human politician would have been booted out of Congress for being too elitist. Not a "man of the people."

The thought amused Vonos. He was a man of the people. He just preferred to eat them.

In any event, the fascination—and fear—that he provoked in the populace was only enhanced by his carefully cultivated style. He was the leader of the Primus, the new, vampire-only, third house of Congress, and his constituents would never respect one who was not more powerful than they.

He finally deigned to notice the humans huddled around the desk. They were gaping at him like a particularly mindless species of carp. However, one who possessed, possibly, an iota of intelligence bowed deeply. "My Lord Primator. To what do we owe this honor?"

"Honor is an interesting word, human. May I call you human? Or do you prefer to tell me your name, which I will then immediately forget as I do most petty annoyances?" Vonos smiled widely enough to show his fangs and was amused when one of the men, a skeletally thin man with a very bad haircut, collapsed into a faint.

But the man who'd first spoken and must be some sort of leader had more presence of mind. "You may call me whatever you wish, of course, Primator Vonos, but my name is Rodriguez."

"Of course it is. How fitting. Do you know that I first resided in your lovely environs back when it was Spanish territory? They called it Northern Louisiana, I believe." He smiled at the memory, but then frowned as the pleasant recollection of simpler times and plentiful humans to feed on gave way to another, far more disagreeable memory. This wasn't the first time Atlanteans had confronted him on this turf. More than two centuries ago, a band of them had come to town and, with the help of both the colonial settlers and the native Illini, viciously murdered nearly all of his blood pride. Naturally, faced with the death of his vampire family, he'd been forced to flee. Discretion, valor, et cetera, et cetera.

"I will never flee again," he said, his nails digging into the edge of the desk so hard the wood cracked.

The human flinched. "Sir?"

"Never mind. I have learned your group is very ambitious when it comes to gathering members of the Apostates, Mr. Rodriguez."

A measure of the man's nervousness subsided, and he

leaned forward eagerly. "Yes, it has been my privilege. I hope to be at the forefront of a new wave of converts. We can definitely see the future, and it involves interspecies cooperation."

Vonos was always amazed at the human capacity for utter and complete denial. Somehow, in the sheep's mind, subjugation had become cooperation. Well, as they said, whatever gets you through the day.

"We find ourselves unhappy with the actions of the local vampire and his blood pride," Vonos said. "From this moment on, you will coordinate all recruiting efforts through my office and through my local representative, whom I will introduce to you in the coming days."

One of the men cowering behind the leader muttered something that was too garbled for Vonos to make out. "Would you like to repeat that?" Vonos asked. "By all means, share with the group."

He did so enjoy these quaint human concepts.

"I didn't . . . I don't . . ." The man was stuttering too hard to get the words out. Fear tended to destroy conversational ability in the sheep.

"Please tell me," Vonos said, calmly polite, with a slight emphasis on the word *please*. Then he aimed a gentle, encouraging smile at the man. "Or I'll rip your tongue out by its root, and you won't have to worry about telling anyone anything ever again."

The sheep fell to his knees, babbling something incoherent, and Vonos sighed.

"Truly, he is starting to annoy me," he said to the man in charge. "Perhaps you would care to translate, before I lose my patience and kill every one of you?"

"He's afraid of what the local vampires will do to us if we stop cooperating with them," the leader said hastily. "We're—"

"I am uninterested in your rationales," Vonos said, cutting him off. "Be advised that the local vampires will never again be a threat to you or anyone else. We were unhappy with their carelessness."

Vonos's cell phone rang, and he held up one finger for silence. The sheep were at least good with their technology. He did so love his iPhone. Maybe he should convert that Steve Jobs fellow? Hmmm. Idle thoughts for another time.

Vonos glanced at the caller ID and noted that it was his personal assistant, one of the very few vampires that he trusted. He flipped open the phone. "Yes?"

"You have an urgent call from the human leader of the Apostates in Ohio," his assistant said. "He claims he has knowledge that you need."

"I'm growing astonishingly weary of these humans," Vonos said into the phone, while scanning the row of men cringing away from him. "Knowledge of what type?"

"I know it sounds insane, but he claims it's about Atlantis. He says an Atlantean warrior kidnapped one of his colleagues right out of her office. You told me to watch out for anything we could use against the Atlanteans, as insurance for when they want to negotiate with the U.S. government. This could be it."

Vonos narrowed his eyes and thought for a moment. "The story sounds unlikely. The Atlanteans have been far too careful to allow anyone to witness something so lacking in finesse as a kidnapping."

"He swears it's true," his assistant said, excitement in his voice. "The Atlantean did something to him, some form of mind control that knocked him out, but he didn't stay out for long. He just lay there on the floor pretending to be unconscious and heard the whole thing. He says he knew that news like this would be crucial to our mission."

"He actually said that, did he? Crucial to our mission? These humans and their sense of melodrama."

"Well, this guy has been flagged for a while. He's a climber; wants to move up the hierarchy and be in line to be turned eventually."

"Ah. Immortality. The elusive prize at the end of all the sheep's rainbows. It does, however, cast a certain shade of doubt upon his claim. Perhaps he exaggerates in hopes of gaining accolades," Vonos said skeptically, but he allowed himself a tiny bit of cautious optimism. Anubisa would reward him well for building a strong case against the Atlantean advent into international politics. State-sponsored kidnapping of American scientists was certainly a good start.

"I believe I will visit this man myself," Vonos decided. "Who is he and where is he?"

The sound of shuffling papers came over the phone for a moment, and then Vonos's assistant came back on the line. "Here it is. Dr. George Grenning at Ohio State University."

Chapter 19

Rebel regional headquarters, St. Louis

Alaric stepped through the portal into a scene of controlled
chaos and immediately looked around for the Atlanteans.
Alexios, blood matting his golden hair into heavy clumps,
stood near the stark concrete front wall of the warehouse
headquarters, shouting orders to the heavily armed humans as
they rushed back and forth, many of them limping or carrying
wounded comrades.

Alaric grimaced at the acrid tang of gun smoke in the air.
Christophe leaned against a graffiti-covered wall, bent over,
with his hands on his thighs as if propping himself up. Alaric
detected the faint residual glow of blue-green energy that surrounded Christophe; the warrior must have expended enormous amounts of energy quite recently.

Denal was nowhere to be seen. Nor Reisen, Jack, or Quinn.
Something in Alaric's chest tightened painfully at the thought
of Quinn, but he refused to allow it to overcome him. She
would be fine. She had to be fine.

If Quinn were to die, he would have no reason to continue
existing.

Although she'd made it very clear that she had no place in
his future, just the knowledge that she was alive and walking

through the same time as he made the bleakness of his life somehow more bearable.

He was a high priest imprisoned by the dictates of a god's whim. She was a rebel leader tortured by the memory of a dark deed. There was no way they could be together, no potential realm of the future that promised any hope.

But the idea of her death held the extinction of *all* hope, and he could not countenance it. He rapidly crossed the room to Alexios, who took one look at Alaric's face and immediately stopped issuing commands.

"She's alive, Alaric. She was wounded, but it was minor," Alexios said, a rough compassion in his voice.

A strange weakness raced through Alaric and he had to fight his own lungs to draw breath. Quinn was wounded.

"How minor?" he snarled. "Tell me, *now.*"

"Relax. It's just a scrape. An overenthusiastic shifter caught her with a claw or two. Denal patched her up, and the two of them and Jack took off after the vamp leaders. Just to reconnoiter. They're going to find out where they hole up, so we can go after them in full force later. They sent Reisen off somewhere else."

Alaric narrowed his eyes. "Tell me nothing about the traitor."

Jack had been Quinn's partner for some years. They were coleaders of the North American rebels, and Jack also happened to be the fiercest shape-shifter Alaric had ever seen. But then, tiger shifters had never been known for their meek natures.

Jack was boldly confident, and Alaric suspected the tiger was developing more than a fellow-warrior attachment for Quinn. Not that it was any of his concern what Quinn did, he reminded himself, even as the pain of it stabbed through him.

He wrenched himself out of the poisonous thoughts. Alexios was wounded, and yet the priest who should be his healer was mewling like a cursed youngling. "Your head. How bad is it?"

Alexios jerked his head away from Alaric's hands. "It's nothing. A scratch. You know how head wounds bleed. I didn't even pass out this time."

Alaric caught the warrior's gaze with his own, while he called the healing power. "If I had the time to cosset stubborn warriors, I would go through the usual exchange with you, since I know how much you and the rest of the Seven need to prove how fierce and unstoppable you are. But we need you whole, so stand still before I lose the final shreds of my temper."

With ill-concealed bad temper of his own, Alexios snarled something about "meddling priests," but did as Alaric had asked. It was definitely more than a simple scratch, and Alexios had been quite fortunate to escape without losing consciousness. Alaric healed the wound quickly, making sure to flush out any lingering grime and blood, channeling a stream of pure water to encircle and cleanse the warrior's head.

Alexios stepped away from him the moment he'd finished, still muttering under his breath, but then he flashed a grin. "Gotta admit that feels a lot better. I guess you temple rats have your uses, after all."

"Glad to be of service," Alaric said dryly. "At least you refrained from sulking, unlike Denal—"

Denal. The thought of the young warrior, gone with Quinn, turned his blood to ice in his veins. Was he experienced enough in battle to be of any assistance should Quinn really need him? He tried to frame the thought in a voice gone suddenly hoarse. "Denal?"

Alexios shook his head. "Don't even say it. We all think of him as the youngling he used to be. But don't forget Denal gave his life for Conlan's future queen. Only her own sacrifice, in turn, brought him back. The battles he has seen in recent months have aged him. Even beyond that, Conlan and Ven did not choose the fiercest warriors in Atlantis for the Seven by random drawing."

Before Alaric could respond, one of the rebels, a dark-eyed, golden-skinned human female, approached them. "Alexios, we need to move the wounded to the hospital. Are you confident that we're good to go?"

The woman barely glanced at Alaric before dismissing him, but gave her full, respectful attention to Alexios. She wore the bow and quiver of arrows strapped to her body as though she were very familiar with the weight of such a weapon, and the daggers strapped to both of her long, lean thighs had well-worn tape wrapping their hilts.

"We're good, Grace. Jack took care of the shifters who were blocking the Jeeps before he and Quinn left with Denal. Tell the others we're moving out. You drive and I'll ride shotgun," Alexios said.

She nodded and then quickly walked away, leaving Alexios staring after her. "It still seems wrong to me that so many females must take up weapons in this battle," he said, so quietly that Alaric nearly missed his words.

"And yet it is their future, and that of their children, that is being corrupted by the vampires and rogue shape-shifters. What power is more formidable than that of mothers acting in concert?" Alaric replied.

Alexios said nothing. He continued to watch the woman as she directed the others to gather up the wounded. Finally he wrenched his gaze away and turned back to Alaric. "I've got to go. They need protection in case we've got some threat waiting for us on the route to the hospital."

"Do you have need of me?" Alaric lifted his hand and a shimmering ball of pure energy coalesced in his palm. "I would be most pleased to teach a few of the attackers a lesson or two in the power of Poseidon," he said, the rage and frustration of the past few days searing through his nerve endings.

Alexios stared at him, eyes narrowed, then shoved his matted hair away from his face. "What I need is a shower. If I had five extra minutes, I'd call a freaking thunderstorm and scrub the stench of their blood off of me. Damn these marauding bastards to the nine hells, anyway. We can't keep fighting them on so many fronts without reinforcements. Conlan and Ven had better step up their plans to increase warrior training."

Alaric agreed, but simply nodded. It was neither the time nor the place to discuss war strategy.

The woman, Grace, approached them again, this time holding a deadly-looking pistol pointed at the floor. Even Alaric, who had little use for human weapons, recognized a topnotch weapon when he saw it.

"It's time. Michelle is going to bleed out if we don't get her to surgery," she said.

"If you will allow me, I will heal her," Alaric offered.

She looked startled. "I—I don't know."

"Just enough to get her to the hospital, Alaric," Alexios said. "You're going to need to conserve your strength in case Quinn . . ."

Alaric felt the words like a blow to his chest, but forced the emotion into a locked chamber in the back of his soul. Quinn was a survivor. He would heal this human, and Quinn would be fine.

He knelt by the stretcher and spread his fingers wide over the injured woman. She was slight, no larger than a child, with short dark curls. Her size and dark hair reminded him of Quinn, and for an instant he saw her face superimposed over Michelle's. Then startlingly blue eyes opened and Michelle gazed up at him with a spark of humor in her gaze in spite of the hideously gaping bite wound in her throat.

"I'm going to die, aren't I? That's just brilliant. My first mission and I go out with a bite, so to speak," she joked, surprising him with a crisp British accent. "Bloody vampires are even worse here than they are in London."

Her humor touched a spark of warmth buried deep inside him, and he attempted a smile. "You're not dying today. Consider this my version of diplomatic relations between countries."

He called power and, as always, thanked Poseidon for gifting his high priest with the power to heal. As the sizzling blue-green energy sifted through his body and poured out from his fingertips, down into and over her wounds, the sluggishly pulsing gash in the woman's throat sealed itself shut and the color returned to her cheeks.

As he sat back on his heels, the healing done, she blinked and a dazzling smile spread across her face. "If ambassadors actually looked like you, love, I think we'd have much better international relations. Any chance you'd be free for a cup of tea now that I can drink it without it coming out of the hole in my throat?"

An unexpected burst of laughter escaped from his throat,

and Alaric lifted her hand to his lips. "Another time, brave one."

Before he could rise, she caught his hand in her own, and her face turned somber. "Thank you. I didn't think I'd make it to the hospital, and . . . well, thank you. If you ever need anything, please call me. Grace can find me."

At the oddest times—moments that came so rarely during the centuries—a human would do something that gave Alaric hope for the future of their species. This was one of those times.

He could do nothing but give her courage its due. He stood up and bowed deeply as the others helped her to sit. "I am always grateful to find an ally, especially one so brave. Thank you, my lady."

Grace fell to her knees beside Michelle and hugged her, then looked up at Alaric with tear-drenched eyes. "Thank you. Anything. Anything you ever want, anytime, I'm here for you."

Suddenly uncomfortable at the unnecessary outpouring of gratitude, Alaric inclined his head and strode toward the door and a strangely grim Alexios, who was staring at Grace and Michelle.

"We need to go, now, Grace. There are plenty of our people with minor wounds who are better off going to the ER than draining any more of Alaric's strength," Alexios commanded. "Alaric, you should get going, too. Let me know what you find and if you need me."

Alaric simply nodded, unable to decide what, if anything, he would do next.

Alexios gestured for the first group to head out the door. "Let's do it."

Grace lifted her gun and, one arm around Michelle, led the way out of the door. The others, carrying the wounded, lined up behind her.

Alexios unsheathed his daggers and started to follow, then turned back. "Alaric, go after her. Since Daniel forced the blood bond on her, Quinn has been different. Lost. She deserves better than for you to abandon her and, priest or no, you know it."

Alaric lost all control at the thought of the vampire—their sometimes-ally—Daniel, who also called himself Drakos, who'd saved Quinn's life even as he'd tied her to him. Alaric hurled the energy sphere at the wall farthest from the humans and watched with grim satisfaction as the windows exploded outward into the empty street.

"What Quinn Dawson deserves is far more than I could ever provide, whether she is blood bonded to a vampire or not."

"Three exchanges, Alaric. It takes three exchanges for a human to become a vampire. He saved her life by doing it, but it was only one." Alexios shook his head, clearly disgusted. "I have no time for this. Do as you will. I'm gone."

He ran out the door, weapons drawn, after the last of the humans. Alaric started to follow. Stopped.

Took another step. Stopped. For perhaps the first time in all of his centuries of existence, he was nearly frozen with indecision.

Every instinct he possessed screamed at him to go after Quinn. Logic dictated that he assist Alexios. Emotion battled reason. Longing warred with rationality.

Emotion kicked logic's ass.

He was going after Quinn.

Chapter 20

Atlantis, the cavern

Keely fought her way back to consciousness, feeling the aftermath of the most intense vision she'd ever had kicking her butt like a tequila hangover. She was trapped; something was holding her down. Something . . . or someone.

Her eyes snapped open, and she looked up into his face. The face she'd known for years, even though they'd only just met. Her hand automatically went to the fish carving, still safely under her shirt.

The image of his infant self swam through her memory, disorienting her. She couldn't help herself; she needed to touch his face. Justice flinched a little at her touch, but then leaned his head into her hand, his arms tightening around her. She realized she was lying in his lap and wondered why it felt so completely right.

Part of her knew that she should move away. The rest of her wanted to stay right there in his arms for a very long time.

She felt safe in an entirely unsafe situation, no matter that it was crazy. But, then again, she'd just lived through centuries of his life, and she knew him on a more fundamental level than she'd ever known anyone before.

"You are well?" His voice was husky, and his black, black

eyes were warm and unexpectedly gentle. "You have been unconscious for several hours. If I had harmed you in any way—"

He left the sentence unfinished, but his face hardened and his eyes iced over with self-recrimination.

"No," she managed. "It was the sword. You had no way to know. I . . . I get visions from touching objects. Especially ancient artifacts that have so much violent and emotional history attached to them. I've never reacted to anything as intensely as I did to your sword."

Justice glared at the sword, his lips curling back from his teeth, then he blinked. "You are an object reader, then? That is a Gift we had thought lost millennia ago."

"That's what Liam called it, too. I guess it's as good a name as any. There's a talent called psychometry, which has to do with picking up impressions of a person from touching an object that belongs to him or her. But what I do is far more specific. I almost always only pick up one scene, and it seems to be the one that had the most emotional resonance for the object. It's an entire scene, complete with dialogue and action, too."

"So you could not—"

"I couldn't hold a shirt belonging to a missing child and know where he'd been taken, for example," she said, remembering the pain and frustration when she'd tried once to do just that. Tried to make her gift valuable to society in more ways than learning unprovable facts about ancient artifacts. "What I'd get is more likely the scene where he first met his new puppy, wearing that shirt, because of the overwhelming joy that would resonate in the fibers of the cloth. Or the pain and grief if his puppy had died . . ."

"I understand. I am sorry."

"It's okay. I have to admit it's kind of a relief to talk about this with somebody who believes me. I don't really want to end up in the Atlantean version of the nuthouse."

He pulled her closer to him until her head rested on his chest. She felt somehow comforted by the reassuring beat of his heart beneath her cheek.

"By nuthouse, I'm guessing you mean insane asylum? Has

anyone ever threatened you with such a place, simply because you have a Gift that is out of the ordinary for humans?"

His arms tightened even further, as if in response to a threat, and she made a small noise of protest. He instantly loosened his hold, and she took a deep breath. "Not exactly a threat. More like a long history of being institutionalized. My childhood—well, let's just say it wasn't all that much fun."

Keely realized that sitting in Justice's lap, no matter how seductively comforting, was perhaps not a position of strength for her. Suddenly she was telling him things she'd never told anybody before and didn't really want to start talking about now.

She shifted, putting her hand against his chest to push away, but froze when she noticed the hardness nestled under her bottom. Her breath caught in her throat and heat seared through her, melting her defenses. He clearly desired her, and there was a tiny part of her that wanted to stand up and cheer.

Except—except he'd been in the Void for so long. She didn't know what it was, but it didn't sound like the sort of place where you could go out and meet women. So what did that make Keely other than a convenient outlet—a woman who was handy and available? There was nothing more to it than that. Embarrassment flushed her face.

No. A zillion times no.

Her physical strength was no match for his, so she stopped trying to push away from him. "Please let me go, so I can get up now," she said quietly.

For the space of a heartbeat, he didn't move. Then he sighed and she felt the warmth of his breath in her hair. When he released her, she scrambled away from him, snatching up her gloves and pulling them back on her trembling hands.

"Thank you. For catching me when I, well, when I went under."

"Please don't thank me, when it was my action that sent you into that painful vision," he growled, leaping to his feet and beginning to pace the floor. "If I had only known—an object reader forced to touch, unprepared, the instrument of such violence over so many centuries. I don't know how you could endure it."

He snarled a long burst of the language she remembered from her vision. From the sound of it, she'd just heard quite a lot of choice Atlantean swearing. She nearly grinned in spite of the circumstances; her scientific side was itching for her laptop or at least a pen and paper so she could start transcribing.

This was better than the lost library at Alexandria. This was a living speaker of an ancient dead language. Phrases like "kid in a candy shop" or "pig in mud" rushed through her mind. This was the find of the decade. The century, even.

If she happened to survive it.

The thought drove her to her feet. She needed to be on even ground with him. "It was fairly difficult," she admitted, ruefully recognizing that her confession was probably the understatement of the year. "But it wasn't all violence. At least, it wasn't all battlefield violence. The scene with your mother—"

He whirled around. "Did you say my mother?"

She almost retreated when she saw his eyes. They'd turned a fiery blue-green color again, nearly feral. Burning.

"What do you know about our mother?" He sprang across the floor toward her and this time she did take a step back. He was all warrior now, the gentleness she'd seen earlier gone as if it had been a mirage. "Tell us. Tell us everything."

He was back to the plural self-reference again. She considered options, and then finally went with the simplest. The truth. "Yes, I saw your mother. I tried to help her, but he . . . he—" She shuddered to a halt, shaking her head in denial.

This wasn't a story she wanted to tell him. Not now, not ever. Especially not when Justice was "they" again. She wondered who the second personality was and where it had originated.

She wondered if it were something he could ever heal.

It wasn't anger, but rather wonder tinged with awe that crossed his face as he fell to his knees on the floor in front of her. "Tell us," he repeated. But this time it was a plea, not a demand. "Please tell us."

She couldn't resist him. Couldn't resist the naked pleading on his face. Couldn't resist the sound of the lost little boy in his voice.

She knelt down next to him, took his hands in hers, and she told him everything, heedless of the tears pouring down her face.

~~~~~

Justice listened to Keely with a growing sense of sorrow. Of loss. He'd kept a tight leash on his pain and wrath all of his life. Ever since his older brother, son by birth of the man and woman Justice had thought were his parents, had told him the truth in a fit of pique. That he'd been adopted. That his real parents hadn't wanted him.

That nobody wanted him.

But his brother had been punished for lies, and Justice had been hushed and comforted by the woman he'd begun to suspect was no blood kin to himself. In spite of her reassurances, he'd been old enough to realize that none of them had looked anything like him. Although, to be fair, he'd never met another Atlantean with blue hair, and he'd spent most of his first decade of life searching. He'd quit wondering about it after his tenth birthday, of course. Shaved his head in a rage.

Blue stubble had been worse. He'd nearly sustained broken ribs in the three or four schoolyard fights over that one.

When the king himself had confronted him with the truth of his birth, it was almost a relief. Bittersweet, to be sure, and filled with confusion and pain, but still a relief. He wasn't crazy. He *did* fit in, somewhere. Belonged to someone.

He was the son of the king. The king of all Atlantis! But his relief and joy burned to ashes in his mouth almost before it had a chance to be born. The king told him of Poseidon's command, and of the *geas*. Justice could never reveal the truth, or he'd be driven to murder anyone who'd heard the story of his birth and heritage.

Worst of all, the king—his father by blood—had never wanted him. Justice's own father had cast him aside. Had told him his mother had never wanted him, either, confirming Justice's most secret, darkest fear: that he was unworthy of even a parent's love.

It had been a relief to be ordered to the warrior training academy. Constant physical exertion was a civilized way to release the fury that rode him so hard. He'd snarled and spat his defiance at his trainers and fellow students like a wild blue-haired animal, pushing himself to the limits of his endurance and then beyond. Far beyond. The healers all grew to despise the sight of him.

But then, one perfectly ordinary day, everything had changed. He'd met Ven and Conlan. Liked them. Admired them, even, though he'd hated them for having what he would never have—a true family who loved them. A place to belong.

Now this woman, this object reader, this *human* who'd come to represent his soul's salvation, told him that he hadn't been unwanted. His mother had wanted him. He whispered her name. "Éibhleann."

The Nereid, who'd fallen silent, echoed the liquid syllables of their mother's name in their mind. "Éibhleann."

Anguish pounded through them. Éibhleann was an ancient Nereid name meaning beloved of the goddess. What foul irony lay in that?

Keely's voice fell silent. She'd finished her recounting of the visions she'd seen, visions she'd *lived*. Visions of his life.

"Justice? Are you . . . well, it sounds stupid to even ask this, but are you okay?"

The gentle concern in her voice nearly broke him, when centuries of battle had not. She sounded worried for him. For *him*, when she should hate him for what he'd done to her. First abducting her, then putting her in such danger and through so much suffering.

He was a monster. No matter what he needed, she deserved better.

There is none better than us, the Nereid shouted in his mind.

Justice tried to slam the mental door shut, but only partially succeeded. Keely's hands trembled in his; he'd been clenching them far too tightly. "I'm not sure what I feel right now. But regardless of my reaction to this news, thank you. Thank you for giving me the truth that I never knew before."

"Your mother loved you, and she wanted you," Keely said. "Her emotion was very powerful, Justice. What they told you about being unwanted—it was a lie. It was a big, fat, cowardly lie."

He smiled at the outrage in her voice. She was furious on his behalf. Warmth swept through him at the thought. Had anyone, during the entirety of his life, ever been outraged on his behalf before? They'd depended upon him, they fought at his side, and they'd saved his life.

But outrage? No. Never.

Only Keely had ever stood up for him like this.

"So you told him," he murmured. "You told the king of Atlantis himself that he was wrong. I would give everything I own to have been able to see that."

She smiled back at him, and the shared flash of humor turned something over inside his chest. He knew he wanted her; he'd accepted that he hungered for her. But perhaps it was more. Perhaps she was breaching the barriers he'd long since established around his emotions.

Shock reverberated through his mind, and the Nereid broke through again. *Yes, let her in. She told us the truth. My—our—mother was a warrior woman, as all Nereid maidens are. She fought for us, and she died for us. Somehow, she spoke to us through this human. Isn't that enough to let us know that this female belongs to us?*

Justice looked at Keely again, but this time he saw her through the lenses of the Nereid's eyes. Her quiet beauty became sharper, more sensual. The green of her eyes glowed like the most precious jade. The curve of her lips turned sinful, almost begging him to capture them with his own. The pulse beating in her throat fascinated him. He wanted to taste her skin. He wanted to trace the path from her neck to the lovely, enticing breasts hidden beneath her shirt.

With his mouth. With his hands.

Yes. Yes, the Nereid whispered. *She is ours. Take her. Take her now.*

Justice leaned forward, caught almost hypnotically in a web of heated desire. Keely's eyes widened, but she didn't protest or try to evade him. Instead, her lips parted slightly on an indrawn gasp of air.

Lust coiled inside him, sharp-edged and raw. His cock

hardened so painfully that he thought the pressure would drive him mad. He needed her.

He *must* have her.

He lifted his hands and finally, *finally* wrapped them in that glorious hair, and she sighed in either relief or surrender. He didn't know which. Didn't care.

As long as she let him taste her.

Both sides of his fractured soul merged into a single, driving need. "Keely," he groaned, pushed almost beyond bearing it. "Please let me kiss you. Just . . . just once," he said, even knowing it for a lie. He could never take just one taste of her lips.

Never.

She hesitated, and the blackness of an abyss yawned before him. If she denied him, would he be able to accept her wishes? Or would he lose himself and his very soul to the blackness of his hungers and take her, force her, plunder this woman he needed so very much?

She continued to hesitate and, though screaming pain sliced through him, he stopped himself. He stopped both of his selves. He pulled away, even though the Nereid howled in gnashing rage inside him.

Before he could untangle her hair from his fingers, she placed her own hands over his. Stared into his eyes. Parted her lips and nervously moistened them with her tongue.

"Yes," she whispered. "Yes. Just once."

Then she lifted her head and touched her lips, ever so tentatively, to his.

And he was lost.

Flame and longing and soaring ecstasy ripped through him, just from the first gentle taste of her lips. He shuddered and tried to remain still, tried not to frighten her, but she trembled under his hands and leaned into him, and all hope of sanity fled.

He roughly pulled her into his lap as they knelt on the floor, and he captured her gasp in his mouth, his tongue sweeping in to claim, to capture, to conquer. He wrapped one hand, still tangled in her hair, around the back of her head to pull her even closer, and his other hand caressed her back from her nape all the way down to her lovely, firm ass, settling her more fully against him.

The pressure of her weight on his cock made him groan deep in the back of his throat and her answering moan inflamed him beyond all reason. She put her arms around his neck and kissed him back—she *kissed him back*—and he lost all sense and logic, falling into shining waves of pure desire.

Justice kissed her as he'd never kissed anyone before, and reality parted before him as he hurled into fantasy at rocket speed. She tasted like honey and fruit and the finest wine.

She tasted like salvation.

Need pulsed through him, and he kissed her. It was everything, and yet it somehow wasn't enough. He needed her naked. He needed her naked, warm, and willing underneath him. He needed to drive himself into the wet warmth of her body. He needed to taste every inch of her skin until he was imprinted on her like a brand.

He tore his mouth away from hers, panting, unable to catch his breath, no thought in his head but to rip the clothes from her body. She stared up at him, eyes wide, dazed. Her lips were swollen from his kisses and her hair was tangled around her in wild clouds of flame. She looked as though she'd been tumbled in his bed during a long night of wild lovemaking.

By all the gods, that's what he was going to give her.

He grasped the two sides of her shirt, some hazy thought of ripping it off her pounding through his mind, but a strange noise penetrated his thoughts.

A strange, growling noise. He blinked and noticed a pale pink stain flush across Keely's cheeks.

"Um, that was me," she said, biting her lip. "Actually, that was my stomach. Growling. I'm starving."

She sat there on his lap, blushing, warm and flushed and eminently desirable. Suddenly shy. A strange and unfamiliar feeling rippled its way through him and burst out of him as a harsh, rusty sound. It took him a moment to recognize it as laughter. Real laughter, his first in a very long time.

She ducked her head a little, smiling. "Pretty mundane, right? You kiss me in a 'knock the universe off its foundation' kind of way, and all I can think about is my stomach. But I am really hungry." Her smile faded, and she looked around. "Not to mention, in spite of this very lovely little bout of trauma-induced insanity, we're still trapped in here and we have to figure out a way to escape."

The Nereid's howls of frustration rocked through Justice's brain, but he kept the smile on his face so she wouldn't see it. Wouldn't guess that his mind was splitting in two, or discover that one half of him was violent and unstable.

Take her, take her, take her. She wants us; you know she does.

Justice closed his eyes for a moment, concentrating fiercely on sealing his mind against the Nereid again. It was harder this time, but he finally accomplished it.

When he opened his eyes, she was still there. Not a dream, then, but reality far more exquisite than he could ever deserve. "Thank you."

Confusion shadowed her lovely green eyes. "Thank me for what?"

"Thank you for telling me that I was not the only one affected by that kiss," he said and watched her cheeks turn faintly pink again. "And thank you for reminding me of our priorities. Food and escape. Or escape and food. Either way, the discussion we must have is best put off until later."

"The discussion?"

"In solving one mystery for me, you have opened another, Keely. I had forgotten the Nereid vision quest and all of its ramifications. Certainly I had never considered it to apply to me. But there is no other reason that I would have seen your face when I was lost in the Void. You are part of my own personal vision quest."

Smiling a little, he forced out the words he knew she would not want to hear. "I'm glad it was a 'knock the universe off its foundation' kind of kiss, because you are my destined mate."

Chapter 21

Atlantis, the cavern

Keely paced the edges of the cavern, staying as far from the crazy "you're my mate" man as possible. Justice was doing something at one of the walls; she wasn't sure what. After the "mate" announcement, she'd fallen into a shocked silence and then backed away from him, muttering speculations about his need for a nice round of electroshock therapy.

Half an hour later, she was still mumbling under her breath. From the narrow-eyed glances he'd shot her way, he probably had an idea that her remarks were far from flattering. He'd stayed well away, even when she'd washed up as best as she could in the pool and she'd caught him staring at her as if he wanted to devour her.

At least he hadn't tried to jump her. She wasn't sure how far he was likely to try to go with the "mate" thing. For now, they needed to solve the problem at hand.

"We've got to get out of here," she said for probably the twentieth time, but loudly enough to be sure he heard her. "We're *going* to get out of here."

Justice didn't bother to answer, which didn't offend her, since he'd responded the first dozen or so times she'd made the same statement. He was undoubtedly as tired of hearing her as she was tired of saying it. Still, she carefully stayed at least ten feet from him at all times, wary of being in reach after that kiss.

That kiss.

That rock-the-universe, blow-fireworks-through-the-sky kiss. He'd set off the aurora borealis inside her skull, and she'd responded with a growling stomach.

Perfect. Just perfect. Although she'd always been a girl too practical for fairy tales, so meeting a fairy-tale prince didn't change anything. Not even when he was a prince who had the most amazingly beautiful hair she'd ever seen on a man.

Hey, maybe he was insane, Mr. I'm Your Destiny and all, but at least he was gorgeous. Considering what he'd been through in his life, he deserved to be a little nuts. A tendril of sympathy whispered inside her mind as the memory of her vision surfaced. It's a wonder he was anywhere in the same zip code as sanity.

Speaking of which, how many people had thought she was crazy? Nobody knew better than she did that sanity was a spectrum of relativity. Anyway, it had been so long since she'd been naked with a man that maybe she needed to lower her standards. Crazy? No problem, so long as he had great hair.

She sighed and snuck a glance at him from under her lashes. His hair was dry now. Silky, glossy, and gorgeous; it flowed in waves of blue down his back, clear to the top of the finest butt in the history of mankind. Or Atlantean kind. Or whatever.

He wasn't Prince Charming; he was Prince Tall, Dark, and Deadly. Justice was no perfect, plastic prince, but a very real man with a very damaged psyche.

However, she, as she kept reminding herself, was no shrink. So maybe she should keep her distance, regardless of her hormones playing marching band.

He finally spoke up from where he was prying at one of the gem-encrusted walls. "I thought this was a hidden door to another passageway, but it's nothing. Just another secret compartment that's full of a whole lot of nothing helpful."

He held something up in his hand, and the light from the

lanterns flashed off it like paparazzi flashbulbs on Swarovski crystals. She couldn't help herself. She was an archaeologist, after all, and professional curiosity was killing her.

"What is it?"

"More gems. Everywhere we turn in here, it's more and more and more worthless gemstones," he said, hurling them on the ground.

She walked over, careful not to get too close. "I'm not sure *worthless* is the word I'd use," she said, bending down to select a sapphire the size of her palm from among the gems littering the floor. "I feel a little bit like Indiana Jones discovering an ancient treasure. This rock alone is probably worth more than a year's salary for me."

He shrugged carelessly. "Your salary is no longer important, as we will be sure you have everything you need. Take the sapphire if you want to. Take all the gems you want. To us they're only stones, as you say. At best, instruments of healing now that we have a gem singer."

A bitter taste like rotten grapefruit soured the back of her mouth. He thought she wanted his gemstones. He thought she would raid the most incredible archaeological site she'd ever set foot on.

He didn't know her very well.

She decided to take the high road and ignore the comment, and she held the gem up to the light, examining it. "This reminds me of the one that Liam sabotaged me with back in my office. The companion stone to the Star of Artemis that Nereus was talking about."

Justice reacted as though she'd shot an electric current through him. "What? The Star of Artemis? Nereus? Tell me everything, and I will give you every gem you could possibly want in a dozen lifetimes."

Okay, that did it. Again with the buying her off with gems. She knelt down and very carefully placed the sapphire on the floor next to the other gems. Then she stood up and folded her arms across her ever-more-loudly growling stomach, lifted her chin, and put pure defiance into her stare. "I don't want your stupid gems. What I want is a pizza. Or a plate piled high with pancakes, dripping butter and hot, sticky syrup. I'm not sure what you think you mean by telling me my salary is no longer important to me, but guess what? I'm trying not to be offended. I'm going to pretend I don't even care about any of this right now. All I want is to get out of here and find something to eat."

Almost before she finished her sentence, he leapt across the space between them and clasped her wrists in his hands. A wild excitement burned in his eyes and he smiled down at her. "Say it again. Say it again, just like that. Except add more descriptive terminology."

"What are you talking about? I don't want your hard, blue, shiny gemstones."

He shouted out a laugh. "No, Keely. My beautiful, brilliant Keely. The pancakes. Describe the pancakes again. With butter and syrup and the smell and the sight and the taste."

She sighed, shaking her head. "You've gone over the deep end, haven't you? It's sad, too, after everything you've gone through in your life, that the simple description of pancakes was the final straw."

He laughed again, then leaned over and kissed the top of her head. "No, I'm not insane. Breakfast food has not driven me over the deep end, as you call it. I'm discovering the scope of my Nereid powers, and I think I found one that's related to the transport power that brought us here. I'm as hungry as you are, Keely, and when you described the pancakes, I could almost smell them."

He released her wrists and stood back, just a half step. "Describe them again, please. I think, somehow, I can bring us to the pancakes."

Keely raised an eyebrow, thinking that there were a few things wrong with the plan. "Okay, not to be a naysayer, but there are just a couple of teensy little issues I'd like to bring up before I start waxing lyrical over Mrs. Butterworth. First, what pancakes? Where? What if we show up in the middle of breakfast at San Quentin?"

"That would be a problem?"

"I'm guessing you didn't see *Walk the Line*. Prison, Justice.

San Quentin or some other prison, or maybe in the middle of a shape-shifter breakfast party." She paused. "Do shape-shifters even eat pancakes?"

"I don't know," he said dryly. "What I do know is that *anywhere* that is not a cavern deep underground, blocked off by a cave-in, would more than likely be an improvement over our current circumstances."

"Point taken."

"Hold my hand," he commanded.

She clasped her fingers in his and closed her eyes. Speaking of crazy, she must be right there next to him in the padded cell to go along with this. "What the hell. Fat, fluffy pancakes, with steam rising into the air from the top of the stack. Butter—real butter, not the margarine stuff—melting down the sides. Maple syrup fresh from Canada pooling on the pancakes and running over the edge of the plate—"

His shout interrupted her, but she didn't feel any of the temporal displacement that had accompanied their journey into the cavern. Her eyes snapped open, only to find that nothing had changed. Still in the cavern. Still no way out.

He hadn't transported them to the pancakes, no matter that her imagination was providing that rich, buttery maple smell. Her shoulders slumped for an instant, but then she tried to be upbeat for Justice. "It was only the first try. We can try again," she said, injecting a little optimism into her voice.

But he wasn't paying a bit of attention to her. He was staring at the ground. She looked down and started laughing.

A flowered tablecloth lay, spread out perfectly, on the floor next to them. Platters of pancakes, bacon, eggs, and sausage covered every inch. An opened newspaper lay next to an empty plate, neatly folded to the financial pages, and a pair of eyeglasses rested on top of it.

"Well," she said diplomatically. "At least you brought the pancakes to us. Next time, maybe you could work on bringing the coffeepot, too."

The expression of sheer outraged indignation on his face sent *her* over the edge, and the laughter poured helplessly out. She bent double, clutching her stomach with both arms, and laughed until tears leaked from her eyes. Maybe it was hysteria, maybe it was exhaustion or the culmination of way more stress than a mild-mannered archaeologist should have to endure, but it all caught up to her at once and she laughed until her ribs ached.

At some point, a quiet sound caught her attention and, wiping her eyes, she looked up to see that Justice was chuckling. Not a full-fledged laugh, not even a small one, but at least a chuckle.

It was a start. The man had a sense of humor. She could work with that.

Taking deep breaths to calm down before her laughter turned into hiccups, she plopped down on the edge of the tablecloth and picked up a fork.

"Hey, if we're going to end up in jail for pancake theft, we may as well enjoy them."

His eyes warmed to the color of molten jade, and her breath caught in her throat. Strange how something as simple as eye color could touch her emotions this way.

"I agree. Also I'm starving."

As he sat down on the other side of the tablecloth, Keely stuffed a forkful of maple bliss into her mouth and practically purred, sending up a silent thank-you to the cook who was probably standing in the middle of her kitchen with her mouth hanging open at that very moment.

"Oh, wow. This is wonderful."

He nodded, looking pretty happy himself. "They didn't exactly serve home-cooked breakfasts in the Void," he said, his voice cracking a little.

"Oh. I didn't . . . I didn't want to pry. But if you want to tell me about it, I'd be glad to listen," she offered, placing her fork down on the edge of her plate.

His jaw clenched, then relaxed. Something dark flickered in his eyes before he finally nodded. "Maybe. Maybe you deserve to know. I wasn't always a kidnapper of lovely archaeologists, you know."

The smile he aimed at her was tentative, but it signaled huge progress, and she couldn't help smiling back at him.

"Eat, or I won't tell you any of it. You look like a gentle wave would knock you over," he admonished.

"I'll have you know that I'm stronger than I look," she said, but she picked her fork back up and dug into a fluffy pile of scrambled eggs.

Justice worked his way through a healthy portion of breakfast in silence, then pushed his plate aside. "You saw my . . . the king."

She nodded. "Your father."

A grimace twisted his face. "Yes, if you like. Not that the man ever showed me anything but loathing. In any event, you know about the *geas*—the curse—upon me never to reveal the circumstances of my birth."

"But you did, didn't you?" she said, piecing together everything she'd heard from the others during the craziness at the portal. "You told them, when you sacrificed yourself to save your brother and everyone else."

"Sacrifice is too noble a word. I did what anyone would have done, after taking the measure of the situation and developing a strategy."

"Right. Of course. So many of us would voluntarily turn ourselves over to a . . . What was it? A vampire? No, wait, a vampire *goddess*. To save the lives of other people. Yeah, you're right. That's not noble. I do that every day before breakfast. Twice on Fridays."

He narrowed his eyes. "Don't think I don't see what you're trying to accomplish."

"Oh, good. I so rarely even know what I'm trying to accomplish myself, so it's good that you can see right through me," she said, widening her eyes in mock innocence.

It made him laugh, which inexplicably made her very, very happy. She decided not to overanalyze it. "Go on. You're not noble, you're off with the goddess, and then?" An oddly unpleasant thought crossed her mind. "Goddess, huh? I bet she's pretty beautiful."

"She is possessed of a terrible beauty that is almost inconceivable to human imagination," he said grimly. "Every inch of her is a study in dark and glorious perfection."

"Great. Goddess. Inconceivable beauty and perfection. We could probably move on now." Okaaay. That's one way to measure up short in the comparative looks department: go up against a goddess. She'd thought it was bad when one of her dates had been obsessed with Jessica Alba.

At least Jessica was human. Ish.

Justice was clutching the end of his braided hair so tightly his knuckles were white. "You don't understand. Her attraction is like the flame to the moth, or the snake to its prey. She is death and despair and madness, somehow packaged in the dark fantasies of a deranged mind."

Any childish thoughts of jealousy vanished in the face of his obvious struggle to explain it to her. "Is yours? Deranged, I mean? What did she do to you?"

His face hardened and he almost imperceptibly shook his head. "No. I won't tell you that. I won't tell anyone that, ever."

Justice was silent so long that she thought he'd changed his mind about talking to her. But then he nodded, as if coming to some internal decision.

"Breaking the *geas* shattered my sanity. The curse was such that I always assumed I'd die if I ever broke it, but maybe something in the Void changed its nature. I don't know. I just know that Anubisa wanted . . . She wanted me. She wanted me to do . . . things. Unspeakable, hideous things. But my mind fractured into a thousand pieces when I was unable to fulfill the *geas* and I came very near to dying. She wouldn't let me die."

The lump in her throat made it hard to talk. No one should have to endure so much as he had, centuries of life or not. She forced out the words. "And then? When you didn't die?"

A smile so terrifying spread across his face that she almost physically recoiled from it. "Then she cast me into the Void, and said that she would take my brother in my place."

"Do you have another brother? Besides Ven and the high prince?"

"No. She held Conlan prisoner for many long years of torture, so I know she's planning to go after Ven again next. But now I'll be here to stop her."

She didn't point out the obvious: that there wasn't much they could do stuck in the cave. More and more she was starting to believe that they would make it out.

She was starting to believe in him.

"Will you be able to overcome the damage from breaking the *geas*? I mean, you do reference yourself in the plural sometimes," she ventured.

"My mother was a Nereid, Keely. You saw her. She gave me qualities and, evidently, powers from her lineage. Powers that I don't know anything about, yet. I think when my sanity fractured, it somehow let loose the Nereid side of my soul. He battles me even now, because he wants—"

He broke off, and a dark flush swept over his face.

"He wants?" she prompted, even though she was suddenly sure she didn't want to know what the Nereid wanted. Not when it made Justice's face turn to icy marble like that.

"He wants you," he said flatly. "He wants to strip you bare and get you under him, whether you agree or not. He wants to take you, Keely, and I'll die before I let him."

Her gasp echoed in the silence between them, and she nearly tripped over her own feet stumbling to move back and away from him.

Anguish tightened Justice's features, and his eyes darkened to black as he sat, perfectly motionless, watching her. "So now you know, at least some of it. You know the darkness, the death, and the despair. There has been light, as well, but I would judge that you won't be able to hear of that now."

Some part of her responded to the pain in his voice and wanted to comfort him, but the reality of just how isolated she was—trapped with a self-confessed madman—was coming back to the forefront of her awareness. No matter what sympathy or even empathy she had for him, she couldn't do him any good if she were dead.

Or brutalized by the evil side of his nature.

It took every ounce of her skill and training, but she managed to speak calmly. "Of course I would love to hear about the happy times, but you're right. Now isn't a good time. We should work on finding that way out of here, don't you think?"

As he rose gracefully to his feet, she was extremely proud of herself for not flinching. When they escaped this cavern, after this experience, she'd be able to face anything.

If they ever escaped this cavern.

Firmly silencing the foreboding voice in her mind, Keely turned toward the cavern walls again. There had to be a way out, and she was going to find it.

Chapter 22

Justice roamed around the cavern, searching in vain for a way out. Whatever power he'd managed to call on earlier to transport them was silent, as if mocking him. An option had occurred to him, of course. But he wasn't yet willing to unleash the Nereid trying to possess his mind, just so they could discuss strategy.

It might come to that, though. Hells, it *probably* would come to that. But for now, with he and Keely at least fed, he'd try one more time for a passageway he'd missed before. Desperation didn't feel quite as sharp-edged with a full belly, even though he'd scared her into silence. Now she avoided him entirely, and he couldn't blame her for it. But truth had seemed the best option at the time.

Even though now he regretted it, fiercely.

He glanced over at where she sat on the floor, the dishes pushed aside and a collection of jade figurines from one of the compartments spread out with mathematical precision on the tablecloth. To one side of the figurines, the collection of gems he'd tossed aside earlier were lined up like toy soldiers awaiting their general's command.

She'd tied that wealth of hair back away from her face, and

a little furrow had appeared between her silken brows as she concentrated on the objects. She hadn't spoken in quite some time. Perversely, even though something about her fierce concentration appealed to him, he found himself resenting the ease with which she could dismiss him from her mind.

It would have been impossible for him. Every step he took, every thought he had, was wrapped in the knowledge that she was nearby. The flash of resentment had a now-familiar effect: the Nereid strained against the shields in his mind, growing stronger with every passing hour.

The cavern lay directly underneath the temple of his Nereid ancestors, and that half of his soul continued to cry out that it would not be denied. Justice shoved his hand through his hair, wondering how to defeat one side of his very nature without destroying his entire psyche.

Had he escaped the Void, only to find that its madness had followed him? Dwelt within him? Pharnatus's sacrifice must not be in vain.

Frustration spiked into helpless, irrational fury. Keely could ignore him so easily, and he couldn't even ignore a voice inside his own head. The realization flared inside him— a flash fire of rage—no less powerful for being unreasonable.

Pain caught his head in a vise grip. Steel spikes drove through his temples, heralding the Nereid as it broke through his shields. *She casts you aside like you are nothing, Atlantean. If we had taken her, she would be tied to us forever.*

Justice shook his head, denying it, but the movement only worsened the headache squeezing his skull, and he gasped. "No. We will not . . . *I* will not force her. I promised her."

Then I will not share with you the Nereid art of using matter transference, and we will remain here, trapped, until we die.

Matter transference? But even as he turned the phrase over in his mind, he knew. It was the method by which he'd brought the food; stolen, no doubt, from very surprised and hungry people.

Far more important, it was how he'd brought Keely with him to his long-forgotten hideout.

Yes. The way in, and the way out. Simplicity itself, when you know the key, the Nereid whispered seductively.

Closing his eyes, he waged a brief but furious war with his other half, to no avail. He was seriously considering pounding his skull against one of the gem-covered walls to bash the information loose, when Keely called out to him.

"Justice? I may have an idea of how we can get out of here."

Keely sat cross-legged on the floor, contemplating the figurines. Priceless objects, all of them, and incredibly important to any serious study of the Atlantean past. Even through her gloves, the sheer age of the carvings pressed on her mind and sizzled along her nerve endings. What she was considering was unbelievably self-destructive. Possibly suicidal.

But she was trapped between the proverbial rocks—of the cave-in—and a very hard place.

Justice didn't know how to get them out. He didn't even understand how he'd brought them there. Fine. She'd been inside his past, through the sword vision, and she knew enough of him to know his integrity. His honor. Even the pain he kept so tightly controlled.

He wouldn't lie to her. He'd die before he let the Nereid hurt her. She would accept those facts as proven hypotheses.

So it was up to her.

He crossed the room, resembling nothing so much as a sleek panther, muscles flowing in a graceful, deadly stride. He took her breath away and muddled her neatly ordered, scientific thoughts.

She should be more afraid, especially after what he'd admitted to her, but somehow she trusted Justice enough to feel safe.

Kneeling down across from her, he retied the loosened piece of leather cord at the end of his braid. The cord probably came from one of the compartments, used to tie off yet another bag of gems. She shook her head, amused at herself. Here she was, sitting inside a treasure trove that would be a jewel thief's wet dream, and all she could think about was escape.

Practical, pragmatic Keely.

Except, staring at Justice, wishing his strong hands had been on her skin instead of in his hair, she didn't feel at all practical.

"If you continue to look at me like that, I will allow myself to entertain fantasies of what I would like to do with the remaining maple syrup and your lovely, lovely body," he said, voice husky and nearly growling. His smile was strained and a muscle jumped in his clenched jaw. "There is much difference between a forcible taking and a willing surrender."

As the hated blush swept up from her chest to her cheeks, she bit her lip and tried not to do it. She really tried, but she couldn't help it. She just couldn't.

She looked at the syrup.

This time he really did growl, and the primal ferocity of the sound unleashed a primitive yearning in Keely. Liquid heat spread from the center of her body, and she had to fight against squirming where she sat. Suddenly her pants were too tight and the lace of her bra rubbed unbearably against her sensitive nipples.

If he could do all that to her from a growl, she was in trouble if she ever got him naked.

"Focus," she gasped out, deciding to put it out on the table. Or floor. Whatever. "I don't know what this crazy attraction is between us, but we need to focus. I don't want to trigger your . . . your problem, either."

He froze and then carefully changed position to sit, cross-legged, a cautious distance away. She took a deep breath, lifted her chin, and confronted the issue directly. Ready to discuss the problem logically.

But his dangerously potent smile and the sheer masculine arrogance that shone from his eyes played havoc with her intentions. "You admit it, then," he said calmly. "The attraction, as you call it, though I would name that a very tame word. This has nothing to do with the Other inside me, Keely. This is the desire that surges like a tidal wave between destined mates."

She caught her breath at the heat his words evoked. "I'd have to be a fool or a liar to deny it. At least the desire part.

But it's simply a reaction to a stressful situation. An adrenaline-based hormonal reaction."

He raised an eyebrow, and those fascinatingly changeable eyes flashed from black to palest green. "I think not, my Keely. I will prove it to you. Count on it."

Trying to ignore the heat that sizzled through her at his deliberately provocative words, she asked the question she'd been wondering about for some time. "Your eyes. Liam's did that, too, the eye-color-change thing. Does Atlantean eye color correlate to your emotions? Like a physiological mood ring?"

He stared at her for a long moment before answering. "Perhaps. What colors have you seen in my eyes?"

She shrugged. "I haven't exactly been cataloging, but they've gone from black to midnight blue to a glowing teal, and now they're this beautiful pale green that reminds me of spring. Oh, and sometimes when they're black, they have an intriguing little blue-green flame at the very centers of your pupils."

His mouth dropped open a little before clamping shut into a thin line. The irises of his eyes darkened to black as she watched, like night falling suddenly on a lovely spring day. She nearly smiled at her own whimsy. Maybe she should have taken more poetry classes. She could write "Ode to an Atlantean's Eyes."

"Just now, for example," she pointed out, trying to suppress her grin. "They changed from a vivid green to black when I made that comment about the flames."

"Well, do not panic or jump up and pace the cavern again, please, but it would appear that you have been claimed by both halves of my nature, Keely," he said, drawing the words out slowly as if she'd torn them out of him. "You may be in more trouble than I thought."

She opened her mouth to make some wisecrack, but then she realized that in no way was he joking. Ice shivered down her spine, which worked wonders for that focus she'd been wanting to find. "Both halves of your nature. I'm guessing that has to do with the 'we' persona you go into and the Nereid?"

Before he could answer, she shook her head. "No. Not now. When we're out of here, I promise you, we'll talk about all of this. I won't run screaming for the hills for at least an hour or two."

His face darkened, and he narrowed his eyes. "You won't run away from me, Keely," he said, steely command in his tone. "There is no place you can go that I will not follow. Know that now."

"Yeah, well, *you* should know that I'm not so good at taking orders," she fired back. "Instead of fighting about it, though, why don't we do something productive? Like escape?"

She selected the largest of the sapphires and lifted it to show him. "I think I have a plan."

Placing the gem carefully back down on the cloth, she decided the time had come. "There's something I need to tell you. About the vision I had when I touched Liam's sapphire."

"Liam?" It was just one word but it carried a wealth of danger. Suddenly he was the feral predator again, and she didn't know why. Perhaps he and Liam had bad blood between them. Now wasn't the time to go into it, though.

"Yes, Liam, but he's not important. You need to know my vision. I was in the room with your high priest Nereus and his wife, Zelia, while they discussed the Star of Artemis."

"That's impossible. Your vision must be wrong. I know this name, Nereus, but he couldn't be married. Poseidon deemed that his high priests could never marry. If they don't remain celibate, they suffer an enormous loss of their powers. Nereus was one of the most powerful priests in our history, so he could not have wed."

She shrugged. "Maybe the marriage records got lost in the files somewhere. I've lived with these visions since I was a child, and they are never, ever wrong. Nereus was married to Zelia."

She recounted the story of her vision of Nereus and Zelia, and what they'd said about the Star of Artemis. As she concluded her tale, an important detail struck her. "Justice, it has the power to heal fractured minds, they said. Maybe you could—"

Horrified at what she'd almost blurted out, she cut herself off mid-thought. She had no right. No right at all.

Justice's clenched fists rested on his thighs, but when he spoke it wasn't to tell her to stay the hell out of his business, like she expected and, to be honest, richly deserved.

"He knew? Liam knew this experience would harm you and yet he sent you into it with no warning?" The tone of his voice had changed—went deadly.

"Well, no, he—"

"He is a dead man," he said flatly. "Each breath he takes is a debt owed to the nine hells."

A shiver raced down her spine at his words, which weren't delivered as a threat but more like a known fact. Keely spared a sudden sympathetic thought for Liam. "Well. That's very poetic, but not fair in any way. He had no idea that the vision would affect me so strongly."

"He should never have touched you," he responded, implacable. "I will kill him for it."

"Right. Okay. Going just a little bit overboard, don't you think? Nobody's killing anybody. Anyway, what I was getting at was the intense emotional connection I seem to forge with any Atlantean objects I read. I was thinking—"

She stopped and tried to fill her suddenly empty lungs with air, then began again, forcing the words out past the lump of fear in her throat. "I was thinking that I could start reading objects, one after another, until possibly one of them gives us some information about a way out of here."

She pasted an optimistic smile on her face and tried not to think about all the things that could go wrong. Tried not to think about getting trapped in a maelstrom of never-ending visions. Tried not to wonder if this would be the time she died in one, finally proving one way or another whether vision death equaled reality death.

Of all the hypotheses she'd ever formulated, this was the one she was least anxious to prove.

Since her thoughts were whirling around like a hamster trapped in a wheel, she threw it in Justice's court. "Well? Did you hear me?"

He sat, silent and still, his features icily pale. "In what possible delusional state could you believe that I would let you risk yourself in such a manner?"

Fury rode the hardened planes and angles of his face, and for an instant he looked like an avenging god himself. She refused to be intimidated, however.

Much.

"We don't have a better option; you said so yourself. You don't know how you got us here, and you don't know how to get us out. We have to try something, Justice. I'm a scientist, and I explore different avenues, different hypotheses, until I find one that fits."

Feeling a little like she was following a lion into his lair, she leaned forward and touched his arm. "It might not be so bad. As long as I meditate and prepare, my visions are usually not as intense as these most recent ones were."

"It. Might. Not. Be. So. Bad," he bit off from between clenched teeth. "Really."

With a blur of preternatural speed, he grabbed her shoulders and yanked her across the figurine-and-gem-covered cloth and into his arms. "I forbid it," he said, ice still coating every syllable. "I will go to battle against the other half of my own soul before I will let you take this chance with your health or your life."

He rested his head on top of hers and embraced her so tightly that she almost couldn't breathe. She was about to protest when she realized he was trembling against her. The internal battle he was waging must be one hell of a fight, and the worst part was that she didn't know how to help him.

There was only one thing she could think of, and it was the simplest. She slipped her arms around his waist, and she hugged him back. A violent shudder shook his body and he eased up the slightest bit on the death grip he had on her ribs.

They sat, unmoving and silent, for several minutes, and then he raised his head. "I know what I have to do. I must make a bargain with a demon and hope we don't all end up in hell."

Chapter 23

Atlantis, the palace

After a long, hot shower and a change of clothes, Alexios headed down the immense tapestry-lined corridor to report in to Conlan. The intricate weaving and brilliant hues of Atlantean history—scenes woven over the course of thousands of years—barely registered as he headed for the war room.

The war room. Its walls had listened in, silent and without judgment, on the plans of Atlanteans for more than eleven thousand years.

Alexios wondered if walls could laugh.

Plans, plots, never-ending meetings to discuss never-ending wars. They were all merely chess pieces in a game played by gods, and even the strongest of the Warriors of Poseidon rarely rose higher than pawn.

That pawns were the most frequently sacrificed had crossed his mind a time or two.

Finally arriving, he stopped short, surprised to see guards posted at the door. Conlan—or, more likely, Ven—must be wary of treachery that could reach into the palace itself. It was unthinkable, and yet the presence of the guards demonstrated that someone had been thinking exactly that.

"Lord Alexios," the elder, a battle-hardened veteran, said. "Prince Conlan and Lord Vengeance await you inside."

The other pulled the heavy door open, and Alexios entered the room, glancing up at the walls as he did so. Silent witnesses, he mocked himself. Plaster and marble and wooden beams, shaped by tools into something of function.

Much like himself.

Shaking his head to disrupt his grim thoughts, Alexios looked around. Conlan and Ven leaned over the long, scarred, wooden table in the center of the room, poring over maps. Ven moved to one side, sliding his finger down a map and muttering something, then glanced up and acknowledged Alexios with a nod.

As Alexios crossed the room, he got his second surprise. The human woman Tiernan Butler, clad in jeans and a white shirt, her dark hair pulled back from her face, stood between the two brothers. Judging by the expressions on their faces, whatever they were discussing wasn't good.

Conlan and Ven wore simple clothing: dark shirts and pants similar to his own. Nothing in their attire shouted out the fact that they were royalty. The high prince, soon to be king, of Atlantis and his younger brother, next in line to the throne, never traded upon their heritage to put themselves above others. Even so, royalty and the aura of unflinching command radiated from them, a silent herald of their birthright.

The birthright—at least by half—of one other. One gone missing, yet again.

"News of Justice?"

Conlan shook his head. "None. And no contact with Alaric, either. Do you have news of him?"

Alexios whistled, low and long. "I'd thought he'd make it back here before me. He went after Quinn; she was wounded in the battle."

Ven's hands fisted, crumpling the map he held. The prince respected Quinn for the warrior she was but, more than that, she'd become his friend. Indeed, she was family, now that her sister Riley would wed Conlan.

Human marrying Atlantean. He thought of Bastien—
Atlantean marrying shape-shifter. Ever more twisting skeins
of yarn for some future tapestry that one day would decorate
the palace corridors, perhaps foretelling the final end to those
never-ending wars he'd mused on earlier.

"It was a minor wound," he assured them. "But you know
Alaric. He and Quinn have a . . . bond. He followed her, in
order to make sure of her well-being." He quickly filled them
in on what had occurred in St. Louis. "Quinn, Jack, and Denal went after the vampire leaders."

Alexios didn't elaborate as to what the trio would do to the
vamps when they caught up with them. He didn't need to.

Conlan shot a glance at his brother then nodded. "If Quinn's
wound is minor, Alaric should return soon. There is nothing
we can do to track Justice until that time, so we should focus
on the matter at hand. Tiernan has given us much news of the
plans for the Apostates."

Alexios's gaze settled on the human, then returned to his
prince. "Is that wise? Especially considering where we found
her, are we going to trust that what she tells us is truth and not
some elaborate sort of trap, with her as bait?"

Instead of becoming defensive, Tiernan smiled at him.
"You'd make a good reporter, Atlantean. Never believe anything you hear. Fact-check, fact-check, fact-check."

She paused, and her cheeks flushed a dull red. "The truth
is that I got in over my head. I thought I knew the setup; I
went in as part of the catering staff. I knew they wouldn't
start the festivities until the caterers left, but I thought I might
hear something useful. Instead, I got blindsided."

"Forced to take your clothes off and be part of the orgy?"
Alexios said, not believing a damn word of it.

"No, I . . . The caterers were in on it. I was ordered to take
a load of empty platters down to the catering van and not
come back. But I took a detour to the bathroom and then managed to hide behind that couch when nobody was looking."
She touched her bruised face. "Got this shiner when somebody tossed a bottle back there and it hit me. It was tough to
keep from crying out. But one of those nasty old men saw me,

and I had to play along and pretend I was shy and it was my first party. It would have been dangerous for me to run; he was suspicious. So I had to undress while the pervert watched. Then he took my clothes and said he'd be right back. I was trying to figure out how to get out of Dodge when you guys busted in."

"Rather convenient timing, isn't it? If anything you're saying is true," Alexios said. "Maybe we'd better triple-check your version of the facts."

"Which is exactly what we're going to do, with every piece of information she gives us," Ven said flatly. "But she was right about the Void, and what she's telling us now confirms information we have from independent intelligence. So far, so good, in other words."

Tiernan pointed at one of the maps, and Alexios moved closer in order to see. "They're starting in the most populated areas and working their way out. Big cities—major metropolitan areas. New York, of course. Boston. Seattle. Jacksonville, Florida, of all places. Urban sprawl hits vampires, too, I guess," she said. "We've been working on this story for nearly three years. The Apostates, and the cult of Algolagnia."

"Who is *we*?" Conlan asked.

"Yeah, I find it hard to believe that your bosses at the *Boston Herald* are encouraging you to go after this story," Ven said, shaking his head. "Last we heard, that paper was one of nearly three dozen in the United States run by a consortium of shape-shifters."

Tiernan looked up at him, a smile quirking at the edges of her lips. "You seem to hear a lot. Is it true that Donald Trump is a shape-shifter, or is that just an unsubstantiated rumor?"

Ven snorted. "With that hair?"

Alexios couldn't find it in himself to be amused. Not after escorting half of the rebel team to the emergency room. "Perhaps we could leave the attempts at humor by the wayside, until a more appropriate time." He heard the snap in his voice, but made no apology. To apologize would be to dishonor the wounded . . . and Grace.

Conlan's gaze rested upon him for a moment, considering,

and then the prince nodded. "Alexios is right. But again I must ask, who is this *we* to whom you refer? We have heard of no human investigation into the Apostates."

"If you'd heard of us, it would mean we weren't doing our jobs," Tiernan retorted. "We're investigative reporters, and we work underground. We gather sources, facts, and solid evidence. Then and only then do we take the story live. This is going to be the biggest story of my career when it breaks."

Alexios decided to try a bluff. "We've heard of you, too, reporter. We've heard that you're a glory seeker who thinks Pulitzer is her middle name. We've heard you're unreliable and sloppy. Why would we possibly want to work with you?"

For a split second, so quickly that Alexios almost missed it, Tiernan's dark eyes went hazy and unfocused. "That is a lie," she said, her voice almost eerily calm. "You have never heard of me, and you haven't heard of my investigation, either. You don't know who to trust, and you're worried about your friend.

"There's more," she said, turning toward Conlan. "You're afraid that whatever he did—Justice—with or *to* that archaeologist is going to have repercussions for Atlantis. Terrible repercussions."

Suddenly she blinked and shuddered a little, like a water bird shaking droplets from its feathers, and pasted a grin on her suddenly pale face. "Don't bluff a poker player."

A heavy silence freighted the air. Something odd had just happened, but Alexios wasn't sure what. All of his senses were telling him that Tiernan was merely human.

Then again, so were Quinn and Riley. Human and *aknasha'an*. Emotional empaths after thousands of years. Erin—a gem singer. No one was surprised by the merely *odd* anymore.

"All right, let's operate on the assumption that you're telling the truth," Conlan said. He pointed at the map. "Show us."

In rapid succession, Tiernan pointed to a dozen heavily populated areas. "All of these. The cult of Algolagnia is recruiting heavily. Unfortunately, their version of recruiting is a lot more like what we would call the draft."

Ven swore viciously under his breath in ancient Atlantean, no doubt in deference to Tiernan. Regardless of the language, however, the meaning was clear. "So what you're saying—"

"Is that it's not voluntary," Tiernan finished his sentence. "Not very many people, no matter what you think of us humans, sign up to have their brains turned into mashed potatoes."

"Vivid imagery, but how appropriate is the analogy?" Conlan asked. "Are you saying Anubisa and her acolytes are enthralling the humans? As distasteful as that is, it's a temporary measure. We have seen this for centuries. Indeed, millennia."

"There is nothing temporary about this," Tiernan said adamantly. "We have evidence of actual permanent distortion of brain patterns. We've got brain surgeons, neurologists, and neuropsychiatrists working with us. MRIs of the brains of affected individuals are far, far different than scans of people merely suffering from temporary enthrallment."

She paused, staring at each one of them in turn, as if to emphasize her point. "Anubisa is creating an army of human minions with shattered minds, who will never, ever be able to return to themselves. She's playing Sudoku with our brains, and somebody's got to stop it."

Unless she was an actress far better than any Alexios had ever seen on the stage, Tiernan was telling the truth. The passion and pain in her voice had nearly caused it to break, but there was steel in the woman. Steel honed in outrage rather than fire, perhaps, but steel nonetheless.

"Shattered minds can be healed," Conlan said.

Ven stared at him. "The Star of Artemis? But that's—"

Conlan made a subtle hand gesture, cutting his brother off mid-thought.

Ven narrowed his eyes, but complied. Then he slammed his fist on the table, startling them all. "It's always back to her," he snarled. "How is the universe so out of balance that Poseidon sits idly by and lets the vampire goddess roll the dice with the futures of three races?"

"You speak blasphemy, I feel compelled to point out, even though I can't disagree," Conlan said. "Perhaps, for now, we should focus on what direction we can take in this battle, rather than flailing at the actions of gods."

Tiernan gasped a little. "Are you saying that Anubisa is actually a goddess? And by Poseidon, do you mean the mythical sea god?" She narrowed her eyes. "I came to you about a *real* problem, with *real* information about your friend, expecting *real* help. Is this your idea of a joke? Let's feed fairy tales to the human?"

Alexios swept his arm out in a gesture encompassing the room in which they stood. "You're in Atlantis, Tiernan Butler. The mythical lost continent of Atlantis, as your kind likes to call it. Do you really want to discount the existence of the sea god when you stand in his realm, far beneath the surface of the oceans?"

Tiernan opened her mouth as if to respond but then snapped it shut. After a moment she grinned, and a flash of the carefree woman she might have been in easier times shone out at them. "You do have a point."

Then her smile faded. "Your other friend . . . the one who went kind of crazy in Boston. Is he okay?"

Alexios looked to Conlan, who nodded. "Brennan is fine and has no memory of any uncharacteristic behavior. We find that we must keep him some distance from you, however, since there is clearly something about you to which he is reacting . . . adversely."

"Gosh, you boys sure talk pretty," she drawled, eyes sharp. "Reacting adversely. Interesting way to put it."

"We don't have the *time* to explore it now, even if we had the inclination," Ven snapped. "Brennan stays away from you. You stay in Atlantis while we check you out."

Before she could utter the protest that was so clearly forming on her lips, Ven shot a wicked smile her way. "Fact-check, fact-check, fact-check, right? From your lips to my ears."

"Fine," she said flatly. "I guess I'll agree, since I don't really have any other options. I don't even know how we got here, and your castle staff aren't exactly forthcoming to the human prisoner."

"You are our guest, Lady Tiernan," Conlan said, and once again the royal bearing was in evidence. "Not our prisoner.

But we would be remiss if we did not verify your story, as you yourself do understand. Give us a few days, and we'll return you to Boston to continue your work."

"If you're telling the truth," Alexios felt compelled to add.

"Truth. Always truth, shining in the shifting sands of nuance, intent, and deception," Tiernan murmured, staring off into the distance. "I tell the truth in ways you wouldn't even believe, Atlantean."

A shiver snaked across Alexios's spine. Definitely something off about Tiernan Butler. Perhaps something they should investigate.

Conlan inclined his head. "We hope that is the case, for all of our sakes. If vampires have progressed to actual human brain-pattern destruction, then we must step up our response."

The prince bent his head to study the map again. "Perhaps you will have your Pulitzer yet."

Tiernan began to respond, but Alexios had recognized the dismissal in Conlan's words. "If you'll come with me, Tiernan, I'm sure we can find you a comfortable—"

"Erin wants to see her," Ven interrupted. "She's at the Temple and said she'd give Tiernan the tour."

"Temple?" Tiernan's eyes brightened with what Alexios was beginning to recognize as journalistic zeal. "What Temple?"

"The Temple of the Nereids," Alexios said, gesturing to the door. "More of those mythological beings you were talking about earlier."

As she fired questions at him, Alexios managed to herd her toward the door. He held it open for her to exit before him and then turned back toward Conlan and Ven. "I stand ready, for whatever you decide."

They nodded in unison, looking in that moment more like identical twins than mere brothers. "We know," Conlan said. "As soon as Alaric returns, we'll plot out our next steps."

"Justice first," Ven said, and the determination in his voice had the resonance of a vow. "Then Anubisa and the Apostates."

Alexios nodded, in total agreement with that plan. He

pulled the door shut behind himself and went to rescue the guards from Tiernan's interrogation, repeating the vow in his mind.

Justice first, and justice second.

Even the reporter would like that. It had the ring of a front-page headline.

Chapter 24

Atlantis, the cavern

Justice forced himself to do willingly what he'd fought against for hundreds of years. He opened the shields in his mind and released the Nereid half of his soul. At first his response was only silence, as if the Other mocked him.

As if he'd waited too long.

However, ever so gradually, power curled like liquid fire through the resistant spaces of his mind. Heat filled his body, sparkling and shimmering through his veins and arteries like champagne-filtered blood.

Finally. Finally you call to me, and invite me to demonstrate my power. The Nereid's voice resonated through his mind with the thundering of percussion drumming out a triumphant march.

"I call on you to *share* your power," Justice said aloud. "If we can't escape this cavern, it does you no more good than it does me."

Keely's forehead furrowed as she gazed up at him quizzically, and he realized what his half of the conversation must sound like.

"I'm not crazy; I'm only talking to myself," he offered. "The only way we'll get out of here is if the Nereid half of me can teach me powers I've never known. It wasn't an Atlantean gift that transported us down here. I'm not sure what I did or how I did it. The Nereid knows, and so I will learn."

"This is probably a subject for another time, but it doesn't seem all that healthy that you're talking about the other half of *yourself* in the third person. Of course, earlier you were referring to yourself as 'we,' so I guess it's all relative," she said, smiling weakly. "I'm good with whatever gets us out of here."

Justice smiled at her in a way that he hoped was reassuring, and then he closed his eyes and sank into the duality of his consciousness. Swirls and spirals of shimmering color danced in the darkness inside his mind, as if his Nereid half were a prism reflecting the brightest gemstones in the cavern.

Though he didn't understand the scope of the power released, he could certainly feel the magnitude of it. He'd always been possessed of superior usage of the Atlantean magics, but this was different. Darker. Not more powerful, but simply *other*. Clay shaped by a sculptor with mysterious intent.

His mind shuffled through the new concepts. New constructs. A different view of ordering the universe.

Matter transference. The knowledge and technique gleamed before him. It was so simple; of course he *could* do it. Of course he *had* done it.

Of course he could do it again.

It was a simple process. He offered up his being into the fabric of the universe. It was a loan—no more. A momentary return to the energy of creation. He pictured himself and Keely where he wanted them to be, and they would travel through the waves, as particles of that flow.

He could see it. He could hear it, touch it, taste it. Everywhere he looked, energy beams danced and played, sweeping through the fabric of life itself. It would be so easy to sink into the energy. To catch a ride.

He turned toward Keely and, truly *seeing* her, laughed, suddenly joyous. Brilliant oranges, yellows, and reds floated, sparkling, around her. She existed inside a kaleidoscope of all the colors of the sunset, crowned by the flame red of her hair. She was strength and wonder and innocence, and yet there were darker hues, as well. Flashes of sienna fading into deepest mahogany, indicative of some negativity. Pain in her past.

He had no reason to know it, but he did. He was no longer only Justice. Or even only Justice and Nereid. He was part of the web of all existence in the galaxy, and traveling within it would be as effortless as swimming in a quiet pool.

Not so easy as that, the Nereid cautioned. *You cannot fall into that trap. Limitless possibilities exist to seduce the unwary. If you give yourself to the universe without reservation, there is the chance you'll never return.*

Justice recoiled at the idea of limits, but then leashed his denial. Forced himself to listen to the Nereid.

Keely. He needed to protect Keely. Remove them both from this cavern in which they were trapped. Focus on the practical; the magical could wait. He turned to her. "I know how to do it. He told me, and it's so simple—well. It's simple once you have the knowing of it."

"You can really get us out of here?" Fragile hope shone on her face and for a moment he paused, stunned by her beauty.

"Yes. I would ask where you wish to go, but I believe one destination is mandatory. We have explanations to make. *I* have explanations to make. We'll go to the palace. It must be the beginning, although we don't yet know the ending."

Keely took a deep breath and nodded. "Part of me wants nothing more than to go home, have a hot bath, and drink a bottle or two of wine. But we need to tell the prince about the Star of Artemis and the Trident. All of Atlantis could be in serious danger if they try to ascend without the full set of gemstones."

He held out his hand and she twined her fingers in his, and a fountain of sparkling light merged into a geyser around them. Entranced by the hypnotic allure, he almost missed her next words.

"Just tell me this is safe," she said, attempting a smile. "I know we did it once before, but I can't help but feel a little bit like a guinea pig. I really don't want half of my atoms going to Borneo while the other half end up in the palace here in Atlantis. I watched *Star Trek* on DVD, you know. That transporter was not exactly reliable."

From somewhere in his past, he found an echo of humor that hadn't yet been beaten out of him by years of battle—or months in the Void. "I hear Borneo is nice this time of year."

Somehow, against all odds, Keely started laughing. Justice called to the magic of his Nereid ancestors and, holding her in his arms, he stepped off the edge of reality and into the tapestry of the universe. They dissolved into pure energy, and both halves of himself—Nereid and Atlantean—marveled at the brilliance of captured sunlight that he held so carefully in his arms.

∿∿∿

Keely melted into nothingness, again—or maybe not. In some nearly indefinable way, this was different. She felt herself more an active participant in the process, although it certainly wasn't her bringing the magic. As a scientist, she tried to observe and catalog. Sensations, reactions, experience as experiment.

But the matter transference defied description. At least, it defied any rational description. Any sane explanation. Magic consumed her, swallowed her up. She could only hope it would spit her back out, whole, when she got to the other side.

Colors and sounds clashed around her, as though she'd taken a mind-altering drug and fallen into the middle of a symphony. It was beautiful and terrible; sensation piled upon sensation until she thought she would go mad.

And then it was over.

They fell, whether down or up was unimportant, but they fell out of the currents—out of the maelstrom—and back into reality. As they landed, ever so gently on their feet, in a room Keely hadn't seen in any of her visions, she wondered why reality suddenly seemed so dull.

Startled shouts rang around her, and before she could get her bearings, the business ends of two daggers and a sword were pointing in her direction. Pointing at Justice, actually.

Justice's arms tightened around her and then he moved to shield her so quickly that he was a blur.

"How dare you raise weapons against us?" His voice was little more than a growl, but she understood the words and intent clearly enough. She could see the trembling in his muscles that told her he was nearly incoherent with rage.

Keely knew she had to do something. The Atlanteans were threatening the fragile peace Justice had brokered with his Nereid half, and she wasn't going to stand for it.

She stepped out from behind him and held up her hands in surrender, looking toward Conlan, who stood slightly in front of Ven. "Hey, I come in peace. Keely McDermott, archaeologist. *You* invited *me*, remember?

"Thanks," she said, putting a hand on Justice's arm. He was making a low, bestial growling noise in his throat as he scanned the room, eyes narrowed and teeth bared. He looked exactly like the predator she'd thought him to be; but now she knew he was that and so much more.

After years of archaeology, Keely was no stranger to dealing with foreign governments. This one might be more foreign than any of the other ones she'd encountered, she thought with grim amusement, but the principle still held true.

The room was a simple one, bare of any trappings of royalty. This was a working space, it was clear. She glanced around, openly curious. "This is some kind of strategy room, isn't it?"

The prince's brother nodded, but still no one spoke. So much for small talk.

"Justice," she hissed, "I'm not making much headway here. You need to help me out."

Conlan and his brother slowly lowered their weapons, identical expressions of shock on their faces. They exchanged a glance she couldn't decipher, and then Ven tossed his sword on a table.

"You're here, and you're safe," Ven said fervently. "Thank the gods you're both safe."

Conlan bowed his head, and Keely saw his lips moving but couldn't hear the words. When he looked up, he smiled at Justice. "I, too, thank the gods that you have returned safely from the Void, my brother. And my apologies, Dr. McDermott. Are you well?" He sheathed his daggers and took a step toward her, and Justice's growl ratcheted up a notch to an actual snarl.

"I'm not hurt," she said. "Although I wouldn't turn down a

hot meal and a bath. But we need to talk first. Justice is having a hard time, as you can see. I don't really understand it entirely but he had to make a deal with the Nereid half of himself in order to figure out this matter transference thing that allowed him to transport us here."

"From where? Where did you go?" Conlan ran a hand through his hair in a gesture of pure frustration. "We cannot begin to tell you how sorry we are for this. Certainly we did not mean for your visit to Atlantis to be marked by kidnapping. Are you sure you are unharmed?"

Keely noticed that Ven never took his eyes off Justice. Ven's pale face and tightly clenched jaw told her that he carried his own load of guilt over his brother's sacrifice to Anubisa.

Beside her, the growling noise abruptly shut off. "Are you so unconcerned for *my* welfare, Brother?" Justice asked, mockery in his roughened voice. "After four long months in the Void, do you not query after me?"

Keely saw the anguish that shadowed Conlan's face. He took a step forward, toward his brother, but Justice backed away, pulling her with him. "Forget it," he sneered. "We are unimpressed by your efforts on our behalf. We spent far too long as captive of the vampire goddess, but you know something about that, don't you, Conlan? She seems to have a preference for Atlantean princes, doesn't she? Even when one of them is the unwanted bastard who was never acknowledged by his own family."

"We never knew," Ven said through gritted teeth. "We never knew. Damnit, Justice, don't you know us better than that after hundreds of years fighting side by side? I've called you brother even not knowing about the blood tie. Could you possibly think that, knowing it, I'd do any differently? Any less?"

Keely noticed that Conlan was less direct. He studied Justice but said nothing, and he'd schooled his face to blankness.

"Must be something they teach you in prince school," Keely said, trying to lighten the unbelievable tension in the room. "That poker face."

Conlan laughed, surprising her. "You are the second woman to bring up poker in our war room in the space of a very short time. Perhaps this table would be more suited to games of cards, rather than games of countries and kings."

Justice put an arm around her and pulled her close. Only the knowledge that he was so near to losing control kept her there, in spite of her frustration at his caveman tactics.

She'd noticed the recurrence of the word "we" in what he'd said. The Nereid was growing stronger, then, and she wasn't sure she wanted to see what would happen if *he* took over.

"Aargh! Now I'm doing it," she said, glaring up at Justice. "I'm even *thinking* of you as two separate people. You need to get hold of yourself, or your *selves*, as best you can. We need to tell them about the Star."

Conlan jumped on it. "The Star? The Star of Artemis?"

Beside her, Justice drew in a deep, shuddering breath and seemed to gather his self-control along with the oxygen. "The Star, yes. The one that we've long been taught has the power to heal fractured minds. Its value was far greater than even we knew, however. We need to find the Star—we need to find all the lost gems of the Trident. Without them, Atlantis cannot rise."

Chapter 25

Justice's words fell, echoing like falling stone in a newly unsealed tomb. He watched grimly as Ven and Conlan physically recoiled from their meaning.

Conlan recovered first. "What do you mean, Atlantis can't rise without all of the gems returned to the Trident? It cannot be true. When the ancients sent the gemstones to the seven corners of the globe, they had not discovered the portal at that time. If only the use of the gems together with the Trident would allow Atlantis to ascend to the surface, they had in effect just doomed the Seven Isles."

"There's no logic in it," Ven said. "Conlan is right. Without those gems, how could the ancients ever have hoped to return to the surface? It doesn't make sense, Dr. McDermott."

"I don't know," Keely said. "I don't know about logic, or your ancients, as you call them, or any of that. Politics has never been my forte. Maybe they saw the future and knew you'd find a way to travel to the surface. But I saw it in the vision, and my visions have never, ever been wrong. That sapphire must be in place in the Trident, along with all of the other gems, or you will destroy Atlantis when you try to ascend."

The skepticism was plain in their faces. They didn't know Keely. They hadn't seen her nearly crushed in the throes of one of her visions. They were going to need proof.

Even as everything in him balked at the idea, Justice realized that, in their place, he'd want the same.

But the Nereid inside him scoffed. *Everything you do will always be less, to them. Why should they take your word for any of it?*

Keely sighed, and her shoulders slumped. "You're not going to take this on faith, are you? You don't know me from Adam—or maybe from Poseidon would be the better expression—and you're going to want evidence."

The resignation in her defeated posture touched Justice deep inside, in a place he'd believed long buried. "No. No, they do not want or need evidence. Your word is good."

He folded his arms and confronted the men he still hadn't become accustomed to calling brothers. "You haven't seen her during a vision. You haven't heard the truth and the history that spills forth from her lips."

He put his hand behind his back and briefly touched the hilt of his sword. "She's an object reader, and she read my sword. She named it. It's called Poseidon's Fury, and our father gave it to me."

Ven and Conlan exchanged glances and suddenly he reached an unpleasant conclusion. They were unsurprised by the news.

"You knew? All these years, you knew?"

Conlan shook his head. "No, not that. We never knew that you were our brother. But the sword, yes, of course I'd seen my father with that sword. At first he told us he lost it, but then one day I saw a stringy little blue-haired boy carrying a sword that was far too big for him, and I recognized it."

"I wanted to take it away from you," Ven said, a faint grin playing at the edges of his mouth. "We were about the same size. I told Conlan I was going to kick your ass and take that sword back."

"But I was the wiser, as usual," Conlan interjected dryly. "I dragged Ven back home so that we could ask our father about it."

"What did he say?" Justice leaned forward, though he despised himself for his eagerness to hear even a single kind word from his long-dead father.

They looked uncomfortable. "Is it really the time to talk about the past, when Atlantis's future rests on the truth of Dr. McDermott's vision?"

Keely laughed, but it was a bitter sound. "Trust me, Your Highness. My visions are all about the past. And from what I've seen of what your father put Justice and his mother through, it's no wonder you don't want to talk about it."

"His mother? What do you know of his mother?" Ven asked.

"It was in my vision," Keely said. "I saw her, lying in pain—in labor with Justice—on the floor of what must be your throne room. Carved dolphins on the back of the throne?"

"Justice could've told you that. Hells, Liam could've told you that," Ven challenged.

Justice felt his tenuous grip on his temper fading. "You, who plan to wed a gem singer who stepped straight out of the waters of time, question the word of an object reader?" He looked from one to the other, realization dawning. "That's why you wanted her to come here as an archaeologist, isn't it? I wondered at the choice when you announced the list of invited scientists. What is there to excavate on the Seven Isles?"

Keely pulled free of his hold. "Is it true? Only for that?" Raw anger edged her voice. "Only for something I hate in myself? How did you even know?"

"As to how we knew, one of your colleagues on the Lupercale dig is a friend to Atlantis. As to the second, do you always hate your Gift, Keely McDermott?" Conlan's voice was gentle. "I would have thought it served you well in your chosen profession. Why would you choose to explore the past if you are so determined to deny yourself?"

Keely clenched her fists against her legs and slowly inhaled and exhaled a very deep breath. "Okay, I can't deal with this right now. I'm running on adrenaline and pancakes. Here's what you need to know."

She turned to Justice and looked up at him, a question in her eyes. He knew what she was asking and, although he despised the idea that his brothers would hear about the humiliation that had destroyed his childhood, he nodded assent.

"I think I need to sit down for this," Keely said.

Conlan hastened to indicate that she should sit, apologizing for his lack of manners. Justice remained at her side, sitting next to her on the battered couch that had seen so many planning sessions.

Almost without meaning to, he found himself taking her hand in his own. He needed the contact. Needed the warmth of her touch in order to endure the revelations she was about to give.

Conlan poured tall glasses of water from the tray sitting on a sideboard and carried them over. Keely took a long drink of the sparkling cold liquid, and then she began to talk. Quietly, concisely, and in chronological order, she told them of the visions she'd had. She began with the one Liam had forced upon her, of the Star of Artemis.

Ven interrupted at one point. "Nereus? But—"

Conlan waved him to silence. "Later," he told his brother. "Please continue, Dr. McDermott."

The telling seemed to last for an eternity, especially when waves of shame washed through Justice with the heat of Hellsfire. Keely finally finished her recounting and drained the water from her glass, then looked up at Conlan and Ven.

"So. Any questions?" Defiance underscored the weariness in her voice.

"I have so many questions that I don't even know where to begin to ask them," Conlan said. "But I have a feeling that you need rest. Food and rest. So we'll adjourn this meeting and postpone our questions until the morning. Perhaps by then our high priest will have returned."

"Alaric is gone?" Justice asked, surprised by the news.

"He couldn't reach you, so he went to St. Louis to help with a certain matter that required his assistance," Conlan said, leaving the details to Justice's imagination.

Justice knew there were deeper reasons that Conlan wished for Alaric's return. The high priest had the role of testing anyone suspected of being compromised by the vampires. Even Conlan himself had undergone it.

Justice was sure that he was next. What he wasn't sure of was what Alaric would make of his dual nature.

Do not worry about this priest, the Nereid whispered in his mind. *We will present a united front for the testing.*

A hint of relief winged its way through Justice at the thought, and wary caution followed closely behind. Now, so soon, he was planning to deceive his fellow Atlanteans for the foreign presence that squatted inside of him?

Better to cut it out of himself like a cancer.

You cut me out and you die, the Nereid reminded him, arrogant command in his tone. *I would have expected gratitude, not censure. We are out of the cavern, are we not?*

Yes. There was that.

"Yeah, we had a little vamp and shifter problem," Ven added, cutting into Justice's internal battle. "It didn't go all that well for the good guys, either. Quinn was wounded, and Alaric went after her to be sure she was okay."

Justice wanted to ask for further information, but Keely leaned against him, drooping with exhaustion.

He carefully rose, pulling her with him. "Rest. As you say, we need rest. Food and a bath, and then a good night's sleep should go a long way toward restoring us."

Keely only nodded, her eyelids drifting shut as she stood there. He wanted to carry her, but knew she'd hate it, especially in front of Ven and Conlan. So he contented himself with walking beside her down the corridor toward the guest wing.

Giving in to the burgeoning paranoia that grew with every step he took farther into the palace, especially since Ven had accompanied them to "help out," Justice examined every inch of the room they'd offered Keely before he let her step so much as a foot into it.

Finally, he turned toward the doorway where she leaned, all but falling over from tiredness, and he nodded. Heaving a sigh of relief, she crossed to the bed and flung herself down on it, face-first into the pillows, her silken hair in wild disarray around her.

"I'll call for some food for you," he promised and strode over to talk to Ven, who still hovered in the corridor.

"You can't stay here with her," Ven said, his face and voice equally grim. "You know that, don't you? We need to know— gods, man. What you did for me—" Ven stopped, the words strangling in his throat.

The emotion in Ven's—in his *brother's*—voice twisted something inside Justice's gut into a painful knot. "I don't need or want your gratitude," he warned, his own voice rasping with feelings better left unexpressed. "You would have done the same for me. Hells, you *have* done the same for me."

Ven scrubbed at his eyes with the back of his hand, and they both pretended that two of Poseidon's fiercest warriors had not come very close to shedding tears.

"Food. Keely needs food," Justice said, desperate for something to change the subject.

Ven glanced over Justice's shoulder and pointed into the room. "Actually, I'm guessing she doesn't."

Justice turned to look and saw that Keely was sound asleep on top of the coverlet, still fully dressed down to her boots. He touched a pressure panel on the wall and the room darkened, and then he quietly walked over to the bed and stared down at her. Even disheveled and exhausted, she was more beautiful than he ever could have dreamed a woman could be.

Ven's voice came from directly behind him, startling him. "She's a pretty courageous woman," he said quietly.

Justice's initial instincts had him clenching his fists to protect her, but that faded as the meaning behind Ven's words sank in. "She's braver and far more beautiful than I could ever deserve," he admitted. "But she's mine."

Ven sighed, and then laughed softly. "I had a feeling that might be the way of it, as soon as I saw you two together. Remember, I just went through this with Erin. It feels a lot like being knocked over the head with a very heavy sword, doesn't it?"

Shaking his head, Justice leaned over and gently removed Keely's shoes, then pulled the side of the coverlet over her. Because he couldn't resist—because he *wouldn't* resist—he bent and pressed his lips to her forehead. She made a sound like a tiny hiccuping snore and then settled more deeply into the pillows.

As they reentered the corridor, closing the door behind them, Ven clapped a hand on Justice's shoulder in a gesture of camaraderie that felt familiar. Like something Justice himself might have done only four short months ago.

Four *long* months ago.

Now it took everything he had not to flinch from the contact. He warded the room with healthy, familiar Atlantean magic, forcing the voice of the Nereid to silence in his head. None would enter Keely's room while she slept; the powerful wards would ensure that. The dawn would bring what it would, especially if Alaric were back. But for tonight, at least, Justice could rest.

Rest, and pray to all the gods that he would not dream.

∽〰⤳

Keely woke up facedown in a pile of cloud-like silken pillows, still fully clothed except for her boots. Bolting up out of bed, she stared wildly around the room that she'd been too tired to really get a good look at the night before.

She was entirely alone and didn't want to look too closely at the little twist of relief—or was it disappointment?—in her stomach. Certainly it couldn't be *regret* that Justice was nowhere to be seen.

Or at least so she tried to convince herself.

Wandering around the room, she felt a feminine delight in the pale green silks and complementary cream furnishings. It was a study in understated elegance that enriched its occupant instead of making her feel inferior. Some sort of interior design psychology, no doubt. Or maybe it was an Atlantean gift. Beauty everywhere she looked.

And the view out the window was a Cinderella fantasy dream. The palace gardens stretched for acres and acres of dazzling color and lush greenery crisscrossed by paths of multicolored stone. She wanted, more than anything, to climb out the window and escape to the peaceful serenity of the gardens. Away from warriors and craziness and tension.

Instead, she resigned herself to putting on her Dr. McDermott face and finding out what they wanted and—just maybe—how she could help them.

Help *him*. Justice was never far from her thoughts, as much as she might wish otherwise. Or did she? Her own mind was becoming as divided as his was.

A knock on the door saved her from any further internal examination, and she opened it to find a silver-haired woman wearing a simple belted cotton dress and comfortable shoes. She had one hand on a wheeled cart. A housekeeper, perhaps.

"I've fresh clothes and a tray of coffee and juice for you, my lady," the woman said, smiling.

"That's wonderful. Thank you so much. And it's Keely, please. Just Keely."

Keely held the door open, trying not to bliss out at the lovely aromas, as the woman rolled the silver cart into the room. There was definitely some delicious coffee in Atlantis, so one worry at least was resolved.

"I'm sure you'd like to freshen up, Keely," the housekeeper said, warmth in her voice and smile. "I'll return in half an hour to escort you to the princes." She pointed to an inset panel on the wall, and the second button on it. "Just push this if you need anything further before then."

With more smiles and nods, the housekeeper left the room, closing the door behind her.

Keely spent several minutes enjoying a couple of cups of coffee with plenty of sugar and cream swirled into the rich depths while she stared out the window, taking in all of the wonders of the view. Again and again, her gaze was drawn to the dome that covered the entire city. It was awe-inspiring. Whether magic or technology had fashioned it, it was simply amazing. The force of pressure of the water that must bear down on it, day after day . . .

Well. There were certain things a girl didn't need to freak out about before she had a shower.

Sometime later, showered, caffeinated, and feeling almost human again, she checked out the clothes. Remarkably, they were all her size or close to it. She chose a simple green shirt and tan pair of pants and pulled her own boots back on over a clean pair of socks, putting aside all the lovely dresses and skirts and other frilly clothes the housekeeper had brought. It made her feel more in control to dress in something akin to her standard work uniform. She'd learned early on that nobody took seriously a scientist who wore lace or frills.

Of course her gloves were safely in place. Even touching something as neutral as the walls in a place this ancient would likely send her into a trance.

The housekeeper returned, as promised, and led her through corridors whose walls were covered with the most glorious tapestries she'd ever seen. She'd love the opportunity to spend hours, or even days, studying them.

Later, perhaps. If they'd let her.

When they arrived at a door guarded by two somber-faced warriors, the housekeeper knocked and then ushered her into the same room she and Justice had wound up in the night before.

Conlan and Ven were already there.

"Please be welcome. I trust your rest was undisturbed?" Conlan said, bowing slightly.

"Honestly, a train could have roared through the room and I probably wouldn't have noticed," she admitted, grinning. "I was pretty tired. I'd had a little excitement, you know."

Ven grinned back at her. "Way to bounce back, Doc. You're my kind of scientist, I can tell." He gestured to the laden side table. "Please help yourself to breakfast. We've already eaten."

"Riley sends her regrets, but she is having a difficult time with the pregnancy, and Erin is with her, as well," Conlan said.

"I'm sorry to hear that," Keely said. "Riley is your wife?"

"She will soon be my lady wife and queen, yes. Evidently we are having a priest or an Elvis," he said dryly, but the warmth in his voice and the heat in his eyes told her that Riley was very loved, indeed.

A tiny twinge of regret pinged deep inside Keely's chest. No man had ever looked that way when he'd talked about her.

She shook it off. She wasn't usually so sentimental. Must be something about being in Cinderella's castle that made her think about Prince Charming.

Or Prince Tall, Blue-Haired, and Deadly.

While she ate, they pored over maps on the long table, speaking quietly and casting the occasional glance at her. Keely dove into the food like the starving woman she was. When the roar in her stomach faded down to a warm rumble of contentment, she took another sip of coffee and then carefully placed her fragile, almost translucent china cup on the table, resisting the urge to turn it over and examine it like one of her ancient artifacts.

Anyway, *artifact* was probably the wrong word to use. An artifact was something long buried and forgotten, hidden in the mists of time. This delicate china, fired by a process she'd never before seen, was part of their breakfast dishes. It boggled the mind.

The archaeologist in her wanted to cheer or stand up and do cartwheels. Certainly, she was itching to go get her tools from her pack that she'd reluctantly left in the bedroom, go outside, and dig somewhere, just for the heck of it.

The excitement suddenly drained out of her like helium from a punctured balloon. They hadn't invited her there for digging. They knew what she was. They probably had certain artifacts already lined up for her.

They'd called her an object reader, as though the term had precedence in their history. It was both shocking and wonderfully validating to be accepted for something that was so integrally a part of her. However, just as she used tools in her work, she recognized when someone else wanted to use her. She had no intention of being a chisel in their hands, at least not until she got some answers. Foremost among them: where was Justice?

She poured herself another cup of the delicious coffee and then sat back in her chair, casting a measured glance at Ven and Conlan. It took less than a minute for them to feel the weight of her stare, and they both looked up at her.

"Is there something else we might get for you?" Ven's smile was utterly charming and totally guileless. It might even have fooled somebody who'd been born yesterday.

Keely wasn't that gullible. "Yes, actually. I'd like to see Justice. I'd like to see him right now."

"We're sure he'll be along any moment—"

She cut Conlan off, choosing not to worry if there were any penalties for interrupting royalty in Atlantis. "Right. You said that. Nearly half an hour ago. How do I know you don't have him locked up in some Atlantean dungeon?"

Ven raised an eyebrow and grinned. "No wonder Justice is so crazy about you. Not much frightens you, does it?"

"Lots of things frighten me. Global warming. Poverty in Third World countries. Genocide. Snakes. I hate snakes," she said flatly. "But you two don't scare me, and if you've harmed Justice in any way, you're going to have to answer to me."

Ven smiled at her as if he were a teacher delighted with a prize student. "Snakes, huh? Is that common to all archaeologists or have you just watched too many Indiana Jones movies?"

She stood up, pushing her chair back and out of the way, and bared her teeth at him in the fiercest expression she could muster. "Keep laughing at me, and I'll see if I can find a whip, Your *Highness*."

It was Conlan's turn to smile as Ven clutched at his heart with a mock expression of pain on his face. "Oh, that's just hitting below the belt. Don't Your Highness me, if you want us to be the good friends I know we're going to be," Ven said.

"I don't need any more friends," Keely said, enunciating clearly. "I'm sure *you* don't need any more enemies, not to mention any international incidents. So tell me where Justice is—right now—or you're going to have both on your hands."

Chapter 26

She felt Justice before she heard him. Warmth seemed to flow into the room and wrap itself around her, carrying the scents of salt water and sea air. Pure relief combined with utter contentment swept through the tension in her nerve endings, calming and soothing. She could almost feel the whisper of his breath in her hair, the sound of his voice in her ear.

Justice had arrived, and her reaction was so simply and unreservedly joyous that it scared her even more than those snakes they'd been discussing. Her body and heart seemed literally to sway toward him, like a flower turning to the sun. How had he broken through her defenses so easily and so powerfully?

The hard length of his body was suddenly pressed against her back as he wrapped his arms around her. "Even after everything I have forced you to endure, you fight for me, *mi amara*. I have done nothing to deserve you, but I will never let you go," he murmured in her ear.

She stiffened and tried to pull away, the primitive claim he'd staked on her setting off all her warning alarms, but his arms were like steel bands holding her in place against the heat of his hard body. A struggle would only cost her a measure of dignity and do nothing to reassure Ven and Conlan, who were staring at Justice with a mixture of gladness and wary reserve.

She *knew* Justice, knew him more than she'd even known anyone, in spite of the short time since they'd actually met. She'd lived with his presence for years, and she'd seen the horror of his life and his terrible loneliness through her visions. It wouldn't harm anything to let him believe she was completely on his side, no matter what. That she wasn't afraid of him.

She wasn't entirely sure that it wasn't the truth, anyway. If they could use the Star of Artemis . . .

"That's it. We need to use the Star," she burst out. "It can help him. I saw it in my vision."

Conlan and Ven exchanged glances, and she caught the skepticism.

"You don't believe me."

Conlan shook his head. "It's not as simple as that. Although there are legends that the Star of Artemis can heal a mind broken by the stress of battle or through some injury or illness, none of us know whether the legends are true. The Star was one of the seven gems scattered to the far reaches of the earth before the Cataclysm. Only two have been returned to us and those only quite recently."

"We have no idea where it is," Ven added. "And although we have a fair idea that you're right about the Star, some of the rest of what you're telling us is impossible. Nereus could not have had a wife."

"I know, I know. Priesthood, celibacy, whatever," she said, rolling her eyes. "Times change. You admit you don't know where the Star is. Isn't it possible that Poseidon's priests used to be able to get married, and you just don't know about it? Liam told me that Nereus lived eight thousand years ago. It's not exactly like you have eight-thousand-year-old wedding photos lying around, do you?"

Justice finally relaxed his hold on her, and she gently pulled away from him and began to pace up and down the room, thinking out loud. "Anyway, it's not just the Star of Artemis. You need to have every one of those gems in order for Atlantis to rise. That is, if you *want* Atlantis to rise. By the way, what ocean are we underneath? How far down are we? Why haven't submarines picked you up with their technology? Or naval aircraft, or even satellite imaging?"

She looked to Justice, but his gaze had turned inward and his fists were clenched at his side, as though he were fighting another internal battle. She only hoped he'd continue to win, because she didn't want to know what would happen if the Nereid took control. Especially since Justice wore his sword sheathed on his back, the hilt rising behind his shoulder. The Nereid let loose with a sword.

That would be bad.

As though he heard her thoughts, Justice smiled at her briefly, reassurance in his eyes. He was trying to let her know that he was winning the battle, so she flashed him a brilliant smile of support and belief in return.

It wasn't all that hard to smile at him, crappy circumstances or not. He was so beautiful it actually hurt to look at him, even in his simple white shirt and dark pants. He looked like he belonged in princely robes or carved in marble and up on a pedestal. She allowed herself to spend a moment simply savoring the sight of him.

His hair was braided back again and, for a moment, she let herself imagine the tactile pleasure of slowly unbraiding it. Feeling the blue waves slip like silk through her fingers and fall like a curtain over her body.

Heat washed through her and she abruptly turned to examine one of the walls so that none of them saw her telltale blush. A couple of deep breaths later, she put her game face back on and still wanted those answers. "Well?"

Conlan took a seat at the table and poured himself a cup of coffee. She noticed he had a large, sturdy mug, not one of the delicate china cups. So maybe that *had* been the guest china she'd been served from.

Or maybe her brain was trying to distract her with trivia to take her mind off the fact that she was arguing with Atlantean royalty underneath the ocean somewhere.

Way to go, Keely.

"Those are questions and answers for another time," Conlan said quietly, but with a hint of steel in his voice. Definitely giving off a "don't push your luck" vibe. "We haven't survived for millennia by disclosing our secrets so easily, even to such a brilliant scientist as yourself."

"Charming, while giving me nothing. You guys are good," she said, putting a healthy dose of admiration in her voice. No matter. She was patient. She could wait.

"In regard to your visions, although my instincts tell me that you are speaking the truth, or at least the truth as you believe it to be, I would be a poor leader, indeed, if I were to take your word for something so critical," Conlan said slowly. "However, if there were some way you could prove to me the validity of your visions—"

"Yes," Keely said. "Sure. If you—"

"Absolutely not," Justice said harshly. "We have caused Keely to suffer far too much. We will not allow you to bring her to any further harm."

Keely whirled around, her heart in her throat. She heard it in his voice, never mind the plural self-reference again. The Nereid was back, and Justice's fury over the potential threat to her was dangerously near to causing his fragile control to topple. She took a step toward him with some thought of comforting or helping, but he moved with a blur of speed and was suddenly across the room from her, still clenching his fists.

"Do not," he growled at her, the words suddenly rich with a liquid accent she'd heard before—from his mother in the throne room during her visions. Then he turned the force of all that rage on his brothers. "We have seen Keely for centuries in our vision quest. She is ours, and you will not harm her."

Before Keely could move, Ven had somehow positioned himself so that he stood between Keely and Justice. He spoke calmly, as if trying to soothe a frenzied animal.

Or simply a brother who'd gone insane when a *geas* shattered.

"Justice, you know we don't want to hurt her. You know we want to do everything we can to help you. Am I talking to both of you now? Have you gone *Sybil* on me?"

Suddenly, shockingly, Justice threw back his head and laughed. It was a warm, hearty, normal laugh, with nothing chilling or alien about it. A wave of relief hit Keely with such force that her knees weakened from the onslaught. He'd done it. He was in control.

When Justice stopped laughing, he looked at Ven and grinned. His eyes were clear again. "You and your damn movies. The Nereid has no frame of reference for *Sybil* or *Dawn of the Dead* or *I Was a Teenage Werewolf*, either. Maybe that's the trick. I can battle the other half of my soul with B movies."

Ven very subtly moved so that he was no longer blocking Justice's view of Keely. "You see? All these years, you goons mocked me for my excellent taste in quality filmmaking, and now it just might save you from losing your marbles."

Conlan folded his arms across his chest and looked at Keely. "I thought having *one* little brother was bad enough. Now I've got two of them to deal with. I may abdicate the throne and move to Fiji, where it's quiet."

Keely snapped her mouth shut, from where it had been hanging open down to about her kneecaps. Staring at them in disbelief, she put her hands on her hips. "Are you kidding me? Justice's sanity and the fate of all Atlantis might be at stake here, and you're making bad jokes?"

"We're guys," Justice said, still grinning. "It's what we do."

It was the sanest, most absolutely ordinary thing that he'd said in the entire time she'd known him, and that grin on his face transformed his features from dark and terrifyingly beautiful to drop-dead, fall-at-his-feet-with-her-clothes-off sexy. She couldn't do anything else but stand there smiling back at him like a giddy coed with a crush on the professor. She didn't know how much time passed, while they all stood there grinning at each other, but of course like all good things in her life it was too soon over.

Conlan drained his coffee mug and put it back down on the table. "I have devised a plan that will both test at the veracity of your visions and also perhaps give us the information we need in order to track down the missing jewels, Dr. McDermott. You will object read the Trident."

Keely stumbled and fell back against the wall, then slid bonelessly down until her butt hit the floor. "Oh, sure. No problem, Your Highness. For my next trick, I'll read the sacred object of power—of a *god*."

She couldn't help it; she started laughing helplessly. "After what Poseidon's sword very nearly did to me . . . oh, hell. You may as well call me Keely instead of Dr. McDermott. Why be formal when I'm going to be dead soon?"

∽⌇⌇∾

The Nereid tried to break free again, and Justice ruthlessly shoved him back into a corner of his mind, but the mere thought of Keely in danger threatened to smash his control to jagged shards.

"She will not touch the Trident, you godsforsaken son of a squid," he gritted out, trying desperately to keep from going for his sword. "Brother or no, I will kill you if you try to harm her in any way."

Conlan slammed a fist down on the table, but before he could reply, Ven started laughing, lightening the tension in the room a fraction. "Son of a squid? Really? That's not bad. Points for the nasty visual, man."

Keely, her head jerking back and forth as she tried to look at everyone simultaneously, suddenly started laughing, too. "I know I'm an idiot, but now all I can think of is Squidward from *SpongeBob*. Did you know they have a movie called *Atlantis SquarePantis*? One of my American colleagues on the Lupercale dig had a young son who watched it over and over until I thought my ears would melt. You guys should get a copy."

Ven whistled. "*Atlantis SquarePantis*. Nice. I'll have to pick that up next time I'm up top. Too bad UPS doesn't exactly deliver down here."

Justice, calmer now, still wasn't seeing the funny. He glared at Keely. "You joke when your life is in danger?"

She blinked and then grinned at him. "I'm an archaeologist. It's what we do."

Hearing her toss his own words back at him unlocked a hidden door deep in the frozen recesses of Justice's heart. That this woman could possess such incredible courage in the face of such fantastically bizarre circumstances—that she could still smile and joke—astonished him.

She astonished him. She was more than the sum total of her beauty and intelligence. She had courage, compassion, and humor beyond any he'd seen before.

He would never let her be harmed.

"She touches the Trident over my dead body," he said flatly.

"Nice. Pithy, yet melodramatic," Ven said. "But it doesn't solve our problem here. Your woman just hit us with some news that could mean the destruction of our whole world, if we don't pay attention to her."

"I'm not his woman," Keely said.

"Right, Doc. Keep telling yourself that," Ven shot back. "We need some answers. If she could somehow not only prove what she's saying is true, but maybe find out more for us—"

"Never," Justice snarled. "You didn't see her. She went into a trance that was coma-like. Her pulse slowed down to nearly nothing and her skin turned cold, just from touching my sword. If she touches the Trident, she could die. Hells, even those who are not object readers have died from touching the Trident. Poseidon's magic is fickle and deadly."

"Offer me an option, then," Conlan shouted. "Offer me an option that helps us understand this. Dr. McDermott just told us—"

"I'm in the room," Keely shouted back at him, pulling herself to her feet. "I am *in the room*. Quit talking about me like I'm not, you bunch of . . . of . . . royal cavemen."

Silence. All three of them stared at Keely in shock, as if they'd forgotten she was there. Justice was torn between wanting to laugh and wanting to toss her shapely ass over his shoulder and get her far, far away.

"That's better," she said, no longer shouting, but not exactly calm, either. "For your information, I'll touch whatever object I want, but I'm not suicidal. I do have a suggested option, if any of you pigheaded brothers are ready to listen."

"We're all ears," Ven drawled.

"The Trident. Does it rest in a case of some sort? In the past, when an object held emotional memories that were too violent for me to comfortably handle, I'd touch its case or container, or even the dirt or rock where it had been found."

"That's kind of brilliant. No wonder you're the famous archaeologist," Ven said.

"No," Justice said. "It's still too dangerous."

"That's perfect," Conlan said. "The Trident rests on a silken cushion in the Temple. Without Alaric here to bring it to us, I suggest we go to it."

You see? They ignore you. They treat you as if you are nothing, and they will put our woman in jeopardy. We must take action, the Nereid whispered inside Justice's mind.

Action was good. Slowly, saying nothing, Justice unsheathed his sword. The unmistakable hiss of steel released from leather sang through the air, which immediately dropped several degrees in temperature.

"Keely," he said, stalking toward her with the sword pointed in the general direction of his brothers, "is not going to Poseidon's Temple. We will not allow her to take that risk."

Unfortunately, however, he made the tactical mistake of looking into Keely's bright green eyes. The warm understanding and determination he saw there almost buckled his knees. Even the Nereid fell silent inside his head.

Keely placed her hand on his arm. "If there is any chance that it can help you—both of you—I'll take that risk," she said softly. "I don't really understand it, but you've become pretty important to me in a very short period of time. There aren't many people who are important to me, Justice. Please don't ask me to be a coward when a little bit of my courage might mean an awful lot to you."

He was undone. He, who had conquered thousands of enemies and survived countless bloody battles, was shattered by the gentle words of a human. She wanted to risk herself for him.

He couldn't help himself, and the fact that Conlan and Ven were in the room be damned. He caught her with his free arm and pulled her close, then pressed a brief, hard kiss to her mouth, only forcing himself to stop when the soft warmth of her body nearly caused him to forget the danger they faced.

"You honor me beyond words, *mi amara*, but I must forbid it." He gently pushed her behind him, faced Conlan and Ven, and raised his sword a little. "Defy me in this, and brother will be forced to battle brother in this room."

Conlan's face hardened. "I'd hoped it wouldn't come to this." He nodded once, sharply, and a narrow ribbon of glowing blue-green energy sliced through the room from behind Keely.

Before Justice could move, the energy encircled him, trapping him. Fury smashed through him, and he called on the Nereid for help to escape the trap, but Conlan and Ven raised their arms and added their own strength to whoever had sent the first attack.

He was bound, unable even to speak, though he struggled furiously and called on both Atlantean and Nereid power. The Nereid shrieked its defiance inside his brain, but could do nothing against the combined onslaught.

"What are you doing? Are you hurting him? Stop it!" Keely shouted. "Stop it! I'll do whatever you want; just let him go. Can't you see he's having a tough enough time controlling the Nereid side of himself without you betraying him like this?"

Regret washed over Ven's features, and for an instant Justice understood what they were doing to him and why. Then rage seared understanding to bitter ashes and he shuddered under the force of returning madness.

"If we let him go, he won't let you help us. You heard him, Keely," Ven said.

"If you *don't* let him go, I will never read one damn object for you. Ever. Do you understand me? Never," she shouted, tears running down her cheeks. Then she turned to face Justice. "Listen to me, please. I can do this. I can safely touch the cushion, or I never would have suggested it. But I need you sane, so you can hold my hand while I do it. Please, Justice. I need you."

Justice was shocked back to reason by the sight of her tears. She cried for *him*.

She needed *him*.

Abruptly, he stopped struggling. He instantly could speak again, as if the magic holding him recognized his acceptance.

"We won't fight you if you can promise that all precautions will be taken to keep her safe," he said to Conlan.

Conlan nodded and lowered his arms, releasing the bonds of power. Beside him, Ven did the same. Finally, Christophe materialized in the corner of the room and the magic he'd been directing at Justice faded. Some dark part of Justice was bitterly pleased to see the stark white pallor of Christophe's features. Holding him had not been so easy, then, even with three of them.

He sheathed his sword and then opened his arms, barely daring to hope. But Keely only hesitated for a moment before she walked into his embrace, put her arms around his waist, and buried her tearstained face in his chest. He held her as close as a whisper of breath, as gently as a cherished hope.

She was both breath and hope to him.

"We will allow it, then," he told Conlan and Ven. "We will go to the Temple, and you will discover the truth of her visions. Then we will leave Atlantis, and you will never bother us again."

"You're our family," Ven said, the anguish plain in his voice, but Justice hardened his heart against it.

"We were never your family. You've proved it again this day. And you should be warned: if ever you try to trap us again, we will not be caught so easily. Both Atlantean and Nereid souls swear this to you."

Ven started to speak again, but Conlan cut him off with a gesture.

"To the Temple, then," Conlan said tiredly. "One crisis at a time."

Chapter 27

Poseidon's Temple, Atlantis

Keely couldn't speak. She was, literally, stunned speechless by the sight of her surroundings. The outside of the Temple had been awe-inspiring enough, with its polished marble and gold and copper inlay. But this . . . this was beyond an archaeologist's wildest dreams of avarice.

They'd walked by room after room filled with historical treasures; one room was piled floor to ceiling with objects made of shining gold and encrusted with gems. Offerings to Poseidon from centuries past, Justice had told her. The "old stuff" was in arena-sized rooms below, he'd said.

The "old stuff." Her throat seized up at the thought of it. Another room was stacked, wall-to-wall, with ancient-looking leather trunks filled with what she imagined must be amazing things.

Room after room filled with statues and paintings that had to be thousands of years old. The corridor they were traveling was lined with the most magnificent artwork she'd ever seen. A friend of hers who was a museum curator would be having cardiac arrest right about now.

A library as big as the Ohio State football stadium. As

they'd passed the entryway and her eyes had widened at the sight of hundreds of robed men and women working at long tables, Justice had casually murmured something about restoration work on the rescued scrolls from Alexandria.

Alexandria.

Rescued scrolls.

From Alexandria.

She'd almost fainted on the spot. Luckily, she was made of tougher stock, and she'd only suffered temporary light-headedness.

Because, you know, they were only *scrolls.* Rescued from *Alexandria.* Only quite possibly the greatest archaeological find of lost historical documents since . . . well, *ever.*

Her stomach fluttered again, and she forced her mind away from the scrolls and the art and the "old stuff" to concentrate on the task before her. She also needed to focus on not tripping over her own feet, as Justice dragged her by the hand down the extremely long corridor, following Conlan and Ven at a pace designed for long Atlantean legs, evidently.

"Hey! I do work out. I even run, but you're annoying me with this forced march. Can I catch my breath a little?"

Justice slowed but didn't stop and didn't even look at her. His profile was grim, his features hard as the statues they kept passing. In fact, there was a certain similarity. The proud, nearly arrogant expression. The elegant nose and cheek-bones.

"So are these all statues of Atlanteans?"

He stopped so abruptly that she ran into his back, face-first.

"Hey! A little warning next time?"

He whirled around and glared down at her. "You're on your way to risk your life, and you want us to discuss statues with you?"

She caught her breath at the fiercely glowing blue-green flames in the centers of his black pupils. Even though clearly both of him—or them, or however that plural might be constructed—were present and accounted for, he didn't intimidate her anymore.

"Scientist here. Curious, okay? Occupational hazard."

Before Justice could respond, Ven called out to them from about twenty feet farther down the hall. "Are you two coming or not? The sooner we get this over with . . ."

He left the sentence unfinished, but Keely didn't need a translator. The sooner they could be sure that she was telling the truth and get on with whatever they needed to do to find the Star and heal Justice's mind so Atlantis could rise and bring peace and little fluffy bunnies to all mankind.

Or something like that.

She realized that fear and the stress of being wound so tight she might explode at any second was making her giddy. *Hysteria*: her word of the day.

Justice clenched his jaw, tightened his hand around hers, and began to walk toward his brothers, pulling her along with him. "We're coming. Do not press us."

As they approached the doorway, he stopped again. This time the look he aimed at her was pure determination sheathed in ice. "You do not have to undertake this trial. If they need proof of your visions to believe you, then to the hells with them. They will suffer for their disbelief. You have no need to prove anything to anyone. We will force them to release you from Atlantis and we will leave with you."

She stared at him in surprise, but then the truth of his words sank into her and nearly shattered her. He was offering to give up his home and family—his entire world—to protect her.

This warrior who fought viciously against others sacrificing for *him* was prepared to give up everything for *her*. It was more than she could comprehend, so she took refuge in humor. "Well, you'd fit right in on campus with the blue hair, but you might have asked me first about coming home with me," she said, attempting a smile. "You're not exactly a stray cat, and I have a really small apartment."

His eyes narrowed and he made a low, threatening noise deep in his throat. "We have claimed you, Keely. Perhaps now, when our grasp on calm and balance is so precarious, is not the time for your jokes."

She sighed, but said nothing. He was back to the claiming again. When she'd done what she could for him and for Atlantis, she was going to have a long talk with him about the twenty-first century. Or maybe she'd send him a nice, safe e-mail from a safe few thousand miles away.

Safely.

Not that she feared Justice. But the Nereid was an unknown quantity, and it was better that he and she weren't in the same time zone.

She ignored the pain in her chest that accompanied the thought and started walking again. Toward Ven and the room that evidently held the Trident.

Was it blasphemy to go poking around at the sacred objects of a god, even if you didn't worship that god? She touched the fish carving that rested under her shirt on its chain and wished that she'd added a gold cross to the necklace. A symbol of her own faith. Although the fish could do double duty. Didn't a fish also serve as a symbol of Christianity? Jesus fed all those people with only two fish, after all.

She briefly closed her eyes and offered up a prayer that she would survive whatever lay in front of her. Survive and be able to help Justice. As if he could read her thoughts, he squeezed her hand briefly and a shiver of heat flared between them. She trembled as the sensation shuddered through her body, and the memory of his kiss back in the cavern shot into her mind, so powerful and potent that she stumbled.

The memory flashed heat through her, but it wasn't sexual or even sensual. It was the warmth of simple joy: the taste of icy lemonade on a hot desert dig, the sight of a brilliantly colored sunset over the ocean waves, the sound of bells sparkling in a child's laughter.

The warmth of coming home. To the kind of home she'd always wanted.

He caught her before she could fall, and she shook her head at the question in his eyes. How could she tell him that her heart had chosen now, of all inconvenient and inappropriate times, to fall fearlessly over the edge?

Taking a deep breath, she put her Dr. McDermott face

back on, gently pulled her hand free from his, and strode through the open door to face whatever lay inside.

～～～

Justice and the Nereid watched from their shared eyes as Keely slowly circled the pedestal upon which the Trident rested on its peacock-blue silken cushion. She'd done nothing else for what seemed like a very long time. Simply walked round and round the pedestal, never taking her gaze from the Trident, with its five gaping holes where the remaining of the seven gems should rest.

None of them seemed to want to be the one to disturb her concentration, though. There was something in the way she held her body; her muscles clenched so tightly that he could see her hands trembling and her chest barely rising and falling with the shallow breaths she was taking. If he hadn't seen the real thing, he would have guessed that she was in a trance now.

But he *had* witnessed the real thing, and the prospect of her going through such trauma again, on a far grander scale, froze the marrow of his bones with terror. She'd promised him she could do it. That touching the cushion would be bearable.

Even he, fiercely protective of her as he was, had to admit that the cushion itself had never seen battle or committed a single blood-drenched act. So it made sense that it would be bearable for her. Also, Keely had sworn that if he held her hand and gave her his support, she could do this.

He could do no less than match her courage. But they needed to get on with it before his own courage faltered again at the risk she was taking, even though the fate of his own fractured mind might rest on discovering the location of the Star of Artemis.

Finally, she stopped walking and stood, head bowed, her fiery red hair falling forward to hide her face from view. His fingers ached to stroke the silken strands away from her forehead as he pulled her close to him.

His arms ached to hold her and never, ever let her go. Lean on her strength to help him fight the battle waging within him. Her calm was the check to his madness, her light the balance to his dark.

She was his Keely. *Our Keely,* whispered the Nereid. *Ours and only ours, forever. Let her do this one small task, and then we will leave this place until we gain the strength to use our combined powers to conquer. It is our rightful place, as heir apparent to Atlantis.*

Justice recoiled and drew on all of his mental reserves to lock the Nereid away in a far corner of his mind. He didn't know how long he could keep it under control, but he would never listen to treasonous plans from the poisonous stranger who lived inside his head.

Inside his soul.

He was doomed, and he was damned, and the only faint hope he had of surviving with any of his sanity intact lay in the strength of this human female.

"I'm ready," she said quietly. So quietly he almost didn't hear her. "I'm going to take off my glove now and touch it, but only with one hand. Sometimes that lessens the force of the impact. I'm not sure why."

Slowly, reluctantly, she pulled off her left glove and dropped it to the floor. Turning to Justice, she attempted a small, wavering smile. "Hey, wanna hold my hand?"

She lifted her right hand, still gloved, and he leapt forward to take it.

"Always," he said.

Her green eyes briefly shone with a flash of happiness or, perhaps, hope. Then they darkened again with grim resolve. "Okay, let's do this thing."

She closed her eyes and took several deep breaths, visibly relaxing the tension in her body as she prepared herself. Then her eyes snapped open and she grinned. "Feels like I should say something important or ceremonial here, but I got nothing."

Before he could think of a reply, she reached out with her left hand and grasped the edge of the cushion farthest away from the Trident itself. Then her eyes widened until he could see white rimming her entire pupils. Her hand clutched spasmodically at his, and then a bolt of pure energy shot through her body and slammed him across the room. He crashed down on his back but was up in a second.

Keely screamed so loudly and with such anguish that acid seared through his stomach as he shot across the room toward her. Ven, swearing a flaming streak in Atlantean, headed for Keely. Conlan dove at the cushion to yank it out of her grasp.

But some kind of completely transparent energy shield, like nothing Justice had ever encountered before, bounced them all away from her and on their asses on the cold, hard marble floor.

Keely, still standing there with her hand grasping the cushion so tightly that her knuckles were white, shuddered and shook, still screaming. Her eyes rolled back in her head until he could see nothing but white, and he snarled and leapt toward her again.

He must reach her. He must protect her. He'd promised to hold her hand, always, and he was failing her.

The energy shield smashed him back again, and this time his head cracked against a wall a dozen feet away. He put a hand to his scalp and it came away bloody, but it wouldn't stop him if it took a hundred tries, or a thousand tries; by all the nine hells and even those deeper, he would save Keely or die trying.

Suddenly, her screaming stopped. The unexpected silence cut through them like the sharpest blade. Keely's eyes returned to normal, but emerald fire blazed from them as though something or someone more than just Keely looked out.

"He took it," Keely said, her voice steady and clear, in spite of the convulsions racking her body. "Reisen took the Trident so that he could become the king. The House of . . . Mycenae. The House of Mycenae should rule. Poseidon made him pay for his arrogance. He . . . something about his hand. The vampires took Reisen's hand."

"How could she know that?" Conlan asked, awe infusing his voice.

"Justice could have told her," Ven said, but Justice saw the doubt in his brother's expression. They were starting to believe.

Another shock visibly raced through Keely, and she threw

her head back, the cords in her neck straining. Still, her voice came through in measured cadence, no hint of the stress her body was under showing in her tone or in the suddenly lyrical rhythms of her words.

"Atlantis must sink beneath the waves, in order to survive the Cataclysm. *Ragnarok.* The Doom of the Gods. The burning. We will rise again. Send a full measure of the best and brightest of us out among the humans. Send them to the corners of the world. Each of seven groups shall take one of the gems of the Trident. The Dragon's Egg. The Nereid's Heart. The Star of Artemis. The Vampire's Bane. The Siren. The Emperor. And, finally, Poseidon's Pride. Only when all are together again will Atlantis be allowed to rise. If the gems are not together and the Seven Isles attempt to rise to the surface, no matter the magic or technology of the future, Atlantis will be destroyed."

As she spoke her final words, she released her hold on the cushion and sank, unconscious, to the floor. Justice dove for her as she fell and encountered no resistance. The energy shield had vanished as suddenly as it had appeared.

"Now do you believe me?" he demanded of his brothers, as he cradled her limp form in his arms. "Now do you see that her visions are true?"

Solemnly, both Ven and Conlan nodded. Such simple words to convince them all.

Such simple words, spoken plainly and fluently, but not in English. Nor in any other modern language that Keely could possibly speak.

She'd delivered her chilling pronouncement—flawlessly— in the language of the ancient Atlanteans.

None of them could doubt her now.

Chapter 28

Atlantis, the war room

Keely woke from a fractured dream of glittering gems and sun-splashed jungle to the sight of Justice staring off into the distance. Dark circles lay like bruises beneath his eyes, which had changed color again and were now blacker than a tomb robber's heart. Fury rode the hard planes and angles of his face, and she shivered.

At her movement, he realized she was awake. He stared down at her with a pained expression of joy, relief, and anger. Warmth and color swept across his face like spring following the icy dread of winter, and his arms tightened as he pulled her against his chest, murmuring something too quietly for her to hear. She realized she was sitting in his lap, on one of the couches back in the palace war room, but she was too exhausted to waste energy on being embarrassed at the intimate position. Someone had pulled her glove back on her hand, and she was grateful for that small kindness.

"So, I guess I survived the Great Cushion Experiment, huh?" She forced a grin, but nobody returned her smile. Ven and Conlan stood in oddly identical positions a few feet away, with their hands behind their backs in a sort of parade rest. At her words, though, Ven dropped into a crouch so that he was on eye level with her and blew out a huge breath.

"Hey, Doc, you scared us. Are you okay?"

"I'm fine. Just a little shaky," she said distractedly, already searching through her memories of the vision for something useful.

Justice lifted his head from where it rested on the top of hers. "Never again," he said harshly. "Never again will we allow you to go through that."

She lifted a hand to his face, and he stilled at her touch. "There you go with the *allowing* again. I'm not very good at taking orders," she said huskily, her throat raw.

Why was her throat raw? Oh. Right. There'd been screaming. *She'd* been screaming. She'd almost forgotten the pain, in the wonder of the vision, although she couldn't imagine how. Pain had sliced through her until she'd been sure her arms and legs were being wrenched off her body. Slowly. By somebody who was seriously pissed off.

"Dare to mess with a god's toys, and see where that gets you," she said, shuddering. "Anyway, as far as touching anything that is *anywhere* near the Trident, you don't have to worry about me trying that again."

"Worse, it was all for naught. We now know nothing more than we did," Conlan said grimly. "I offer my sincerest apologies that our trial put you through so much pain, Dr. McDermott. It is even more regrettable since we've learned nothing new."

"Well, that's not exactly true," Ven said. "We learned the names of all the gems. We knew we were looking for the Star, which is a sapphire, and the Vampire's Bane, a yellow diamond. We knew that the emerald we already possess is called the Dragon's Egg, and that the ruby is the Nereid's Heart. But evidently the aquamarine, amethyst, and tourmaline still missing are called the Siren, the Emperor, and Poseidon's Pride, although which is which is anybody's guess."

"Alaric may know more about the gem names," Conlan said. "You are correct, of course. All knowledge is power, and now we have more of it. However, we still have no idea of the location of any of the missing gems."

"That's not exactly true, either," Keely said. "I know where the Star of Artemis is. Or at least I know where they took it when they left Atlantis."

"What?" Conlan and Ven said at the same time.

"Oh. Sorry. It wasn't a typical vision," she said slowly, trying to be as clear as possible so they would understand. "Usually I'm an observer to an event that had violent or deeply emotional resonance regarding the object. Sometimes I actually become part of one of the people in the room. It's like I inhabit their body as an extra consciousness, if that makes sense."

Justice loosened his arms a little so he could lean back and look at her. "Oh, I think I grasp the general concept," he said dryly.

She blinked up at him for a moment, then the connection clicked in her frazzled neurons and she laughed. "Does this mean we were made for each other?"

The humor in his eyes deepened to some darker emotion. "Keely, you have no idea."

She forced herself to turn away from the promise—or the threat—in his gaze, faced Conlan and Ven again, and even laughed a little. "You don't know how wild it is to actually talk to somebody about this without them trying to lock me up in a rubber room. Anyway, this was different, as I was saying. It was like I was watching an insane version of TV where all the channels were playing at once in HD, three-D, four-D, or supersonic-D."

She shoved a hand through her hair, pushing it away from her face. "I saw where all of the gems went, but mostly just in flickers. I didn't recognize any of the places, except one. The ruby is in some dark, smelly cave, for example. A really damp place, but there's no way for me to know where."

Ven and Conlan exchanged glances and then looked at her with growing respect. "Yes, we found the Nereid's Heart in a cave under a mountain in Washington state," Conlan said.

"The only place I'm absolutely sure of is where they took the sapphire. The Star of Artemis. I saw the mural on the wall," she said, remembering the vivid colors in the vision. "I have a print of that mural on the wall in my office. A colleague was involved in the excavation. It's the San Bartolo site."

From the blank expressions on their faces, she was guessing they didn't get the archaeological trade journals down here.

"San Bartolo," she repeated, going into lecture mode. "It's a pre-Columbian Mayan archaeological site in northeastern Guatemala. It's mostly jungle today, but there was a large population during the Maya Preclassic Period. Dr. William Saturno from the Peabody Museum discovered a mural room in the base of the pyramid in 2001. They carbon-dated the murals to 100 B.C., which made them a hugely exciting find. They were the oldest and finest Mayan murals that had been discovered at the time, and—"

She stopped, midsentence, and gaped at them. "Oh. Oh, that must be it. Your ancestors. The ones who settled all over the world before the Cataclysm. They must be behind some of the world's creation mythology. There is always a flood, and—"

"We know of the creation myths," Justice said impatiently. "What of San Bartolo and the Star?"

"The mural. It's the Mayan creation myth. They show images of gods, sacrifices, and trees. One of the sacrifices is fish, which some believe represent the oceans of the underworld."

The smooth weight of the fish carving resting against her chest seemed to warm, but she didn't pull it out from under her shirt, just filed the impression away in a corner of her mind and continued. "The one I found very interesting was the maize god. He's looking behind him at a kneeling female, while another female figure with flowing black hair floats above the kneeling woman. They—"

"Anubisa," Justice gritted out. "She delighted in images of her dominance over the male gods."

Keely gasped. "Really? You believe that could be her? Even from way back then?"

Justice shrugged, his powerful muscles tensing and then relaxing against her. "It's not that long ago, right? You said 100 B.C.? Hells, we just defeated Barrabas, and he was young by her standards."

"Fine. Glamour shots of Anubisa on a mural with the god

of popcorn. We get it," Ven said, standing up again. "But what about the Star? If it can really help Justice, we need to know where it is. Not to mention the part about Atlantis not rising without it."

Keely leaned back against Justice, suddenly exhausted. "I'm sorry. I got distracted. The Star is hidden in a niche in the rock. It's placed precisely behind the eye of a fish."

Justice stiffened and then jumped up, still holding her in his arms as though she weighed nothing. "Then we go there. Now. We recover the Star and—"

"Not so fast," Conlan cautioned. "There must be Guatemalan guards on site, and the excavating team. Not to mention how are we going to explain that we want to deface an important historical site to pull out our astonishingly valuable, enormous sapphire and remove it from the country? I'm sure the Guatemalan government will have something to say about that."

Keely struggled in vain against arms like iron bands and finally gave up. She fixed her fiercest professorial glare on Justice. "Let go of me, now."

To her surprise, he did. But he kept an arm around her waist, almost as if he couldn't bear to lose contact with her.

To her further surprise, she didn't mind that at all.

"Government, guards, whatever. It's not like they can keep us out, with Poseidon's magics on our side," Ven said.

Keely shook her head. "You don't understand. The government doesn't control the site anymore. A band of rogue vampires took over the entire Peten region a few years ago. Nobody has been able to get them out, even Interpol's P Ops division. Too much jungle and too many hiding places. Without burning down the entire jungle, there's nothing anybody can do. The nearest village is only a couple of miles away from the site, and they've been cut off from civilization for some time. From what I understand, they've been given up for dead."

Justice started pacing the room, tension in every line of his body. "It's Nereid in origin, isn't it?"

"What?" Ven said.

"The Star of Artemis. Doesn't the legend hold that it was originally a gift to Poseidon from the Nereid high priestess?"

"Yes, that's true," Conlan said. "Some of us paid attention in class, Ven."

Ven rolled his eyes. "I paid attention when it mattered. Ask me about the twenty-eight ways to kill a vampire without a weapon."

"Twenty-eight ways?" Keely started a mental count, but could only come up with five. "Really? Can you show me—"

Justice blurred across the room until he was blocking her view of his brother. "If you think you will ever get close enough to a vampire to try any of those techniques, you are sadly mistaken," he said, his voice pure silken menace.

"Hey, some of the worst grave robbers are vampires—"

"If it is of Nereid origin," Justice continued, cutting her off, again, which was really beginning to be a very bad habit, "then I may be able to track it. If I go to the Guatemalan jungle and find this San Bartolo, even if the Star has been moved, perhaps I will be able to sense it."

"Unless somebody found it and stole it thousands of years ago and it's long since been cut up and set in a couple dozen necklaces and earrings," Keely pointed out, a decided bite to her voice. "Also, quit interrupting me."

"In any event, it is of no matter," Conlan said. "You cannot go anywhere until Alaric has time to . . . visit with you."

"Time to trespass in my mind, you mean," Justice said darkly. "I'm in control for now. I've reached an accord with the Nereid. Do not force me to do something that might breach the fragile nature of that agreement. I will travel to San Bartolo and see what I can discover."

"If you're going, I'm going with you," Keely said, and all three of them glared at her, turning the full power of their arrogant Atlantean warrior attitude on her poor little human female self.

Boy, did they have a lot to learn.

"Not happening," Ven said.

"I forbid it," Conlan said.

"Not a chance," Justice said. But then something glittered in his eyes and his face . . . changed. Somehow took on a darker, more predatory cast. A dangerous smile crossed his face, and a look of such purely sexual intent filled his expression that she actually shivered and took a step back.

"Yes," Justice who was no longer only Justice said. "Yes, you will go with us."

Before she could reply, the room exploded into action. Conlan threw his hands in the air and channeled that blue-green energy again. Ven dove across the room toward Justice, no weapons in his hands but grim purpose in his eyes. Justice dropped to the floor and swept out a leg, knocking Ven's feet out from under him. As Ven bounced back up, crouching into a fighting stance, Conlan threw two perfect spheres of energy at Justice.

Justice laughed and almost casually raised one hand. The spheres burst into showers of harmless sparkles. Then he pointed a single finger at Conlan and shot a stream of silvery green fire at him, knocking the prince clear across the room and smashing him into a wall so hard that Conlan stayed down for a moment.

Ven took the opportunity to lunge at Justice, but Justice was ready for him. He threw his hands into the air, shouting a word of power, and fastened a spiral coil of shimmering water around Ven, imprisoning him within it. No matter how hard Ven fought to get out, the spiral adjusted to his efforts and held him firm, arms trapped at his side.

Ven snarled something at Justice that Keely was pretty sure was downright nasty, but she was in such a state of shock from the sudden violence that she just stood there, helpless, wondering what kind of defenses she could put up against magic like that.

Only one came to mind.

Compassion.

Justice roared out a sound of utter dominance and triumph, and she knew the Nereid had taken over. Somehow, she had to get through to the Atlantean Justice.

Her Justice.

She stood, perfectly still, only trembling the tiniest bit, as he stalked toward her like the predator he was. She had no intention of being prey, however.

When he came close enough to touch her, she tried her only weapon. "Justice, I need your help. You have to fight him, for my sake. I'll do anything I can to help you, and I'm glad to go to San Bartolo. We'll find the Star of Artemis together. But you have to be in control. I'm afraid of the Nereid."

He stopped, arms held out in front of him, reaching for her. His muscles shook with the force of the internal battle that must be raging inside him. Finally, long moments later, sanity and reason returned to balance the hunger and possession in his eyes.

"I'm in control, for now," he said roughly. "But I need you. You must come with me, or I'm afraid I'll lose this battle forever."

So Keely, who had rarely made an unplanned move in her life, threw caution to the Atlantean winds and stepped forward into his arms—and into her future. "Just try to keep me away. Mayan murals? A pyramid? Possibly an eleven-thousand-year-old sapphire with magical powers? Hey, what archaeologist could resist?"

The lines around his mouth deepened and he looked at her with stark, burning hunger. "For me, Keely. I need you to come for me, not for science or for pity or for any other reason. I need you to come for *me*."

"Yes," she said, giving in finally to the inevitable truth between them. No matter what happened, she wanted this one moment of honesty. "I'm coming for you. Only for you."

He shouted out a wordless cry of triumph and swept her into his arms. Then, just as before, the world dissolved around them in a cascade of potential realities, and she closed her eyes and hung on for the ride.

Chapter 29

Holy Ghost Cemetery, St. Louis

Alaric had long since lost any tenuous grasp he'd had on his temper. After an entire night of searching the city for any sign of Quinn, Jack, and Denal, he'd finally caught a faint glimmer of conscious thought from Quinn's very interesting mind, only to track it here to this place of death, a few short hours past dawn, and then lose it again almost as soon as he'd arrived.

He floated as mist above the grave markers; so many of them dated in early 1849. Some illness, then. Probably another cholera epidemic. He remembered doing what he could for the humans of that time with Atlantean medicines and healing. Some of them had thought him the angel of death, come to carry them away.

He'd laughed at the idea then, but it was true that too many times he *had* delivered death. He'd always confined the killing to the enemies of the humans, though. Too many times he'd been called upon to work with the warriors. Too many times he'd healed and healed until his powers were exhausted, and then been forced to watch warriors and humans die horribly.

It was never enough, never enough. He'd given up all for power, and even the power was never enough.

The power rushed through him as if called by its naming or drawn by his fury. Both power and fury needed an outlet. He channeled water and threw it in a series of intricate arrow shapes against the fence that circled the cemetery, out of pure frustration. After the first blast smashed a section of fence into splinters, he forced himself to calm enough to curb the power. The next barrage drove a century's worth of dirt and grime off the wooden boards that remained standing.

None of it made him feel any better. Still he could not find Quinn; the faint shimmer he'd sensed of her emotions that had led him here had vanished again. She and her sister Riley were *aknasha'an*—emotional empaths. As such, not only could they read the emotions of others but they had the ability to project their own emotions in a way other humans—and even other Atlanteans—had long since been unable to do. He'd been able to reach out to Quinn, no matter the distance, ever since the moment he'd first met her and saved her life.

The connection to Quinn had only cost him a small price: pieces of his blackened heart and chunks of his desiccated soul. She didn't even know she'd claimed them, emotional empath or no.

Her ability was a Gift thought lost in the waters of ancient time, but then again, many such Gifts were returning to prominence during these dark and deadly days. The world seemed caught on the cusp of a change so huge and hideous that it might rival the Cataclysm that had sent Atlantis to the bottom of the ocean. Every act taken and every decision made swung the pendulum toward the light or dark side of the future.

If only Poseidon would give them a clear path to follow. The gods, however, were never so straightforward. Except in matters that he, Poseidon's high priest, could wish would be colored more in shades of gray than strictly black and white. Such as the vow of celibacy and promise never to wed he'd sworn to the elders when they'd invested him with the high priesthood.

He'd vowed to live his entire existence starkly, bleakly alone, in exchange for the chance at limitless power and access to a god. But the favoritism of the sea god offered cold comfort, and power for its own sake no longer held any appeal. His past, present, and future rolled in an unending coil of solitude. No hope of warmth or comfort.

No hope of Quinn.

To break the vow would mean the diminishment of his powers; no longer could he lead the Temple or serve as counsel to the high prince. No longer could he protect Atlantis when it was on the brink of its ascension back into the world of the landwalkers.

Now that his people needed him most, he could never abandon them, no matter the personal cost. The choice was clear: he could have Quinn, or he could keep his world intact. Not much of a choice, in any event, when she'd made it clear she would never have him.

The rebel leader and the priest. It sounded like the punch line to a very bad joke. A match made in the lowest of the nine hells, yet never to be a match at all. The gods must have laughed the day they had fashioned Quinn to be the woman for whom his soul had always yearned. They must still be laughing now.

But none of that mattered. Quinn was simply another rebel warrior, an ally in the fight to save humanity from the rogue vampires and shape-shifters who wanted to turn them into sheep to be herded and devoured. Another ally. She could be nothing more and nothing less.

And if only he could convince himself of that, perhaps his heart would cease slowly and torturously dying inside his chest.

He took a deep breath, finally rematerializing into his corporeal form. This reverie gained him nothing; obsessing on what could not be changed never did. He merely needed to find Quinn—find them all—and ensure that they were safe. He'd gained no sense of Denal during the long night, either, and he should have been easily able to track the warrior's thoughts on the shared Atlantean thought path.

But there was nothing. It was as if they had vanished from existence. Not that he would have been able to find Jack. Weretigers had brains far too animalistic for an Atlantean to track. Jack preferred it that way, ally or no. A red haze crossed his vision at the thought of Jack. Quinn's partner had deeper feelings for her than he admitted, and the thought of the two of them, always together, sliced through Alaric like a razor's edge through flesh.

Before he could destroy any more of the innocent fence, a shimmer of emotion not his own—anger mixed with pain—glanced a featherlight touch at the edge of his consciousness. The unique colors entwined in the emotional resonance told him the source instantly. It was Quinn. She was alive. The deep twilight, silvery gray, and wine red of her emotional aura were unique colors among those of any humans he'd ever encountered.

Relief, longing, and a joy so pure it burned seared through his veins. She was alive.

Quinn was *alive*.

And now he knew exactly where she was.

He drew power to him and blasted the door off of a stone mausoleum, shattering the heavy door into shards of shattered wood and the padlock into twisted bits of melted metal. She was alive, and no door or lock ever made would keep him from her, with all respect to the Denham family who'd carved their name into the lintel.

Not even bothering to transform into mist, he strode through the open doorway to the crypt, unsurprised to see a dark opening at the back. Crossing the stone floor, he offered a brief nod of respect to the long-dead inhabitants. At the opening, he found a steep wooden staircase that circled its way down into the dark.

Of course the vampires would have a home base in tunnels under a graveyard. Vampires were nothing if not predictably clichéd.

Alaric bared his teeth in a fierce approximation of a smile and headed down the stairs. He could feel Quinn, and she was down there. Neither dead bodies, nor vampires, nor the risen demons of the nine hells themselves would keep him from her.

She was an ally. She was his heart made flesh. She was his woman in some alternate reality where his own future was not bleak despair, solitude, and a lonely death.

He projected his thoughts to her along their unique mental connection. *Quinn, I come for you. Are you injured?*

Her thoughts came back to him, strong and holding not a hint of fear, but perhaps something of vulnerability. His warrior woman.

Alaric? Somehow I knew you'd come.

Are you injured? He sent the demand more urgently as he picked up his pace and started running at a blurring rate of speed. Her answer, when it came a few moments later, pushed him to run even faster, calling power as he ran.

Not yet, but Jack and Denal are. We're about ten feet away from that door, but it's guarded by vamps. Feel free to blow it out of its frame.

Straight ahead, Alaric saw the barricaded wooden door at the end of the tunnel. He called even more power and smashed through the door with approximately the speed and force of a tropical typhoon. Shattered boards imploded inward, and one had the impossible fortune to land dead center in the heart of one of the guardian vampires.

One down, only a dozen or so to go.

He scanned the layout of the room while still on the move and didn't stop until he had swept Quinn up from the floor where she was sitting, holding one arm at an awkward angle. He shot across the dark and dank room and gently lowered her slight body, which seemed to weigh almost nothing, until she stood with her back to the wall, as he called a shield of water to block her from any danger.

Whirling around to face the room, he noted Denal and Jack's positions. Jack was in human form, unconscious or dead, on the ground in a corner. Denal lay in a crumpled heap near Jack, but Alaric could at least sense Denal's life force, strong and steady.

Ten vamps crouched in varying stages of threat, fear, or obeisance, all oriented toward one very fashionably dressed vampire who leaned against a very old coffin in the center of the room.

"I find myself wounded that you did not invite me to your party, Quinn," Alaric said dryly, never taking his eyes off the vampires. "Furthermore, we will discuss the meaning of 'not injured' later."

Quinn laughed, although he could hear the edge of pain in

it. Her arm was definitely broken, but he had no time to heal it just yet. "Hey, you know me. Always a party girl."

The foppish vamp raised one eyebrow, then deliberately yawned and adjusted his French cuffs. "You must be another of the famed Atlantean warriors. Really, is Poseidon so weak that he chooses the likes of you? Not to mention that you send a little girl to do your dirty work."

Quinn tried to break free of the water shield protecting her, but it was designed as much to keep her in as to keep others out. Alaric knew her that well, at least.

"I'll little girl your *ass*, you—"

"Quinn," Alaric said quietly. "His aim is to ignite your temper. Perhaps you might allow me the chance to assist you this one time?"

"Fine, but you seem to be making a habit of it," she shot back. "We can discuss that later, too. Be my guest."

The vampire threw back his head and laughed. "Having trouble keeping your humans in line, are you? You Atlanteans must be desperate." He gestured toward Jack. "Working with shape-shifters, too, I see. This one stinks of the jungle, so I'm guessing he's no wolf, although we didn't give him time to demonstrate his . . . furry side."

Alaric called power and negligently bounced an energy sphere in his right palm, smiling as the vampires other than the leader cringed away from him. "You'd be another of Anubisa's minions? One wonders if she has a warehouse somewhere."

"Stupid Vampires R Us," Quinn said, snickering.

"I am Vonos, and I am the Primator," the vampire said, his fangs lengthening as he seemed to lose a little bit of his deliberate calm.

"Oh, yes. Another minion to replace Barrabas, after we . . . vetoed his political career," Alaric replied, rolling the energy sphere around in his fingers.

Vonos abruptly stood to his full height and lifted a leather-wrapped package that had evidently been on the coffin behind him. Holding it in the palm of one hand, he pulled the cord that tied the top of the package together and the edge of the leather wrappings fell open just a little.

"I find that now I'm bored with this conversation," Vonos said.

Before Alaric could react, Vonos aimed the top opening of the package toward the semicircle of vampires surrounding him. "You disobeyed us, and now you'll die. I've always favored a scorched-earth policy myself."

A blinding yellow light burst from the package with the intensity of a sun flare, and Alaric threw up an energy shield around Jack and Denal and widened the water shield protecting Quinn to include himself. With the speed of light, the searing radiance struck all of the vampires other than Vonos. Any vampire in the path of the light exploded into sizzling drops of acid which rained down all throughout the room. Luckily, the shields surrounding Quinn and the Atlanteans held firm and they were untouched.

Vonos whistled and then rewrapped the package and calmly surveyed the destruction. "For once, the rumors were not exaggerated. This gem can never fall into the wrong hands, now can it? I'd say it's so hard to get good help these days, but I do so hate clichés. Lovely to meet you, Atlantean. I look forward to our next encounter. Oh, and thanks for the little toy. This group has kept it secret from our goddess for hundreds of years, which is fairly annoying, but what can you do?"

He flashed a fang-filled smile of pure triumph at Alaric and held out the package as if to taunt him. "I believe your kind call it the Vampire's Bane? Fitting, isn't it?"

With that, the vampire lifted his arms in the air, still holding tightly to the package, and vanished.

A jolt of pure electricity raced through Alaric. If that were truly the fabled yellow diamond known as the Vampire's Bane, then it was one of the missing gems of the Trident. Conlan must know of this immediately.

Behind Alaric, Quinn stumbled and fell against his back, and all thoughts of strategy and gems and magic fled. In an instant, he had her in his arms again, cradling her against him, careful not to jostle her injured arm. He called power and sent the force of the healing blue-green energy into and through her until her bone was mended and every bruise and scrape on her body, no matter how minor, was repaired.

She opened her eyes as he withdrew the healing power from her. "That seems to be another habit of yours. I get broken, and you fix it. You're ruining my reputation as a tough rebel leader," she murmured.

"Ruined," he repeated, his voice rough as he remembered another conversation at another time. "I can do no other than protect you and see you made whole, with all apologies to the state of your reputation."

Her dark eyes were enormous in her pale face and, only for an instant, the searing heat of some powerful emotion burned in her gaze. Then she lowered her lashes and turned her head away from him. "Thank you again. I'm healed now; you can put me down."

He'd faced trial by fire with less reluctance than he did the act of releasing her. Every stolen moment, every purloined touch, was one he stored against the day—against the century—when he faced the nights alone, after her mortal life was long over.

The moment her feet touched the ground she stepped back and away from him, her hands clenched into fists at her sides. As she stared at the ground, he took the opportunity to drink in the sight of her. As always, he was slightly surprised that his heart had chosen her as his destined mate. He'd always thought some regal and serene beauty would eventually catch him in the grasp of his one great unrequited love.

But Quinn . . . was Quinn. She'd never known a day of serenity in her adult life, and as to her appearance? She was thinner than ever, all hard lines and angles, as if the battles of the rebellion drained not only her energy but her substance. Her short dark hair still looked like she cut it with the blade she kept in her pocket, and her clothes were ragged and threadbare, probably scrounged from some bin of discarded items.

By all the gods, she was beautiful.

It was the force of her personality, a fervor and charisma that shone out at him with all the strength and glory and brightness of her soul. Her soul called to his so powerfully that she was a beacon in the darkness of his existence.

Finally, she looked up at him and met his gaze, and she

gasped. He knew what must be visible on his face and therefore did not try to deny it. "You know," he rasped out. "You have always known, and you will always know that I am yours, and yet never can be. I am the most powerful high priest Poseidon has ever appointed, and yet I am too weak to hide the depths of my feelings for you."

He dropped to one knee before her and bowed his head. "Denounce me if you must, but I can no longer hide from this need I have to see you. To touch you. I will keep my distance as much as I am able to do so, but please allow me these brief glimpses of what I can never have."

Quinn made a strangled sound somewhere between laughter and a sob, and fell to her knees in front of him. "If only life were a fairy tale, then I could be your princess to rescue. I look into your eyes, and see the happy ending that I will never, ever deserve. The pain of seeing you can't be any worse than the pain of lying in my cold, empty bed, night after night. Longing for you. Wanting you. Needing you."

She lifted a hand to touch his cheek, but stopped with her fingers mere inches away from his skin. "Even now, when I should check on Jack and Denal, my mind and heart are filled with you. You override my duty, and you override my common sense."

Alaric knew the same was true for him, but he was far beyond caring. "And you are the emotion that brings music and light to my world, and an anguish almost beyond bearing to my heart."

In the corner, Jack stirred, and the motion broke the trance they'd fallen into, staring into the secrets of each other's eyes.

"I would give a century of my life for a single taste of your lips, but I will not defile the memory of your kiss with these surroundings."

She leaned in toward him, staring at his mouth, and for a moment all thought of honor fled and he didn't give a damn about Denal or Jack or that they were surrounded by the remains of dead vampires. He wanted her more than he wanted his next breath.

But Denal murmured some small pained sound and Quinn

blinked, then glanced over at Denal and leaned back. Oceans of regret filled her expression, but she pressed her lips together and stood, careful not to touch Alaric.

As if one touch would ignite the flames ready to leap into a conflagration between them.

He had no doubt that it might.

He, too, stood and moved toward Jack and Denal, relieved that they were both alive. Ashamed that he hadn't made certain of that fact earlier.

Devastated at the loss of her nearness.

As he called the energy of Poseidon to heal Denal and the tiger shifter, he also sent up a silent plea for the strength to resist the overwhelming desires of his very soul.

Then tried to pretend he didn't hear the god's mocking laughter.

Chapter 30

Northeastern Guatemala, the jungle

Justice opened his eyes when the sensation of falling through a vortex faded. Bright sunlight shone down in patches through a thick cover of trees. The verdant jungle surrounded them, lush with thickly crowding plant life.

For a few seconds, utter silence surrounded them, but then the native wildlife evidently decided he and Keely were no threat, despite their unusual arrival. Several species of birds trilled, sang, and scolded them for the disruption, and he heard at least one family group of monkeys chattering excitedly nearby.

Keely still clung to him, her eyes tightly closed, and he had no desire to move away from her. He slowly stroked her back from nape to waist, and the feel of her lithe body trembling against his was enough to harden his cock to the point of pain.

He had to have her. Soon. Desperate need shook through him, and he pulled her to him more tightly. He had never needed anything more than he needed the feel of her naked body underneath him, welcoming him as he plunged into her.

But he couldn't take the chance. His hold on the Nereid

was growing ever more precarious, and the Nereid's desires were darker. Rougher. Not anything he would ever do to Keely. His Keely.

She opened her eyes and looked up at him, and the awareness in her eyes nearly broke him in two. She knew he wanted her, in the way a woman always knows. One word from her, and he would be lost.

So he must prevent her from saying that one word.

"We're here," he said harshly, releasing her and stepping back. "Wherever here is."

She blinked up at him, and a flash of hurt crossed her features. But her words were strictly professional. "You were aiming for northeast Guatemala, and from the heat and the looks of this jungle, I think we made it."

They scanned their surroundings but saw nothing in view that would indicate any ruins or dig site. The fierce heat beat at them like a physical force; breathing was like drawing air through a wet blanket.

"Well," Keely said, shrugging, "it was probably too much to ask that you'd somehow transport us directly to the mural. You're just learning how to do this, after all. Think of the pancakes. At least you brought us to the jungle instead of bringing the jungle to us."

She smiled at him, and the force of it punched into his chest. He tensed, waiting for the Nereid to react, but the other half of his soul was either exhausted or in hiding and was blessedly silent for a change.

"Can you feel it? You said the Star of Artemis was of Nereid origin. Is there some way you can do some Atlantean or Nereid magic and scan the area? I know I'm probably reaching, but I have no idea exactly what you can do. If there's some way we can orient ourselves toward San Bartolo and get an idea of how far away it is, that would be a good thing. Especially since we have no food or water. It's somewhere between the high nineties and maybe a hundred and five degrees, I'd guess, and we'll get dehydrated fast."

Justice nodded and tried to send his senses out into the jungle to detect the Star of Artemis. But it didn't work. Every bit of power he possessed, both Atlantean and Nereid, had been drained over the past few days.

Calling on every ounce of stubbornness he had, he pushed harder. Forced his mind to wring reserves of power he'd never used before and channel it to his purposes. He felt something in his brain twist and buckle, and a thundering headache caught his skull in a vise grip. But underneath the pain a tiny pulse of awareness flickered. Somehow, he knew what it was.

"I found it," he told Keely. "I found the Star, and I know where we have to go. It's going to be quite a walk, but we can probably make it in a day or so, unless my reserves of energy come back sooner and I can use the matter transference technique again."

Keely stared at him steadily, as though taking his measure. Whatever she saw evidently reassured her, because she nodded decisively. "I've walked through jungles before, but never without drinking water. We'll have to take it slow and easy until you get your strength back and can at least bring us some water bottles and something to eat."

"I should be able to do something about the water soon," he said confidently, in spite of the fact he had no idea how soon his powers would replenish—if ever. Keely didn't need to know how unsure he was of the Nereid magics. She had enough courage for any warrior, but there was no need to continue to test it.

She started walking, then stopped suddenly and laughed. "I guess it would help if you told me which way we're headed. Also, when it comes to those water bottles, be careful not to teleport them from the packs of some poor, unsuspecting hikers or tourists who will be left freaking out, wondering what in the heck happened to their water."

He pointed toward the faint beacon of magic that still flickered faintly in his mind. "The Star lies in that direction. As to the other, I will do my best," he said, wondering when the sound of her laughter had become more beautiful to him than any music. He surreptitiously adjusted his pants so walking would be less uncomfortable and started forward, resolutely pushing all thoughts of Keely, naked, out of his mind.

He glanced back at her, and caught his breath at the excitement glowing in her green eyes. Okay, he'd at least try to push *most* thoughts of Keely, naked, out of his mind.

As he'd told her before, he was a guy, after all.

∽——∾

Three hours later, Keely called a halt. She was tough, and she'd vowed to herself to keep up without complaint, but hiking any farther with no water was suicidal and she was no idiot. In the fierce, furnace-room heat of the jungle, moisture was being lost from their bodies at a rapid rate. Maybe Atlanteans, being sort of water people, could handle it better than mere humans, but she needed a rest.

Also, she was tired of staring at his backside as he led the way through the thick vegetation. Not that he didn't have a very fine backside. Broad shoulders tapered down to his narrow waist, not to mention that tantalizing braid of his that she really, really wanted to loosen so she could run her fingers through those long strands of silky hair. His butt was so firm and muscular that she'd entertained brief fantasies of biting it, about an hour or so back, when she'd still had the energy for that sort of thing.

Wonder how the tough Atlantean warrior would have responded to that? She laughed out loud, and he whirled around with one of those bursts of inhuman speed and stared at her.

"What is it?"

"Justice, I need a break. In the shade, preferably."

"Why is that funny?" He stared at her suspiciously. "What are you plotting?"

She clamped her lips together, but the laughter escaped anyway. "Oh, trust me, you don't want to know. Anyway, we need to stop. I can tell I'm getting dehydrated, and we're walking through the hottest part of the day. I recommend we find some shade and wait out the afternoon until it's cooler this evening."

He moved again in another blurred flash of speed and suddenly he was standing near inches away from her. "I'm so sorry. I was lost in contemplation of our options and our ultimate goal and didn't spare a thought for how you were faring. Please accept my apologies for my thoughtlessness."

But his nearness played havoc with her wits, and she didn't really catch the meaning of his words, just stood there staring up at him wishing foolish things. Wishing her life hadn't turned into an adventure novel. Wishing he would just kiss her.

Wishing she was the type of woman brave enough to just kiss him.

"I . . . you . . . what?"

"Sorry. We Atlanteans tend to drop back into formal speak in tense situations," he said wryly. "Translation: I'm an idiot. We should've stopped sooner. There seems to be some shade up ahead under that overhang."

Keely gave herself a mental slap and nodded briskly. "Right. Shade. Ahead. Great." She took off at a determined march, and he fell into step beside her.

A grin quirked at the edges of those beautifully sculpted lips of his. "Is there any reason you seem to have lost the use of verbs?"

The low, husky tone of his voice sizzled across her nerve endings, and suddenly the jungle was a whole lot hotter than before. "I have a strict 'no verbs in jungles' policy, of course. If we stay here much longer, adjectives will go by the wayside next," she said, flashing an innocent smile. The kind of smile that said "nobody here wants to rip your shirt off and lick your bare chest."

She hoped.

What was wrong with her? It must be some weird kind of jungle pheromones. Mix one Atlantean with one crushingly hot jungle and you get mad sexual desire. Of course it didn't hurt that he was the hottest man she'd ever seen in her life. The memory of Justice in the cavern, naked and dripping wet, flashed into her mind, and her mouth dried out even further than mere lack of water had caused.

Great. She'd die in the Guatemalan jungle of dehydration brought on by sexual fantasies. Wonder how they'd word *that* on her tombstone.

She reached the overhang a few paces ahead of him. It was a niche carved into the side of a small hill, and it smelled a little musky, like animals had made it a home over the years. It didn't seem to hold any now, but it stretched farther back into the hill than she'd expected and she couldn't see all that far back into the darkened interior.

Justice put a restraining hand on her arm. "I'll enter first and ensure that no animals are inside and jealous of their territory."

She swept her arm out in a "go ahead" gesture. "Be my guest, sword guy. I'll just wait here at the side, in case something comes barreling out."

He grinned at her and suddenly bent down and pressed a kiss on her lips. "You continually surprise me. Every time I expect you to disagree with me, you say something practical. Every time I expect you to go along without question, you tell me why I'm wrong. Life will never be boring with you, will it, Dr. Keely McDermott?"

With that, he entered the small cave, leaving her to stand there, fingers pressed to her lips, wondering how a future life with her had become such a firm assumption in his mind.

Wondering why the idea of it didn't scare her one bit.

"It's clear, but there's an opening back here and you're going to want to take a look," he called out to her. "I'd say we made a discovery, but it's obvious that somebody was in here before."

She bent a little to enter the cave, and was relieved to find that it opened up into a room with a fairly high ceiling. Looking around, she discovered something else.

It was no cave.

The walls were just that—walls—made of stone. They'd found an ancient building of some kind, possibly even a Mayan temple or pyramid, considering the height of the small hill.

The familiar chill raced up her spine. A piece of history that very few had seen in perhaps thousands of years lay before her. *This* was what she lived for—what she needed as much as she needed water to drink. She automatically reached for her pack, only to remember that it was safely ensconced in her room back in Atlantis.

Where it didn't do her a damn bit of good.

Biting off a few choice words, she followed the wall to a doorway carved into the back of the room. A faint blue-green glow emanated from the doorway.

"Justice? Is that you?"

"I've recovered enough of my strength to give us a little light, Keely. You're going to want to see this."

She followed the light and the sound of his voice into the chamber and stopped, stunned. Three of the four walls were uncovered from the dirt and vegetation that covered the fourth, clearly the product of centuries of neglect. On each of the three walls, a mural spread in vivid, dramatic colors.

"This isn't San Bartolo, but this is definitely another rendering of the *Popol Wuh*," she said. "Oh, Justice, why wasn't this reported? This is such an important find!"

He crossed to stand next to her and she realized the light came from a glowing sphere that floated over the palm of his hand. He held it up like a lantern and leaned in to study the first wall with her. "The *Popol Wuh*?"

"It's the Mayan creation myth. Their creator, K'ucumatz, the mother and father of all life, first fashioned men from clay or mud. But they were weak and dissolved in water, like this. Do you see this first image of the man figure dissolving in the river?"

He nodded and pointed to the next image, sounding almost as excited as she was by the discovery. "And this? The tree being carved into a man?"

She nodded, her hand reaching of its own volition to touch her fish carving. "Yes, K'ucumatz tried next to make men out of wood, but they had no hearts or minds, so they couldn't praise their creator. That never flies with gods, you know."

She smiled at him, but he was lost in contemplation of the image. "I have sometimes carved figures that almost seemed as if they could step out of my hand and fly or swim or run away," he murmured. "But of course they had no hearts or minds, either."

Keely thought of all the tough times that her carving, and the visions of Justice, had helped her through over the years. "I've seen your carvings, and I wouldn't be so sure of that."

He turned to face her, holding the energy sphere up. She could see every detail of his features in the softly glowing light and realized that somehow, in such a short time, her heart had memorized his face. She caught her breath, afraid of what her own expression might reveal to him.

He studied her for a moment, then shook his head. "I don't understand. How can you have seen my carvings? I give them away as soon as I finish them."

Her hand tightened on the fish. She wanted to tell him, wanted to let him know how much he'd meant to her over the years. But something stopped her. Some remnant of rational Keely before she'd fallen through the looking glass.

They needed to find water. They needed to find the Star of Artemis and use it in whatever way they could to help Justice heal his fractured mind.

Then she could tell him amusing stories about a small wooden fish and be careful not to let on just how pathetic she was that she'd let a simple carving and visions of a long-ago warrior take on such importance in her life.

She forced her fingers to release the carving and dropped it beneath the neck of her shirt again. "I don't know. I'm just hot and tired and probably remembering something Liam said to me about carvings," she said, forcing a laugh. "Anyway, look at this. The final, and successful, attempt was when K'ucumatz mixed white and yellow maize—corn—to make the flesh and blood of humans. This time it worked. One of the most important figures in the Mayan culture is the maize god, which you see on that wall."

He studied the second wall, luckily distracted from her remarks about his carvings. "This is similar to the maize god you told us about in the mural with Anubisa in it?"

"Yes! Yes, it's clearly from the same artist or group of artists. I'm almost sure of it. Of course, without side-by-side comparison of photographs, I can't be—" She swayed a little, suddenly overcome by a wave of dizziness, and started panting, unable to catch her breath.

He caught her with one strong arm around her waist. "Keely? You are unwell?"

She pushed her hair away from her face and tried to

breathe, but the heat and dehydration, probably combined with the events of the past few days, had taken their toll. He released the energy sphere, lifted her into his arms, and moved them both out of the chamber and back to the mouth of the cave, where the outside air was much fresher.

She leaned over, pulling in slow, steady breaths, until the dizziness and hyperventilation passed. "I'm fine," she said finally. "Just really could use some water."

Unexpectedly, he smiled. "Although the Nereid still hides from me, or is recovering from the use of so much power, I find that my Atlantean gifts are returning. If water is what you want, my Keely, then water you shall have."

He strode outside and stopped in the middle of the clearing, legs braced apart and arms held up in the air. The sunlight shone down on him as if he were some primitive god himself, returned to his people and ready to accept their worshipful homage. He was beautiful and stern and primal, and something deep inside her stirred, shaken and moved by the sight of him. Her breasts tingled and her nipples hardened, craving his touch, and her thighs tightened as liquid heat pooled in her center, readying her for him like some ancient virgin to be sacrificed to a lusty god.

Her face flamed at the thought and she tried to remind herself of the biological imperative that caused women to be attracted to powerful men in dangerous situations. She was a scientist. She of all women couldn't fall prey to something so primal.

Even as she tried to resist the siren call of his intense sexuality, he lowered his gaze from the sky and stared straight into her eyes. His own had darkened to black with blue-green flames dancing in the exact centers of his pupils. "Poseidon, hear me," he called out in a voice filled with tempest-tossed waves and gale-force winds, never taking his gaze from her. "Bring water to me that it may give life and health to my woman."

"I'm not your woman," she whispered, but this time even she didn't believe it. At that moment, with winds circling Justice like a typhoon, whipping through the clearing to center on him, energy crackling around him like miniature lightning bolts in shades of silver, blue, and green, she could deny him nothing.

"For Poseidon," he roared, throwing back his head. Somehow his braid had loosened, and long strands of hair whipped around his face and shoulders; blues all the spectrum of possibility caught in the strands of his hair flew in the wind as it danced to his call.

She looked up, following his gaze, unable to doubt him for even an instant. He had called for water, so it would come. She knew it, and when the swirling, twirling coils of crystal-clear water tumbled through the air toward him, she laughed with delighted joy.

"Come to me, Keely," he said, and the heat in his eyes seared through her until she wanted to tear off her clothes and throw herself on the ground in front of him, a pagan offering to be taken right there in the downpour that he had created. But instead she stumbled forward, hands clenched at her sides, until she stood a mere breath away from him.

He laughed down at her and shouted out another word, a beautiful word, a word she did not know. The water turned into a spring shower, falling onto them and into their open mouths and down their necks and soaking into their filthy clothes.

Keely closed her eyes and turned her face up to the rain and laughed, drinking in as much of the clean, sweet-tasting water as she could. It was the purest water she'd ever tasted. Purer than mountain spring water, purer than the most expensive bottled water.

She swallowed as fast as the rain fell into her mouth and then, finally sated, she opened her eyes and smiled up at him, raindrops clinging to her eyelashes. "That was amazing! You can do that whenever you want? Wow, that would solve so many—" She fell silent, her torrent of words failing at the intent way he stared at her mouth, as if he must taste her or die.

His mouth came down on hers, and he pulled her so tightly against him that the heat of his body steamed against her through their wet clothes. There was nothing gentle in it; it was a kiss of claiming, desperate wanting, and need. She murmured a sound, lost in his mouth, and his hands clenched on her skin, pulling her tighter, still. His muscular body shuddered violently against hers and she drew back, alarmed, and looked up at him.

He clenched his jaw shut and tightened his grip on her even more, until it seemed that every inch of her body was touching his. "I need you, Keely. I have to have you right now. Please," he said in a low and guttural voice that shook with the force of the passion behind it. Then he loosened his hold a fraction and dropped his head, inhaling deep gulps of air. "No. We can't. I'm afraid that the Nereid will take over. You must tell me no."

The lightning began to shoot through the air again, lighting up the still-falling rain with its thunderous cracks and silvery blue glow. Behind and above the rain, she could see the sun, still shining brightly in a clear sky. No cloud had anything to do with this downpour, and no other woman had anything to do with his desperate need.

It was all for her. Only for her. The realization and the heat flamed through her, making her womb clench and her knees buckle. He was holding her so tightly that it didn't matter, though. She couldn't fall. He was there for her.

Still waiting for an answer. A desperate plea in his eyes, but whether it was for her to say yes or no she couldn't tell.

"Yes," she said, jumping into the abyss. "I want you, too. Together we'll tame your other half."

He lifted her into the air and shouted out his joy, swinging her around in the middle of the raging Atlantean storm. Then he pulled her close again and bent his head until his lips were a breath away from hers.

"Together. We can do this together. Kiss me, Keely. Kiss me so that I can know you want this as much as I do."

No power on earth could have stopped her—not reason, not logic, not any thought for what the future might hold. She needed him more than she needed water or air and for once in her life she was going to take exactly what she wanted, consequences be damned. She caught his face in her hands and smiled.

Then she kissed him.

Chapter 31

Keely's soft, tentative kiss touched Justice so deeply that he felt as though his soul were being torn in two. Half of him wanted nothing more than to tear her clothes from her body and make love to her for hours, while the other, more honorable half of him wanted to run and hide somewhere far from her.

Far from temptation.

Far from the danger that the Nereid would take over and harm her.

I am part of you, the Nereid whispered in his mind. *The sooner you come to terms with that, the sooner we can join forces to be more powerful than ever you have dreamed.*

Justice lifted his head from Keely's and stared down at her. "I want you more than I have ever wanted any woman. But—"

Take her, you slug-ridden bottom feeder! You know you want to fuck her until she screams our name.

"No!" he shouted.

Keely's puzzled look turned to one of understanding. "He's fighting you, isn't he?"

"Yes. He wants you as much as I do, but in darker ways. I cannot—I'm not sure I can control him," Justice admitted.

Keely's smile, though tremulous, held a wealth of trust that humbled him. "Tell him . . . no. Let me tell him—tell you both. I want you. All of you. You don't need to be rough or overpower me. Just make love to me. Please."

The Nereid's angry, driving need faltered, turning into confusion. *How can she want me? Even you, who are the other half of my soul, do not want me.*

Justice gave the question the careful consideration that it deserved, then responded out loud so that Keely could hear him, too. "Perhaps I am wrong in this. Perhaps I need to accept that we are both parts of the same whole."

Dark laughter rang in his mind. *If we get her, I am willing to try anything.*

Then somehow, some way, something changed. For the first time in his life, Justice felt—even without his mental shields—a tentative truce. A kind of peace settled over him and his mind achieved a form of calm it had never known.

Keely looked up at him, a question in her eyes.

"Yes," he said, his voice husky. "Yes, both of us—both of *me*—all of me wants you."

He bent his head and kissed her, holding nothing back, and the vortex opened around him. Her mouth tasted like honey and home and everything he'd ever wanted. His tongue dove in and he took, feasted, drank her mouth and lips. He rained kisses on her cheeks, nose, and forehead the way he'd caused water to shower down on her before.

The wonder of her touch humbled him. The touch of her lips inflamed him. The feel of her body tightened his own almost to pain. His cock hardened until he thought he would explode from the merest touch. He wanted her; he needed her. She would become his and remain his forever.

"You are mine, Keely," he said, desperate for her to admit it. "My vision quest has shown me, and the flame of Poseidon you've seen in my eyes confirmed it. Your soul is the destined mate to mine."

She pulled back a little, but he tightened his arms. He would never let her go. She had to see that, had to understand it.

"Justice, this is too much. I want you, too. I've never felt like this before. But can't we talk about destiny and vision quests later?" She twined her arms around his neck and lifted her face to his, and her silken brows were drawn together in frustration. "I can't believe I'm saying this, but can't we get naked now and talk about the future later?"

He couldn't help it. He shouted out a laugh. "Your wish is ever my command, lady. But first, we need to take care of this."

He released her and removed his sword and placed it on the ground, then stripped off his clothes, tossing them away from him so fast that he had no idea where they landed. When he finally stood naked in front of her, he smiled. "Now I plan to do the same thing to you."

Keely stared at Justice and remembered her offhand comment about statues come to life. His powerful body, sculpted in long lines and perfect, muscular curves, was enough to make her gasp. His erection was as big as the rest of him and, as he looked at her, it bobbed against his abdomen, very visual evidence that he wanted her.

Nothing was more potent than the knowledge of being truly desired, and Keely's nipples hardened until the lace of her bra was unbearable pressure against them. Her muscles jerked in a spasm of delight and her thighs tightened against the heat flooding her core. "You—" Her mouth was too dry to get the words out, so she tried again. "You plan to throw my clothes all across the jungle?"

He flashed that very wicked smile and started toward her, slowly stalking her as any predator would stalk his prey. A fierce, almost feral heat burned in his eyes and she caught her breath at his plain intent. He wanted her, and he was going to take her. He was pure dominant alpha male, and she wanted him like she'd never wanted anything or anyone before.

When he reached her, he pulled her to him and kissed her with such possessiveness that she felt the heat of it sear through her to her soul. His tongue dove into her mouth and he kissed her as though he would die if he didn't. He twined his fingers in her hair, his hand cupping the back of her head, and drew her to him more tightly, until not even a breath of air could have fit between them.

Passion soared through her; heat and pure crazed desire threatened to buckle her knees. "More," she breathed against his lips. "I need more of you."

He put his hand on her butt and pulled her closer so that his penis fit between her legs and the hard bulge of it drove her further into wanting and need. "Now?" he asked.

"Now, now, now," she said, beyond embarrassment or reason.

In one smooth movement, he whipped her shirt up and over her head and tossed it aside, and then bent his head to look at her.

And she froze—she'd forgotten the carving.

Justice stared down at Keely's beautiful breasts, barely covered by scraps of lace, her nipples jutting out and making him want nothing more than to taste them, bite them, suck on them. Her necklace hung down in her pale, lovely cleavage as if drawing his eye. The pendant was a wooden carving of . . . a fish.

His fish. One he'd carved hundreds of years ago.

He lifted it and examined it, sure he must be mistaken. But there was no mistake. "This is mine. But how is that possible?"

Keely bit her lip and a pink flush heated her cheeks. "I meant to tell you about that. I found it several years ago and I—well, I had a vision of you. Carving it. By a fire. I thought you were a warrior from centuries ago, and you, well, *it*, sort of became my talisman. Someone I could think of when times were difficult."

He stared into her eyes as the truth of her confession slammed into his heart. She'd had a vision quest of her own— of him. She'd relied on *him*.

"You are mine, Keely McDermott," he said, his voice coming out as little more than a growl. "I'm going to have you right now."

He stripped off the rest of her clothes in seconds and took a moment to hold her at arms' length and marvel at the glory of her body. Lithe and toned, she was no hothouse flower but a woman who used her body and treated it well.

"I love your legs," he murmured.

"Thank you, I—"

"I need them to be wrapped around my waist."

She gasped a little and he caught her lips with his own again and pulled her up so he could feel all of her against his body. She lifted her legs and wrapped them around him and he raised her even higher, his hands supporting her wonderful ass, until his cock was centered under her warm, wet center.

"I need you now, Keely," he said, pushing against her just a little, straining every muscle to force himself to wait.

"I need you, too." She kissed him and he drove into her as far as he would go, thrusting his cock into her tight, wet heat, feeling her sheath clinging to him and clasping him until he was sure he would explode right away like some untried youngling.

Keely cried out at the feel of him. His thickness filled her, stretching her so much that her nerve endings seared with a heady combination of pain and pleasure. But she was so wet from wanting him that her body accommodated his length and width and bucked wildly against him, needing more.

Needing him to move.

"Don't stop," she panted, lifting herself up and sliding back down on the velvet-encased steel of his penis. He was so hard and so long that he touched some spot deep inside her that drove her crazy. "Please, more."

He devoured her mouth with hot, hard kisses as he thrust into her deeper and harder, rocking into a rhythm that made her whimper in delirious need. Heat and sheer urgent hunger shot through her until she was desperate for him, desperate to come, desperate to sate the almost unbearable need.

She bit his neck, driven beyond reason, and he growled something in Atlantean, then plunged into her so deeply that she cried out, so close to the edge that she almost couldn't bear it.

He stopped, holding her in place, buried inside her, and held still until she looked up at him, dazed and barely coherent. "What? Why did you stop?"

An expression of sheer masculine triumph swept over his face and something feral glittered in his eyes. "Mine. Tell me.

Tell me you're mine, and I'll fuck you until you scream my name."

The crudeness of his words thrilled through her even as she recognized what he was doing. Laying a claim. Asserting his possession. Forcing her to admit, finally, that she was his woman.

But, ultimately, giving her the choice. She could refuse.

Something in her heart twisted at the thought. No, she couldn't. Couldn't refuse. As she looked into his eyes, which now held wariness and perhaps the beginnings of pain as the moment stretched out between them, she knew what she had to do.

Admit the truth, no matter the consequences.

She raised her head to meet his gaze. "Yes. I'm yours."

He shouted out his triumph and then kissed her again, thrusting into her body again with even more power than before. When he raised his head, she could barely breathe over the rising intensity that threatened to explode in every inch of her body.

"And you're mine," she managed to gasp out.

"Always," he said. "Always, *mi amara*."

Then he made good on his promise and drove into her over and over until she came, screaming his name.

Justice shuddered at the strangely erotic feel of Keely's gloved hands digging into his shoulders as her entire body tightened around him. Her legs were clamped around his waist like a vise, and she exploded, screaming out his name, her body clasping his cock in a series of spasms so intense that he had no hope of outlasting her. He pushed into her as far as he could and his release took him like a tidal wave, shooting out of him with more power than he'd ever experienced. She kept coming, shaking with her orgasms, and every tremor squeezed more and more out of his cock. He was sure his knees would give out from the sheer ecstasy of it, but he'd be damned if he'd go down without a fight. He braced his legs and pulled her even more closely to him.

And then the world itself exploded around them, and he fell into a whirlwind of colors. Greens and golds swirled around him. Somehow he knew that he was seeing her aura—seeing her true self. He marveled at the rich, bright beauty of it, and then he fell into her soul.

Everything that she was and everything that she'd experienced flashed through him with a burning fury. He saw her painful childhood; felt the agony of a small child whose parents thought her a freak. Burned with impotent fury against parents who could hurt their own child in such a way.

He saw her goodness and enormous capacity for generosity, felt her wounded in a thousand ways over the years as unfeeling friends and colleagues painted her different. An outsider.

His heart ripped apart when he felt her anguish over the man who'd left her, and silently he vowed to find the bastard and rip his limbs off of him. Slowly.

Knew instantly that Keely would hate it if he did so. She was light and goodness and caring, the bright side of the moon, in contrast to the dark well of his own soul. He fell and fell, into the corners of her soul, and into love. She was his, and he would never, ever let her escape from him.

Keely cried out as the spasms of aftershocks continued to rip through her body. She'd never had an orgasm so powerful or one that had lasted so long and she was almost afraid of the intensity of it. It was too fierce, too strong; it opened her up too much. She knew better.

Opening up only gave someone the opportunity to reject her.

Justice's big body shook with the force of his release and she came again from the feel of it, clinging to him, holding him. Wanting him never to let her go. She felt wetness on her cheeks and realized she was crying, not from pain or sadness but from the power of the moment. She started to say something— anything—to try to find her way back from the earth-shattering intimacy, but then the ground opened up beneath her and she fell into the stars.

It was as if a door in his soul opened up and ushered her into his very essence. Everything she'd seen before in her visions of him—and much, much more—enveloped and enfolded her until she was bathing in the stream of his consciousness. She saw his fierce honor and pride, and his love for his family, even though it was a love he'd never allowed himself to feel. But, more than anything else, she felt his emotion for her.

It was love, and lust, and need, all wrapped up together and blazing in flaming blues and silver. A conflagration of emotion, all of it directed toward her. And, almost unnoticeable, a darker hue in the center. A dangerous presence inside the colors of his soul.

The Nereid.

Is that you? she hesitantly thought the question. *You are part of him, you know.*

Am I? came the sardonic response. *Yet you love him and fear me.*

Love? She wanted to protest but the soul allowed for no prevarication. Only for the barest of unvarnished truths.

Yes, love, she admitted. *You are part of him, so I love you, too.*

A hesitation flowed through the colors toward her, but then a sense of denial. *No. You could not love me, for I don't deal in love. I will eventually overpower him, and I will take you in every way that I like.*

He flashed scenes at her, scenes of raw, furious sex. Images of her submitting to him in every way possible.

She recoiled, but then the warmth of Justice's colors surrounded her and supported her again and she sent back images of her own to the Nereid part of his soul. *I will take you, as well,* she told him and sent him thoughts of warm and gentle lovemaking, interspersed with deliberately provocative scenes of wild and unrestrained passion.

His aggression changed, tumbled into fierce desire, and then became joy.

Yes, we will have each other, the Nereid said.

Yes, I am yours as much as you are mine, Justice said.

Their voices swirled together in the colors of Justice's soul, and Keely laughed and cried and crashed through her last fragile bit of hesitation into love.

Finally, finally coming back to some sense of reality, she

realized she was still clasped in his arms and his penis was still inside her. She lifted her head from his shoulder and started laughing. "We're stark naked in the middle of the jungle. This is something that has never happened to me before on any expedition. Not to mention that I have no idea how your legs are still holding both of us up."

He gently lifted her just a little ways and she felt his penis hardening again as he slid her back down his shaft. "Strong legs from long years of warrior training will serve me well, because I find I need you again."

She laughed again and pulled off her gloves. "I kind of forgot these before."

He bent his head and stared intently at her breasts, and heat rose in Keely again, shocking her since she would have guessed she wouldn't have the strength to feel desire again for at least a week.

"How is it that I did not take the time to taste these lovely breasts?" he murmured, and then lifted her high enough that only the very tip of him was still inside her. As she squirmed, wanting him, needing him back, he caught her nipple in his mouth and sucked hard.

Keely cried out, and her hot cream bathed the head of his cock. He needed her again and again and again; he would never have enough. He lifted his head long enough to spot a pile of their clothes and strode over to it, still holding her, his cock thrusting deeper with every step. Then he pulled out just long enough to lay her gently down on the clothes, rearranging them so that her delicate skin wasn't touching the vegetation. She stared up at him, her lovely emerald eyes glazed with passion, and he wondered for an instant if he were caught in some magical spell where every dream he'd ever had was coming true in the form of this lovely human.

If dream or fantasy, he decided he didn't care. She'd touched his very soul and tamed the Nereid side of him, and he needed no reality except the one where he was so far inside her she could never forget him.

He lifted her knees, positioned the head of his cock at her glistening entrance, and drove himself home, sheathing himself to the hilt until his sac smacked into her lovely ass and she cried out. Resting his weight on one forearm, he reached between their bodies and touched her, rubbed her own slickness against the center of her nerve endings until she cried out again. "I can't take any more," she said, panting and whipping her head from side to side. "Justice, it's too much. Too much pleasure."

"Never," he said, entranced by the way her nipples had hardened into two rosy peaks. "Never too much."

She lifted her hips, matching every stroke, making delicious moaning sounds that drove him insane with hunger, and he rode her—they rode each other—in a frenzied rhythm. He felt the exact moment her body tightened around his and knew she was on the edge, so he thrust harder and faster, murmuring endearments to her in a stream of frantic Atlantean. She had to know how much he wanted her.

How much he needed her.

This time, he yelled *her* name as he came, shuddering with her in a blinding explosion of power and heat and color that drove him to the edge of consciousness. As he collapsed, careful to roll to the side a little and avoid crushing her, he started laughing. "I think you may have accomplished what no enemy has been able to do in all these centuries. I think you've killed me."

She lay panting, holding him tightly. Finally she caught her breath and she, too, started laughing. "That makes two of us. If it's always like this, we're in trouble."

Her laughter faded and she turned her head to look into his eyes. "What was that with the colors? Justice, I . . . I felt like I was inside your soul."

"It was the soul-meld, Keely. The soul-meld is a gift from Poseidon and allows an Atlantean and his true mate to see inside each other's souls. When you said you saw the flame of Poseidon—the blue-green flame—in my eyes, I knew. The soul-meld brands a warrior's heart as permanently as the mark of Poseidon marks our bodies."

She traced the brand on his arm. "This? What does it mean?"

"Poseidon's Trident bisects the circle representing all the peoples of the world. The triangle is for the pyramid of knowledge from the ancients. All of Poseidon's warriors bear this mark as testimony to our vow to serve Poseidon and protect humanity."

She kissed the mark and then his chest, nestling against him for a moment. Then she pulled away from him and sat up.

"You know, I hate to be mundane at a time like this, but we're in the jungle with no clothes on, and there are bugs. I really, really don't want bug bites on my butt."

He blinked at her, stunned by her matter-of-fact practicality, then started laughing again. "Not to mention any moment your stomach is going to rumble, isn't it?"

She grinned. "Well, now that you mention it . . ."

Chapter 32

He called water again and they showered, unable to keep from touching each other. Keely knew from what she'd seen in Justice's soul that the truce with the Nereid was temporary. He'd have to find a more permanent way to incorporate both sides of himself into a cohesive whole. Maybe the Star of Artemis really could help with that.

She felt like she was pinning all her hopes on a magic rock, which was way out there in fairy-tale land. But, as she kept reminding herself, she'd just traveled through space and time to the Guatemalan jungle with an Atlantean. Hard to stay in denial after that.

"We need to go," she said finally, after they were both dressed.

He kissed her until she was breathless and then released her, a look of grim resolve on his face. "Yes, we do. We need to find the Star of Artemis for far greater reasons than merely my own. Although I do feel some hope for the future since the glory of your lovemaking has tamed even the Nereid inside me."

She felt the heat climb into her cheeks. "You're pretty glorious yourself, but if we start talking about lovemaking, we'll never get out of this patch of jungle."

He closed his eyes and held his hands up into the air, and she knew he was using his senses to reach out and try to feel the Star of Artemis again. It only took a few seconds.

"I feel it. Its call is stronger now. I must be gaining strength." He pointed in a northeast direction. "It's coming from there."

She nodded, hoping her shaky legs would carry her on another long walk. Her entire body felt limp and sore in unusual places after their intense lovemaking. She just hoped there wouldn't be chafing.

She laughed out loud. Practical Keely was right. Justice would crack up if he heard her thoughts now. He turned and raised a quizzical eyebrow, which only made her laugh harder. "Nothing. Just a random thought. Lead on, then. It's going to be a long, hot walk."

"We're not walking," he said, beckoning to her. "We're traveling in style. Atlantean style."

She could only watch, dazzled, as he transformed into a sparkling rainbow of mist that somehow had form and substance enough to lift her into the air.

We're going to fly, he said in her mind, and she soared up through the canopy of trees on a magical carpet of water droplets that contained the shape and consciousness of the man she'd just held inside her body.

Magic rocks would seem mundane after this.

They flew over the jungle, skimming the treetops like a child's fantasy of flight. Keely gasped at the sight of fiercely scolding monkeys and laughed in delight at the brightly colored birds who flew along with them, clearly wondering what kind of new strange cousin shared their skies.

"Archaeology was never as much fun as this before," she sang out, hoping he could understand her in that state, somehow sure that he could. She couldn't take in everything fast enough, and her head whipped back and forth on her neck so rapidly as she gazed around that she'd probably give herself whiplash.

We're very nearly there.

She nodded absently, staring down through an opening between treetops at a sleek jaguar pair crossing the ground, fluid muscles moving under their dappled coats. "They're so beautiful."

Beautiful and deadly, he said in her mind.

"Rather like you," she replied, smiling.

In retaliation, he tossed her into the air so that for a moment she was falling, unsupported, shrieking with surprise, but he caught her again so quickly she never had a chance to become afraid. "Now that's just mean," she scolded. "Wait till I get a chance to—"

The sight of the smoke stopped her midsentence. Thick clouds of rolling, ominous black smoke a little ways in front of them. Finding the Star might not be as simple as they'd hoped.

The jungle was burning.

∽∽∽

Justice smelled the smoke before he saw it. He immediately took them back down to the ground, a safe distance from the jaguar pair, and rematerialized. Automatically, his hand checked to see that his sword had made the transition with him. Reassured, he pulled it from its sheath.

"Keely, I need for you to stay here while I check it out."

She shook her head. "That's not happening. The two of us will investigate together."

He glared down at her, giving her the fierce look that had caused many warriors to quail before him. "This is my area of expertise, Dr. McDermott. You will do as I say and stay out of the path of danger."

The obstinate set to her jaw told him that he didn't intimidate her in the slightest. By all the gods, she was magnificent.

"Yes, well, my area of expertise involves not getting myself killed on expeditions," she snapped. "You're the one with the fighting skills and the weapons. I'm the one who is not going to wait alone for you here, in the path of who knows how many hungry jaguars or raiding mobs of criminals. The State Department doesn't issue travel warnings about Guatemala for no reason, you know. This is a lovely country with wonderful people, but it holds real danger, and I don't even have my passport with me to back up my identity."

She was right. He hated to admit it, but to leave her there might expose her to even more danger than to take her with him. "Fine, but you do exactly what I say when I say it. I will be very unhappy with anyone who puts you in any danger, and that includes you."

She lifted her chin. "I'm not an idiot or a stupid coed from a cheap horror flick. I'm not going to run screaming into the arms of the guy with the chain saw. I'll do what you say, as long as it makes sense."

He wanted to shake some sense into her. He wanted to kiss the sense *out* of her. He'd finally found his true mate, and she was annoying the *miertus* out of him.

"Fine. Let's go. Stay behind me." He took off, nearly running. Something about that smoke raised a sense of dread in his gut. He'd seen too many burning battlefields, too many towns and villages razed by predators intent on herding the humans into the waiting jaws of vampires and shape-shifters.

She'd said vampires had taken over the San Bartolo site. Maybe they'd decided to expand their territory. After all, a formerly lost Mayan temple wouldn't offer them any chances to feed, but a Guatemalan village, cut off from any governmental protection, would.

He turned, still running, and lifted Keely into his arms. They'd move faster this way, and suddenly he had an urgent need for speed.

Chapter 33

Keely stared in shock at the scene that lay before them when Justice stopped running and put her down. A small village—or what was left of the village—lay in ruins, smoldering and still burning in places.

"What happened here?" she whispered.

"More like *who* happened here, I'd guess," Justice said flatly, his fury-darkened eyes scanning the area. "It's a common vamp trick; burn out your prey when they try to hide out. Vamps can't enter sanctified places, as you probably know. So they burn the churches first."

He indicated the largest of the smoking piles of rubble, and Keely gasped when she saw the charred remains of a large wooden cross.

"But . . . the people? Do you think they got them all?" Tears ran down her face, unheeded, at the thought of the villagers being burned alive in the church.

The unmistakable sound of a shotgun shell being chambered came from behind them. "No, señora, they did not get us all. Do you and your friend intend on finishing us off?"

Justice snarled a string of words so harsh and guttural that she was sure she never wanted to understand what he'd said.

He whirled around, placing himself between her and the man with the shotgun.

"We are not your enemies, but if you threaten my woman, you will welcome the return of the bloodsuckers in comparison to what I will do to you and yours," Justice growled. "What is your name and what is the name of your village?"

Keely peered over his shoulder at the man with the gun. He was lean, with shaggy dark hair falling into his eyes. He wore jeans and a torn white shirt that gleamed against his bronze skin. His facial features bore the clear evidence of his Mayan heritage.

The man shrugged, either unimpressed or too weary of violence to respond to Justice's threat. "My name is Alejandro and you are in Las Pinturas. As to the rest, I care little for your threats, sword or no. However, I do not harm women, unlike those vampire bastards who attack us again and again."

"Why are you still here?" Justice asked. "You're fools if you think they won't come back again and again."

Alejandro's eyes turned to ice. "You think I would not have removed my people from danger if I could? The first things they destroyed were our vehicles." He indicated a smoking pile of metal nearly hidden behind one of the buildings. "We have our radio, and we've radioed for help, but there is apparently a wave of violence occurring right now and we are low on the priority list."

"We'll help, won't we?" Keely said, putting a hand on Justice's arm. "We have to do what we can."

Justice said nothing but gave a slight nod, his expressionless face giving away nothing of his feelings. Keely tentatively tried to reach out with her emotions or her mind, but encountered nothing but darkness. He'd shielded his mind from her, and she didn't know enough about the soul-meld to understand how to break through. She moved her hand to clasp his, anyway, and the slight pressure of his fingers reassured her. He'd gone into protective warrior mode; that was all.

Looking around at the destruction, she couldn't exactly blame him.

Alejandro's gaze skimmed over Keely and Justice, and whatever he saw seemed to reassure him, because he lowered the gun and called out, "They are safe enough. You can come out now."

At first one, then another, then finally nearly twenty adults came out from wherever they'd been hiding behind the smoking burnings. Only after they had completely surrounded Keely and Justice did six children cautiously appear to join their parents.

Keely's heart plunged at the sight of the children's terrified faces. "We won't hurt you," she called out in fluent Spanish. "*Somos amigos.*"

One small girl, no older than five or six, pushed between the rank of adults and stood staring up at Keely with enormous dark eyes, clutching a dirty stuffed animal in her arms. None of the villagers rushed to claim her; in fact, many of them looked at her with varying degrees of suspicion, and one old woman even surreptitiously made the sign against the evil eye and then spat on the ground. The girl flinched and Keely suddenly, fiercely, wanted to slap the superstitious old bat's face.

"Eleni," Alejandro called sharply. "Don't get too close to them."

"But Justice will put the fires out with his water," Eleni said. "And Dr. Keely will help us find Mama."

Keely gasped. "How did you know our names?"

"Eleni often . . . knows things," Alejandro said in English. "She doesn't speak any English, though, so I will use your language to tell you that her father died long ago and her mother has been dead for several weeks. The vampires took her and left her head for me to find. We have tried to tell her this, but she either cannot or does not want to understand."

The lines on Alejandro's handsome face deepened and the fury in his eyes promised vengeance. Justice wore a matching expression on his face. The two warriors were nearly a mirror of each other, though from vastly disparate cultures.

Or, perhaps not. If the Atlanteans had settled in Mayan lands more than eleven thousand years ago . . . Keely shook her head to clear it of the random musings. Now was certainly not the time to lose focus.

Eleni made some small sound and looked up at Keely,

deep wells of loss and sadness in her eyes. The girl made no move to come closer, but just huddled into herself as though fearing a rebuff. Keely was completely unable to maintain any kind of detachment looking at this poor child who reminded her of another little girl, so long ago.

A little girl whose own parents were afraid of what she was.

But at least Keely had had parents, even though they were unable to provide much in the way of emotional support. Poor Eleni had lost both of hers. Keely dropped to her knees and held out her arms to the girl, who came willingly to her and laid her small head on Keely's shoulder and held up the stuffed animal for Keely to see. Keely felt a sharp wrench in her stomach when she realized it wasn't a toy at all, but a fuzzy, well-worn slipper matted and stained with blood.

"Mama left her slipper, you see," Eleni confided trustingly. "I'm worried that her poor feet are getting cold."

~~~~~

Las Pinturas, twilight

Justice carried the last load of useable goods to the single house that had been left relatively unscathed by the vampires' destruction and handed them to the women who were organizing the stores. Some of the canned goods had survived. Several charred-at-the-edges but still serviceable blankets. Various personal items that the villagers had pulled from the wreckage.

What the fires hadn't ruined, he had. He walked back to look at what was left of the village, and self-disgust roiled like acid in his gut. He'd had no choice but to call water to put out the fires. They'd have lost everything if he hadn't. But the sight of that little boy clutching his soaking-wet collection of half-burned baseball cards had turned his stomach.

Or wrenched an organ further up in his chest, not that he'd admit it.

These people reminded him of the American colonists he'd been fighting to save back on that long-ago night when he'd carved Keely's fish. Brave and stubborn. Willing to live their lives here in the wild, by no man's—or government's—rules or constraints. They were farmers eking out a subsistence living, but they were proud. Alejandro perhaps the proudest of them all. He'd done the work of ten men, ordering and cajoling his people to work quickly to save all that could be saved and barricade the building so they could hide the women and children inside when darkness fell again. Proud and courageous, both. Alejandro would make a fine warrior.

They are fools, the Nereid sneered in his mind. *No protection from the Guatemalan Paranormal Ops patrols this far out. They're nothing but bloodsucker bait.*

"They radioed P Ops this morning after the vamps left," Justice said. Then he realized that he'd just answered himself out loud. "Okay, now I'm ready for the Temple protective rooms; that's for sure."

Keely walked across the charred ground toward him. Her face was smudged with dirt and ash, but to him she glowed like a flame. She'd tied her wealth of hair back away from her face, and he wanted to let it loose and bury his face in the silken strands. Inhale her sweet scent after so many hours of the smell of burning filling his nostrils and lungs.

"Did you say Temple protective rooms? What are those?" she asked, always the inquisitive scientist, even bone weary as she must be.

He bent his head to kiss her, because he could do nothing else. A feeling so huge coiled inside him that the pressure would surely burst his rib cage. There was nothing more important than Keely, no moment in his life from this day on that he would not spend thanking all the gods for her. He closed his arms around her and pulled her so close that he could feel her heart beating against his chest.

But a warrior preparing for battle must plan strategy with his head, not with his heart, and so he reluctantly let her go.

"I want to get you out of here," he repeated for the twentieth time since they'd first arrived. "I have tried and tried to call to the portal, and it will not answer my call. Perhaps I am too damaged and the Atlantean magic will not recognize me again."

"Never," she said firmly, sending a wave of warmth

through him. She believed in him, and though he could not credit her with any good sense for doing so, he offered his thanks to Poseidon that she did.

"I can't reach Conlan or even Alaric, either," he admitted. "They are too far, or perhaps they have turned against me. They know we are here; you told them the Star was in San Bartolo. I cannot believe they have not come to our aid, unless I truly am exiled."

"They're your family, Justice. They won't give up on you," she said. A flash of remembered pain crossed her face, but she shook her head at whatever thought had caused it. "I know about families and abandonment, and your brothers were willing to die for you. Don't give up on them, because they won't give up on you. I can feel it."

Hope tried to send up a tentative flare, but he ruthlessly crushed it. Better to be surprised than to have to live with the anguish of shattered expectations. "We can discuss that another time, *mi amara*. If the vampires return again, I cannot bear for you to be anywhere near this place. If you are harmed, then I will drown the earth itself in my rage. Perhaps not even these villagers will be safe."

She folded her arms across her chest and lifted her chin. "I trust you. You just worked all afternoon to help them; you'd never harm them. Don't make me have this discussion with you again. I'm not going anywhere until you can get us all out of here, and you admitted that your energy is nearly gone."

It was true. He'd used the Nereid power of transport to take a wounded child and his mother to the nearest medical clinic, and the use of his new power had exhausted him so much that he'd nearly lost himself in the energy stream on the return trip. Once the particles of his being had been scattered and spread across the universe, he never would have returned to himself.

Never could have found Keely ever again. Terror knifed through him at the thought. No, he would not risk travel in that manner until he was sure his energies had returned.

She put a hand on his arm. "If you could travel by mist again, or do that super-speed thing, or anything that would help move these people, that would be one thing. But you're not superhuman—"

Suddenly she stopped speaking and laughed tiredly. "I guess you are superhuman, though, aren't you? It's not like the average human can do any of the things you've done today. Eleni even calls you Señor Superman."

"Yeah, well, my cape is at the dry cleaners," he said savagely. "I'm no superhero, Keely; I'm a monster. Part of me thinks these people are fools and sheep who deserve to be abandoned."

Stepping closer to him, she put her hands on his cheeks and pulled his head down to hers. "But you won't do it, and the choice is what makes you different from the monsters."

Slowly, smiling up at him, she lifted her face and kissed him gently. He let her take the initiative and stood perfectly still, exquisitely sensitized to the feel of her lips on his. She feathered kisses on his lips, chin, and jaw until a flash of heat seared through his body like a stroke of lightning, and he couldn't bear it anymore. He lifted her in his arms, flashed across the clearing as quickly as he could, and withdrew to a spot a few feet within the trees, so they were blocked from view.

"Justice," she said with a little gasp, but he swallowed her gasp and lifted her, pressed her back against the tree, and caught her mouth with his own. He kissed her and every ounce of finesse, every art of gentleness he'd ever known deserted him so that he was as rough and clumsy as a schoolboy.

He wanted her more than he'd ever wanted any woman. How could he be so unrestrained? The need was too great, too overpowering, and if he didn't have her wrapped in his arms and naked underneath him soon, the pain would take him again, back to madness and burning and the dark. Every ounce of his being was centered on his lips as they devoured her and on his cock as he bucked against her.

He must have her, or he would be lost forever.

But he was saved; he was whole. She was his well-being and his heart and his home. She was *kissing him back*, and all was right with his world. The warm taste of her mouth, sweet from the cup of hot chocolate she'd drunk with their meager dinner of canned goods, teased and tortured him and swept sea-tossed tempests of longing and hunger through him. His body actually shuddered with the enormity of his need, and he raised his head, gasping for breath.

"Keely, I need—I need—"

"Señor Justice?" The small voice came from behind him, but it took a moment for it to register in his frenzied mind.

"Justice, put me down," Keely whispered urgently. "It's Eleni."

He clutched her tighter for an instant, then reluctantly released her, breathing hard and trying to regain his equilibrium. Keely ran over to the child and knelt down in front of her.

"Are you okay, Eleni?" she asked in her beautifully accented Spanish. "Is anything wrong?"

Eleni clutched that pitiful slipper to her and shook her head. "They're coming, Keely. The bad ones are coming back and they're almost here."

Chapter 34

Keely lifted Eleni into her arms and wished desperately that she could take the child far, far away from danger and superstition.

Justice's face hardened and he drew his sword from its sheath, grimacing at the blackened blade. "I would have thought they'd be sated from last night's raid for at least a week," he said grimly. "Either there are more vampires in this blood pride than Alejandro knew, or these are very greedy bloodsuckers."

Eleni shivered and Keely shook her head at Justice. The child didn't need to hear about it; she'd lived through it and lost both parents to the vampires. He inclined his head in acknowledgment and then strode out of the trees and back toward the village. She followed, holding Eleni, who clung to her like one of the native monkeys, her painfully thin legs and arms clutching Keely and the ever-present slipper, stinking of the rust-like smell of old blood, between them.

The village was almost tranquil in the dusky shadows of twilight. A few scattered people moved about or stood in small groups, talking quietly. Two men stood guard, shotguns at the ready, scanning the perimeter. They reflexively raised their weapons when they saw Justice and Keely, then lowered them again, nodding their recognition.

Alejandro appeared suddenly, almost materializing out of the dark. "I am not of a mind to rest our guard until we are safely ensconced in the vehicles of the P Ops unit," he said. "I know you have done the work of five men, and I do not know how much using such amazing powers tires you, but would you be willing to take a shift? Your sword—"

"They're coming," Justice said flatly, cutting him off. "Eleni warned us, and we're going on the assumption that she's right. Round up every able-bodied man—"

"And woman," Keely interjected. "It will take all of us to fend them off."

Justice glared at her but didn't respond to her comment. "You said there were no more than a dozen last night, Alejandro?"

"Yes, and that was the most they've ever sent. I think that was the entirety of the blood pride."

"A dozen vampires is what we call 'a good beginning' in Atlantis," Justice said, grinning wolfishly. "You and I and two or three of your best marksmen will easily handle them and make them regret ever stepping foot in Las Pinturas."

The white gleam of Alejandro's teeth flashed, startling in the growing dark. "I find that I like you very much, although I reserve judgment on your claim to be from the continent beneath the waters."

"Yeah, well, let's get all girly and talk about our feelings later," Justice said. "Keely, to the safe house. Now. Take the girl with you."

"She can stay with the others," Keely protested. "I'm a damn good shot and I can help."

"I don't care if you can shoot out the eye of a bloodsucker at two hundred yards," Justice snarled. "You need to be safe or I will lose my precarious hold on sanity and destroy everything and everyone that moves for miles around."

Alejandro froze, his hands tightening on his shotgun. Then he turned to Keely. "I do not doubt that he means it, señora. Please do as he says."

"Fine," she snapped. She wasn't going to waste valuable time arguing when the minutes until the vamps arrived were ticking down. She'd get Eleni to safety then find a gun. No way was she huddling in a corner like a scared rabbit.

As she ran across the clearing, she heard Justice and Alejandro shouting orders behind her. The men came running, weapons in their hands and grim determination on their faces.

One of the women met Keely at the door and held her arms out for Eleni. "Come to me, little one," she soothed. "Let the doctor be for now."

Eleni cried out and dug her heels into Keely's kidneys. "No, no, no. Want Keely!"

"It's okay," Keely said, moving into the room and looking for a pile of blankets where she could deposit Eleni. "Eleni, you have to listen to me. I need to help Justice—"

"Señor Superman does not need our help," Eleni said mutinously. "You stay with me."

Keely knelt down on the floor and tried gently to pull Eleni's arms from around her neck. "Please, sweetheart. I promise to come right back to you, okay? But even Superman needs help sometimes."

Abruptly, Eleni let go of Keely, wrapped her arms around herself and started rocking. "You won't come back. Nobody ever comes back to me."

Keely hugged the child, but she'd gone as stiff and unyielding as a board. "I will. I promise you."

But Eleni's eyes had gone wide and shocky; she began humming a discordant tune to herself and Keely knew she didn't have time to break through to her. Only returning as she'd promised would reassure the child.

The kind woman who'd met them at the door knelt down beside Keely, a shotgun in her hands. "I will care for her, Dr. McDermott. I am not as superstitious as these others. You take this and help protect us from these devils."

Keely nodded her thanks, unable to speak over the lump in her throat. She pressed a kiss to the top of Eleni's head and then took the shotgun from the woman and ran for the door, hoping she wasn't too late.

Justice called for water and was relieved when it immediately answered his call, trembling in wait at the edge of the clearing as he'd commanded. At least one of his Atlantean powers had not been lost, then, even though the capricious magic of the portal to Atlantis would not respond to him. Twilight had turned to full dark and the rich, earthy smells of the jungle pressed in on him, counteracting the residual stench of burned buildings and charred dreams.

Alejandro knelt behind an overturned cart a dozen paces away, leveling his shotgun in the direction that the attack had come from the night before. Of course even bloodsuckers knew enough to vary their methods and directions of attack, but it was a matter of seconds to turn to meet the threat.

"I can hear them coming," Justice said quietly. "Be ready."

Alejandro nodded and passed the word to the other men, who stood strong and resolute, even though their faces were pale with dread. All of them had lost family members to the vampires. They knew what they faced, and they had no powers other than their simple shotguns and a pile of wooden stakes next to each man.

The trick was getting close enough to use one of those stakes.

I have a surprise for you, if you insist on helping these pathetic humans, the Nereid said smugly.

What is it? And it had better be fast and useful, Justice warned.

You decide, the Nereid replied, then flashed a series of visions—of *knowledge*—through Justice's mind so fast that he nearly stumbled with dizziness.

Suddenly he knew. It was as if he had always known. Known how to access the power of his other half, of his Nereid ancestry. He could wield water as an Atlantean.

He could wield madness as a Nereid.

As both, he could bring utter destruction to the vampires who chose that minute to soar through the trees and land on the ground not ten feet in front of him. Madness and confusion, and it would be so easy.

Still, he did love the feel of his sword in his hands.

"You do not belong here," the vamp in front of the group hissed at him, as Justice counted nine more laughing and skulking around to try to flank their group. "You are no villager, nor even native to this land."

Justice raised his sword and the vamp took a step back, suddenly hesitant. "I belong nowhere and everywhere, bloodsucker. You, though, bear the stamp of the Mayan heritage, yet still you torment these countrymen and women of yours. That is the worst kind of treachery."

Alejandro stood up, leveling his shotgun at the vamp's head. "I propose a barter," he said calmly.

The vamp barked out a chilling burst of laughter. "What barter could you—"

The shotgun bucked and roared and exploded the vamp's head into acidic chunks of skull and meat. Justice shot a look at Alejandro, who shrugged as the vampire's headless body fell to the ground, dissolving in a flood of slime. "My shotgun shell for his head. Seemed fair to me."

Then he aimed almost without looking and took off another one's head, still with that eerie calm.

Justice raised his sword and yelled a battle cry. "Las Pinturas!" Then he dove toward the vampires, hacking, slashing, and slicing, a study of grace in motion, centuries of training and practice evident in every move. No matter what Anubisa had done to him, no matter what battles the disparate sides of his heritage fought over possession of his mind and soul, he was an Atlantean warrior. A Warrior of Poseidon.

And these vampires were all going to die.

Two of them dove for him in a coordinated move, and he sidestepped the first, slashing into its neck as it flew by him, then circled around in a smooth motion to drive his sword into the next. As the vamp screamed and died, a rush of power so hot and powerful shot through the sword's blade and rushed into Justice's arm that he nearly lost his grip on it. Instead, he raised his arm into the air and shouted out his fierce joy as the sword gleamed with an inner light; first the symbols on the blade that he'd seen in the Void and then the entire blade transforming from the hated dull black to silver-blue fire.

"For Atlantis!" he shouted, and then he called the water that he'd held at bay and threw his left arm forward, pointing at a group of the remaining vampires. The water obeyed his command and shaped itself in deadly arrows of glittering ice and shot toward the vamps in a hail of sharp-edged death.

As the three fell, their heads rolling off to the sides, he heard the sounds of two different shotguns going off. Alejandro had claimed another, blowing its head off, and another villager had punched a hole in one of the vamp's chests. Unfortunately, it had missed the heart, and the wound was closing before their eyes.

A third shotgun blast sounded, this time from behind him. Justice whirled around to see Keely standing in front of the door to the safe house. Not five feet away from her, another vampire dissolved into the ground in a pool of green slime.

Keely stood there, shaking, her hands firmly holding the shotgun to her shoulder, her eyes enormous as she looked up and met Justice's gaze. "I . . . I got it," she said in a shaky voice that unleashed the fury of a thousand monsters in Justice's mind.

Hatred larger than the world swelled within Justice at the idea that one of them had come so close to her. Fury deeper than any ocean pulsed through the Nereid in waves of ice and fire.

"We're done playing with you," he said, and he dropped his sword, lifted his arms into the air, and roared out a sound that shook the trees themselves. Slicing his arms down through the air, he blasted a shock wave of concussive force through the clearing, knocking the villagers on their asses as it traveled straight to the vampires.

Like water crashing against the rocks, the wave of his fury smashed through the remaining vampires, and every one of them exploded into a bloody shower of acid and flesh. Justice heard screaming but he didn't know if it came from someone else or from his own throat as the force of the power he'd harnessed tried to shake his mind free from its moorings.

Madness laughed at sanity and the power, the power, oh, by all the gods, the *power* of it beckoned and seduced until he began to whirl around, dripping with acid and chunks of spattered vampire, laughing and laughing and laughing. The cosmic stream of the universe flowed through him and around him, inviting him to dance a waltz of the ages.

Why didn't you tell me? We are all-powerful! We will kill them all and take anything and everything we want! Justice demanded of his Nereid half.

The Nereid was strangely silent for a long moment. Then he finally replied. *But what if everything we want is something that must be given to us, not taken?*

Justice stopped spinning, frozen to immobility by the words. Then a quiet voice broke through the madness.

"Justice, come back to me. We need you. I need you. Please come back to me."

He forced his eyes to focus on what was right before him, instead of gazing out at the energy stream of the universe. He released the colors and light long enough to figure out why the voice called to him so powerfully.

It was her. It was Keely, and she was crying. "Please. Please come back to me. You're frightening them, and me, too."

The sight of her crystalline tears tracing a path down her cheeks cut directly into his heart. Abruptly, he released the power and pushed through the madness.

The Nereid inside him offered up a sensation of intense joy and need. *She is ours, and she has given us her love. What else can matter?*

Justice held out his arms, and Keely walked into them, heedless of the mess covering him. "Is it true?" he demanded, not caring that several villagers were surrounding them, many with shotguns held at half-mast. "Do you love me?"

She clutched his shirt for a moment, then stepped back from him and looked up at him, disbelief plain on her face. "Do I love you? Do I *love* you? Are you freaking kidding me? Do you think I'd go through hell like I have for the past few days for just anybody?"

Turning on her heel, she started to stalk away, but he raced forward and caught her arm, knowing that he must hear the words. "Tell me now. Is it true?" he repeated. "Do you love me?"

"Yes, I love you," she said, all but spitting the words at

him. It wasn't how he'd envisioned her declaration of love, but it was a start.

"Keely, you must know that—"

"Oh, shut up," she cried, and then she hauled off and punched him in the face.

Chapter 35

Justice rubbed his jaw, which actually ached. For a scientist, she packed a hell of a punch. A smile spread over his face, which made his split lip hurt, but he didn't care.

By all the gods, she was magnificent.

Alejandro lowered his shotgun and whistled, staring after Keely. "If I'd seen her first, you'd have quite a fight on your hands," he said admiringly. "That is one fine woman."

Justice narrowed his eyes and growled at the upstart. "Go near my woman and I'll—"

"Yeah, yeah. If you're done going crazy on us, we have a hostage," Alejandro said, cutting him off. "And if there's any way you can teach me that explosion thing, I'd give my right arm to know that trick."

"That trick, as you call it, is a power granted to me by my Nereid heritage," Justice said, for the first time in his life claiming his mother's people with pride. Something inside him warmed and expanded at the realization. "I cannot teach it to one who is not Atlantean and Nereid."

"Too bad," Alejandro said with a rueful grin. "But thanks for not exploding all of us. I was afraid when you saw Keely was threatened that we were all going to be collateral damage."

"It was a valid fear," Justice admitted, then looked around. "Did you say a hostage?"

"Over here," one of the men called, and two of them walked up, dragging one of the vamps between them. It was the one who'd been shot in the chest, and the wound was still closing. "He must have fallen to the ground from the injury, so he escaped being caught in that wave of death, or whatever you call it," the man said, bowing his head a little toward Justice but staying a careful distance away.

Alejandro cocked his shotgun. "Easy enough. Stand away from him," he ordered his men.

"No," Justice said. "I have a better idea. We send him home with a message."

"Fine. Here's a message," Alejandro said, lifting his shotgun and firing in one smooth motion. Half of the vamp's right upper leg disappeared and it started shrieking.

"I actually meant a verbal message, but that works, too," Justice said, admiring the man's handiwork. "You're pretty good with that shotgun."

"We will kill you all," the vampire shrieked. "We will come back with all of our blood pride and tear you into tiny pieces and—"

"Do you want me to let him take your head off with that thing?" Justice asked, tilting his head to one side as if truly interested in the answer.

The vamp stuttered to silence, clutching his wounded leg as it began to heal and shooting death glares at all of them.

"Good. So here's the message. You and yours stay away from Las Pinturas forever. If we ever see even the slightest sign of any of you, we will hunt you down and destroy you, and believe me when I say that the exploding vampire technique was only a party trick compared to the destruction I will rain down upon your bloodsucking asses," Justice said.

His calm tone seemed to terrify the vampire, who bobbed its head and tried on an ingratiating smile. "Yes, I hear you. I will give the message," it whined. "If you let me go now, I will hurry to spread your message to the four corners of the region."

Justice looked at Alejandro. "Are you satisfied?"

"I can live with it. Can I shoot him again?"

Justice shrugged. "Your town, your call."

The vamp screamed, then fell to the ground and started crying red, bloody tears. "No, please no. I can't spread the message if I'm too wounded to move," it blubbered.

Alejandro stepped forward and kicked the vampire in the face. "You have killed the last of my people, you undead bastard. Mind that you never, ever return or I will personally cut your balls from your body."

"Yes, yes, I mean, no, no, whatever you say," the vampire gibbered and Alejandro motioned to his men, who put even more distance between themselves and the vamp.

"Then go, and don't forget to spread that message," Justice said.

Still sobbing, the vampire backed away from them, dragging its wounded leg, greenish brackish blood pouring down its face from its broken nose. "Yes, yes, yes," it kept saying until it reached the trees, and then it gave one harsh cry of rage or defiance and sped off into the night.

They stood staring after it for several long moments, and then Alejandro raised one of his arms and stared at the globs and spatters of vampire slime that coated his sleeve and skin. "So, about that trick with the water you did earlier on the burning houses. Does that work for a shower?"

Justice laughed and channeled the water that came so eagerly to his call. "All part of the service. Exploding vampires; hot and cold running showers."

As they washed themselves the best they could under the gentle, welcome rain, Justice realized he still faced his most terrifying encounter ever.

He had to go apologize to Keely.

~~~~

Keely cleaned herself off with water from a bucket before she went in to Eleni, so as not to traumatize the child even more. She was so angry that it was surprising that the water didn't boil into steam the second it touched her skin.

Questions crashed through her mind, faster and faster. Did she love him? Did she *love* him? He was a stupid, blind, sorry excuse for a human being. Or Atlantean being. Or what the hell ever. Damn him, anyway. Did she really have to say the words? Hadn't she proved how she felt about him, over and over? What about that hours-long sex romp in the jungle? Did he think she went around having wild sex in jungles all the time?

Energy sizzled up the nape of her neck even before the sound of his footsteps alerted her to his approach. "Stay away from me, Justice," she warned. "I'm in no mood right now. I just killed my first vampire—my first anything—and that's pretty traumatic. Then I had to deal with you and your stupid questions."

"Keely," he said. Just that. Just her name.

But there was so much pain and longing in the sound that she bowed her head, surrendering her rage to a gentler emotion. The anger disappeared as if she'd never felt it, and she carefully considered what to say, still with her back to him as she knelt by the bucket. "Justice, I know. I know you're fighting this battle, and I know that you sometimes can't control the Nereid, but I kind of need for you to take some things on faith. Can you do that for me?"

She waited, but only heard silence. A healthy dose of mad started up again and she stood up, kicking the bucket over in frustration. "Look, you have to meet me halfway—"

She whirled around, ready to give him a very detailed list of grievances, just in time to see his eyes roll back in his head as he fell backward to the ground. She jumped forward but wasn't quick enough, and his body and head hit the dirt with two solid thumps that had her wincing in empathy. Oh, man, was he going to have a headache when he woke up. He'd told her using the Nereid power drained him. She had a feeling that the shock wave trick had used huge amounts of his power and energy.

She heard more steps running toward them, and then Alejandro rounded the corner and skidded to a stop. There was a long silence as he stared back and forth between Justice and Keely.

"I must revise my opinion, Dr. McDermott," he said gravely, although there was a certain glint in his eye. "You are far too much woman for me."

"I didn't do this," she protested, but he just nodded, holding up his hands as if in surrender. She couldn't help it; she started laughing helplessly. The terror, anger, and exhaustion had drained her completely. She laughed and laughed until tears started rolling down her cheeks, and Alejandro crouched down next to her and touched her cheek with one hand.

"You are very courageous, Keely, but even the strongest steel can find its breaking point. Let me assist you in carrying your man to a better place to rest."

"He's not my man; he's a thickheaded buffoon," she mumbled, scrubbing at her face, and it was Alejandro's turn to laugh.

"All men are buffoons at times," he said gently. "The heart of a good person cannot lie, and your heart shows plainly on your face whenever you look at him, as his does when you are near."

She just sighed. He called out, and one of his men came over to help. Between the three of him, they managed to lift Justice's heavy form and get him inside to a pallet of blankets in one corner. As soon as she saw them, Eleni wiggled out of the arms of the woman who'd been holding her and ran to them.

"Señor Justice, Señor Justice! You cannot be hurt. I did not see you hurt," she cried out. Then she hurled her tiny body on top of Justice's chest and put one arm around him, still holding that awful slipper in the other, and cast a reproachful glance at Keely. "Except when you hit him. You should not have done that. Hitting is wrong. We must use our words to resolve our differences," she said in a singsong voice, clearly parroting something she'd heard many times.

Alejandro and the other man strode off, probably to return to guard duty, and Keely dropped to her knees next to Justice's still body. "You're right, Eleni. It was wrong of me to hit him, and I will apologize when he wakes up. Is that okay?"

Eleni nodded, the tracks of tearstains shining silvery in the dust coating her cheeks. "I was so afraid. Even though I did not see you being injured, I was so afraid. But you came back, like you promised."

Keely soothingly patted Eleni's thin back and rashly made

a promise—to herself and to the child. "I will always come back, Eleni. If you like, you can stay with me from now on."

But Eleni was drifting off to sleep, still clinging to Justice, and she didn't respond. Probably hadn't heard, which was all for the best. Keely wondered if she was going crazy. Falling in love with a magical warrior and then punching him. She'd never punched anyone before in her life. Promising something to a traumatized child that probably would be impossible to achieve.

Still, she'd seen the impossible on a daily basis since the moment Liam had walked into her office talking about Atlantis. Surely arranging for one orphaned child to come home with her couldn't be that difficult.

Firmly putting all of it out of her mind, she curled up next to Eleni and Justice and put her arm over both of them. She was exhausted and needed sleep. She'd think about the rest of it in the morning. As she fidgeted, trying to get comfortable, she felt Justice's warm hand pull hers to his chest, so that it rested on his heartbeat. Comforted by the feel of it, strong and steady under her palm, Keely finally let her mind and body sink into the warm darkness of sleep.

∾——∾

Several kilometers away, in the temple at San Bartolo, the wounded vampire finished telling the leader of his blood pride the tale of the events of that night. Enraged, the leader's yellowed fangs lengthened so fast that they slashed bleeding ribbons in his lips. He bellowed out a howl that was so long and loud that all of his pride members in the area dropped to their knees and cowered.

"They dare? They dare to threaten me?" he screamed. "We shall see who lives to threaten whom after this night!"

"Perhaps," ventured the vamp whose leg was still trying to heal, "we could wait for the rest of us to return at dawn from hunting and go in strength when night next falls?"

The leader swooped down on him, eyes glowing red and savage. "You dare to question me?" he hissed.

"Never, never, my lord. But if you could have seen the power of the explosion . . . I only suggest that we return with sufficient force that no hint of danger could come near to touching you."

The leader drew back, a calculating expression on his face. "Perhaps you are right. A true leader never risks himself; I am far too valuable to take any chances of facing the true death."

He slowly turned to face the mural of the goddess Anubisa preparing to feast on the puny maize god of the ancient Maya. "We will destroy this new threat in your name."

Behind him, the others mewled and whined varying noises of agreement but he ignored them. One day he, too, would be a god, as vampires before him had been worshipped by these Mayan sheep.

One day quite possibly as soon as tomorrow.

Chapter 36

Keely woke slowly, climbing up through stages of sleep as though her weary body and mind were protesting every step. When she finally opened her eyes, it was to see sunlight slanting through the building and falling like bars of gold on the wooden floor. Justice and Eleni were gone, but a blanket had been neatly tucked around Keely's shoulders. She sat up, grimacing at the foul taste in her mouth, and an equally foul smell coming from somewhere nearby, and wished for a shower and a toothbrush, in no particular order.

"Señora would like to accompany us to wash up?" Keely looked up at the question and found the shy woman from yesterday sitting at a battered wooden table, folding clothes and sorting them into piles. "We thought you might enjoy a change of clothing."

Keely's nose wrinkled when she realized that the foul smell was coming from herself. Hiking through the jungle, having vampires disintegrate all over you . . . it was no way to keep fresh as a daisy.

"Yes, I would love that," she said gratefully. "I'm sorry, I don't know your name."

"I am Maria," said the woman—girl, really. She couldn't

be older than eighteen or nineteen years old. "Follow me, please."

Keely followed Maria out into the bright sunlight and automatically glanced up at the sky. It had to be mid-morning. She couldn't believe she'd slept so long. She scanned the clearing as she followed Maria to a path that cut into the trees, but there was no sign of Justice or Eleni.

"Maria, do you know where Justice is?"

Maria glanced back over her shoulder and smiled. "He and Eleni went with Alejandro to patrol. That one is such a man, no? You are lucky to be his woman, and he, too, is lucky to find a woman with fire in her spirit as well as in her hair."

"I'm not his woman," Keely grumbled, picking her way through trees and over wildly overgrown plant life on the path. Suddenly she looked around and wished for her shotgun. "There aren't any jaguars that like to take this path, are there?"

Maria laughed. "No, they stay away from the village and our paths. The smell of cooking fires . . ."

Her voice trailed off and Keely knew they were both thinking of other fires.

"I'm so sorry," Keely said. "I can't begin to imagine how much you've suffered."

Maria's shoulders slumped but then squared again. "Alejandro will take us out of here. We have only ever had random attacks before; a single vampire would try to take one of us. This has only happened twice in the entirety of my life. But this— this is organized warfare and we cannot stand against it. If your man were to stay with us and guard us . . . I heard of his magic. But you cannot stay, can you?"

She turned to fix a measuring stare on Keely, hope mixed with resignation in her eyes.

"No, I'm sorry. We will stay until your P Ops unit comes, but we must finish up our . . . mission and return home."

Maria nodded. "We understand. Alejandro will save us."

The words fell from her lips like a benediction, and Keely, who rarely noticed interpersonal relationships, had a sudden flash of insight. "He's *your* man, isn't he? Alejandro?"

"I would like that," Maria said, blushing. "But he still thinks of me as a child."

They rounded a curve in the path and a stream lay in front of them, sparkling in the sunlight that danced on its surface. Keely stopped and took a deep breath, content to see something beautiful after the night's terror and death.

"We will wash up and you can wear these clothes, if you like," Maria said shyly, holding out the bundle in her hands. "They are mine and we are very nearly the same size."

Keely looked at Maria's voluptuous curves and doubted her own less bountiful shape would fill out any of the other woman's clothes, but didn't let anything but thanks show on her face as she gratefully accepted the fresh clothes. Well-fitting clothes, after all, were the last thing on her mind, even if the teensiest bit of vanity wanted Justice to see her looking at least almost as pretty as the beautiful Maria.

They stripped down to their underwear and waded into the stream to wash, sharing a bar of soap that felt like silk and smelled like delicate jungle flowers. Keely washed her hair, too, and nearly cried with the sheer relief of being clean again. When they were done, they headed for the stream bank, chatting about inconsequential things, striving for mundane and normal as a respite from horror and death.

The loud crack of a branch breaking rang in the air, and they both froze. Maria started crying, and Keely put her arms around her. "It can't be vampires, not in the daytime," she soothed, while wondering what other dangers they'd overlooked in their little bathing adventure.

But it was no unknown danger that stepped out from the jungle, but Justice and Alejandro. Justice took her breath away, again, as if she were seeing him for the very first time. He'd changed into different clothes, simple jeans and a dark T-shirt, but his glorious blue hair hung loose and damp all the way to his waist, and the muscles of his chest and arms filled out the shirt in a way that had her wanting to tear it off and climb all over him.

Naked.

She crossed her arms over her chest when she realized her nipples were poking out through the wet fabric of her bra in response to the heat pouring through her body. All she had to do was look at him to want him.

Smiling a little goofily, she finally met his gaze—and flinched. Fury darkened his eyes to black, and his clenched jaw gave Keely the feeling that he was fairly upset.

Possibly at her.

She lifted her chin and stared defiantly at Justice. "Why are you glaring at me like that? If it's about that punch last night—"

"Did it occur to you, for one second, that it could be dangerous to be out here alone and half naked?" He bit off the words from between clenched jaws, and his gaze swept her body from head to toes and back up again, leaving her feeling as if he'd just stripped her bare.

From the look in his eyes, he wanted to do just that. Or yell at her for an hour or two. She wasn't in the mood for the latter and it was not exactly a good time for the former, no matter how much her hormones were jumping up and down at the thought.

She glanced at Alejandro, suddenly realizing that Justice wasn't the only one seeing her in wet and nearly transparent underwear, but she could have been part of the scenery as far as he was concerned. He was staring at Maria as if he'd never seen her before, and Keely bet that he'd certainly never seen her like that. Maria's lush body strained at the lacy scraps of her bra and panties, but she made no move to cover herself, although a flush rode high on her cheekbones.

"Do you like what you see?" Maria asked him, her voice quivering a little but strong.

"*Dios mio*, you should be—you should be—" Alejandro broke off as if unable to form a coherent sentence, and heat flashed in his eyes.

Keely smiled. At least some good might come from this day, if these two found each other. Before she could say a word, however, a blurred flash of speed that might have been a man with blue hair lifted her off her feet and raced through the jungle with her.

By the time Justice finally slowed to a stop and put her down, she'd worked up a full head of steam and was ready to lay into him. "Okay, I've really had it with this caveman act. You are not my boss, you are not my father—"

"Thank Poseidon," Justice said fervently as he stared intently down at her breasts.

She lost her train of thought for a moment as he bent toward her breasts, lifting them in his hands, but she gave it a valiant effort. "You are not . . ."

He licked her nipple and sucked it into his mouth.

She threw back her head and moaned, but tried again. "You are not . . ."

He pulled her panties down and slid his fingers through her wetness, then rubbed his slick fingers back and forth across her clitoris and her knees gave out.

He caught her with one strong arm, still rubbing her rhythmically as he sucked on her nipple, and she was reduced to wordless moaning, forgetting what she possibly could have been trying to say. All of her focus was centered on what he was doing to her body, and she knew if she didn't have him inside her very soon, she was going to go mad.

"Justice, please," she said, almost begging, not caring, only caring that he didn't stop, never stopped, oh, God, he was sucking on her other nipple now and driving first one, then a second finger into her, then across her clit, over and over and over until she bucked against him, clenching his fingers inside her heat. She cried out as she exploded against him, but he didn't let her go or remove his fingers.

Instead, he lifted her up in his arms and kissed her, slanting his head at the best angle to thrust his tongue inside her mouth in the same rhythm as he was thrusting his fingers inside her body. Tension began to rise in her body, coiling in her nerve endings again, centering on her breasts and between her thighs, and she couldn't speak, couldn't think, could only moan.

"Please, please, I need you," she pleaded against his mouth and he stopped kissing her, his breathing harsh and his muscles clenched as hard as rock under her hands.

"I need you, too, *mi amara*. The sight of you all but naked in the sunlight and the thought that anyone could have come upon you like that . . ." He shuddered against her. "I need you so much I may have to fuck you all day long, just to get over that scare you gave me."

She laughed, then whimpered as he drove his fingers inside her again, thrusting in and out until she was boneless with need and wanting.

"I need to taste you, my Keely, my woman. I need to drink you in as you come in my mouth," he said roughly. He fell to his knees on the soft carpet of grasses and, before she could think or protest or yell "Hallelujah!" he put his mouth on her and she cried out.

He kissed her and licked her and sucked her clit into his mouth with the same intense pressure he'd used on her nipple, still thrusting into her with his fingers, and she shuddered and shook and grabbed his lovely hair with both hands, holding him to her as he took her thoroughly with his mouth and his hands. She felt the tension and the need and the glory of it take her, and she exploded again, screaming, not caring if the entire village heard her, unable to bear the intensity of the pleasure.

She came and came and he kept licking and sucking her, not stopping, and she came again and again, in a never-ending orgasm that wrenched through her and lifted her into the sunlight and rocketed her, spasming, through the clouds. Finally she collapsed, falling forward so that he had to catch her, boneless and weak with satiated pleasure.

"You . . . I . . . Oh, God," she whispered.

He smiled down at her, a smile filled with hunger and smug male satisfaction and a darker edge of need. "You taste like ambrosia," he said, and just from his words an aftershock shivered through her and she gasped.

"Now I need to be inside you," he said and he unzipped his pants and shoved them down, kneeling there on the ground, and pulled her down so that she straddled him. "Take me, Keely. I need for you to ride me and show me that you need me even a fraction as much as I need you."

Slowly, so slowly, she slid down on his enormous erection and gasped at the feeling of his thickness sliding into her. She was so wet, so drenched, that he fit in her more easily than before, although he still stretched her to a marvelous feeling of fullness. She took all of him inside her until her thighs rested on his and she lay her head on his shoulder for a moment and took a deep breath. Then she lifted her head and looked into his drowningly beautiful eyes, midnight blue with green flames in the centers.

"Now," she whispered. "I need you now." She rose up and then slid back down, soon getting into a rhythm older than time, older than Mayan ruins, older than dreams of creation. She took him because he was hers, and she had to feel him inside her or she would die from the loss. She took him, and her body began to respond again, against all odds, rising with such urgency that she knew she was near to shattering around him.

Justice felt Keely's hot, wet sheath clutching him and knew she was near to coming again. He also knew that the feel of her orgasm would cause his own to pour out of him and he wanted to wait, to last longer for her, but he was as helpless as a youngling to fight the tide of pleasure that ripped through him like a tsunami. He grasped her hips in his hands and drove her into a faster rhythm, lifting his own hips to drive his cock deeper and harder into her with every stroke, until he couldn't tell where he left off and she began. They were joined as one and they always would be, and he hadn't been exaggerating when he said he might have to fuck her all day to get over the fear of losing her. Only when she welcomed him into her body did he feel truly safe from the fear that she would leave him.

She will never leave us, the Nereid said. *If she ever tries, we will track her to the ends of the earth.*

"Never," Justice growled, thrusting harder. "You will never leave. Promise me."

Keely moaned and released her grip on his shoulders, and then, she caught his face in her hands and stared into his eyes. "I will never leave you," she said breathlessly, since he continued to thrust into her and she was so close to the edge. "Now stop issuing all these ultimatums and just keep . . . just keep . . ."

Her body arched backward, rigid, and her thighs clenched as her sheath convulsively gripped his cock in a series of spasms and she cried out. "Justice! It's . . . Oh, God. It's happening again."

One final thrust, and his balls drew up even tighter and exploded, shooting his release into her so deeply that he had a second to wish that he'd gotten Poseidon's blessing so that he was giving her his child. Then the wave took him and knocked him down and the current swept him into the colors of her soul, roaring out his fulfillment.

The soul-meld took them and tossed them through stormy, sunlit seas until, holding tightly to each other, they came back to reality, still joined. Keely's tender skin bore evidence of his kisses and his bites, and a primal flush of fierce joy raced through him at the idea that he'd marked her as his own. Then he felt remorse that he might have hurt her and kissed each of the marks on her neck and chest, one by one.

The emotion that had grown and built inside him while they were making love forced their way up through his chest to his throat, demanding to be released. He had to say the words that were near to exploding directly out of his heart. "Keely, *mi amara*, I love you."

She looked up at him and started laughing, startling him. Then she grabbed his face and planted a loud, lip-smacking kiss on his lips.

"Justice, my big, strong warrior. I know."

Chapter 37

Keely and Justice took their time making their way back to the village, enjoying the stolen moments of calm. He'd told her that Eleni had complained of a slight upset stomach, but that it wasn't serious and the child had wanted a nap, so Keely didn't feel the need to rush back.

The vampires were no danger during the sunny heat of the day, when they had to go to ground. She and Justice and the villagers would be ready for them again by evening, but just for an hour or so, the two of them had needed to capture a tiny bit of peace. The P Ops unit should finally arrive in the morning and transport the villagers to safety.

Justice's shirt hung down to her knees, so they walked toward the stream hoping to find her clothes. Or, more accurately, *Justice* walked toward the stream, carrying her, since he didn't want her to hurt her bare feet on the ground. Keely was torn between appreciation and exasperation by his protectiveness, but she imagined there was only so much chivalry that a centuries-old Atlantean warrior was going to give up. She was a big fan of picking her battles, and this wasn't going to be one of them, especially since she loved the feel of his bare chest against her cheek.

She was turning into a hedonist, and it didn't bother her one bit. Wonder what Dr. Koontz would have said about that?

She laughed out loud, and Justice paused. "What is funny?"

"Oh, it would take too long to explain and it's about a totally unimportant person, anyway. But I sure hope Maria actually left the clothes at the stream."

"I like you in my shirt. I think you should always wear nothing but my shirts," he said, his deep voice amused as he began walking again.

"I'm sure you do, but I don't want to have to walk back into the village wearing nothing but your T-shirt. Not that everyone there doesn't already think of me as your woman anyway, but let's just say that I'm not an exhibitionist."

"This is good, since I would have to kill any man who saw you naked, and Conlan hates it when we kill potential allies," he said calmly, and she couldn't tell if he was kidding or not.

"Are you—"

But he cut her off by raising his hand and making a shushing noise. "The stream is just beyond those trees. I hear Alejandro and Maria talking. I'd hoped they'd be gone by now. Let me go in quietly and fetch your clothes and shoes."

He gently lowered her to her feet, then kissed her, stepped away, and transformed into sparkling mist. Her eyes widened in wonder. She'd never get over the awe of seeing him do that, if she saw it a million times. It was so magical and beautiful that it literally took her breath away.

In less than a minute, he was back, a miniature, iridescent rain cloud balancing a pile of clothes and her shoes somehow on the surface of his misty shape. He dropped the clothes into her arms, then shimmered back into his corporeal form. For a split second, he was surrounded by radiant light like a full-body halo, and she caught her breath at the almost spiritual glory of it.

"What the hells is wrong with that man?" he grumbled, bringing her back down to earth with a thud.

"What do you mean?"

"They're still going at it," he said in disgust.

She laughed, covering her mouth so Maria and Alejandro wouldn't hear. "What's wrong with that?"

"Nothing," he snapped. "Get dressed."

She slipped his shirt over her head and handed it to him, then pulled on the loose white skirt and scalloped red blouse Maria had provided, trying to puzzle out why he was so annoyed.

Suddenly, she blinked. "You're jealous?"

"What? Don't be ridiculous! Jealous of what?" he growled.

"That Alejandro has so much . . . stamina," she suggested, barely able to keep a straight face. "You shouldn't let it bother you, honey. After all, you *are* a few hundred years older than he is. They say that's the first thing to go . . ."

He narrowed his eyes. "You are not nearly as amusing as you believe yourself to be, woman."

She cracked up. "Oh, yes, I am. You should see the look on your face."

"I am *not* jealous of that human's stamina, or anything else!"

The horrified denial on his face just made her laugh harder. When she could finally catch her breath, she let him off the hook. "You know, it probably took them quite a while to start 'going at it' as you so elegantly put it. Maria said Alejandro had never looked at her as anything but a child before. I'm sure that changed when he got an eyeful of her in those wet underthings."

"What?" he said blankly, his eyebrows drawing together. "What about her?"

The snarky remark she'd been ready to say died on her lips when she looked into his eyes and realized that he wasn't kidding. He really hadn't noticed. Beautiful, voluptuous Maria. He hadn't even looked at Maria, because every atom of his laser-like focus had been zeroed in on her.

She threw her arms around his neck and pulled him down for a very passionate kiss. When they finally came up for air, he tilted his head.

"Not that I'm complaining in any way, but what was that for?"

"For not noticing Maria," she said, handing him back his T-shirt but regretting when he covered up his magnificent chest with the fabric. "You know, there should be a law that you have to walk around naked all the time."

Then she turned and started toward the village, humming.

Behind her, Justice made a strangled choking noise and then followed her. "Women," he muttered. "I'll never understand them."

Keely just smiled.

~~~

Justice was content to follow Keely down the path, enjoying her strangely happy mood, though he had no idea what had caused it. Well, he knew what had caused *part* of it. He grinned, watching her lovely ass, wondering if she'd go along with another detour before they reached the others.

Probably not. He blew out a breath, weighing the pros and cons of simply grabbing her and speeding off to another isolated spot. Before he could talk himself into the result he wanted, he heard one of the men on patrol call out a greeting. Keely answered, and something about her lovely voice pronouncing the round vowels and liquid consonants of her fluent Spanish made him hard. He shifted in his pants. Maybe he could ask her to speak Spanish the next time they made love. He stopped dead when another thought struck him with the force of a tidal wave. By all the gods, when she learned Atlantean, he was doomed. He'd be chasing her around all day long, every day of the week.

"Justice," she called back to him. "Are you coming? I'm going to go check on Eleni."

He forced himself to put away thoughts of Keely whispering Atlantean endearments and shook his head. "Go ahead. I will take my turn on patrol."

She flashed a huge smile that nearly dazzled him with its warmth and headed toward the safe house, and another realization hit him belatedly.

She'd called him honey.

When he sauntered into the clearing, grinning like a fool, the men shot knowing grins his way but said nothing. He waved and wandered over to the table where some of the women were setting out a midday meal. As he came close enough to smell the delicious aroma of spicy vegetable stew, his stomach rumbled, reminding him of Keely.

Of course, everything reminded him of Keely. Maybe he did need to have Alaric examine his mind and find out why he was turning into a love-struck fool.

Alaric. The portal. His smile faded as he realized he hadn't tried yet that day to call the portal. Part of him knew his reluctance was due to fear that the magic would not answer him.

Part of him just wanted to avoid the consequences if it did.

Which part am I, then? the Nereid, who had been silent since the previous night, asked him. *Your conscience or your goad?*

Neither. Both, Justice replied. *You are a part of me that I cannot deny and remain whole.*

He closed his eyes and centered his consciousness, reaching for the portal's magic to respond. Something shimmered at the very edges of his mind, just out of reach, taunting him with its nearness but still unavailable. If he could just focus more strongly, he would have it. He clenched his hands into fists and leaned forward, physically pouring his will into his effort. It was just there . . . just there . . . He could almost touch it . . .

And then Keely's screams shattered the air.

Chapter 38

Keely clutched the shredded blanket in her hands, unable to believe the evidence although she was staring at it. She screamed again.

"I'm so sorry, señora," the woman said through her tears. "She was sleeping, and we were all working very near this building, so we didn't worry at all about leaving her alone."

Keely couldn't answer her. Should have been able to think of something reassuring; tell her it wasn't her fault. But she couldn't. Because it was Keely's fault. She'd left poor orphaned Eleni alone.

The love-struck archaeologist had wild sex in the middle of a crisis, leaving an abandoned child to be captured and hurt. She would never forgive herself.

She didn't deserve to be forgiven.

She couldn't think, couldn't react, couldn't bear the slicing, rending pain that ripped through her body.

So she screamed again.

Justice smashed the door open and ran in with his sword drawn, then skidded to a halt. "What is it? Are you wounded? Tell me, *mi amara*."

Keely finally stopped screaming and mutely held up the

torn remnants of the blanket so the words on the sheet beneath it were clearly visible. Hateful words drawn in black charcoal, as if to mock the survivors huddling in the burned-out village.

WE HAVE THE CHILD.
SAN BARTOLO AT TWILIGHT.
OUR TURN TO BARTER.

Justice lowered his sword, but his sword arm was shaking as if with some immense inner pressure. "They took her. Eleni."

Keely nodded, unable to force words out past the pain-filled lump in her throat. Then she pointed a shaky finger at the object that had caused her to scream. There, lying half hidden in the tangled sheets, was Eleni's poor dead mother's bloody slipper.

But some of the blood on it was fresh.

Justice roared, a hideous, wrenching sound of fury and pain, and Keely flinched and covered her ears. She couldn't hear him. Couldn't bear it. Couldn't stand this feeling that her heart, finally given freely, would be ripped out yet again.

Her brain stepped in and ruthlessly clamped a lid on Keely's emotional meltdown. Coldly, logically, she began to plan. Because there was no way in hell she was going to sit there on her ass when there was a child to save.

She blinked furiously to clear her vision, scrubbed the tears she hadn't known she was crying from her face, took a deep breath, and stood up. "So now we figure this out," she said flatly.

"Now we figure this out," Justice echoed, ice coating his voice.

～～～✦

An hour later—an hour closer to dusk—and Justice wanted to kill something. Real bad.

They'd huddled all the remaining children into the building and set armed guards inside and out. They'd ignored the old women who'd tried to bully them into eating. One of them, a sour-faced crone, had attempted to put forth the idea that Eleni was some kind of devil child and not worth saving. Keely had lit into her so savagely that the old woman had run away, muttering something about "guarding the children who deserved to be protected."

At the table, they'd argued, they'd planned, they'd wasted sixty precious minutes, but they still hadn't reached an agreement as to how they would handle the so-called barter.

Keely and Alejandro were to the point of shouting at each other when he'd finally had enough. "That's enough."

The words came out harsher and louder than he'd intended, but right at that moment, he didn't give much of a pile of *mi-ertus*.

Everyone fell silent, staring at him. He realized his hand was on the hilt of his sword and forced himself to release it. These people were not his enemy.

Finding one lost child is also not our mission, the Nereid said. *We need the Star of Artemis. To return it to the Trident and take our rightful place as prince of Atlantis. The child's fate is unfortunate, but children are dying all over the world. We can't save them all.*

"We can save this one," Justice said fiercely. Alejandro, Keely, and the others turned puzzled faces to him, and he realized he was doing it again. Arguing with himself out loud.

We can save this one, he repeated, but this time in his mind. *I hate to pull out a bad cliché, but you're either with me or you're against me, and I'm just a single one of Alaric's mindfucks away from getting rid of you forever.*

The Nereid fell silent, so Justice decided to talk to all the people who *didn't* live in his brain.

"Look, we've been over this and over this for an hour. This discussion is useless and mind-bogglingly irrelevant."

He pointed at Alejandro, whose dark eyes were flashing fire and vengeance. "*You* want to bulldoze our way in there, guns blazing, with every man we've got. Go before twilight and surprise them and snatch Eleni. Have I got that right?"

Alejandro nodded. "*Sí.* It's the only way. We overpower them and—"

Justice cut him off. "It's the only way, all right. It's the only way to get the rest of your men killed. Vampires never take stupid chances. Their sense of self-preservation is matched only by their cowardice and depravity. They wouldn't have taunted us with that note unless they had far superior numbers. Obviously they've got human or some kind of nonvamp help, or they couldn't have taken Eleni during the middle of the afternoon. They sure as the nine hells won't be sitting in the middle of the meet place playing jump rope with her."

He looked at each one of them in turn. "We go in hard and fast and they kill us hard and fast. Then they kill her, wherever they've hidden her. Then just for kicks they come here and slaughter the rest of your people."

Keely nodded, rubbing her reddened eyes. "I've been telling him—"

Justice cut her off, too. "You've been telling him that we threaten the vamps. Reason with them. Tell them that the P Ops patrol should be here tomorrow and if they give us Eleni, we won't rat them out. Is that about right?"

Keely nodded, her eyes narrowing. She probably figured she wasn't going to like what he said next.

She was right.

"Vamps don't do logic and reason when they're angry and want revenge. We can threaten them with P Ops, sure. They'll cut their losses and move on somewhere new, to a nesting ground where we can't find them. Of course, they'll drain Eleni first and leave her dead body for us as a present, but they'll be gone."

Keely's face went dead white at his cruelty, but he just added it to the list of his sins, the inner whip of self-flagellation cutting mercilessly into him. Yeah. He was a foul bastard who'd abandoned these poor villagers for an afternoon of selfish pleasure, and a tiny child would pay the price.

An orphan, like he'd been an orphan. But he'd at least had adoptive parents who'd loved him. Eleni had nothing but pain, torture, and death in front of her, unless he fixed it.

He was good at fixing things.

He unsheathed his sword and carefully placed it on the table in front of him. "This is the plan. Either get on board or get the hells out of my way, but this *will be* the plan. They want me, I'm guessing, since I'm the one with the nifty explosive trick."

Alejandro slammed a fist down on the table. "They want me! The use of the word 'barter' was deliberate. If you are planning any solo trip to the vampire camp, you are mistaken. These are my people, and I failed them while I . . . while I—" he shot an anguished look at Maria who sat, sobbing, at the end of the table. "While I shirked my duty," he finished, a dull flush on his cheekbones.

Justice met Alejandro's gaze in a moment of perfectly shared understanding. They were both warriors who had failed to protect their charges. They both would die to make it right.

Fine. Let him come.

"What *is* the plan, then?" The bruised-looking skin under Keely's eyes emphasized her stark, drawn pallor. "You're the mighty Atlantean warrior, so why don't you tell us all about it?"

Where there had been love and laughter in her eyes only a few short hours before, now there was nothing but desolation. Keely's guilt must be as crushing as his own, he realized.

Not only Atlantean warriors carried the weight of innocents on their souls.

"They want to barter, so we barter," he said flatly. "Me for Eleni."

A chorus of dissent broke out around the table, but Keely looked down at her hands resting on the table and said nothing, although she flinched as if from a blow.

"They'll kill you," Alejandro said. "Kill you first, then Eleni, and then the rest of us. I have no illusions that we can hold off a blood pride of angry vampires with a few shotguns."

"Maybe. But if so, I plan to take them with me," Justice replied, never taking his eyes off Keely. "Anyway, plan A is that nobody dies but vampires. I suddenly have a lot to live for."

Keely finally looked up at him, and the black emptiness in her eyes scared him more than the idea of facing a hundred vampires.

"Give me a shotgun," she said.

"You will not come anywhere near that nest," Justice began. "I'll—"

But it was her turn to cut him off. She ignored him as completely as if he didn't exist and turned to Maria, who was still weeping. "If you can shut up for five minutes, get me a shotgun," she said with icy disdain. Then she lifted something from her lap and placed it on the table in front of her in an eerie echo of Justice's action of mere minutes before.

It was the bloody slipper.

Maria, shocked into silence, traded a long look with Keely and then squared her shoulders and hurried off. Keely selected a piece of bread and started chewing it with grim determination.

"We need to eat," she said, still in that utterly flat tone. "We haven't eaten all day. It's still an hour until twilight, and I won't fail Eleni again because I was too damn stupid to put fuel in my body before I went to rescue her."

Justice, who could function at full capacity for up to six days with no food, decided to follow her lead. Maybe letting Keely feel in control of something, even something as meaningless as the decision to eat bread and cold stew, would help her find her way back from her own personal hell.

She swallowed the piece of bread and began on her previously untouched bowl of stew, slowly and methodically eating one spoonful after another. It was like watching a zombie or one of those robots in the movies Ven liked to watch. There was nothing of human emotion about it, no trace of fear or sorrow.

Just spoonful after spoonful of cold stew.

His mouth dried out so much he was almost unable to swallow the bread. If by his folly he had lost both the child and Keely, there was nothing left for him. His mind tortured him with visions of a world without Keely, and a Void blacker than any Anubisa could conjure yawned like an abyss at his feet, beckoning.

Alejandro looked from Justice to Keely and then nodded as if reaching a decision. He broke off a hunk of bread and started chewing.

Keely dropped her spoon in her bowl and metal rang against metal; a hollow, haunting sound. Then she turned those dead eyes on Justice again and something in his soul shriveled.

"You told us what you're going to do," she said. "Now tell us how we can help."

Chapter 39

Just before twilight, San Bartolo

The men from the village had hidden themselves as best they could in the trees and grass surrounding the temple, but the plan for them to cover Justice with protective gunfire was a dismal failure. The topography didn't lend itself to any real cover; in order to see their targets clearly they'd have to come into the open or they'd be firing blind and take the chance of hitting Justice or Eleni.

Of course, if the vamps forced him to take the meeting inside the temple where the mural was, all bets were off. He'd be entirely on his own.

Keely, shotgun ready and aimed, lay on the ground on her stomach just over a slight rise in the ground, hidden by the tall grasses. Alejandro flanked her, kneeling, and between the two of them a pile of ammunition lay ready for reloading. Justice had tried to hold her, just for one last embrace before he went down to face the vampires, but she'd been stiff and resistant in his arms. He'd kissed the top of her head and let her go, hating that their last moment together would be like this.

He crouched down beside the two of them. "It's time. Are you ready?"

Alejandro swore virulently, shaking his head. "No, we're not ready. We're nearly useless here. I need to go with you."

"No. We've been over this. If I fall to them, I'll need for you to come get Eleni and keep her safe. Keep Keely safe. I need your word," Justice said.

Alejandro looked like he wanted to argue, but finally nodded. "You have my word. I will protect the child and your woman with my dying breath. Right now I'm going to check that everyone is in place. I'll return within two minutes."

Justice nodded and Alejandro slipped away as silently as one of the jaguars that roamed the jungle.

Keely watched him go, too, and then looked up at Justice, that flat, dead look still in place in her emerald eyes. "I can protect myself, and I'm nobody's woman. You do what you need to do. We'll take care of our end."

Justice wanted nothing more than to take her and fly away from this miserable place, far from vampires and death and stolen children. He'd finally found the true mate to his heart, to his soul, and he would lose her so quickly. He knew the optimistic plan he'd fed the others had no chance of succeeding. The vampires would be more than ready for him.

He'd stepped into situations like this before, but always with his brothers and the rest of the Seven at his side. They could handle all of it as long as they were together.

Alone, he was nothing but vamp fodder.

There were so many things he wished he'd had the time to say. Abruptly he stood up, forcing himself to move. "Keely, know this. No matter what you are thinking or feeling, you have no blame in this. It was I who stole you away for those hours, I who failed to protect this village and the child. I am tasked with protecting humanity, and yet I chose selfishly instead of honoring my duty."

A flicker of life moved behind her eyes, and she slowly shook her head from side to side. "I knew how much she was suffering, Justice. She's just like me, except she was orphaned and treated like a pariah. I knew, and still I abandoned her."

Tears welled up in her eyes, but her face was hard and unyielding. "If you fall, I will follow you and rescue that child, no matter what it takes."

He took the shotgun from her hands, pulled her into a fierce embrace, and kissed her with every bit of love and longing his soul cried out to give her. Forcing himself to release her was the hardest thing he'd ever done in his long, bleak centuries of existence.

She caught his arm as he turned away. "Justice," she said, so quietly he nearly missed it. "I love you, too."

He said nothing. Words were beyond him, as his soul prepared for death. He simply began the solitary walk down to the San Bartolo temple, a condemned man walking to his own execution.

But he'd save the child first. When they remembered his worthless life, they would know that Eleni lived.

There was only one final act he must at least try. He stopped walking and closed his eyes, mustering every ounce of energy and power he possessed, and then he called for the portal.

This time it answered his call. Fickle godsdamned thing. As the familiar ovoid shape appeared and shimmered and stretched into shape, he saw the startled faces of the guards on the other side as they recognized him and lowered their weapons. When he made no move to enter, one of them called out to him.

"Lord Justice? Your brothers will be very happy to know that you're back. The portal hasn't opened for any of us, not even Alaric, since you left."

Ah. That answered one question. They'd known he was in San Bartolo. Part of him had hoped—no, expected—that they would show up to save the day, as Ven liked to say.

"My lord? Are you entering?" the other one asked him. "Is there trouble?"

"Yes," Justice finally answered. "Yes, there is trouble. Tell Conlan and Ven . . . Tell them to send help. Tell them we need reinforcements. Tell them the Star of Artemis is here but it's guarded by a nest of vampires."

"We will cross over right now to assist you," the first guard said. He took a determined step forward and the portal's magic shot something that looked and sounded like a high-wattage electric jolt at him, smashing him back and onto the ground.

"No, it looks like you won't," Justice replied, oddly unsurprised. "For whatever reason, the portal wants me to do this on my own, which makes me think Poseidon has set me some particularly vicious test."

"But—"

"Tell Conlan and Ven . . ." Justice had to force out the words. "Tell them that I love them. Tell them that I'm proud to be their brother and that I'm sorry. That's all."

"Lord Justice!"

But Justice simply shook his head and walked away, not even watching to see if the portal closed behind him. While he talked to the Atlanteans, it had fallen full dusk. Eleni was waiting. If she even still lived.

If she did not, he would set the earth itself on fire with the power of his fury.

The Nereid spoke in his mind, in the resigned tone of one who has accepted his fate. *So now we die, but at least we die gloriously. It has been an honor being part of you, Justice of Atlantis.*

"It has been an honor being part of you, Justice of the Nereids," Justice said, realizing as he spoke the words that he truly meant them.

For our final grand gesture, I propose that we truly merge into one being, more powerful together than either of us could ever be apart, the Nereid said, a dark glee in his tone.

"If you're going to go, go big," Justice said, laughing. "Let's do it."

As one, both sides of his being—both halves of his soul—crashed open the doors and shields and walls they'd built up between them over the long years of his existence. Power, finally unfettered, raced through his body and energized him with the towering force of a typhoon.

Laughter burst out of him at the sheer joy of so much power sweeping through his body—waves and waves of pure, silvery power. Suddenly, he knew what he might be able to do.

There was a chance. A tiny one, but still a chance that he was going to live through this.

Just one final thing. Bending down, he found a smooth stone on the ground, far from the riverbank where it had been polished by the water. Opening up his heart and his soul, he focused all of his emotion to absolute truth and poured it into the stone. *I love you, Keely, and will love you until all of the oceans vanish from the desolate plains of the earth. Know now and always that you are my heart, my soul, and my life.*

He clenched the stone so tightly in his fist that it hurt and then slowly opened his fingers. If his plan failed, it would be enough.

It would have to be enough.

Chapter 40

Justice was still laughing with the joy and force of the power crashing through his body when he reached the front of the temple. The two vampires who stood at the entrance sneered at him.

"Laugh now, mortal, for our leader will kill you slowly."

"Nice. Original with just that hint of melodrama," he said, thinking of Ven's usual responses to situations like this. "Now give me the girl."

"Move back and kneel to your better, fool," the uglier of the two vampires said. "He comes now."

"I kneel to none but Poseidon," Justice said calmly, drawing his sword. Poseidon's Fury gleamed like polished silver under the twilight moon. "Bring me the girl now or the two of you shall die cursing your names."

They looked uncertainly at each other, clearly hearing the promise in his voice. But then the sound of many voices came from the entrance, and a swarm of vamps came out of the temple.

He'd been way, way off in his estimation. There were nearly one hundred of them, give or take a dozen.

He was a dead Atlantean walking.

But by all the gods, he could bluff.

"Bring me the girl now," he repeated, this time talking to the peacock of a man in the pseudo-ancient Mayan getup. Maybe he thought it made him look more important. Kingly, even.

Justice didn't give a damn what he looked like. He just wanted Eleni.

"Bring me the girl, or I will cause the biggest shock wave you have ever seen to explode every single one of you into an oozing pile of slime."

The peacock bared his fangs. "I am Gultep'can, and you are a petitioner at the feet of my greatness."

Justice shrugged. "Not much for feet, greatness or otherwise. I only petition to the greatness of Poseidon, and not very often."

"Your sea god is a puny weakling compared to the glory of Anubisa," Gultep'can sneered.

"I know your goddess, up close and personal," Justice said with loathing. "But we can play 'my god is greater than your goddess' later. Right now, you have ten seconds to bring me that girl, alive and unharmed, or you are all going to face the true death on the eleventh."

Gultep'can's eyes flickered just enough for Justice to realize that he was buying the bluff.

"Bring the girl," Gultep'can ordered. "I am the mighty Gultep'can and I proposed this bargain, and so I do decree that it will be so."

Yeah, way to save face. But Justice didn't care how it happened, so long as it happened. For now, the vamps were keeping a healthy distance. Clearly they'd heard what had happened to their buddies the night before.

But that wouldn't last long if he didn't back up his threats with action. And the problem was that he just didn't know if the shock wave would kill Eleni, too, if he released its power. Last night it had only killed vamps, but had that been a fluke? Until he could fully understand and control his new, unified powers, he would not risk her life. If she still had a life to risk.

Finally, his mental countdown at nine seconds, he heard the most wonderful sound in the world. Eleni's tiny voice.

"Señor Justice! You came! I knew you'd come!"

One of the vamps came out of the entrance, dragging her by her thin dress, and then let her go at a gesture from Gultep'can. She ran toward Justice as fast as her little legs could carry her and jumped into his arms. He hugged her quickly and then put her down at his left side so his sword arm was free.

She trustingly slipped her hand in his and looked up at him. "When you make the beautiful waterspouts, can I watch?"

He squeezed her hand. "Eleni, I don't have time for games right now. You are going to head back to the village for me, over that ridge, okay?" He pointed up the slope exactly at the point where Keely and Alejandro lay, hidden from view.

"But I want to stay and help," she said.

Justice tried to be patient with the traumatized child in spite of the fact that dozens of vamps were skulking closer and closer to them. He put the stone in her hand and folded her fingers over it.

"You are a very brave girl, but you can help me most by doing what I ask. Give this to Keely for me, Eleni. It's very important. Now, please go and find—"

"Keely and Alejandro, yes, I know. They're right over that hill," she said artlessly, tightly holding on to the stone. "Will they let me help load the shotguns?"

Her innocent question, born of her psychic gift, galvanized the vampires like a lightning strike through water.

"You dare to try to betray our bargain?" Gultep'can roared. "Kill them!"

"Run, *now*, Eleni," Justice shouted over the din. "I'll protect you while you get away. *Run!*"

Eleni ran. He barred the way to her, sword flashing and striking death into any vamp who tried to get past him. He fought like he'd never fought before, but there were too many. They came at him from all sides, striking and biting and clawing, and soon he bled from a score of wounds, but he managed to keep any of them from following Eleni.

"We're here!" Keely's voice rang out and Justice saw her step out from behind a tree, shotgun braced against her shoulder. "Eleni, come to me! Run faster!"

Gultep'can screamed out commands and his minions went

running in every direction. "Get her! Get the child! Kill Justice before he can bring the earth's anger again!"

Four of them rushed Justice, grabbing him by each of his arms and legs and sinking four sets of fangs into him. He threw back his head and howled out his pain and rage, but they were vampire strong, and he was bleeding from dozens of wounds. Four against one was too much.

Yet another wrenched his sword out of his grasp, but the hilt set the bloodsucker's hand on fire and the flames rushed up its body until it was a stinking pile of ash with a sword lying on top of it.

Justice watched in anguish as more of them started up the hill toward Keely and Eleni. "Keely," he roared. "Get out of here."

Eleni reached Keely as he watched and immediately dropped into a ball at Keely's feet. The thunder of shotgun fire boomed out; first once, then twice, and Justice saw that Alejandro was in the game, too. As he watched, every one of the villagers stepped out of their hiding places, guns aimed and firing.

They thought they were protecting Keely, he realized, despair flooding him. All they were doing was getting themselves killed, and her with them.

∞~~~∞

Keely's heart started beating again when Eleni reached her, safe and seemingly relatively unharmed. But it stopped again when she realized Justice was buried under a sea of vampires who were slowly biting and clawing his flesh from his body.

There was no way anybody could survive that.

With shaking hands, she settled the stock of the shotgun more firmly into the hollow of her shoulder, aimed at one of the vamps holding Justice, and fired. The report nearly deafened her, and she reflexively flinched. When she opened her eyes, she saw the now-headless vampire's body falling to the ground.

Another shotgun blast sounded from very near her, and another vamp's head exploded. Alejandro.

She turned to him and he gave her a thumbs-up, smiling

grimly. "If we're going to go out fighting, let's at least give them a fight," he yelled.

She nodded, no time or energy for talking, and took aim again.

∿——∾

In the space of seconds, two of the vamps holding him had been blasted to the true death. Justice grinned at the sight of Keely and Alejandro standing practically shoulder to shoulder, firing on the vamps.

Two to one was great odds, never mind the blood pouring down his face from a head wound. He slumped into a sudden deadweight, going down and taking his two remaining captors with him. It was a simple trick to snap one's neck and then roll over the other one, grab his sword, and chop through its neck. In a flash, he was back up on his feet and back in the fight, slicing and stabbing and hacking.

Gultep'can waded into the battle, his eyes glowing a vicious red, and tossed his own vampires away from him so he could clear a path to Justice. "I will kill you myself," he snarled.

"Come and get me," Justice taunted, beckoning.

A space cleared out between and around them, just like it had in the schoolyard battles Justice had fought as a child. What a circle life was. He'd started out fighting bullies in a ring and now he would die that way.

But he was taking Gultep'can with him.

He shifted a little, so he could see Keely. The vamps had stopped stalking her as they all rushed over to watch their nasty-ass leader mop the jungle floor with Justice.

"Read the stone," he shouted as loudly as he could. "And get the hells out of here. Now!"

A rushing movement at the corner of his peripheral vision alerted him, and he turned fast, but not fast enough to avoid the dagger Gultep'can hurled at him. He caught it in the ribs and staggered back. He ripped the dagger out of his chest and hurled it on the ground, then started laughing again. "Is that all you got? Big bad vampire god wannabe and all you got is a little knife?"

Gultep'can, enraged beyond all reason, howled and screeched

and dove straight at him. Justice blocked the worst of the blow and sliced his sword out as best he could in the close quarters, slicing a long gash up the vamp's abdomen.

"You'll die slowly for that one," Gultep'can screamed, holding in something that looked a lot like a piece of his intestines.

Justice laughed again, just because he could. The wounds were finally taking their toll, overcoming the burst of adrenaline-fueled strength. He'd always been immune to vampire bites but sheer blood loss could get him. He stumbled, suddenly dizzy, and the vamps took it as their cue. They all swarmed him and he went down in a tangle of arms, legs, and slashing, ripping fangs.

The last thing he heard was the fading echo of the Nereid's voice. *We don't have to die like this.*

∞～～∞

Keely saw Justice go down under what looked like hundreds of vampires and she fell to her knees, the gun falling from her nerveless fingers. Something fragile ripped wide-open in her chest, and she cried out in anguish.

Eleni sat up and leaned against her, throwing her arms around her in a fierce hug. "Don't cry, Keely. The water god is coming, but first Justice will make the pretty blue waterspouts."

The child pressed something round and smooth into Keely's hand, and she automatically closed her fingers around it. A rock. Eleni was so traumatized, she was babbling nonsense and had given her a rock to comfort her. Keely didn't know whether to laugh or cry.

Then the full force of Justice's love swept into her from the rock, so powerful it permeated her glove, lifting her up and washing her away with the currents.

∞～～∞

"I. Don't. Want. To. Die. Like. This," Justice gritted out, as he ripped one of them off him by the jaw. The vamp's fangs took a chunk of skin with them, but at least that was one fewer. He smashed his elbow in the face of another, and suddenly his arms were—for just a moment—free.

He threw them up in the air and roared out a single word. A word in the ancient language of the Nereids. A word he didn't even know that he knew, but that had suddenly swelled in his heart and soul, dangerous and sharp and deadly.

The word called power to it and turned tangible as it left his mouth, hanging in the air above the place where he lay on the ground, dying.

Being murdered.

He watched, his life's blood draining out of him from so many, many wounds, as the word took shape and became real and raised in dark and terrible beauty the fearsome power of the universe.

A thundering boom shook the land and the trees and even the sky, and a shock wave visibly poured out from the word in concentric circles and turned the world to crystalline shades of blue and silver.

All around him and on top of him and even somehow underneath him, the vampires exploded, not into their usual acidic slime but into fountains of clear, pure water.

He raised his head with the last of his energy and looked around and saw that everywhere the same thing was happening. Miniature geysers of pure water sprang up wherever a vampire had stood. Last to go was Gultep'can himself, who screamed his defiance to the very end.

"Some grand gesture," Justice said, his head thumping to the ground as his neck could no longer support the weight of it. He turned toward the small hill and saw Keely, his beloved Keely, glowing like a flame. She had her arms around Eleni, but she was starting down the hill toward him.

So they lived. They both lived. It was enough.

Justice smiled a little, full of regret but also content. He'd saved them.

It was enough.

Chapter 41

Keely stood in awe as the vampires exploded, one after another, into beautiful whirlpools of silvery blue water. Justice had done it somehow. She knew it.

Then she saw him, lying on the ground, so bloody that it was impossible that he still lived. She started downhill, picking up pace until she was running, barely even noticing that Eleni ran behind her.

"Justice! Don't you dare die on me! You have to live. You have to live for me!" She kept yelling meaningless nonsense all the way down the hill, until finally she skidded to a stop in front of him and fell to the ground.

At first she thought he was dead, and pain knifed through her so intensely that she doubled over from the force of it. Then she saw his head move, just a fraction of a centimeter, but it was a movement.

"Please, please, please, come back to me," she begged, stroking the top of his head, which seemed to be the only uninjured part of his entire body.

Alejandro ran up to them. "Is he—"

"No!" Keely shouted. "No, he is not. And don't you dare say it!"

"Keely, you should take Eleni back to the village," Alejandro said, kindness and sympathy warm in his voice. "There is nothing we can do for him. That one gash is so deep, it must have cut into his lungs."

"No. I won't leave him. You take Eleni back." She kissed Eleni's forehead to reassure the girl, as much as she could be reassured after an experience like this. "I'll come back for you. But right now I must be with Justice so he's not alone." Her voice broke and she hugged Eleni, her bitter tears falling into the girl's hair.

Alejandro spoke again, but somehow this time it was not Alejandro. Keely didn't know how she knew this, but she did. She jerked her head up to stare at Alejandro, who suddenly seemed to shine with silvery light.

"I CHOSE WELL WHEN I GIFTED MY SWORD TO JUSTICE," thundered a voice that held all the power, glory, and mystery of the seas.

"Poseidon?" Keely knew. She'd heard that voice before, in her visions.

"YES, OBJECT READER. I AM THE SEA GOD WHO CLAIMS THIS WARRIOR AS MY OWN. KNOW ALL PRESENT THAT NOW THE SWORD THAT FULFILLED ITS DUTY SO WELL AT HIS HAND SHALL SERVE TO HEAL ITS WIELDER."

The silvery light spread from Alejandro and formed an iridescent dome over Justice, Keely, and Eleni, and the icy cold of the ocean depths suddenly seared through her skin and bones. Eleni gasped and huddled closer to Keely, burying her face in Keely's shirt.

Justice's sword, lying nearby, lit up. The sigils on the blade glowed with a silvery fire so bright that they all had to shield their eyes. After long moments, the glare that filtered through Keely's eyelids faded and she dared to sneak a narrow-eyed glance.

The light was gone. Alejandro still stood frozen, unmoving, but the light was gone.

"I like it not that I nearly died, and my woman is already looking at another man," Justice said, amusement in his husky tone.

She whipped her head around, almost afraid to look. What she saw made her cry out in wonder. Justice sat up, whole and uninjured. Even the blood that had coated him was gone.

"You . . . you . . . you—" she stuttered, then threw herself into his arms.

"That's more like it," he said, then caught her lips in a soul-melting kiss. It was a kiss infused with heat and wonder and awe, and it lasted a very long time.

"SO," the voice like thunder said, startling them out of their embrace. "YOU HAVE CHOSEN WELL IN YOUR WOMAN, BUT TELL HER TO KEEP HER HANDS OFF MY TRIDENT. SOME SECRETS ARE TOO VIOLENT FOR AN OBJECT READER TO EVER KNOW AND SURVIVE."

Justice stood up, pulling Keely to her feet beside him, and he lifted Eleni into his arms. "What was it?" he asked Alejandro, who was not Alejandro. "Was it a test? After these hundreds of years of loyal service, you test me now and put my woman and these innocents in such great danger?"

"IT WAS NOT I WHO PUT THEM IN SUCH DANGER, BUT IT WAS FOR YOU TO PROTECT THEM. POSEIDON'S FURY IS MINE TO GIVE AND MINE TO RECLAIM, AND EVERY FIVE CENTURIES I DECIDE WHO SHALL HOLD IT AND PASS IT DOWN."

The sea god's voice was haughty beyond arrogance, commanding beyond dispute. Keely supposed that, being a sea god, it came with the territory.

"Thank you," she said, not knowing if it was allowed for her to talk to Poseidon, but needing to say it. "Thank you for his life."

"YOU GAVE HIM HIS LIFE, DR. KEELY McDERMOTT OF THE LAND OF OHIO. I SIMPLY HEALED A FEW WOUNDS."

Poseidon held up Alejandro's arms and glanced down at his body. "THIS ONE IS STRONG. I WOULD NOT HAVE MINDED HAVING ONE SUCH AS HE IN MY WARRIORS," he said, and it was so odd to hear and see it that Keely almost laughed, but figured that might be some kind of blasphemy.

"ENOUGH. I MUST GO NOW," Poseidon decreed. "BUT FIRST, ONE FINAL THING."

He reached out with one of Alejandro's hands and touched Eleni's face. "YOU WILL GROW UP TO BE VERY WISE, YOUNGLING, AND A COUNSELOR TO KINGS. MIND THAT YOU REMEMBER THAT."

She laughed and clapped. "Can I come play with the dolphins with you, Señor Sea God?"

Poseidon's laughter rang in the air. "MOST DEFINITELY, YOUNGLING. MOST DEFINITELY."

Alejandro stumbled, then looked around wildly, raising his shotgun. "What? What happened? Where is he?"

Justice tightened his arm around Keely. "Now we get some rest, and then we get to work."

"Work?" She had no idea what he was talking about.

"The Star, Keely. We must find the Star of Artemis and take it back to Atlantis."

"The Star," she repeated. "You know, I'd almost forgotten about it."

Deep voices sounded from inside the temple, and they all reacted instantly, going for weapons. When Ven, Conlan, and Alaric appeared at the entrance, they were greeted by several shotguns and a sword pointed directly at them.

Keely smiled a little, remembering another surprise entrance. Turnabout was only fair play.

"We thought we'd lend a hand," Ven said cheerfully. "But it looks like you've got things well under control."

Alejandro, shotgun pointed at Conlan's head, glanced at Justice. "Do you know these men, or shall I propose another *barter*?"

Justice laughed. "No, my friend. These men are . . . my family."

Alaric gave them that narrow-eyed stare. "Much more has happened here than is apparent at this time, I think."

Conlan inclined his head. "I think you're right. Does anybody want to tell us what in the hells has been going on here?"

Justice and Keely started laughing like loons, and the three Atlanteans looked at them though they were crazy.

"I'll tell you the story of San Bartolo and the league of

extraordinarily vicious vampires," Justice told his brothers and Alaric, when he could finally speak. "We'll have food, rest, and talk. And then we'll all come back here and find the Star."

"The Star of Artemis is here? We will find it now," Alaric commanded.

"Justice almost died," Keely told him with some asperity. "The Star has been safely buried in that rock for thousands of years. One more night isn't going to hurt it."

Alaric started to respond, but Conlan held up a hand. "No, she is right. At this time, I find that I would like to have a meal with my *brother* and his woman."

Justice clenched his jaw and fierce emotion shone in his dark eyes, but Ven held up his hands in mock protest. "Oh, hells no, Brother, don't call her his woman."

Keely lifted her face and kissed Justice's jaw, then smiled at Ven. "It's okay. I surrender. Since even the sea god himself called me Justice's woman, I've decided to just go with it."

Justice flashed her a look of such powerful love and acceptance that her knees nearly went weak. It was a look of belonging—a look of home. "*Mi amara*, you are mine and I am yours. Forever."

"Forever," she said.

Then, holding Eleni and each other, they led the way to food and rest.

Epilogue

Two weeks later, San Bartolo

Keely walked out of the temple into the bright afternoon sunshine and smiled at the sight of Justice playing catch with Eleni in the clearing. Her big, tough warrior was a softie where the child was concerned.

"You will work with us on this?" Señor Hector asked. As Guatemalan director of archaeological affairs, he was thrilled that the vampires were gone from the site and anxious to resume work.

"No, I'm sorry, but since the head of my department mysteriously disappeared, I have a lot to do back at Ohio State. Plus, I have another project in mind," she said. "I'm sure you and the original team will have a wonderfully exciting time, though. Please do be sure to keep me updated so I can hear all about it."

He nodded and hurried off to supervise the members of his staff who were unpacking the tools and supplies. She headed for Justice, her smile growing every step of the way.

"Are you two kids having fun?"

Justice lifted her into the air and swung her around. "Do you want to play?" he said silkily, his eyes going dark and very intent. She could always tell when her man had sex on the brain.

Of course, it was almost all the time, so maybe it wasn't all that impressive, as psychic talents went.

"Later," she said, laughing. "Now put me down."

He did, after kissing her breathless.

"When will Alejandro be back?"

Justice tossed the ball to Eleni, who promptly dropped it and ran off to chat with the grad students. She was slowly blossoming, in spite of everything she'd been through, and Keely hoped that time, that great cure, would help to eventually give her a normal, happy childhood, and that the shadows in Eleni's eyes would one day disappear. Now that they'd begun the process to officially adopt her, which she'd been assured would be considered with all speed, taking into account the best interests of the child and the great service Keely and Justice had performed for the people of Peten, Eleni was finally starting to believe that she would really have a new home and family.

A few days earlier, she had come to them and asked them to help her bury the slipper and hold a memorial service, just the three of them, for her lost mother. Keely had cried right along with Eleni after they put flowers on the tiny mound of dirt and said good-bye to Mama in heaven with Papa. Even Justice had had a few tears trailing down his face. He'd told Eleni that no brave warrior should ever be afraid to show her feelings, and that she honored her mother with her tears. Keely hoped that the ceremony had brought some measure of peace to the child so that the healing process could begin.

"Alejandro is still in training to lead the P Ops team that will guard the site," Justice said. "He should be back in a week or so, but we'll be gone by then."

"What about Alaric? What did he say when he examined your mind?" The thought of it still made her shudder, but she supposed it was better than what she'd gone through as a child. One short session versus years of psychoanalysis and drugs.

He shrugged. "He can't figure me out; the duality of my soul is too strange to him. Mostly I think he's just going to leave me alone."

She hugged him. "Sounds like the perfect resolution to me. Speaking of resolutions, are you ready?"

He hesitated, then nodded. "Yes. As ready as I'm ever going to be."

Keely glanced across the clearing and met Señor Hector's eyes and she nodded. He looked somber, but he nodded in return. They were all set.

Hand in hand, Justice and Keely entered the temple and walked up to the breathtaking mural. Even though they'd seen it so many times, it still inspired awe and wonder.

"That people living so long ago could create such beauty in the middle of building their civilization," Keely said. "It astonishes and humbles me."

"Wait till you see more of Atlantis," Justice said, grinning. "It's going to rock your world."

She laughed. "Always one for breaking a mood, aren't you? Anyway, you rock my world."

Turning serious, she pointed to a small crevice in the mural, directly in the center of the eye of one of the fish. "This is it. I've excavated enough for you to use your water power to gently sluice it out with a minimum of damage."

"Still can't believe Hector went along with this. Or that Alaric and Conlan put up with the delay."

"Well, Hector kind of owed us," she said. "Without you, they'd never have gotten access to this site again. And don't get me started on Alaric."

He called water, and a thin, delicate stream spiraled through the air and into the crevice with the precision of a scalpel in the hands of a master surgeon. They waited, holding their breath, and within a minute or two that lasted forever, a shimmer of something appeared at the mouth of the crevice.

She cupped her gloved hands underneath the opening and water poured into them, followed by a golf ball–sized sapphire that gleamed with the brightness of a lovers' moon.

"Oh, Justice," she whispered. "It's so beautiful. The Star of Artemis. At long last."

"I still cannot believe Conlan and Alaric did not forcibly smash through the mural and take the Star," Justice said, his lips quirking at the memory of *that* argument.

"Well, they owed you one, too," she said fiercely.

"And you are so quick to defend me, *mi amara*."

She held out the Star. "Now we can discover what it really does. If it heals fractured minds."

He stared down at it for a long time, then slowly shook his head. "No, my love. My mind is no longer fractured, and I have no desire to perhaps learn that the Star would rend me in two again."

He leaned down and pressed a brief kiss to her lips. "Your love has healed everything that was broken in me, and I have no need of this rock. Now or ever."

Keely touched her necklace and closed her hand around the tiny fish. "I can't believe that this little fish showed me the face of the man who would become my universe. You've healed everything that was broken in me, too. I cannot imagine a life without you. Now or ever."

Their words carried the resonance of vows. Keely realized that centuries of battle, honor, and courage, combined with the horrors of his childhood, had unleashed not only one but two beasts in Justice. Now, through the power of their love, the beasts were joined together to form one whole. The man she would love forever.

She twined her arms around his neck and kissed him, the promise of an eternity of love on her lips. Seconds or minutes or hours later, Eleni's impatient voice came from the entrance to the temple.

"Come *on*, already," she demanded. "I want to play ball, please."

Laughing, Keely and Justice pulled apart and, hand in hand, walked out into the sunlight, toward their child and their future, together.

Turn the page for a special preview
of the next book in the
Warriors of Poseidon series

ATLANTIS UNMASKED

By Alyssa Day

Available July 2009 from Berkley Sensation!

Leaving regional rebel headquarters, St. Louis

"It's almost impossible to shoot a bow while driving."

Grace Havilland clenched her fingers around the steering wheel of the Jeep and waited for the Atlantean warrior riding shotgun to respond to what she thought had been her very reasonable point.

Waited. Waited a little longer. She'd met Alexios months ago and seen him sporadically since, but she'd never been in such a small space with him. It felt like being trapped in a cage with a lion that'd just eaten a full meal. Deadly, dangerous, and exhilarating, but maybe—just maybe—you'd live through it.

Unless he suddenly felt like a snack.

She wrenched the wheel to the left when she saw the deceptive DEAD END sign appear in the headlights and then took the deserted side street. Alexios finally turned to face her, his golden hair brushing the tops of his shoulders and sweeping forward to hide the scarred left side of his face. Reinforcing the lion imagery so strongly she flinched a little.

He raised a single eyebrow.

"The sign keeps people out," she explained. "HQ escape route and a shortcut to the hospital. Since we're a little behind everyone else, I wanted to catch up."

A weak but warm voice floated up from the backseat. "Shortcut would be good."

"How are you doing, Michelle?" Grace asked, not daring to look over her shoulder at this rate of speed.

"Well enough, considering that nasty vampire nearly ripped my head from my neck. Lucky for me that your dishy Alaric popped in with the magic healing powers. My first mission with you Americans and the rebel headquarters gets attacked. Bit of a bad penny, me."

Alexios made a strangled snorting sound. "Dishy Alaric. Now there's something I bet he's never heard in his nearly five hundred years. Alaric, the dishy high priest of Poseidon's Temple." In spite of the rich, dark amusement in his voice, he never once quit scanning every inch of the deserted street as they raced through it. Always on guard. Always alert.

A warrior in every facet of his being.

Grace slanted a glance at him. Six feet and a few inches of pure, primitive male, all hard lines and curved muscle. He'd fought like an avenging angel back at HQ when their strategy meeting had been viciously destroyed by the wave of vampires and shifters crashing through doors and windows in a multi-pronged attack. She'd loosed arrow after arrow, each one finding its target, but Alexios and his sword and daggers were everywhere at once, stabbing, slicing, and slashing. All the while, his expression had remained utterly calm and controlled. Even as he'd circled around her, ripping heads from vamps and . . .

A realization seared through the memory. Always around *her.* He'd fought in a perimeter around her, leaving her room to shoot her bow, but never straying far from her side. Anger started a slow burn.

"Were you protecting me in that fight?" she asked, slowly and carefully, trying to put a lid on her temper. Not good to accuse and attack the fierce warrior ally unless it was true. "Because you know that I don't need protecting. I've been doing this for a long—"

Michelle made a loud shushing noise. "Oh, let's not get our knickers in a twist. So, Alexios. You don't look a day over thirty. But if Alaric is nearly five hundred years old, how about you?"

Alexios's dark gaze touched Grace's face for an instant, hot, predatory, tangible as a caress, before returning to vigilance. She wondered if his eyes were blue or black or one of the many shades of jewel-like green, but couldn't tell in the dark vehicle. Atlantean eyes were like mood rings. Unfortunately, they didn't give out the handy decoder chart.

"How about me, what?" he finally answered Michelle.

"How many centuries?"

"A little more than four. Grace, watch that hole in the road."

She swerved to miss the pothole and began to slow for the end of the road and the busy intersection it dumped into. "You're more than four hundred years old? Really?" Okay, maybe a man *that* old had a few preconceived notions about fragile females that could be forgiven.

"Well, you look lovely for your age," Michelle called out. "He's maybe a little old for you, Grace, though. You've only just turned twenty-five, after all."

Heat burned through Grace's cheeks. "What? Michelle, I—"

Before she could stammer out any convincing denials, on the order of, "No, I wasn't casting Alexios in my own personal fantasy," the man himself pointed his gun directly at her head.

She slammed on the brakes, too stunned to react coherently. Alexios and the Atlanteans were *allies* to the rebel cause; they wouldn't . . .

"On the left, Grace. Get down!"

Instinctively, she obeyed the tone of command in his voice and ducked, covering her head with her arms. The explosion of sound and glass tore through the Jeep a split second later, and Michelle screamed.

Over Grace's head, Alexios fired the Glock she'd loaned him when he'd realized his daggers and sword wouldn't be of much use in a moving vehicle. He spat forth a stream of words that absolutely had to be Atlantean cursing; she'd fought with warriors for enough years to recognize the cadence. If the Ice King of Calm was swearing, it had to be bad.

The realization brought her to a snap decision of her own. Grace wrenched the parking brake up, released her seat belt, and threw herself underneath his arms in a twisting half turn toward the backseat. Alexios slammed his hard chest down on her back, though, capturing her in a contorted embrace.

"No. If you lift your head, the attacker on the roof of that building is going to shoot you," he breathed in her ear.

"I need to get to Michelle. Now."

"I will not lose you," he said as he slowly pulled away. The words were so quiet that she nearly missed them. She snapped her head to the left and found his face a breath away from her own. Fury rode the high cheekbones and hard angles of his face. "I'm going out there," he said. "When I give the signal, you put this vehicle in gear and get the hells out of here."

He dropped the empty gun on the floorboard and pulled his daggers out of their sheaths. The movement was fluid and oddly slowed by stress-skewed perception, almost encapsulated in a bubble of time. She noticed the hairs on his tanned and muscled forearms were burnished gold, and she even had time to think it an odd observation to make before dying.

Then, in a move that made her wonder if somehow she'd gotten a head injury in the crash, Alexios simply disappeared. It wasn't sudden. It took maybe three or four seconds. But his body dissolved into a shimmering cascade of sparkling mist and, utterly transparent and nearly without shape, he soared through the open window beside her, leaving Grace with her mouth open in wonder and tiny water drops caught in her eyelashes.

"Oh dear. I think I may have died," Michelle said, moaning. "Either I just saw Alexios turn into an angel, or you and he are going to have some seriously interesting sex."

Stifling her ready retort, Grace resumed her crawl into the backseat to help Michelle, careful to keep her own head down. There was blood everywhere; the gunshot had smashed through the window next to Michelle and hit her shoulder. Glass glittered in her short dark hair, and shallow scratches bled on her forehead and cheeks.

"How bad?"

Michelle tried to smile, but it turned into a grimace. "I won't be wearing any sleeveless dresses for a while."

Grace's eyes burned. If she lost her best friend . . . "Damnit, Michelle, quit with that British stiff-upper-lip crap. How bad?"

In the pale glow reflected from the streetlamp, Michelle's face was whiter than a St. Louis blizzard. "Maybe a little bad. It's just below my shoulder, but I'm starting to have a hard time breathing, and—" As if on cue, Michelle's sentence trailed off into a horrible wheezing gasp.

"It must have punctured your lung. Oh, dear Lord and goddess help us, we've got to get out of here," Grace said, offering up prayers to Diana and to the Christian god. She snatched her bow and half-empty quiver from the back and pulled herself into the driver's seat, fitting arrow to bow with an ease born of long practice. She took aim through her open window and waited to deliver silver-tipped death.

She was a descendant of Diana, and her aim was always true.

"I'm going to get you to the hospital," she promised, scanning the area for Alexios or the attackers.

A dark shadow somersaulted through the air toward the Jeep, and she tracked it without thought, acting purely on instinct and natural talent.

"Didn't you have enough back at HQ, you bastards?" she screamed. "A dozen dead shifters and at least a half dozen dead vamps isn't enough? I'll kill every single one of you if she dies."

The shadow moved almost faster than her eye could follow until it materialized into a coalescing shimmer in the pool of light cast by the streetlamp. She eased the pressure of her fingers on the arrow.

Vamps didn't travel as mist. It was Alexios, transformed back into himself.

He bared his teeth and the expression on his face was so

utterly feral—so inhumanly predatory—that Grace caught her breath, ice skating down her spine.

"Go. Now," he ordered. "I'll be right above you. Get her to the hospital. Now."

"You got them?"

"They won't hurt anyone else," he said. "Now go!"

Michelle's harsh wheezing fired Grace's urgency to do just that. She slammed the Jeep back into gear and, tires squealing, pulled out into the street and away from the remains of whatever had attacked them in the alley.

"Hang on, baby, hang on, please, please, Michelle, hang on," she pleaded in a constant demand and prayer, as she sped the remaining couple of miles to the hospital. Above the Jeep, matching her pace exactly, a soaring cloud of sparkling darkness watched over them.

She bumped over the curb at the entrance to the emergency room parking lot and pulled the Jeep right up to the door, ignoring signs and the shouts from the ambulance personnel standing around the large double doors. Grace leapt out, shouting for help, and raced around to open the back passenger door. Michelle slumped out into her arms, eyes wide and staring, and Grace instinctively screamed, so loud and long her throat burned, for the one person she needed more than she'd ever needed anyone.

"Alexios!"

"I am here." He lifted Michelle out of Grace's arms and began running for the ER doors. Emergency personnel met him with a gurney. He gently lowered Michelle onto it and backed away as hospital personnel rushed Michelle inside, already snapping out competent-sounding medical speak.

Head lowered, Alexios returned to Grace and lifted her into his arms, holding her to him so tightly she almost felt— *almost*, for a fraction of a second—*safe*.

She saw one of her team approaching from the outside waiting area, and she put her hands flat on Alexios's chest to brace herself and push him away. For an instant, his eyes flared such a hot green that she wondered his gaze didn't burn the skin from her face. But then he slowly, inch by inch, lowered her to the ground and released her, almost as if he, too, were reluctant to break the contact.

"I can move the Jeep, Grace," Spike said. He'd been wounded by the first wave of shifters in the door, but the bandages wrapping both of his arms and the side of his face clearly hadn't slowed him down. "Everybody is already getting treatment. Most all of us are going to be fine. We'll hear about Hawk after surgery."

She nodded, glad to hear it but too drained to comment.

Spike's eyes narrowed, and he shot a suspicious look at Alexios. "We thought that dark-haired guy healed Michelle?"

"So he did," Alexios replied, his jaw clenching around the words. "We were ambushed."

Spike was instantly on the balls of his feet, hands hovering near his jacket, underneath which Grace knew he carried at least three guns and several knives. "How many? Do you want us to go after them?"

"They're taken care of," Grace said.

Alexios nodded. "There were only four." Any other man would have been boasting; Alexios merely stated facts.

A flash of respect crossed Spike's face. Grace wasn't the only one who'd seen Alexios in action. She thought maybe Alexios wouldn't want her to mention the mist thing, though. That had been new. Maybe it was meant to be secret.

"Thanks for moving the car. We'll be . . . we'll be inside." She glanced up at Alexios, who started to put an arm around her, then hesitated, as if afraid of being rebuffed. She leaned into him, too tired and afraid for Michelle to force herself to stand alone, yet again.

Just this once, she would lean on someone else. Just this once.

∽∽∽∽

St. Louis University Hospital, emergency room

Alexios looked around the crowded waiting room, remembering the countless times he or another of his fellow warriors had needed to be healed. Unlike the healing chambers in Atlantis, which were an oasis of serenity—all fresh air and sunlight, soft, silken cushions, and masses of flowers from the palace gardens—this room where desperate and injured humans waited smelled of sweat, blood, antiseptic, and despair.

Grace huddled in an orange plastic chair, strangely diminished without her many weapons strapped to her body. He stood across the room from her, leaning against a battered vending machine, and tried to think of a time he'd seen her without them but came up empty. The bow, knives, and guns were part of her, oddly dissonant to her beauty and her name.

Grace. It suited her. She was grace in motion, in and out of battle. Except now, when she hunched in that ugly chair, arms wrapped around her knees, waiting for the bleakest kind of bad news.

After they'd removed their visible weapons, he'd helped her into the ER, trying not to wonder why something deep in his chest ached at the feel of her in his arms. Then she'd pulled away from him and collapsed into that chair, and she hadn't moved since. Alexios had wasted a good ten minutes convincing various hospital personnel that he didn't need to be treated for a head wound, after they'd caught sight of the apparently alarming amount of blood that remained in his hair and on the side of his face. He'd finally snarled something along the lines of "it's not my blood," and they'd backed off, all wary apprehension with a healthy dose of fear mixed in. Ever since then, he'd waited. And waited.

He despised waiting.

Hospital security was there in force, and the police were on their way. Luckily, Grace had excellent contacts within the local Paranormal Ops unit, and Alexios had met some of the officers before. He wasn't worried about the police. P Ops needed to be told about the attack, at any rate.

However, although he didn't want to examine the reasons *why* too closely, he was worried about Grace.

She'd somehow attached herself to him the first time he'd run a mission with the human rebels in St. Louis, adopting him as a mentor without bothering to ask his opinion of the idea.

He'd snarled at her to leave him alone. Repeatedly. When she'd simply fallen back and quietly continued to shadow him, he'd tried a different tactic and ignored her.

If he were honest with himself, he'd admit that he'd only pretended to ignore her. Grace was a hard woman to ignore. She was fiercely independent, dark eyes burning with quiet intensity and a dagger's-edged intellect. Slender, with firm, toned muscles, she was still an athlete, like she'd been as a child. An Olympic contender in swimming at only fifteen years old, Quinn had told him.

But a decade ago the world had changed, and Grace's world had collapsed beneath her. A band of female vamps, celebrating their newfound freedom when vampires and shifters had declared their presence to the world, had run across Grace's big brother in a bar. He hadn't survived the party.

Grace nearly hadn't survived his death.

They'd been alone in the world, their father gone when they were young and their mother dead from cancer not long before Grace lost her brother. Quinn said Grace had been broken. Lost.

But she'd found a purpose in fighting back. Spent the past ten years training for command in the rebel army. He'd seen her in battle, and she was good. Damn good. Her reflexes and strength were incredible for a human, and she was almost preternaturally lethal with her bow. But she'd been running on rage and adrenaline for a decade, and if Michelle died— Michelle, the only friend she had left from the innocence of her childhood—Grace was going to crash, hard.

Alexios had seen the signs in her. He knew it was coming. The only thing he couldn't figure out was if he wanted to be around when it happened. It was bound to be personal, that kind of emotional overload.

Too personal for an Atlantean warrior, sworn to the service of his prince and the sea god, who'd vowed to live his life free of even the most casual emotional attachments.

A doctor wearing bloodstained scrubs pushed through the doors to the waiting room and looked around expectantly. "Nichols? Michelle Nichols?"

The blood drained out of Grace's face, but she jumped up out of the chair. "Yes, that's me. I mean, I'm her friend. What happened? Is she okay?"

The doctor frowned, and Alexios started across the room. It wasn't news he wanted Grace to hear alone.

"She lost a lot of blood, and she had a collapsed lung," the doctor said, wiping his forehead with the back of his hand. "I'm not going to lie to you. We did the best we could, and now we wait and see. If your friend's a fighter, she just might have a chance."

Grace stood, frozen, seemingly unable to speak. Alexios put an arm around her and shut down the part of his brain that wanted to think about how right she felt there. She was merely a soldier temporarily in his command, and it was his turn to stand for her.

"Thank you, Doctor," he said. "We'll wait for news."

The doctor nodded, barely glancing at Alexios, then the man's head snapped up for the customary double take Alexios had grown so bitterly accustomed to over the years. "I hope you don't mind my professional curiosity, but how did you get that facial scarring? And have you ever considered cosmetic surgery?"

Alexios's eyes iced over as he regretted, once again, the fact that he couldn't just stab humans who had balls bigger than their brains. "Your concern is misplaced, Doctor, although I thank you for it," he gritted out, trying not to choke on the words.

Grace turned toward him and rested her head on his chest. It was the first sign of weakness she'd ever shown in his presence, and a wave of fierce protectiveness washed through him.

"I need some air," she murmured. "Please, Alexios, please help me. Get me out of here."

Alexios tightened his arms around her and nodded to the doctor. "Thank you again. We'll wait for any news, as I said."

Losing all interest in Alexios, the doctor started to move off, but then stopped, a trace of sympathy crossing his face. "She's going to be in the ICU for quite some time. You two should go get cleaned up and get some rest."

Nodding again, but not bothering to reply, Alexios steered

Grace toward the exit. The doors opened with a hydraulic swishing noise, and the three men outside turned toward them, hands automatically reaching inside jackets. They relaxed slightly when they saw it was Alexios and Grace.

"All clear out here," said the stocky one who'd moved the Jeep for them. Spike, maybe. Or Butch. One of the odd names-that-weren't-names that the rebels used. "Any news?"

Grace shook her head, but didn't speak. Fine tremors shook through her body, and Alexios knew the meltdown was finally on its way.

"Almost everyone is doing well, as you said," Alexios reported tersely. "Michelle was in surgery a long time, though, and the doctor said she lost a lot of blood. He said she'll make it, if she's a fighter, and we all know that she is."

He addressed the words to the man, but they were meant for Grace. She drew in a shuddering breath, and he knew at least part of the meaning had penetrated.

"She's going to make it," he repeated. "But Grace needs some air. We're going to walk a little bit. You're sure the way is clear?"

The taller man, older, with leathery skin and a hawk-like nose, nodded. "We're good. We were sure with dark coming on that the vamps would start showing up, but we ain't seen hide nor hair of 'em. The boys are patrolling all the way around the hospital for the shifters, too."

Alexios nodded. "We won't go far."

He herded Grace down the sidewalk and away from the lights and sounds of the ER. She walked with a jerking, halting gait, like a marionette dancing on the strings of a drunken puppet master. When they reached a low stone wall, partially hidden by some bushes, he guided her to it. Then he sat next to her, his arms around her, and held her while she wept.

The sound of her sobbing—muffled because she tried to hide it from him—and the feel of her warmth as her body trembled in his arms overwhelmed the careful, rock-solid defenses Alexios had carefully constructed over the past several years. He inhaled deeply, trying for control, but failing miserably when the scent of sunshine and flowers from her hair shuddered through his senses.

She was tough, a warrior woman. She never showed weakness to anyone—ever. And yet here she was, crying in his arms. Needing him to comfort her. The fierce drive to protect and cherish surged through him, and a tsunami of unexpected and unwanted emotion crashed through the barriers around his heart like a tidal wave through a fragile coral reef.

She turned her tear-drenched face up to his when his body shuddered against hers. "Alexios?"

There was only one choice he could make. Only one recourse open to him. He needed to taste her lips more than he had ever needed food or water or even air to breathe.

He kissed her.

He kissed her, and she gasped a little against his mouth, but then she was kissing him back. She was *kissing him back*. She twined her arms around his neck and pulled him closer to her and opened her mouth to his invasion, welcoming and enticing him.

Seducing him with her lips and warmth.

He groaned, or perhaps she did, but either way the sound was swallowed up in the heat between them, and he was tilting her head better to devour her, and kissing her and wanting her and needing her . . .

The red flashing light of an emergency vehicle splashed on the side of the building, at the farthest edge of his peripheral vision. A vision but not a vision. A memory but not a memory.

Flames.

The fires. The pain.

The torture.

He wrenched his mouth from Grace's and stared at the flashing light. Heart pumping. Muscles clenching.

Retreat! Escape! Kill them! Escape! Escape!

"Alexios?" She struggled in his arms, and he yanked her even closer, maddened that she would try to escape *him*.

"Alexios," she said, stronger now. "You're hurting me."

Somehow the words sank in past the memories. Past the waking nightmare.

There was no choice. There was only despair, and the death of hope, and an eternity of loneliness stretched out in front of him. They'd twisted him, and now he was broken. Wrong.

Alexios took the only honorable option available to him.

He left her there, bewildered and alone. Walked, then ran, then flew as mist through the air, desperate to escape. He never stopped, not even once, until he'd traveled all the way back to Atlantis. His throat burned with unspoken words; his eyes burned with unshed tears.

He ran, and he made yet another promise: he'd never allow himself to touch Grace again.

GLOSSARY OF TERMS

Aknasha—empath; one who can feel the emotions of others and, usually, send her own emotions into the minds and hearts of others, as well. There have been no *aknasha'an* in the recorded history of Atlantis for more than ten thousand years.

Atlanteans—a race separate from humans, descended directly from a mating between Poseidon and one of the Nereids, whose name is lost in time. Atlanteans inherited some of the gifts of their ancestors: the ability to control all elements except fire—especially water; the ability to transform to mist and travel in that manner; and superhuman strength and agility. Ancient scrolls hint at other powers, as well, but these are either lost to the passage of time or dormant in present-day Atlanteans.

Atlantis—the Seven Isles of Atlantis were driven beneath the sea during a mighty cataclysm of earthquakes and volcanic activity that shifted the tectonic plates of the Earth more than eleven thousand years ago. The ruling prince of the largest isle, also called Atlantis, ascends to serve as high king to all seven isles, though each are ruled by the lords of the individual isle's ruling house.

Blood pride—a master vampire's created vampires.

Landwalkers—Atlantean term for humans.

Miertus—Atlantean slang for excrement.

The Seven—the elite guard of the high prince or king of Atlantis. Many of the rulers of the other six isles have formed their own guard of seven in imitation of this tradition.

Shape-shifters—a species who started off as humans, but were cursed to transform into animals each full moon. Many shape-shifters can control the change during other times of the month, but newly initiated shape-shifters cannot. Shape-shifters have superhuman strength and speed and can live for more than three hundred years, if not injured or killed. They have a long-standing blood feud against the vampires, but old alliances and enemies are shifting.

Thought-mining—the Atlantean ability, long lost, to sift through another's mind and memories to gather information.

Vampires—an ancient race descended from the incestuous mating of the god Chaos and his daughter, Anubisa, goddess of the night. They are voracious for political intrigue and the amassing of power and are extremely long-lived. Vampires have the ability to dematerialize and teleport themselves long distances, but not over large bodies of water.

Warriors of Poseidon—warriors sworn to the service of Poseidon and the protection of humanity. They all bear Poseidon's mark on their bodies.

The WARRIORS OF POSEIDON
series by *USA Today* bestselling author

ALYSSA DAY

Atlantis Rising

Atlantis Awakening

Atlantis Unleashed

M393AS1208